TOME

TID_ OF SOULS

When I look back, I believe going to the window probably saved my life. It forewarned me – just a little, but enough. Even so, as with much else, I wish I hadn't seen what I saw.

It was the double-decker. The waters were still rising, but the top windows and the people inside remained visible. They were scrambling away to the back end of the bus.

Someone was standing up in the water at the front end, near the staircase. At first I thought he was just fat. Then another figure rose up out of the water and I almost screamed. The bus passengers weren't so restrained. I could hear them from where I stood.

The second shape – its flesh resembled well-cooked meat, falling off the bone. I could see the bone of one arm showing through, and when the thing swivelled sideways for a second, showing its back, I saw the flesh coming away from the spine on each side, baring it like a moth's body when its wings are spread. Then it turned my way. *God. God almighty. That face.* Grinning because so much of the flesh was falling from the skull. And looking at me. The sockets of its eyes were empty. They glared; a greenish-yellow glow, bright. It started forward, the fat shape following – I saw now it wasn't fat, just bloated, from its drowning. And then a third figure rose up into view, climbing up the bus's flooded stairwell, and a fourth... all with those glowing eyes.

WWW.ABADDONBOOKS.COM

An Abaddon Books™ Publication
www.abaddonbooks.com
abaddon@rebellion.co.uk

First published in 2009 by Abaddon Books™, Rebellion Intellectual Property
Limited, Riverside House, Osney Mead, Oxford, OX2 OES, UK.

10 9 8 7 6 5 4 3 2 1

Editor: Jonathan Oliver
Cover: Mark Harrison
Design: Simon Parr & Luke Preece
Marketing and PR: Keith Richardson
Creative Director and CEO: Jason Kingsley
Chief Technical Officer: Chris Kingsley

ISBN: 978-1-906735-14-2

Printed in Denmark by Norhaven A/S

TOMES OF THE DEAD

TIDE OF SOULS

SIMON BESTWICK

Abaddon
Books

WWW.ABADDONBOOKS.COM

To Judith and Roger Bestwick, my parents.

PART ONE

Storm's Edge – The Boatman's Call

I looked upon the rotting sea,
And drew my eyes away,
I looked upon the rotting deck,
And there the dead men lay

Samuel Taylor Coleridge, *The Rime of The Ancient Mariner*, Part IV

CHAPTER ONE

Katja

The rising of the dead was the best luck I'd had in years. A godsend, even. I was lucky to survive, of course; my owners showed exactly how they valued me when they left me locked in a Cheetham Hill brothel to drown. I was lucky they kept me upstairs; I heard the women on the ground floor. I heard them die. Heard their screams of panic, heard them choked off as they drowned.

At least, at the time I thought they had drowned. Hours later, clinging to a rooftop, holding a gun with one bullet left in it and trying to decide which of us to use it on, I wasn't so sure.

My name is Katja Wencewska. Although my family is Polish, I grew up in Romania. It's a long story, none of it relevant to this.

I will tell you what is relevant.

I am twenty-seven years old. My father was a military officer. Special forces. A good, brave man, always very calm. Tall, as well. A tree of a man. An oak. My mother, in contrast, was like a tiny bird – very bright, excitable. I loved them both dearly. I was their only child. They were proud of me; in school I won prizes in Literature, the Arts and Gymnastics. I have two degrees.

None of that helped when they died. A stupid man, driving drunk, late one night. Their car went off the road, into a ravine. My father died instantly; my mother took several hours. The idiot responsible was cut out of the wreckage with barely a scratch. I wanted to kill him, and could have. Papa had often shown me how. He knew the world is full of predators, and taught me to protect myself against them.

I was studying for a PhD at the time, but of course that had to be abandoned. Bills had to be paid, but there was no work to be found. Then I heard of a job in England. For a fee, strings would be pulled, things arranged. A teaching job.

I spoke good English. I thought I would work hard, make money. Eventually I planned to come home – when things were better there, when I had money saved.

I thought I was so clever. I was well-educated and, I thought, streetwise. I could kill with a blow after all, if I was forced to. But the thought never crossed my mind. I had heard of people trafficking of course, but you never think it will be you. Predators would be so easily dealt with if they came to us as predators.

I was a fool.

You can guess the rest. My passport was taken. There was no teaching job. I was to service men for money. When I refused, I was beaten and raped. Worse than rape. Other things were done to me. I will not talk about those things: they are not relevant, you have no need to know. After this I felt defiled and wretched. I did not refuse again. It was made clear to me – to us all – that if we were too much trouble we would be killed. We were expendable; easily disposed of, easily replaced.

I was kept at a brothel in London at first. After six months they moved me to another, in Manchester. I spent the next eight months there. Being able to kill with a blow means little when there are always more of them, when the doors are always locked, the windows always barred, when you have nowhere to go.

I think that is all I need to say about myself.

I was woken that morning by screams and blaring horns.

I got to the window and squinted through the bars. On Cheetham Hill Road, people were leaping onto the roadway to avoid something pouring over the pavement. At first I thought it was water – dark, filthy water – but when I pushed the net curtains aside I could see it flowed uphill. And over the screams and traffic noise, even the horns, I heard it squealing.

I realised they were swarming rats.

It was raining heavily; water gushed down the pavements and the road into the gutters. There'd been a lot of that lately.

There were rats on the road too – all on one side, the lane for city bound traffic, which was deserted. The road out of Manchester, on the other hand, was jammed solid. I could see the people in the cars – wild, terrified faces, fright and fury mixed, fists pounding windows, dashboards, steering wheels, making their horns blare and blare and blare.

The rain intensified until the road blurred. I stepped back from the window, let the curtains fall back into place. My stomach felt hollow and tight.

We had a television there, but I hadn't seen the news in months. We weren't allowed, and besides, we only wanted to watch things that would take our minds off our lives. I had no idea what had, or was, happening, only that something was very wrong.

Soon, I heard banging on the brothel's front door. I looked outside. It was Ilir, our owner. One of his sons came out of the door; he'd been left in charge. Ilir's black BMW was in the traffic jam, doors open. Ilir dragged his son to it. They slammed the doors; Ilir pounded the horn, but the traffic didn't budge. After a minute, they pulled into the deserted city bound lane. Other cars started following their example, and for a short time the traffic moved forward, but then locked up again. So many people, all trying to leave. Some of the other girls had started screaming, pounding on the doors. They'd abandoned us. They hadn't even turned us loose, just left us here.

People were running along the pavement, clutching their belongings, their children. Their eyes were wild.

An hour or so after Ilir and his son left, the answers started coming. Below Cheetham Hill are the Irwell and the Irk, two of the three rivers that run through Manchester. None are very deep; all have high banks. But water was washing *up* the street. Lapping up in slow, relentless waves.

Even then, I didn't really get it. It only really sank in when people started abandoning their cars.

It happened very quickly after that. Water washed round the wheels of the cars and rose higher. It lapped round their skirts. It poured over the pavements. Across the street, water flooded under the front door of the kebab house and across the floor. People were wading the torrents, then began climbing on top of the cars.

For a few minutes, I just watched. None of it felt real. It was like watching some bizarre art-house film. But nothing had felt real in that place for a long time. You couldn't let it, if you wanted to stay sane.

The water now started pouring over the crest of Cheetham Hill, and the rising waters now became a surge. A middle-aged Asian man fell over and was swept along, screaming for help. His arms flailed, and a toupee slipped off his head. I heard myself giggle; it was a jagged, ugly sound. I clapped a hand over my mouth. He went under and didn't come up.

Then I heard the girls downstairs begin screaming in earnest, and I realised the waters were entering the brothel.

We were all locked in our rooms overnight. Each one had an *en-suite* sink and toilet – for convenience, not comfort. The windows were all barred, so there was no escape. Even if the waters didn't flood the upper floors, I could still look forward to starvation.

My father had shown me how to pick a lock. I could've escaped my room easily enough on several occasions. The difficult part had always been what I would do then. There were two front doors, inner and outer, the inner triple-locked. And even if I'd got clear of that, where would I go with no papers, no passport, no way of getting a legitimate job?

But now the rules had changed.

I started searching, trying to find something I could use. The women downstairs were screaming. People on the street were screaming. I blocked it out. It didn't help me to hear it, wouldn't help me do this faster.

I tipped up the wastepaper basket. There were used condoms in it, slimy to the touch.

Ignore them, Papa said.

At last I found a paper clip.

I knelt by the door and set to work. It was a slow job. Trial and error. My fingers got sweaty and slipped on the metal.

Suddenly I realised something.

The girls downstairs had stopped screaming. All but one. Then suddenly, that too was choked off. And there was only silence from the ground floor.

Outside the street was silent. I went to the window. Stopped, and stared.

Most of it was underwater. Brown, dirty water had covered almost all the cars. The roofs of a few vehicles showed. There was a double-decker bus opposite, the top deck still above water. A dozen people were there, slack-skinned faces gazing into mine. Here and there, on the water, I saw reddish stains, dispersing slowly in the current.

There were two other women upstairs in the brothel – Marianna, who was about my age, was praying over and over in the next room. Marta, the youngest of the girls, was sobbing helplessly across the landing. She was only fifteen. A child. Tiny. Dark. Like my mother had been.

I ran back to the door, back to the lock. My fingers shook. I took a deep breath.

Panic is a choice, Papa used to say. *You can decide not to be scared, not to panic. You can decide who's in charge.*

So I chose to stay calm. I could still hear the rain pelting down outside, but I didn't look to see if the waters were still rising. I couldn't think about that. I had to act as if time was not a factor. I just kept working. Even when the thin carpet I knelt on grew cold and wet.

Marta was sobbing and screaming as well now. From next door, Marianna's prayers had blurred into a rising jumble of sound, fast turning into a wail.

The tumblers clicked.

I got the door open. Water filmed the landing, welling up from the flooded staircase. There was a fire extinguisher on the wall. I could smash the locks on the other girls' doors.

Then there were fresh screams. From outside.

I don't know why, but I went back to the window. I suppose I thought the worst of it was past. The door was open. I had time. Or, perhaps, there was something about the screams that alerted me.

When I look back, I believe going to the window probably saved my life. It forewarned me – just a little, but enough. Even so, as with much else, I wish I hadn't seen what I saw.

It was the double-decker. The waters were still rising, but the top windows and the people inside remained visible. They were scrambling away to the back end of the bus.

Someone was standing up in the water at the front end, near the staircase. At first I thought he was just fat. Then another figure rose up out of the water and I almost screamed. The bus passengers weren't so restrained. I could hear them from where I stood.

The second shape – its flesh resembled well-cooked meat, falling off the bone. I could see the bone of one arm showing through, and when the thing swivelled sideways for a second, showing its back, I saw the flesh coming away from the spine on each side, baring it like a moth's body when its wings are spread. Then it turned my way. *God. God almighty. That face.* Grinning because so much of the flesh was falling from the skull. And looking at me. The sockets of its eyes were empty. They glared; a greenish-yellow glow, bright. It started forward, the fat shape following – I saw now it wasn't fat, just bloated, from its drowning. And then a third figure rose up into view, climbing up the bus's flooded stairwell, and a fourth... all with those glowing eyes.

The passengers were still. There wasn't really anywhere to go in any case. The rotting thing seized one of them, a woman in her twenties, and bit into her neck. I heard her scream. The bloated figure grabbed her too and they pulled her down; blood sprayed up and splattered the windows.

It was over for them very quickly after that. Sometimes I think they were the lucky ones.

I just wish, before I turned away, I hadn't seen the child, hands and face against the glass, screaming...

But there was nothing I could do.

I grabbed the extinguisher off the wall and smashed the lock on Marta's door. She stumbled out, then shrieked again as she saw the flooded stairwell.

"What are we going to do?" It came out in a wail.

I pointed to the hatch in the ceiling. "Get into the loft, then out onto the roof."

Luckily I didn't have to tell her everything; she clambered onto the landing rail and I caught her legs, boosted her up. She pushed the hatch up, grabbed the edges and started wriggling up into the loft. I ran to Marianna's door and smashed the lock there too.

Marianna was on her knees praying. I dragged her to her feet and out onto the landing. The water there was ankle deep now.

"Climb!" I shouted to Marianna, and started clambering onto the banister. Marta reached down to grip my hands. Then her gaze drifted past me and her eyes widened.

I looked.

Wished I hadn't.

Down in the dark water, in the flooded stairwell, I could see movement. And lights. Pairs of yellow-green lights, rising towards the surface. And then I could see their faces.

CHAPTER TWO

"Marta!"

Her eyelids fluttered. The tranced state broke and she focussed on me again. She gripped my wrists tightly, then pulled me up through the trap door.

The first dead thing rose out of the water. The top part of its face still clung to the bone, matted hair hanging from the remaining pieces of its scalp. Marianna, frozen on the landing, stared down at it. A second, equally decayed, emerged a second later.

"Marianna!" She looked up, then scrambled onto the banister. The dead thing seized her legs just as I caught her outstretched hands. Screaming, she fell sideways into space, almost pulling me through the trap after her; Marta caught me round the waist.

My grip broke. Marianna fell back onto the dead things, and all three of them crashed into the brown water. Another dead thing rose. A woman, in jeans and t-shirt like my own. Her skin was blue, but she was unmarked. Except for the eyes; the empty sockets were filled with that green glow, and what looked like dried candlewax clung to her cheeks. Her face was blank and slack.

Marianna screamed my name. Not her mother's or father's, or even God's. Mine. Because I always knew what to do. But there was nothing; already she was beyond help.

They didn't kill her, not outright. That was the worst part. They weren't interested in that. They could hold her down, hold her still. The blue female gripped Marianna's arm at wrist and elbow, then leant forward and sank her teeth into the flesh. She shook her head back and forth, like a terrier with a rat. Marianna's shriek was the sound of a drill going into bones. I'd heard that, once. Ilir arranging a punishment, on someone who'd crossed him. He made us all watch, so that we would understand.

Thick blood began pouring out, down Marianna's arm, down the dead woman's chin. The blue woman pulled her head back.

Skin stretched and split, then the muscles and tendons underneath, as Marianna's drilling shriek rose ever higher. I heard them tearing. Blood spurted out in a vivid, unrelenting spray. I glimpsed white through it. Bone. Something ragged hung from the blue woman's mouth.

The water in the stairwell was red. The other two dead things held Marianna's legs, heads shaking to and fro as they bit. Her free arm flailed about, until a fourth pair of hands seized her wrist. A head lunged out of the water and sank its teeth into her breast.

I pulled Marta away from the trapdoor. Marianna's screams faded, became moans. Shock setting in, numbing the pain. There was that much mercy left, at least. But nothing would take away the sight of those things eating her alive. Perhaps, if she was lucky, she was beyond understanding it now.

But I wasn't.

There were other noises, too. Grunting and tearing. A sound like ripping wallpaper. *Skin.* A wet splatter, like piss on stone. *Blood.* And the chewing sounds.

They were eating her. There was still flesh on her bones.

Panic is a choice, Papa said again.

While they were eating her, they were not eating Marta, or me.

Marta – she'd wriggled away, across the bare loft floor, huddled in the angle where it met the wood panelling. Her breath was hitching, rapid. Whimpering. So was mine. Faster and faster. My heart, hammering.

I closed my eyes, breathed in deep, then slowly out. In. And out again. Made myself count to ten. Just thinking about the numbers, not about the things eating their way through Marianna's body or what they would do when they'd finished.

Eight. Nine. Ten.

I opened my eyes. Marta was still huddled and whimpering.

I could get further, move faster, alone. Papa might have done the same.

But I chose not to. I cannot quite explain why. Perhaps because she was a child. Perhaps it was something in myself I refused to abandon. Or perhaps because, small, dark and birdlike as she was, she was very like my mother; it might have been that simple.

I dragged her to her feet, shook her, slapped her face.

"We have to get to the roof. Quickly. Before they –" I hesitated, then said it. "– before they finish eating Marianna."

She gulped a weepy, shuddering breath, face twitching. I touched her cheek. "Take deep breaths. You have to stay calm."

I looked around the loft. Any exit to the roof would be behind the thin plywood panelling. Was there a window? I'd never seen the front of the building; on the rare occasions I'd left or entered the brothel, I'd been bundled through a door at the back.

From below came ripping and munching sounds, and the gristly pop a chicken leg makes when wrenched free of the bird's body. Marianna was silent. Hopefully dead.

There was little time. Too much had been wasted already.

The window would be in the middle.

I prodded the wood panelling. It gave easily. Thin. I stepped back and drove a kick at it.

The plywood split. I yelled and kicked again. On the third kick the panel gave way; splinters stung my ankle and shin.

I grabbed at the edges of the hole I'd made, and pulled. "Marta! Help me. Quickly." She saw what I was doing and ripped at the panelling too. Chunks of it tore away. Behind it, wooden planks were nailed across something.

Thankfully the wood was old and soft, the nails pulling free of the brick work.

Please let there be a window behind this. Please.

There was. A casement, a couple of feet deep, and at the end of it, two panes of grimy glass.

I had to crawl into the casement feet-first to get at the window itself. I kicked out twice, with both feet, smashing the glass. Two or three short jabs knocked away the jagged edges.

It was almost silent. Almost. From below, there were still faint chewing sounds. And things breaking. Hard things. Bones.

Soon there'd be nothing left of Marianna.

The best I could hope was to keep us alive as long as possible. When there was no other option, I would find a way to end our lives. Marta I could finish with a single blow, a twist of the neck. For myself I would need a weapon of some kind. Better that than a death like Marianna's.

"We're going to climb up onto the roof," I told Marta.

"What... Katja, what do we do *then*? They'll just come after us. They –"

"*Marta.*" I put all the authority I could into my voice. It didn't feel like very much, but she stopped talking. "We'll deal with that when we get up there. OK?"

"OK."

"Good," I said, and told her what I wanted her to do.

The biggest danger is loss of nerve. When I slid into the casement, I had to go head-first, on my back. Just as I was about to put my head out through the window, I pictured the water below, teeming with dead things reaching up for me. You can't stop to think in a situation like that, except about your next move, or it will paralyse you.

If I stuck my head out, it would be grabbed, seized in rotting hands. If I was lucky they would twist and tear, and my head would be ripped from my shoulders. If not, they'd drag me out and pull me into the water, where I'd feel their ragged nails ripping away my clothes to get at the flesh underneath, their teeth tearing pieces of my body away...

... while Marta...

"Katja?"

... while Marta was left on her own, waiting to be devoured. Unless she killed herself first.

I hadn't saved Marianna. But I'd been locked in my room to die, and I hadn't. I'd been treated as a piece of meat, but I wasn't. I was alive. Marta was alive. I'd got us both this far.

I was meat to Ilir, meat to the punters; now I was meat to these creatures. Only the appetite was changed.

Ilir – Ilir was probably dead already. Trapped on the flooding roads, in those infested waters.

But not me. Or Marta. We were alive. Now Ilir knew what it was to be meat.

I started laughing. Even to my own ears, in that space, it sounded like an ugly, jagged sound. But I couldn't stop. It was so funny. Ilir was the meat now, and I wasn't. Not yet.

"*Katja!*"

Do it, Papa said. *Now.*

I stuck my arms out through the window and reached for the top of the casement. I wasn't meat now, but I would be if I didn't move.

Nothing grabbed me. I began pulling myself up and out, still laughing. Hands grabbed my legs. I kicked out. Still laughing.

"Katja!"

"I'm sorry. I'm sorry." But still laughing.

The casement jutted out from the slope of the roof. The top of it was flat. With Marta behind and then under me, holding my feet and boosting me up, I was able to climb up on top of it. Then I turned and grasped her wrists as she reached up towards me.

The water lapped around the windows on the floor we'd lived on. Where would it be in our rooms now? Shin, knee, waist deep?

Something bobbed at the edge of the water. A mass of small objects, bristling with brown fur. Rats. Drowned rats. Hundreds of them. Beyond them, the water was full of faces, crammed together, glaring up with dull, impersonal hostility, eyes glowing. Live rats scurried, squeaking, over the roof tiles and guttering.

Water, the deep brown of drinking chocolate, rolled down Cheetham Hill Road and down side-streets and alleyways, frothing and eddying around lampposts and the bus. The bus's windows were steamed up and there was blood on them. Handprints. Shadowy figures moved inside. Eyes glowed behind the windows.

I leant back, pulling on Marta's wrists. She wriggled out of the window and braced first one foot, then the other, on the frame.

Fresh pairs of eyes flickered into life below; new faces swam up through the murk. They were gathering. I mustn't look, mustn't think about them.

Marta was composed now, focussed on the task in hand. I was proud of her. I pulled on her arms, and she walked up the sides of the casement, got a foot up onto the top of it. Then the other. And then she slumped down onto her knees and sobbed, and I stroked her hair and whispered things my mother had said to me when I was little, on nights that were long and sleepless and I saw monsters in the dark.

The casement roof creaked under us. If it broke...

I couldn't hear anything from below. No movement in the attic.

When I looked around and across the street, I saw that others had done the same as us. All the roofs were occupied. Scores, maybe even hundreds, of people. Men, women, children. Babies. Grandparents. All huddled on the rooftops. Some clung to the sloping roofs, trying to hold on, feet wedged in the buckled guttering.

All that remained of Cheetham Hill Road were the rows of buildings that had flanked it, steadily sinking from sight as they descended towards Manchester. A mist was gathering. I couldn't see the city, or whatever remained of it.

It was almost peaceful. The only sounds were the lap and splash of the water, and the low, muffled weeping washing in from the rooftops. I looked back down. The faces were still there. Now and then there'd be a faint splash as arms broke the surface. They were treading water.

So far, we were safe. Safe. That was funny. I giggled. Marta stared at me. I made myself stop, forced a smile.

Above the casement, the roof sloped upwards another two or three metres. Just to our right, there was a chimney stack.

"Marta?" I pointed. "We have to climb."

The roof was sharply angled, the tiles wet. One slip... her eyes darted down.

I caught her by the shoulders. "Don't look at that. Don't think about it. Now, listen to me. You're going to go first –"

"I can't –"

"You're going to go first because then I'll be right behind you. If you fall, I'll catch you. And when you get to the top, you can help pull me up. OK?"

At last, she nodded.

"Alright. Go on. *Now.*"

From below, there was a thumping sound. Marta let out a terrified squeak.

"Don't listen. Just climb."

She spread herself out across the tiles, dug in her toes and pushed upwards. Sobs made her back shake.

From below – *thump, thump.* Something had flopped into the attic space. It was moving around. The thumping got louder. *Closer.* I wanted to look round. I did not. Would not.

Marta fumbled for a purchase on the tiles. Her hands slid. "Katja!"

"Don't use your hands like that. Spread them flat and press down. Use your feet to climb."

"How?"

"Bring one leg up. Get a grip with your trainer. Then push up. Then with the other. Yes, that's right. Quickly now." I kept my voice as level as I could.

Panic is a choice. Panic is a choice. Panic is a choice.

From below, the thumping grew louder still. I ignored it, had to. Watched Marta climb. *Oh please, God, let her make it.* I hadn't prayed in years. I would say a prayer for Marianna when we got up there. Even though I did not believe. She had. And she had been a friend. Or a colleague. Something to me, anyway.

Marta was sobbing. She was just a child. A child. Still. Despite everything she'd already gone through. Now this. No child should have to see this. Nor any adult.

She will never make it. Too young, too small; too fragile, too afraid.

"Keep climbing, darling. You can do it."

She was almost there now, close enough to reach out and grab the apex of the roof. First one hand, then the other. As she did, her feet slipped, and her whole weight fell on her hands. She screamed. Her feet scrabbled and kicked desperately, sliding off the tiles. When I tried to catch them, she nearly caught me in the face.

"Marta, stop kicking. *Stop kicking.*" I heard my voice rise. Sweat trickled down my back. How long could she hold on? If she fell, could I catch her? Would I? Or let her fall?

So easy to let her go. On my own, I could take better care.

Responsibility, Katja, Papa said. *She is one of yours. And besides, she looks so like your mother.*

I lunged out and grabbed her ankles. She screamed again, twisted her head round. Thank God, her grip didn't break. "Marta, keep still!"

This time, she listened to me, and obeyed. I shifted my hands so they were braced under her heels. "I've got you. Alright?"

"Oh god."

"Sh. It's alright, little one." My mother called me that, as a child. "I've got you now. I'm going to push you up. You pull with your arms, and get one leg over the rooftop. OK?"

"Yes."

The thumping was very loud now. "Go on!"

I pushed, and Marta hauled herself up, pulling herself astride the roof. "Katja!"

And the thumping stopped.

Marta grinned down at me, stupid with relief. It lasted for a barely a second. Then she was staring past my shoulder. "Katja?"

I turned. A head stuck out of the window. It was the blue woman. Her glowing sockets stared up at me. Drool welled up in her mouth like blood from a wound. It overflowed and mixed with the blood around her mouth. Marianna's blood. Her hands fumbled at the casement's top edge. Two fingers were without nails.

None of this could be happening. Perhaps my mind had finally given way and in reality I lay on my bed in the brothel unmoving and unaware, a piece of meat at last. What would Ilir do? Probably take me out and bury me in some unmarked grave. Peace of a kind.

"Katja, climb up!"

Marta. She needed me. If this *was* real, and I gave up, she had no chance.

Perhaps that was really why I saved Marta. To save myself.

But I couldn't look away from the blue woman. We stared at each other – for how long? Seconds, perhaps even minutes. It could have been hours, from how it felt. I waited for her to drag herself the rest of the way through the window. But she didn't. She let go of the window's edge and slid back inside the attic.

I stared at the space where she'd been.

"Katja, come on!"

I turned around, spread myself flat against the roof, and started to climb.

It went without a hitch. I pulled myself astride the rooftop and pointed to the chimney stack. We shuffled along until we were against it. I huddled behind Marta, trying to share body heat. We only wore jeans and T-shirts, and it was still raining. After all this, dying of hypothermia would be ridiculous, but entirely possible. Life has a sense of humour; this much I know. That jagged, ugly laughter bubbled up in me again, and I bit my lips until it passed.

A wind had risen, thinning the mist enough to reveal what remained of Manchester. I'd seen the city once before, from a distance. A private party that Ilir hired us out to. They'd taken us out back, bundled us into a van, told us to be nice, to pretend we were having a good time and happy to be there, happy to be doing this. One of the men must've said something good to Ilir, because he'd been kind to me. Kind for Ilir, anyway. He'd driven me into Manchester. Taken me shopping, bought me shoes and a dress. Taken me to a restaurant, bought me dinner. Then taken me back home to his bed, because he'd bought me.

The city wasn't there any more. All I could see – almost all – was water. Higher buildings stood clear of it, like strange, tall islands, the walls like cliffs. There was a towerblock nearby. A tiny stick figure stumbled out onto a balcony. I wondered if it was alive or dead. It stumbled back inside.

In the city proper I could see the CIS tower, sticking out high above the waters, but not the Hilton building; I had no idea what had happened to it. Other towers stuck up. A few tree tops, some of the taller lampposts. But that was all.

The rooftops were crowded. People huddled atop them like pigeons, clinging to each other. The rooftop beside ours was very crowded. A group of Asians; there must have been at least twenty, of all ages. They were trying to spread out along the roof, towards ours. One woman held a baby in her arms. Someone was shouting. Panic in his voice. Some sobbed, others prayed. I remembered my promise to Marianna and mumbled to myself, something like a prayer. It started with 'God' and it ended with 'Amen', anyway.

The sky was black and empty. Rain streamed down. Lightning flashed, a crack of thunder crashing down from almost directly overhead. Thin, bleating cries drifted from the rooftops. I looked for planes, helicopters. Surely the government would send help? They might deport me, I realised, when they realised who I was. But that was for later. I couldn't think that far ahead. Staying alive. That was all I had. Me and Marta. My little family of one.

The creatures seemed to be staying in the water and inside the buildings. They weren't coming out into the open air.

Not yet.

But until they did, we had some rest. Sort of. But that meant time to think as well, and it was all crashing in on Marta. On me, too. I felt sobs hitching in my throat. I had to stop. I couldn't let go now. I had to keep control.

How long ago had I woken up to this? How long had it taken? From getting out of the room, breaking Marta and Marianna out of theirs? It couldn't have been much more than fifteen, twenty minutes. Fifteen or twenty minutes in which to lose a friend and run for my life – or climb for it anyway – from things that could not but did exist.

I had to stop crying, had to stop crying. I took deep breaths. Counted to ten. It didn't help. Not at first. But I kept doing it, and eventually I felt calm again.

"Get back! Get fucking back!"

I looked up. Then I heard the gunshot.

Marta gave a tiny gasp. Screams from the neighbouring rooftop, a thud. A body flopped and slid down the tiles, smearing blood over them. A woman, middle-aged. Still alive. She hit the guttering, scattering half a dozen squealing rats, then dropped.

Instantly the water erupted into churning froth. The woman screamed; the water turned red.

I couldn't see much more than that, but I saw enough. Arms, flailing and clutching; eyes, glowing. The water heaved – they were swarming. Like piranhas. The woman's screams were cut off and for a moment a scrum of bodies heaved on the surface – some rotting, some bloated, some freshly dead – then sank, but the water continued to heave. And the red stain deepened and grew.

"There, you see? That's what happens. That's what fucking happens. You keep away from me you Paki bastards. Fucking keep *away*!"

I peeped round the edge of the chimney stack. A man was crouching at the near end of the neighbouring rooftop. He held a gun. The others on the rooftop were trying to move back from him. One man jostled another. The second man shoved the first.

They fought, and then they both fell. A woman was knocked loose as they went. Oh, God. It was the woman holding the baby.

I didn't look. I heard the splashing as they landed, and then the screams. The screams. And the other sounds. But I didn't look.

The gunman inched backwards. I couldn't see his face. He was white and wore a leather jacket. It looked expensive. He pointed the gun at the knot of people.

"Stay where you are. Don't fucking move."

His voice sounded ugly, ragged and high-pitched. A man with a gun who'd panicked. Nothing more dangerous. How had it started? Who was he? Someone like Ilir, most likely. None of it mattered now. All that mattered was the gun.

That, and one other thing; he was backing towards our chimney-stack. What would he do when he found us? I pushed myself up into a crouch.

"Kat –"

"Sh." I put my finger to Marta's lips.

The gun would come in useful, if those things came out of the water. Even if it was only so that I could save myself and Marta from a death like Marianna's.

"Don't fucking move. Back. Back."

Someone moved. I didn't see who, I was watching the gunman. But he fired again. There was more screaming. Another body – no, two bodies – fell. I saw them from the periphery of my vision. Then I focussed again. It was the man I had to watch.

I crouched and lifted my hands. One would have to grab the gun. The other...

Papa had shown me all the different ways a man could be killed with a single blow, but I'd never used any of them. I'd spent the last year as a slave, not daring to even think of striking back. But now... I didn't feel the same. It hadn't been long, since I'd broken out of that room, but I felt different. I felt like somebody who could use what Papa had taught me. Who could deliver one of those killing blows. I hoped I was right. There would only be one chance.

He was inching back along the roof. His foot slipped. He yelled, flailing for balance. Was he going to go over and save me the job? No; his free hand grabbed the rooftop and he steadied himself. He was shaking. I didn't know if it was fright or fury. Then he was backing up again.

I could hear Marta's tiny, whimpering breaths. I forced myself to shut them out. And the screams of the poor frightened bastards further down the roof. And the sounds from the water. I just focussed on the man with the gun.

He was almost at the chimney stack now. I could hear his breathing. It was wild and gulping and hoarse.

"That's right. Stay where you fucking are. Don't fucking move. Don't –"

He'd reached the stack, grabbed at it with his free hand. Then he stiffened and whipped round. He had a thin face. Sandy hair. Pale eyes wide in shock and rage and madness. He was only in his twenties. He might have been younger than me. But he had the gun. And then the gun whipped up towards my face –

I hit the inside of his wrist with the edge of my left hand. The gun was knocked sideways and fired, perhaps twenty centimetres from my ear. Marta shrieked. The gunshot felt like I'd been punched in the side of the head. I boosted myself to my feet, driving my right hand upwards, heel-first. I knew the exact spot I was aiming for, at the base of the nose. Papa had taught me this; a blow there, from underneath, can smash the bone up into the brain. Result: instant death.

The angle of the blow had to be just right. If I missed, or got it wrong –

Pain shot down my arm. I felt the give of the breaking bone, and sickness burned the back of my throat. The jarring pain of impact as my hand slammed against the skull. The hot, sick spray on my hand and face as his nose exploded into blood and tissue. The gunman's head rocked back and he dropped the pistol. It slid past us.

He toppled backwards, face splashed red, his nose pulp – blood coming out of his eyes – sliding down the far side of the roof and off the edge.

A dozen pairs of green lights gleamed in the brown water where the narrow backyard had been. As the faces began resolving themselves through the murk, he crashed into the water.

I swayed, off-balance. Marta caught hold of my arms and steadied me. He'd been dead before he hit the water. The heel of my hand was bruised and throbbing.

From the backyard, I heard the waters churn and splash, heard things tear and break.

Marta was wide-eyed and crying.

"It's alright," I told her. "It's alright."

The gun had come to rest on top of the casement. Marta saw where I was looking. I looked back at her. "We need it," I said.

I thought she was going to argue, but she didn't. After a moment, she just nodded. She was starting to look less panicked now. Good. It would be easier if she was able to think for herself a little. Not too much. Not so that she started arguing with me or brooding, but enough that I didn't have to explain everything.

It went smoothly enough. When I reached the casement, I felt it creak under my feet, and tensed, afraid it'd give way. I listened out for thumping sounds in the attic, but there weren't any. I crouched and picked up the gun. Found the safety catch and put it on. Thrust it through the waistband of my jeans. And started to climb again.

By the time I reached the top I was shaking. Delayed reaction. And the cold. I managed a smile anyway. Marta smiled back.

And we settled down to wait.

CHAPTER THREE

The rain had slacked off; the waters had stopped rising, for now at least. The creatures were nowhere in sight. Now and again there was a gleam of green light. No more.

Cold was the enemy now. My teeth chattered. Marta's too. We huddled together for warmth.

With stiff, awkward fingers, I tugged the pistol from my waistband and slid out the magazine. Nine rounds. A tenth in the chamber.

I'd hold them off as long as I could. If they could be killed again. Ten bullets. Eight for them. Two for us.

I put the magazine back in and put the gun back in my waistband. I still shook occasionally. Some of it was the cold. Some was what I'd just seen. The rest was what I'd done. I kept reliving the blow, the feel of the man's nose driven back into his brain. He'd pointed the gun at me, yes. But I'd planned to kill him from the first. I would have done it no matter what, because he was a threat.

Was it like this for you, too, Papa, the first time?

Marta stirred and mumbled. I nudged her and her eyes opened; she moaned, glaring at me for disturbing her. But we had to stay awake; it was too easy, in the cold, to drift off and die. On the other hand, perhaps that way wouldn't be so bad. A warm, toasty feeling, then sleep, never waking again. Peaceful. But...

But if *they* came for me while I slept, only waking, when they bit into my flesh like a ripe peach...

I shook my head like a dog shaking water, forced myself to sit up straight. I looked up, praying for an aircraft. Some sign of life. Rescue.

But I knew there'd be none. Manchester was many miles inland. If it was underwater, what of the rest of the country? London was on an estuary. London would be gone. And the government? If they were anywhere, it would be in a bunker, keeping themselves safe, jealously preserving what they had. Wherever you went, that didn't change.

And still the cold, pelting rain fell. Marta moaned faintly again, straightening up. "Easy," I said.

"I'm cold," she said.

"Me too, little one."

Nothing else to say or do. Sit here and slowly freeze. Nowhere to go. I looked up Cheetham Hill Road, the people huddled on the rooftops, hunched on the sloping sides. Most were Asian, women in bright saris, men in shalwar kameez, but I saw people of all colours, in smart dress and casual. But the rain, the cold, the terror made everyone more and more alike. A woman caught my eye, middle-aged and plump, in bright sodden clothing, like a half-drowned tropical bird. She forced a trembling smile. I forced one, then looked away. Little customs. Etiquette. None of it meant anything now. No help would come. We'd been abandoned.

Nothing I wasn't used to.

There was higher ground than this, somewhere. Further above sea level. Relative safety, if we could only get there. But even if we crawled along the rooftops, even if we found a path through the huddled crowds there, sooner or later, there'd be nowhere to go but the water. And in the water...

Eyes open or shut, I kept seeing Marianna, pinned down and torn apart.

So far, they'd stayed in the water, or the flooded buildings. They hadn't come out into the open air, onto the roofs. Were they afraid?

What if Marianna came back as well? Could I aim a gun at her, and fire?

Not that it seemed likely. There would be nothing left of her. Nothing that could move. In a way that was almost worse. I imagined pieces of Marianna – a severed head, a string of vertebrae – bobbing in the water lapping out on the landing, empty eye sockets filled with green light.

Someone screamed. I forced my eyes open. The group to my left. The Asian family. A small, chubby man with a long white beard was pointing downwards.

I rubbed my eyes and looked again. I wasn't sure what I was seeing. My vision must be blurred. But I looked again, and I saw the same thing. The water below, filled with points of glimmering light. Green light. Dozens, even hundreds of pairs. All staring upwards. At me.

I don't know how much time passed. I tried not to look, but every so often my gaze would shift, wandering down to the water, and they'd be there. Once or twice I saw new sets of eyes appearing, blinking on like activated lights.

They were gathering.

My fingers were wrinkled from the damp. Marta was very pale. Perhaps hypothermia *would* get us first. I almost willed it on.

My right hand still throbbed, despite the cold. The heel of the hand. If I fired the gun, that was where the recoil would hit. Christ, that would hurt.

All we could see were their eyes, watching. There were so many of them. And they were already dead. We wouldn't stand a chance. *What are they waiting for? What?*

When the attack came, it was almost a relief.

A face broke the surface, little more than a collection of holes in a clump of greenish-black sludge. Two hands rose, either side of it. More faces appeared. First in ones and twos, then by the dozen and the score. A forest of faces, jammed together. Rotted, grinning ones. Bloated ones, like maggots with glowing eyes. One was little more than bone. And others that hardly looked dead at all. Except for the eyes.

They reached out of the water, clutching at brickwork, drain-pipes, shop-signs – anything that gave them a handhold – and started to climb.

There were screams now, like steel on glass. Deafening. A terrible, helpless sound. But I had the gun. I had the gun.

That made the panic go away; I felt numb, inside and out. Marta clung on to me. But she wasn't screaming. Or crying. I think she'd realised the same as me – with the gun we could cheat the dead things, if nothing else.

I watched them climb with that odd, dull sense of detachment. I wasn't afraid, not then. It had gone out of me. The shock, perhaps. Or perhaps there is only so much a person can sustain before something gives way.

They moved slowly, stiffly. When they brought their arms up and over to grab the latest handhold, it was like watching an old, clockwork machine, badly rusted and winding down.

But with purpose in spite of it all, relentless and inexorable. They climbed over each other – not jostling, not fighting. That was the worst part. They were an army, acting as one. They used one another to advance as a mass. Towards us. A wall of dead, rotting flesh, studded with glittering green eyes.

Hands groped out of the casement, clutched the edge of the frame. A head and shoulders followed. The blue woman.

Dragging herself out, she leant her weight on her arms, and hauled herself onto the casement top. A clumsy forward lunge landed her on the slope of the roof. Crawling on all fours, she began to climb. Her eyes didn't leave my face. It would be easy, if I just kept staring into them. I mightn't even feel anything.

Marta was shaking me. "Katja. Katja. Use the gun."

Screams shrilled across the street. The creatures had reached a rooftop. Brutal, simple tactics. One lunged out, seized hold of someone and pulled. The first brought half a dozen people down with it. Falling, they dislodged others. Pebbles in an avalanche. Three careered straight down the roof's slope and off it into the water, which exploded into churning froth as they were borne under. Others clung to the roofing, tried to stop sliding and climb back up, but more dead things closed on them. A teenage boy slid, screaming and scrabbling, until a dead thing grabbed his arm, twisting it up towards its jaws. Others scrambled in to join the feast.

A dull thudding, behind us. The ones in the back yard. They'd be climbing too.

The blue woman crawled on. Her face opened in a hissing snarl.

"Katja!"

Marta grabbed for the pistol, and I was awake again. I slapped her hand away and pulled the pistol out, took the safety off, fingers stiff and clumsy. The blue woman's hand rose up, clutching and clawing at the air, slapped down on the tiles.

Papa taught me to shoot. So long ago now. I hoped I could still remember.

Aim with both hands, one steadying the other. At the chest, the centre of the body's mass; squeeze the trigger slowly and gently – pull it hard and you'll spoil your aim.

She looked at the gun and cocked her head to one side, almost quizzically.

The gun's bark, jagged in the cold still air. Pain jolted up my arm as the butt recoiled into my bruised hand; I almost dropped it. A brass shellcase tinkled down the roof-slates, and the blue woman reared backwards and fell. Her body slid and rolled till it hit the casement. A hole gaped in the centre of her chest.

Good shot.

The dead things climbing behind her stopped, staring at her. I held the gun ready, smoke drifting from its barrel and breech.

The blue woman's head rocked side to side. She rolled over, showing the ragged exit hole in her back, and started climbing again.

The screams gathered in close, pressing down on my ears like hands. The blue woman's eyes expanded, filling the world.

I aimed at her forehead. If that didn't stop her, I'd turn the gun on Marta and myself, while there was still time for a quick death.

I hardly felt the recoil this time. A small, neat hole dotted the woman's forehead. Dark matter flew out in a spray from the back of her head, like a flock of scattering crows. Her mouth formed an O. She went completely still.

Then her eyes... faded. Like dying lamps. The glow in the empty sockets dimmed, and was gone.

Her limbs locked her in her crouch, then slackened and tipped her backwards, sliding. She thudded to a halt against the guttering, lolling half-over the water. The dead things around her, around us, stopped climbing. One reached out and prodded her. They stared up at us. Then back down at her.

I almost felt a sense of loss. At least the blue woman had been an enemy with a face.

"Katja, behind us," Marta whispered.

It was crawling up the other side of the roof, from the backyard, a tangle of bones and rags clotted with green-black mud that had once been flesh. It suddenly accelerated as if in a speeded-up film, scuttling up towards us like a putrid spider.

I brought the gun across and fired. One eye-socket blew out like a shattered bulb as the bullet snapped its head round. The remaining eye dulled and was extinguished. The remains cartwheeled down the roof, flying apart as they went. They fell into the water and sank. But other faces were filling the flooded backyard.

The blue woman lay where she'd fallen. The other dead things still surrounded her. Then they stepped back and slid down into the floodwater, the lights of their eyes dimming in the murk before disappearing.

When I looked back down at the yard, that was empty too. They didn't come near us; they left us alone.

Just us.

Perhaps if anybody else had been armed... but they weren't. The roofing in the neighbouring building caved in suddenly, collapsing under their weight. The white-bearded man lost his balance and fell in. The rest of his family shrieked. He screamed too. The dead things crawled out of the hole; the ones who weren't busy devouring him. They swarmed up towards the survivors... and just threw themselves forward, bowling the whole mass of them, living and dead, down the far side of the roof. The shrieks were swallowed up, lost in the churning and thrashing of water, the tearing of flesh and the splitting crack of bone.

I had to look away. Even if it cost me my life, I couldn't look. But I could still hear.

I tried to shut it out. Maybe I succeeded. I can't quite remember when I realised the screaming had stopped. At first I thought I'd gone deaf. But then I registered the hiss and splatter of falling rain, the slap of floodwaters against the buildings. The squeak of rats, the patter of their paws. And the wind; I felt it chill me, and I heard it moan. But there were no more screams.

I had no idea what sounds the dead things might make. Did they breathe? They were dead, after all.

I knew when I looked up, they'd be standing around me, silent and motionless, waiting for me to see them, so I'd *know*. Perhaps if I didn't look up they'd let me live.

"Katja?"

"Yes?"

"Do you think they've gone?"

"Who?"

"Those things. Whatever they are. They could be all around us."

Great minds obviously thought alike.

"What do you think?" she asked.

"I don't know."

"I think we should look."

We were going to die anyway, if not by the dead things then by cold, starvation, or disease or just falling off the roof when we fell asleep. If we looked now there might be time to use the gun. "I think so too."

"OK then."

"OK." I opened my mouth to count to three.

"They're gone," said Marta.

I looked along the rooftops, across the street. The dead things *were* gone.

So were the living. Rats scurried along the gutters; two bedraggled pigeons alighted on an abandoned rooftop. But there were no people. None.

Blood splashed the brickwork and tiling; here or there a child's doll lay in a gutter, or a handbag, a shoe, lay on the tiles. The bus's windows, still cracked and blood-smeared, were no longer steamed. The top deck was empty. Anything living had either been eaten or got up and walked, living no longer.

If those things killed us – if we weren't devoured completely – would we become like *them*?

And where *were* they?

"Where have they gone?" Marta whispered.

I had no answer.

We grew colder and colder. Soon we could barely move.

Perhaps this was their plan. We were dangerous, so they'd retreated, leaving the cold to do their job for them. Just waiting.

The thought was almost appealing. I knew I wouldn't be able to keep awake much longer.

Marta's lips were tinged blue. Her teeth chattered.

"So cold," she whispered.

There was a thumping sound from below.

Tiny lights blinked on in the water.

They'd decided not to wait after all.

I tried to count the shots I'd fired. My brain felt thick and slow. Two at the blue woman, one at the other creature. That was right wasn't it? Ten rounds. Minus three. Ten minus three. What was ten minus three?

Seven. Seven bullets left.

Five for them. Two for us.

Thump. Thump.

The ones in the water weren't moving, just watching. There were others, coming up through the brothel. Would they smash up through the roof beneath us? We wouldn't stand a chance.

I drew the gun, fumbled the safety off, looked across at Marta.

"Don't let them get me." Her voice was hoarse and gravelly; she sounded impossibly old. "Please."

I smiled and touched her cheek. Both felt like someone else's movement. "I won't."

Hands groped out of the casement window. They looked normal, not rotted or discoloured. It was only when the rest of the arms groped out, showing big, ragged scallops of flesh missing from the forearms and biceps, that all doubt went.

It pulled itself free of the casement. I aimed at the head. Aimed. Aimed. Couldn't focus.

"Krysztyna?" said Marta.

Krysztyna. She'd been Polish. Blonde, tall. Very beautiful. Punters often asked for her specially. Less beautiful now. She'd been on the ground floor. Her eyes had been blue. They were still there, but clouded and opaque, lit green from within like grimy bulbs.

She crawled up the roof towards us. After her came Elena. She'd come from the same part of Romania as my mother. A village not far from Timisoara. Her eyes had been dark. Not anymore.

Glass smashed behind us. Down the back of the building, another girl was dragging herself out. Anya. And after her, Sonia, and Hana.

Krysztyna was closing in. My hands shook, the gun barrel jerking to and fro. *Shit. Shit. Shit.* She was close. I pulled the trigger.

Shaking too much. Missed her entirely, clipped Elena's shoulder instead. She reared back, arms pinwheeling, then began climbing again. Below, another pair of hands emerged. Gabriela. She was the last one. Unless it was Marianna, but surely there couldn't be enough left.

I aimed again. Krysztyna reached out, her hand coming towards my face.

The bullet hit her just left of her nose, and the back of her head blew out. Her eyes went dark and she flopped forward, then slid down the roof to block Elena's path.

I turned around. Anya reached for my dangling foot. I pulled it back and fired again. The top of her head blew off. She dropped, bounced off the guttering and crashed down into the water in the yard. The surface glittered green.

How many shots now? Three had been fired. That left... that left...

Marta was moving, trying to get up. "What are you doing?"

"Standing up. If we hold onto the chimney... they can't grab our feet."

I nodded and stood. Down in the water, they were rising.

This was it, then.

I perched both feet on top of the roof. Marta got an arm round my waist, another round the chimney stack. I gripped a chimney pot's rim. I'd have to shoot one-handed.

Four left. Four.

They were closing in on both sides. Sonia one side, Elena the other. I'd liked Elena more. So I shot her first. End it for her.

Too low. It blew off the bottom of her jaw. A muffled, strangulated moan came out of what was left of her mouth. I aimed at her nose this time. The bullet punched a hole in her forehead.

I watched her fall.

Two rounds left.

Tears swam in Marta's eyes. Mine too.

"Do it," she said, voice calm and clear. She tilted her chin up. *Ready.*

She closed her eyes.

I put the gun against her temple.

I pulled the trigger.

CHAPTER FOUR

Click.

Marta's eyes opened. "What?"

"Misfire." I pulled back the slide. The bullet clattered down the roof. Sonia was closing in. I aimed down at her.

No.

One bullet.

I looked at Marta.

One bullet left.

Sonia, Marta or me?

I could kill Marta with a blow. I would have to, if I wanted to spare myself a death like Marianna's. I nodded; first Marta, then myself.

I put the gun through my waistband and said: "Close your eyes." Marta did. "Put your head back."

She did, biting her lip, shivering, eyes tight shut. I thought of a young girl about to make love for the first time – how I'd been, the first time. Terrified. The bruised heel of my hand throbbed. I drew back my arm to strike and –

Something wet splashed my legs. A second later I heard the shot.

Sonia slid back down the roof, the top of her head gone. Hana half-turned to look behind her, and blood and matter sprayed from the side of her head too. The shot echoed out as she toppled after Sonia.

The mist was closing in, but something was moving through it. Something long, dark and low.

A narrowboat drifted towards the building. A man crouched in the bow, a rifle at his shoulder. He aimed again.

Marta yelled. Gabriela had seized her ankle. I started to aim at her as she pulled herself towards Marta. Her head came up over the point of the roof and the rifle cracked again. A hole appeared between her eyes and the back of her head blew out, and she slid back down towards the water.

Whoever the man on the boat was, he was a good shot.

The boat came in over the flooded backyard. The man shouted something, then ran back inside the cabin.

It wasn't going to stop, I realised. I threw both arms round Marta and the chimney stack, trying to make my fingertips meet.

The boat thumped into the side of the brothel. The building shivered. I kept hold of Marta, and the chimney stack. *Don't break. Don't break.*

It didn't.

When I looked, the man had climbed back into the bows. He'd slung the rifle across his back; now he carried a shotgun. Another dead thing mounted the brothel's roof; he fired and blew its head apart, pumping the slide to reload.

"Get on board!" he shouted. He was about forty or fifty, with a beard and greying reddish hair. A pot belly, too. An unlikely rescuer; he hardly looked the stuff gallant heroes were made of. Not that I was complaining.

He stepped back, thumbing fresh shells into the shotgun. I jumped into the bow, turned, arms out to catch Marta, but she'd already jumped too, and cannoned into me. We hit the deck.

The man grabbed my arm and pulled me to my feet. The shotgun was shoved into my hands.

"Take this. I've got to get us off here."

He took a pistol from his belt. A lot of guns. Not easily done in this country. Not legally.

Then he ran back through the boat towards the stern. As he did, a dead thing slid down the brothel roof and into the bow. I threw the gun to my shoulder. Papa had taken me hunting when I was a girl. My mother had disapproved, but...

I aimed low. The gun kicked back hard. The dead thing's head came apart and it collapsed against the guardrail. I pumped the slide. How many rounds were left in the gun?

The engine revved. Three more dead things sliding down the rooftop towards the boat. A hand flapped under the port guardrail, scratching at the decking.

The water, full of them. Full.

I walked towards the prow. Marta screamed my name. They landed in front of me, reached out. I fired point-blank, stumbling from the recoil, but at that range two went down. *Pump the slide. Aim. Fire again.* The third fell back over the side, headless.

The boat juddered backwards, turning.

Slap. Slap. The dead thing in the water was hauling itself under the rail. I drove the butt of the shotgun down into its skull. Bone crunched; I felt sick as I felt it give way. But the dead thing went limp and fell away.

Heads poked out of the water, green eyes glimmering. Then the boat turned, and the mist swallowed them.

With the boat moving straight ahead, the man leaned out from the stern and waved to us. I stumbled to the rail, and peered down the cabin side at him. Marta's fingers were tight little claws on my arm.

"You look half-dead," the man called.

I nodded.

"Get yourself in. I'll join you in a minute."

We used the door at the bow end. We stumbled through the galley and a narrow corridor, then out into a wider space at the stern, a cabin about two metres wide. There were curtains on the windows. A carpet. A couch. Ornaments. In the corner, a wood-burning stove.

I collapsed onto the couch. The man's footsteps thumped on the steps.

A pillow against my cheek, a blanket on my skin. I was warm. It felt good.

Awake in my old familiar bed at the brothel, if not safe and sound there. But I was glad, actually *glad* to be back there. After that nightmare. So *real*.

It wouldn't last, of course. By nightfall, I'd be wishing it was real; at least there I could kill some of my enemies, before they –

The blanket.

I opened my eyes.

The blanket was rough, coarse on my skin. My *bare* skin. I was naked. I never slept nude. Stripped for the customers, yes, but at night, when I crawled into bed, I always wore something.

The carpet. My bedroom carpet was a faded blue, nearly worn away. This was thick and cherry-coloured.

There were curtains on the window above my head; bright, floral patterns. A woman's room, surely?

The room rocked gently, side to side. Sick. Dizzy. This wasn't my room. Had Ilir taken me somewhere? A private party? That must be it. Taken to entertain some clients.

The room lurched and I nearly fell to the floor. I yelped, grabbed the edge of the bed. Pain shot up my arm. My hand. My hand hurt. Why did my hand hurt?

"Easy."

I squawked, before I could stop myself. There was someone in the room. The blanket had slipped down. I grabbed it and pulled it back over me.

"It's alright."

Someone sat against the wall. A bench seat. He reached up the wall. *Click.* A lamp came on above.

Fortyish, gingery hair going grey, a beard, balding... a big burly man... a little overweight...

I knew him, but where from?

"It's alright," he said again. "You're safe."

My hand... It was wrapped in bandages. Bruised. How?

"We're out in open water now," he said. "It's far less danger-ous."

Danger. Glowing eyes. Anya and Krysztyna, shot in the head. Sonia too. And Hana. Hanicka, we used to call her. She hated it – she said it was a name for a little girl with her hair in bunches – but we loved to tease her. Affectionately though. She'd been a friend. Marianna... Marianna was dead too. But not shot. Some-thing else. Something worse. *Eaten?*

No, that couldn't be it. Stupid. That was stupid –

Marta. I'd put a gun to her head. No. Not Marta too?

Too?

I'd killed the others. Had I gone mad? What had I done?

"Katja?" He leant forward. "That's your name, right, lass? Kat-ja?"

Speak. Speak. "Yes."

"I'm Derek. You're on me boat. The *Rosalind*. Called it after my daughter. The little one's at the tiller. Taking a turn steering. I showed her how. She caught on fast. Seems to be enjoying it." He gave me a smile; it was quite sweet really. Shy. Awkward. "S'pose it takes her mind off all of this."

"All of what?"

But then I was shaking my head, trying to reject what I was remembering. But no such luck; it all came back. The flood. Picking the lock. Breaking the doors down. The loft. Marianna... Marianna dying. Torn apart. Eaten. Alive. By...

I don't know what name to give the kind of sound I made. A strangled cry, a yelp, a sob, a scream... it was all of these things at once, and wholly none. My hand was on my face, trying, too late, to silence it.

Derek started out of his chair, then thought better of it. "Easy lass. You'll be alright. You're safe now. Got thee out of there."

The boat, smashing into the side of the brothel. Derek picking the dead things off with his rifle, then the shotgun. "I'm... you undressed me?"

He nodded. "You were half-frozen. Nowt I've not seen before."

I remembered *that* part. "Thank you."

"You're welcome, lass. How you feeling?"

My fingers were still stiff, and the bruising still ached dully through the bandages. But I wasn't numb anymore, not shaking. "I feel OK."

And of course, I was still breathing, and nothing had been bitten out of me by something that should've been dead.

"Do you want another brew?"

"Another?"

"We managed to get some sweet tea down your neck before. Do you another if you want."

"I'd love a coffee."

He grinned. "Milk and sugar?"

"Just milk. Thank you."

"Mention it." He moved down the living room, through a narrow passage towards the galley. I could see him, fussing over the gas stove. "Let me know if you need another one, or just help yourself. For now, anyway. Got to keep warm. But after that – well, this is all we've got, so don't go overboard." He grinned again, a boy once more. "No pun intended."

I could feel the tea he'd mentioned clamouring for release. "Is there a toilet?"

"Mm? Oh aye. Loo's through here, first left. Cabin's on your right. My daughter's room. That's for you and the lass when you want to get your heads down."

I held the blankets awkwardly round myself as I went in. When you're naked, you feel like easy meat. I did, anyway. Hence never sleeping that way. Derek seemed harmless enough, but still...

When I came back, Derek had moved a small side-table over to the bed and sat a large, steaming mug on it. He looked away as I passed him. The bed... it had been a couch before, hadn't it? I looked closer – it had folded out. Tidy.

Derek talked about the boat. The *Rosalind* had 'all the mod-cons', as he called them. A generator gave heat and lighting, although it would have to be conserved from now on, as there was only limited fuel. "And we've a long way to go," he added. The wood-burning stove could run on salvaged driftwood, left to dry on the cabin roof. Assuming the weather permitted that.

We sat in awkward silence. Finally I asked: "Do you have my clothes?"

He grunted. "Stuff you were wearing's fit for nowt. I've some you can wear. Claire – the missus – she were about your size."

"Was?"

He nodded.

"I'm sorry."

He shrugged and looked away, blinking fast. "I'm alright, long as I don't think about it. We used to go out on the canal at weekends. I were moored up at Castlefield when this all started. Best place to be, as it turned out. Just slipped moorings and... floated. Pretty choppy." He looked back at me; his smile was tight and stretched. "Tell you, when the waters get rough, boat like this, you don't half feel it. Flat-bottomed, you see. Every time it goes up and down in the water... makes your teeth rattle, I'll tell you."

I smiled back at him.

"Most of the time, I just had my work cut out not going under. Christ alone knew where I'd ended up. Once I could, I started trying to get my bearings. Lucky I'd got a compass aboard. Tend not to need them on a narrowboat, since you just stick to the canals. Then I saw you."

"From that distance?"

"I wasn't far off. Looked through my binoculars. Used to like birdwatching. Not be much of that anymore. 'Cept for ducks and the like, eh? Got the rifle and that out, and... well, you know the rest."

I nodded.

We sat in silence for nearly a minute after that. Then he slapped his thighs and got up. "You'll want them clothes," he said.

I wore jeans and a sweater. And underwear – large white briefs

– and a standard, sturdy bra. Once I would have considered them dowdy, but after two years of thongs and g-strings, push-ups and peepholes, they were a blessed relief. (If you're a man, you'll just have to take my word on this.) My trainers were still usable; he'd dried them out.

I joined them at the stern. Marta held the tiller; he'd found her a stripy jersey, several sizes too large, and an old sailor's cap. She grinned at me, eyes bright. Like a kid out on a day-trip. But that's all she was. A kid. I shouldn't be surprised.

All I could see, when I looked out into the gathering mist, were bits and pieces – tree-tops, the occasional part of a house. "Where are we going?"

Derek slipped a cigarette into his mouth, then offered me the packet. I took one; I'd been trying to give up, not that there'd been much motivation in the brothel. Some of the girls had been on heroin, after all.

"Can I have one?" Marta asked.

"No you bloody can't!" Derek choked on a lungful of smoke. "You're too young. And if I were you, I wouldn't start."

"I've been smoking for two years," she protested.

Derek looked as if she'd just slapped his face. "You bloody *what*?"

"I have," she said, shifting uncomfortably. The way he was looking at her told her she'd made a mistake.

I tried to intervene. "Derek, it's alright."

"Is it hell."

"We both smoked. It was better than what some of the other girls had." I realised he might not realise what we were – had been. "It can't do any harm."

"No harm? Are you mad, woman? Bloody lung cancer and everything?"

We'd be lucky to live so long. I opened my mouth to speak again, but he held a hand up. "No. And that's final." He took the tiller, shouldering Marta aside. "I'd best steer a bit. Get yourself in, lass. You'll catch your death."

She blinked, looking more childlike than ever. "But..."

"Do as you're told, love."

Marta looked at me. I gave a small nod. Something made her hesitate at the cabin door and look back. "I'm sorry, Derek."

He nodded. "Alright, lass. Now get yourself in."

The door clicked shut. Derek kept his hands on the tiller, looking straight ahead. "You shouldn't encourage her."

"Encourage her?"

"Smoking. It's one thing for you, love, but she's just a kid."

I was closer to Marta's age than his, but didn't argue the point. Men tend never to grow up, in my experience; I was a grown woman, and that would tend to erase the age gap as far as Derek was concerned. But Marta was so obviously so young. Part of the appeal she'd had for some punters. Of all the girls at the brothel, I'd been fondest of her. It had been nice having someone else to worry about and fuss over from time to time. Fondest of her, and more worried about her than anything else.

I thought for a second, chose my words carefully.

"Derek... do you know what it was we did? What that place you rescued us from was?"

He didn't answer, just kept staring straight ahead.

"Derek –"

"*Yes.*" His eyes squeezed shut, then reopened. "Yes, I bloody know what it was. I talked to the lass." He thumped the tiller. "Bastards."

I didn't answer. I looked out over the dull brown water. Something bobbed in it. A horse. Dead. Its belly bloated, legs jutting stiffly up, horrible and ridiculous all at once. No people, though. None that I could see. They would be below the water.

Derek seemed likeable enough and – the biggest point in his favour – he'd saved both our lives. But there was something... something not quite right about him, but I couldn't tell what yet. And anyway, I could hardly leap overboard and swim for it.

When I felt enough time had passed, I looked back at him. I started to speak, but he cut me off.

"I know... what you were. Both of you. But it's *were.* That's the one good thing about this. You don't have to be that anymore. Do you?"

I didn't want to think too far ahead; didn't want to consider what might be necessary in order to obtain food and shelter in the future. We only had one thing to sell. Unless I could hire myself out as a mercenary or something like that. Perhaps I could teach Marta how to kill people. God knows what Derek would make of that.

"What?" he said, but he was smiling.

"Mm?"

"You're smiling."

"So are you."

"Because you are."

He looked directly into my eyes when he said that. I looked away.

"Sorry."

"It's alright," I said. "I was only smiling... because I was thinking you were right." Hoping would have been more accurate.

"Aye. We can start again. No baggage. So you can leave all the shite behind. And that includes smoking." He looked at his cigarette – still hanging, unlit, between his fingers – with distaste. "Should bloody quit myself and all. Doubt I'll have much choice before long anyroad."

That was true too. And not just luxuries like cigarettes or alcohol. Vital things. Medical supplies – antibiotics, antiseptics, even plasters and bandages. I looked at my bandaged hand, the cuts there. The floodwater was filthy. Full of silt, effluent. Certainly unfit to drink. Teeming with germs. Full of the dead, walking or not. I thought of the dead horse. Was it only humans who were coming back to life? If it *was* life? Either way, a mouthful of the water could be lethal. A minor cut could get infected and there'd be fewer and fewer things to treat it with. I remembered what I'd thought before – there would be no rescue. Still...

"Is there... do you know if there's anyone else out there?"

"Not seen anyone save yourselves," he said. "Can't pick up owt on radio, either. I can get police and military frequencies and all." He raised his eyebrows. "And there's nowt. I reckon we're on our own, lass."

"I thought the same thing." But there'd have to be other survivors. And the government – they'd have kept themselves safe. In their bunkers. Sooner or later they'd stick their heads out again, if only to get their power back. The only question was how long that would take.

Then I remembered the question I'd wanted to ask. "Derek, where are we going?" He didn't answer. "Do you know?"

"Straight to hell in a handcart, lass." He saw me staring at him, and laughed. "Figure of speech. No, we're aiming north."

"North?"

He nodded. "Further north we head, more higher ground we're likely to find. Better chance of making landfall. Can't keep boating around forever. Lot of farming country that way too, so more chance of finding food. We've tinned stuff here and bottled water, but it'll not last forever. Besides – up that way, it's not very heavily populated, you know?"

I gestured at the water. "Will anywhere be heavily populated, after this?"

"Not by the living, lass."

"Oh." Of course. How stupid could I have become?

"Far as I can tell, they're staying put. Not following us. Sail in among the buggers they might try and climb aboard, but otherwise –" He shook his head. "Further away from the big cities we get, the better."

I nodded. "That makes sense."

He barked a laugh. "Glad you approve."

And I did. But trusting him was a different matter.

CHAPTER FIVE

As we headed north, the wind rose. The mist began thinning out and the visibility improved, but the waters grew choppier, white streaking the brown surface as it crested and heaved. The narrowboat rose and fell; the deck swayed underfoot.

"Better get inside," Derek shouted over the gale. "Get down, hang on to summat."

I nodded and stepped to the door.

"Just one thing."

I looked back. "Yes?"

"Do us a favour? Just put any loose stuff away. There's a cupboard. It's just – some of it was the wife's. I'd miss it."

"Of course."

I went inside.

Marta huddled on the couch; she looked pale, scared and ill. I'd forgotten her. "Are you alright?"

"No!"

I ruffled her hair, grabbed the couch as the *Rosalind* lurched.

"It's alright. It's just a squall." I hoped that was the right word. I hoped I was right.

"It's not that."

"What, then?"

"I'm scared of him."

I looked back at the door. "I think he's OK, Marta. He's just a little – messed–up. We all are."

Her voice rose. "No. There's something wrong with him."

I held her shoulders. "Marta. We don't have anywhere else to go right now. So stay –"

"Stay calm! Stay calm!" She pulled free. "I know. I know." She dropped her voice to a whisper. "But something's wrong with him."

"OK." I nodded. Privately, I agreed, even though I wasn't sure why right then.

Her eyes narrowed. "Don't talk to me like I'm stupid."

"I'm not."

"I'm not stupid. I'm scared, that's all."

"Me too. You did well back there."

"I didn't."

"You were scared at first –"

"I still am."

"But you got yourself together. You watched my back, you kept your head. I'm proud of you."

She scowled, but I could tell she was pleased.

The boat lurched again. A china figure flew off a shelf and hit the carpet. Luckily it didn't break. I wasn't sure how Derek would react if it had. But why hadn't it broken before? Had he put everything away when the floods came? Or before?

There was something wrong there, niggling me. But there was no time now.

"Help me put this stuff away," I said. "Let's keep him happy."

We packed as much away as we could, then climbed onto the couch and grabbed hold.

The boat heaved and bucked, juddering each time it came

down in the water; once we were nearly thrown clear across the room. I don't know how long this went on, but finally the storm eased. The boat bobbed and rocked gently in the water, but I could stand, although my legs shook.

Marta looked shakier still, and queasy. I guessed seasickness was kicking in. My stomach felt a little tender, but nothing bad. I guessed I had good sea legs. That was the English term, if I recalled.

"I think it's calmer now," I said.

She nodded weakly. "I hope so."

I parted the curtains. Outside, brown water slopped against a few protruding treetops, and a thin mist gathered. Without the wind, it would soon thicken again.

There was a cabin, with a double bunk. Apparently it had been his daughter's room.

"He said they used to go out on the canals at weekends," said Marta, pulling off her shoes and socks. "Him and his family. Sometimes a friend of his daughter's."

"Sounds nice."

"Yes." She slumped onto the lower bunk and pulled the covers over herself. "But I still don't trust him."

I went back up on deck. Derek glanced down at me. "Y'alright there, love?"

I nodded.

"How's the kid?"

"Seasick, I think."

"Ah. Poor love. I've some tablets for that, somewhere. Break 'em out later."

I stood next to him in silence. I wasn't that eager for conversation, and I doubt he was either. But I wanted to see where we were going as best I could. It gave me, at least, the illusion of control. "Where are we now?"

"Hard to tell at the minute. At a guess, I'd say somewhere between Bury and Rochdale. But I could be way off."

They were just names to me in any case. "How far along are

we?"

"Along?"

"Towards where we want to go?"

He shrugged. "Not sure, love, to be honest. All I can think at the minute is keeping on northward. Like I said, further we get from towns and cities and the like, the safer we'll be. Best thing'd be a good stretch of land well above sea level, preferably in the middle of nowhere. But at the minute it's pot luck. Just got to keep going long as we can."

"And hope we sight land?"

"Pretty much."

I didn't ask what would happen if we didn't.

Something loomed ahead. It came out of the mist; a church steeple. Near the top, a woman was clinging to it. Her face was pale, eyes tight shut.

"Derek –"

He gripped my arm. "Shh, lass."

"What?"

Too late. The woman had heard me, or us. Or the chug of the engine. Whatever the cause, her eyes flicked open. They were sunken and ringed with darkness; we were close enough now that every detail of her face seemed to jump out. "Oh thank God... help me, please. Please!"

But Derek just gazed straight ahead.

"*Please!*"

"Derek, what are you doing? We can't just leave her."

He glared at me and spoke through his teeth, lips drawn back from them. "How much food do you think we have? How much bottled water? And extra weight means we'll use more fuel. How much of *that* d'you think we've got?"

He kept staring at me, without blinking, till I looked away. I could've asked why, in that case, he'd rescued Marta and I? But perhaps I didn't want to go down that road. He might start to regret his decision. Or I might find out why he'd really rescued us. I didn't believe it was simple compassion. My sense of something badly wrong with him had deepened.

I might be better off knowing the truth. But I didn't think

Derek wanted to get into that, anymore than I did. I'd heard a phrase in a song once – 'comfort-lies'. It's not just men who have those, it's all of us. Or almost all. Perhaps people like me, or Marta, had none of those because we couldn't afford them. Or was that a comfort-lie in itself?

Whatever the case, there's nothing more dangerous than a man stripped of his comfort-lies. And I believed Derek had them, about what he'd done and why. As long as he had to keep believing he'd rescued us out of kindness, we had a degree of safety. But if I made him admit his real motives, that would be gone – and so far I didn't know what his real motives even *were*.

And there was something else.

Derek was right. There would be others like this woman, like us. People who'd climbed onto rooftops or church spires. People on hilltops or little knobs of ground just clear of the floodwaters. None of them safe for us to stay. But all of them begging us to take them on board. Derek's Ark.

That horrible jagged laughter bubbling up in me again; a scream broken up into a kind of manic stutter to stop me going mad. But if I started laughing now I'd never, never stop.

Yes, we could take this woman on board. But what about the next, and the next? There would always be good reason to take another on board, till the boat wallowed low from the weight... running more slowly from it too... using more fuel... the food rationed more and more... and the water too... until very, very soon there was none left at all...

So yes – Derek was right. But that didn't mean he was safe. And it didn't make the woman's screams, increasingly desperate and forlorn as we moved away from her, seeming to get more loud with the distance and not less, any easier to hear.

We heard them for quite a long time. I don't know if we just moved out of her range or if she gave up. I think the latter; for a while I was sure I could hear sobbing. But that could just have been my conscience.

For some time after that, thankfully, we didn't see anything. Just unbroken brown water. The mist was thin and distant, but the light was starting to dim. Visibility, though, was reasonable for us. Neither of us spoke.

I wondered how much food or fuel Derek had on the *Rosalind*. Probably a lot. He seemed prepared for a crisis. Or he'd always expected one. The guns, for instance. Why all these guns on a boat kept for weekend breaks? Yes, we were only alive because of them, but what did they show about Derek?

Still, I could hardly pick and choose. Derek might be paranoid, but so far that paranoia had kept me alive, in comparative safety, with food, water and some degree of protection. Better than the poor woman on the steeple had or was likely to. I would have to cope as best I could.

"You can go below if you like," Derek said after a while. "Getting nippy out."

"I'm OK."

He shrugged. "Whatever. I could murder a brew, though. Tea'd be good. If you wouldn't mind."

I made my way through the boat and ran the wood-burning stove. There was coffee as well as tea; I found I was cold as well, and made myself one. He only had tin mugs, and no tray. The heat seeped through the metal as I carried them through; I gritted my teeth against the pain.

"Ta lass."

I cradled my own in my bandaged hand; the gauze gave some insulation. "What time is it?"

"Getting on for four, me love. We'll need a place to moor before long. No point travelling by night. Could go straight past dry land. Or hit something."

I nodded. *What if it gets dark and we can't find a place to moor?* I didn't ask. There were too many questions like that, with no answer. Or no answer I wanted to hear.

The mist parted and I saw something dark. "Derek, look –"

"Aye, love, I see it."

The boat wasn't built for speed. It took time to reach the island.

Island. Before today it would have been a hill. Now it was a low hump of land, twenty metres square and maybe three, four metres above the surface at its highest point. Tiny, stick-like figures moved atop it.

At first I thought they were trying to hail us and my stomach clenched, imagining what would follow. The woman on the steeple all over again, only worse. But they weren't hailing us; I don't think they'd even seen us then. They were screaming. And minutes later, I saw exactly why.

Eight or nine men and women and two or three children were huddled together on the top. They were the only people on the island. But they were not alone.

The dead things ringed the shoreline, the water lapping around their ankles. Most looked newly dead. Some had pieces missing, bite wounds. One had a dangling arm that was mostly bare bones with a few chunks of meat still clinging to it. They just stood there, staring up at the humans. Eyes glowing. I flinched, and actually drew closer to Derek. I hate that feeling, of dependence on another. Especially for protection. I didn't need a man for that. The ones who'd claimed they were doing so – Papa aside – did anything but.

Derek lifted the edge of his sweater, and I saw the butt of a revolver, tucked into the waistband of his trousers.

I realised something; didn't know how I could've missed it. My gun – when he'd undressed me, Derek had taken it. There'd only been one bullet left, of course, but even that was better than none. The pistol he had wasn't mine, so where was it?

But the dead things didn't move. They gave no sign of having seen us. They just stood there, looking up at the tiny, frightened huddle above them.

Then one of the women on the island saw us and screamed, pointing. The next moment, they were all shouting.

"Fuck," Derek hissed. I didn't say it aloud, but I was thinking the same. I already knew we wouldn't – couldn't – help them. And I hated them for expecting us to. For shouting and pointing and drawing attention to us. For doing exactly what I would have. I hated them for wanting to live.

As the boat passed them, it seemed at first that the dead things hadn't noticed us. Too fixated on these survivors to notice. How long had they been there? Minutes? Hours? I remembered, at the brothel, the long pauses between attacks. As if they were advancing, taking a piece of territory, then consolidating, regrouping, planning the next move. They had plenty of time, after all. The water belonged to them, and there was so little land left. Just as they must outnumber the living.

But then one turned. Just one. It turned and stared, directly at us. Not the boat, but Derek and I.

No. Not at *us*.

At *me*.

I was sure of that. It stared straight at, *into*, me. I had no idea what was behind those eyes. But I knew what it would want to do.

The ring of the dead around the island began drawing in. With those jerky, tottering steps they advanced up the slopes. All of them, except one.

The one who'd been staring at me – it'd been a man once. It wore a smart suit, and I could see the glint of gold on its wrist. He turned all the way round to face us and walked forwards, into the water. Soon he was swimming, a sort of convulsive dog-paddle. The water splashed and churned white about him, but only his head stayed above the surface, his hair – doubtless once neatly coiffured – now a grotesque, straggly bird's-nest.

"*Fuck,*" said Derek again.

The people on the hilltop were screaming as the dead closed in. There was nothing else they could do. Nothing anyone could do – not even us, if we'd been so inclined. They had nowhere to run and no weapons, except for some kind of wooden post one of the men was brandishing at them. Two of them seized one of the women and bore her down as she shrieked. Another woman ran in and tried to pull her free, but another of the dead things seized hold of her, biting into her shoulder. Two others lumbered in, one grabbing her arm, the other catching her round the legs, and she went down.

The two nearest the man with the pole slowed down, lifting their arms to grapple. He swung at them. One retreated; the other lunged forward. A second swing drove into its skull; even at that distance, over the screams, I heard the crunch of bone. The dead thing went down and didn't rise, but the other lunged forward, in one of those sudden, jerky bursts of speed. It seized the pole, and as they struggled for it, three others fell on the man.

I saw a child snatched up by a dead thing and held high. Other dead hands thrust skyward, groping for it. It shrieked and shrieked till the thing holding it thrust it groundwards and they descended.

The other humans went down very quickly after that. I say 'went down', not 'died'. Because they didn't die quickly. They kept on screaming for a long time.

They were still screaming when Derek drew the revolver from his belt and leant out over the railing. The head bobbing in the water, growing slowly closer to the boat, was no longer alone. Four, no, five others were now bobbing in the water behind it. As I watched, a sixth appeared.

"Take the tiller," Derek said. He aimed two-handed, steadying the revolver. There was a dull metallic click as he thumbed the hammer back. I took hold of the tiller, but I kept looking back.

For a long time he seemed to stand like that, unmoving, while the bobbing heads drew silently but relentlessly closer.

Then he fired. The gunshot was so sudden and loud I have to admit I almost wet myself. But didn't.

Water spewed up in a short-lived geyser, about half a metre from the dead thing's shoulder. Derek cocked the gun again. This time, when he fired, a shower of dark fragments flew up, back and out from the dead thing's head. It stopped moving forward and I saw its eyes flicker and fade, leaving it a dark featureless lump in the dying evening light, that slowly sank from view.

The other heads stopped advancing. They were treading water. They didn't follow us; one by one, as the boat moved away, they turned and swam back towards the island. I saw the first of them climbing out of the water onto dry land, dripping heavily, as the mist closed around them. Moving in to join the others at their feast.

A feast whose screams we still heard long after they were lost to sight.

CHAPTER SIX

About half an hour later, with the mist growing thick and the light failing in the east, we found a place to moor.

It wasn't much. The top of a pylon, but there was nothing else man-made in sight. There was no buzz of electricity from it; the power stations were long dead, drowned by the flood.

"With any luck, we're a way from anywhere inhabited," Derek said. "We'll moor here for the night. Not exactly recommended practice, but it'll do."

He'd replaced the revolver's empty cartridge cases with fresh ones. I wanted to ask if he had a spare – in fact I knew he did, he'd carried an automatic earlier, and he still had mine too – but I could guess his response. It made sense we should both be armed, and perhaps Marta too. He'd given me the shotgun without a second thought at the brothel. But that had been then; this was now. He wouldn't have any answer for not arming us, except that he didn't want to. And I didn't want to provoke a direct confrontation as yet.

I watched him clamber in among the pylon struts to tie the mooring ropes. Watched very carefully. I needed to know how to run the boat without Derek, if I had to. Something might happen to him. Or might need to.

He jumped back into the well-deck in the bow and stood facing me, his eyes suddenly empty. Then he smiled. "That's that then," he said. "Who wants dinner?"

I woke Marta up; she'd managed to sleep not long after collapsing into the cabin bunk. She'd been lucky enough to sleep through the encounters with the other survivors.

Derek set up a folding table in the middle of the boatman's cabin and stationed chairs around it. He turned off the lights and lit candles on the table. "Need to save energy anyway," he said, and grinned. I found myself smiling back. Cooking smells wafted from the galley. A microwave pinged.

"Just some frozen stew," said Derek. "But it'll do the job. Might as well use the frozen stuff up first. I've a lot more in tins and suchlike but they'll keep. Fridge takes up gas, so the sooner we get shot of it the better."

The stew came in bowls, with hunks of brown bread. "Eat up," Derek said. "Keep up your strength. Been a long day."

I felt the jagged laughter bubbling up in me again. Yes. A long day. The world as I knew it had ended, I'd seen one friend torn apart and eaten alive in front of me, killed a man with my bare hands and shot several other friends because they'd turned into walking corpses. But I wasn't a whore any longer. I had that much. One good thing. I might be fighting for my survival on a day to day basis, but now that made me no different from almost anyone else. I probably had a better chance than most – not stuck on some isolated lump of sodden turf waiting for the dead things to come out of the water.

Derek poured me a glass of wine, plus a Coke for Marta. He ruffled her hair as he set it down before her. She glowered at him and he laughed. I admit it, so did I. She looked like a kid again, a real kid.

The stew was excellent. Beef, garlic, mushrooms, potatoes, broccoli, carrots, a rich gravy. Probably the best meal I'd had in a long time, except for the time Ilir had taken me to the restaurant; the usual quality of the food in the brothel was lousy. Cheap takeaways and cheaper frozen dinners.

I took a glass of wine, but drank sparingly. I wanted to keep a clear head. Finally I pushed the bowl away. "That was great," I said. "Thank you."

"Mm," said Marta. She was picking over hers. Maybe still a little queasy from the seasickness before. Her glass was already almost empty though. So her stomach couldn't be *that* tender.

Derek smiled and inclined his head. A good shot and a good cook. He definitely had his points. For the first time, I thought I might be wrong about him. Who wouldn't be damaged after something like this? The flood, the dead things, the loss of his family...

His family.

The one subject Derek had avoided. What *had* happened to Claire and Rosalind?

Maybe he hadn't wanted to talk about it. Maybe that was how he kept control. But even so... a dead wife and child? And the ornaments...

That was it – what had niggled me before. Before, when the squall hit – he'd asked me to put the ornaments away. His wife's things. I remembered wondering why they hadn't been damaged before. He'd said the waters had been rough at the start: *"When the waters get rough, a boat like this, you don't half feel it. Flat-bottomed, you see. Every time it goes up and down in the water... makes your teeth rattle..."*

So where had his wife's things been? Packed away already? They had to have been. And one startling absence, now I thought of it. No pictures. No pictures of them at all.

"Katja?" Marta slid her bowl away from her, still half full. Her glass of Coke was almost empty. "Katja? I feel..."

She slumped forward.

"Marta!" I rose.

"It's alright, love," said Derek. "Let the kid rest up."

The Coke glass – I picked it up. There was some kind of sediment at the bottom. "You bastard, what did you –"

"Take it easy, love. No need for that language." Sweat glistened on Derek's forehead. "Just summat to help her sleep. She's been through enough today. Needs her kip."

I put my fingers to Marta's neck. Her pulse was there, regular and fairly strong.

"She'll be fine, Claire." When I looked at Derek, he was smiling tenderly. "Why don't you put the little 'un to bed? Then we can get an early night."

He followed me as I carried Marta to her cabin and laid her on the lower bunk. I pulled off her trainers, but left the rest of her clothes on. I could feel his eyes on my back. He stood a couple of metres away, just out of easy reach, and I knew the revolver was still in his waistband.

I pulled the bedclothes over Marta. She looked younger than ever now; I could have taken her for twelve. I touched her cheek. It occurred to me that she was the nearest thing to family I still had.

"There you go," said Derek. "She'll be fine. Now stop fussing, Claire. Come on."

I turned on him. "Katja. My name's Katja." There had to be some way of reaching him. Had to be.

But he only smiled, his eyes glassy. "Whatever."

"My name is Katja."

"It doesn't have to be," he said reasonably. That was the worst thing, how casual he was sounding, as if we were discussing what brand of toilet paper we bought. "I told you before, love. Fresh start. We can all try again."

He waved me out into the passageway, took a key from his pocket and locked the bedroom door. "Keep her safe," he muttered, and looked over at me. "Got to keep them safe, haven't you? Always got to keep them safe."

I didn't know what to say.

"I was a good husband," he said. "And I were a good dad, and all. Whatever that stupid bitch said."

"Who?" Keep him talking. Try to reach him.

"Claire. Not you, the other one. Stupid bitch I was married to. Dumped me and ran off with some bloke. A fucking *travel agent*. Ran off with him. Took Ros as well. Don't even know where they are. Well, didn't. I know now."

"You do?"

"Full fathom five. Full fathom fucking five. Know Shakespeare, do you?"

"*The Tempest*, yes?"

"That's the one. 'Full fathom five thy father lies, of his bones are coral made. Those are pearls that were his eyes, nothing of him that doth fade but doth suffer a sea-change, into something rich and strange...'"

His voice choked and trailed off. "Only, I'm not the one who's dead, am I?"

"They could still be alive," I ventured.

"Tripe!" His lips curled back from his teeth. "The bitch moved without telling us. Can you bloody believe that? I couldn't even see my little girl. Claire – fuck her, she'd made her choice and buggered off and I don't give a shit what happens to her now. But Ros... No. That's what hurts. She's dead. She's dead and the stupid bitch killed her." He touched the cabin door gently. "But now... Now I've got a family again."

He came towards me. "First time I saw you, on that rooftop, I knew. It was fate, Claire. *Fate*. Bloody fate." He reached out and touched my cheek. I did my best not to flinch away. "If you could see how like her you are, how like both of them you both are. I wasn't going to do owt. But I got my binoculars out and took a closer look, and there you were. It was just you and the girl left by then. I had to think it over. Must've sat there nearly an hour trying to make up me mind. Started getting all your things back out again. Trying to find summat to do. Helped me think."

An hour? Perhaps just out of sight in the mist? All that time, watching us cling onto the rooftop...

"Then they started coming out of the water, and I had to make me mind up. Piss or get off the pot, as they say." He shook his head. "I had all me guns, of course. Shouldn't have 'em on board... shouldn't have 'em at all, really. But fuck that. Knew this was coming. Well, not this. Fucking dead men walking? No-one'd've believed that. But knew it'd all hit the fan one day. The Pakis, global bloody warming – something, anyway, it'd all kick off. So I got everything stocked up. Better on a boat anyroad. You can always move around if things get bad. See? Got it all planned out."

"Yes, Derek. You did."

He advanced, waving me down the passage towards the boat-man's cabin. "Come on, love. Let's get to bed."

"No. Derek. Please." I hated hearing the begging sounds come out of my mouth. Why didn't I kill him then and there? Because half of me pitied him? Because I'd already killed today and every time I remembered the awful crunching feel of his nose under the blow I felt sick? Because if Derek was dead, how would I run the boat? Because if I failed and he killed me instead, then what would happen to Marta?

For all those reasons, I hesitated. And the moment passed. Papa's voice again, coming back to me: *These are not children's games, Katja. To take a life is a grave thing. But once you know you must – do it quickly. If you hesitate, the moment passes, and may not come again.*

"Get in," Derek said.

"Please don't –"

He seized my arm and yanked me bodily into the cabin. I stumbled and broke free, brought an arm up to strike –

The revolver was in his hand and aimed at my face.

"Go on, then," he said. "Try it."

Slowly I let my arm drop.

Derek stepped into the room. I moved back. He kicked the door shut behind him. Dragged the table aside. Pulled the couch back out. Fumbled with it until it folded out.

"Well, then?" he asked.

I knew what he wanted. I had no choice. I peeled my t-shirt over my head, then began to unbutton my jeans.

Afterwards, I suppose, I could have killed him. When he'd finished – grunting and heaving on top of me before collapsing and half-crushing me with his weight – he rolled over and was asleep. The gun was still in his hand, tucked under his body where I couldn't reach.

But I could have done something. If I'd been quick...

But if I'd got it wrong, if he'd woken, with the gun...

But it wasn't even that. I felt... defiled. Disgusted with myself. Much as I'd felt after I'd first come to England, after Ilir and the others raped me. I felt worthless. All too often this is the way. The rage and the hatred do not go outward, where they belong; they turn inwards, on yourself, and they fester there.

I got up. I was sore. Men often wanted to start before a woman was ready. If you were their lover, you could explain these things, work at a common pace, but a whore has no such choice. We have tricks of course, to prepare ourselves beforehand so it doesn't hurt, but he'd given me no time for them. Another reason it felt like the aftermath of Ilir's punishment.

I could feel his stuff dripping out of me. Thank God, he hadn't locked the cabin door. I made it into the passageway and then the bathroom, shutting the door behind me.

I had to clean myself, to get him out of me. But before that, my throat was clenching, my gorge rising –

I reached the sink just in time, before the beef stew and wine came back up.

I coughed and retched and spat, then turned on the taps to rinse the mess away.

I rinsed my mouth with water again and again. After the first couple of times the taste of bile was gone, but it took far more attempts than that before I could no longer taste the sour flavour of his mouth and tongue.

When that was done, I ripped tissues from the toilet roll and used them and the water to clean away all traces of him. I flushed the tissues down the toilet and then sat on it, thrust my hands in my mouth and began to cry for the first time since the end of the world.

CHAPTER SEVEN

I went back to his bed, afterwards; where else could I go? I slid slowly and carefully between the sheets so as not to wake Derek.

He'd made me a whore again. He talked about fresh starts, of new beginnings, but they only applied to him. Marta and I were just clay to make a new family with.

Outside the grimy cabin window it was still dark, thick mist swirling. One of us should be keeping watch. Derek was probably right; we were far from any populated areas, there'd be few if any dead things to contend with, but what if he was wrong? If they boarded us in the night, we'd have no chance.

So? So they would eat me alive, like Marianna. So what? Marianna hadn't been given false hope, a promise of freedom, only to have it betrayed by the same person who'd offered it. It'd be the same ending as hers, only she'd have suffered less. What were all my skills and strengths worth, if that was all the good they did?

But Marta – Marta would die, too...

Even then, I didn't care. Not at that moment. I said I would be honest. I'd said she was the closest thing to family I still had, and I'd meant it. But right then, that meant nothing. I only wanted an end to this. By a bullet, by my own hand – by one of the dead things even, if it came to that.

I looked across at his sleeping bulk, his flabby bare back, pale as a grub. So easy to do something to him – if I could find the weak spots under the fat. It was worth a try, if only to save myself from a repeat performance next time he woke, if that came sooner. Surely if I looked I would find something, a weapon. One sharp thing would be all I'd need.

But I did nothing. I lacked the will. I only wanted the world to go away, however briefly, and leave me alone. So I curled up, my back to him, making sure his greasy, sweaty skin didn't touch mine, and closed my eyes.

As a piece of long-overdue mercy, sleep came.

Thin light stung my eyes and I woke. The cabin window was white with mist.

At first I just stared at it. I felt leaden and numb. I told myself to go and look. But my limbs felt so heavy. Moving them was too great an effort.

Then I heard Papa's voice again. It would be nice to imagine something more mystical, something with a little more hope involved, but more than likely I was only imagining what he would have said. If you know someone long enough, you can imagine almost exactly what they'll say.

Get up, Katja. You don't give up. You're my daughter; surely I taught you better than that?

Oh piss off, Papa. Go away and leave me alone.

Don't speak to your father that way.

Oh, just fuck off, will you? You never had to deal with this. You were never raped.

You're right, of course, I wasn't. But I faced things as bad as this; ugly things that brought me to the point of despair.

And you always overcame them, didn't you Papa? Were you

ever fucking human?

Always, Katja. Another way to look at it is this: you were in this situation before, and you survived.

Yes, but –

But nothing. You thought you'd escaped; it turns out it's not so simple. But this time it is not the same. Think on it and you'll see you're not so helpless. He is only one. He has no sons, no gang of thugs to help him. And you don't have to worry where to go. This place can be your sanctuary, this boat.

But I don't know how to run it!

You're in a safe mooring – you and Marta have time between you to learn. Kill him quickly and be done with it. Don't waste the next opportunity. He is insane; the next opportunity could be your last.

I didn't have an answer for him. I'd never had an answer for him; sooner or later I always ran out of them.

You can do this, Katja. You know you can. But first, look out of the window.

And so I got off the couch-bed. I was still sore, between my legs, but it had faded from a raw burning pain into a dull, persistent ache. I would remember this.

I looked back at the white hump of Derek's body, and started to feel a new sensation, breaking through the cracking pack-ice of my despair.

Anger. It was only a small flicker, a spark amid embers, but it was there to be nurtured. It was like being stranded in an arctic wasteland. Without a fire to warm you, you would die. So you kindled a spark, and you bent your strength to keeping it alive, making it grow.

I felt rage, and I felt humiliation. All the ugly feelings rose. I could have shut them out, retreated from them, into some warm place where I could grow numb again. But I did not, would not. Not this time.

I picked up the bra and knickers and put them on. That was a little better. Only a little, but better. I found my jeans and my T-shirt and I put those on as well. My socks were nowhere to be seen, but I found my trainers and pulled them on, lacing them up as I watched the heavy shape in the bed.

Now I was fully clothed. I felt better still. No longer naked. But he was. And he was asleep. I had a position of strength. I realised how easy it would be. I could see at least two spots where a single blow would cause instant death. He'd never wake. It would be better this way. Simpler.

But first –

I looked out of the window.

The mist was still there, but it had receded, far enough that I could see for quite a distance. The brown water lapped around the pylon. Further along I could just see the top of another one, but nothing beyond that. There was only the wide brown sea, and the mist –

And something else.

Even now, I'm not sure if I really saw it. It registered for a second and then was gone. A brief, momentary gap in the mist? Or an illusion?

Whatever the truth of it, for a second I was sure I saw a low dark hump in the distance. Something that could only be land.

Only for an eyeblink, then gone.

Even if I'd imagined it, there would be land somewhere. There had to be. The seas hadn't, couldn't have covered everything.

But even if they hadn't, the dead things would find it. I'd seen that already. The circle of dead things around the island, closing in. And if anyone was passing by, they'd keep on going. Just as we had. *I'm sorry*, they'd think, *but better you than me.* Just as we had.

One problem at a time, Katja. Deal with each situation as it arises. Now, kill that man.

Yes. While he was still asleep. Quickly, while I had the will –

"Morning, love."

Shit.

I turned. Derek blinked and smiled sleepily at me. His face was kind again. Like any loving husband's, waking up to see his wife's face. "Up already, are you? Seeing as you are, fancy getting us a brew?"

69

I could have killed the Derek of last night without a second thought. But this was the original Derek. The one who'd saved Marta and I. Did he remember what he'd done? Probably, but not as I did. He'd remember me coming to him of my own free will. He'd have erased the chunks that didn't fit with that.

In the galley, I boiled water for the coffee. There was no sound from Marta's cabin, but I could hear Derek thumping about in his. In a moment, he'd be through.

He would be awake and armed. I needed a weapon. And I had little time.

He'd put something in Marta's drink. Where would he have kept that? No, I'd never find it in time.

A knife. There'd be cutlery. Something sharp – a steak knife maybe. I pulled the top drawer open.

"What you after, love?"

Derek lumbered in, barefoot in jeans and t-shirt. The butt of the revolver in his waistband.

Last night I'd had the opportunity, but not the will. This morning it was the other way around. I had to focus on the anger, keep it bright. Wait for my chance and take it without hesitation.

He looped an arm round my waist and kissed my cheek. "After a teaspoon? They're in there."

The gun nudged my hip.

There.

He'd made it so easy.

Now.

I went for the pistol, but for a big man he was quick. I didn't catch him off-guard; it was as if he'd been waiting. One hand caught my arm; the other swept out in a backhanded arc. My lower lip split and I crashed against the cooker.

"Stupid bitch!" he spat at me as I slid down. He drew the gun. "You stupid, ungrateful bitch." He grabbed a fistful of my hair, half-lifting me from the floor; I yelled at the pain, clutching at his wrist. "I fucking saved your life!"

"Katja?" It was Marta. Her cabin door was rattling. "What's going on out there? Are you alright? I can't get out."

"It's alright, love," Derek called out. His flushed, sweaty face twisted back and forth between the rage of a second ago and the kindly rescuer we'd first seen. Trying to be two people at once. "Mummy and Daddy are just messing around, that's all."

"*Katja*! Leave her alone you mad bastard!"

"Shut up!" Derek half-turned to scream at her. He kept his grip on my hair and it felt like I was being scalped, but he'd given me an opening and I took it; I hit him in the groin with everything I had.

He screamed and doubled up, but the gun was swinging towards my face. I grabbed it with both hands, trying to wrestle it away. It fired once; the report was like a blow to the head and for a second I thought I'd been hit. But I hung on.

He let go of my hair. And then clenched his fist and brought it down, in a brutal, clubbing blow to the side of my head.

I vomited. I let go of the gun and fell to the galley floor and I vomited. There was a shrill whining tone in my left ear and through it I heard the bang and rattle of the cabin door and Marta screaming my name.

"Bitch!"

Derek staggered to his feet above me, aiming down. I was on the floor, woozy. I tried to wriggle away. He turned the gun towards me. I kicked out with my right leg, driving the heel out straight. It slammed into his kneecap; I felt the bone crunch, and heard it even over Derek's shriek. He fell; the revolver clattered from his hand. He was howling and sobbing in agony. He lashed out at me blindly and started crawling away.

The gun. I reached for the gun. Picked it up. Managed to stand. My neck was throbbing. God, what had he damaged? He was crawling up the steps, towards the bow door, dragging his ruined leg behind him. One hand fumbled in his pocket –

"Derek!" I screamed, aiming at his back.

He kept crawling. I pulled back the hammer. Aimed. And then fired.

The recoil drove me back, the gun flying up towards my face. I pulled my head aside just in time; the barrel clipped my ear nonetheless. The back of Derek's t-shirt ripped, blood flying out. A bright, vivid crimson fan of it exploded up the steps. There was a splintering crack as the bullet ploughed into wood. Derek's body jerked and fell forward. His legs tremored and kicked. And then he was still.

"Katja?" Marta's voice had grown strangely calm. "Katja?" Now it was small, despairing and forlorn.

"I'm alright," I called out. Probably louder than I needed to, but my ears still rang from the gunshots. "I'm alright."

I let her out of the room. But first I checked on Derek. I had to make sure he was dead.

I was almost certain he was long before I checked his pulse; there was a stench coming off him; shit and piss. A dark wet stain was spreading out from between his legs, dripping down the steps, mixing with the blood. The galley stank of it, of the blood; it overwhelmed the rest. I had to walk into it to get close enough. It squelched underfoot, and my trainers began to stick.

I put the gun behind his ear and cocked it, then reached down and felt for a pulse in his neck. There was nothing.

I uncocked the gun and stepped back. His hand had come out of his pocket. It held a bunch of keys. It took several tries to unlock the door of Marta's room, but soon she was out.

She didn't cling to me, or cry.

"You're OK, then?" she asked.

I nodded.

She looked down the corridor towards Derek's body. Her face stayed calm, like a Madonna. She turned and looked back at me and nodded.

"I told you," she said. "I told you there was something wrong with him."

I put the gun in my waistband and held her. She was stiff to begin with, like wood, but finally she hugged me back. "That's right, little one," I told her. "You did."

We needed to find out where everything was. The bullet I'd fired into Derek had been soft-nosed; it had expended most of its energy on him and embedded itself in the step beneath. The other round had punched a hole out through the galley wall.

We went through the boat to take stock of what we had. In the gas locker beneath the well-deck, we found a rubber dinghy, complete with oars in unscrewed sections. Obviously Derek had liked having a getaway option.

The guns were there too. Two pump-action shotguns, the rifle, the automatic pistol he'd carried and the one he'd taken from me. Both pistols were the same calibre, so I could reload mine.

When I'd done that, I dragged Derek's body onto the well-deck and propped him against the bow. His head lolled back over the gunnels. I tried to tilt it forward but it kept falling back.

I stepped back and drew the revolver. Aimed. Clicked back the hammer.

Now he was dead, my pity for Derek resurfaced. He was no longer a threat, just a man who'd lost too much and been unable to cope with it. He'd saved our lives, even if it had been for distorted and insane motives. We were alive because of him.

And so this was as much to ensure death was the end for him, and that he found whatever peace there was to be found, as for mine and Marta's safety.

So I told myself, at least, as I pulled the trigger.

CHAPTER EIGHT

We restarted the engine and cast off. I left Derek's body in the bows till we were moving, then heaved it overboard, just in case he brought anything to the surface. He didn't sink, just bobbed face down in the low brown swell as we pulled away. The mist swallowed him before he could sink.

"Where do we go now?" asked Marta.

It might have been a trick of the light, an optical illusion, or my worn-out brain seeing what it wanted, needed to, but it was the only clue we had, and we had to go somewhere.

"That way," I said, and pointed.

"Why?"

"Because I think I saw land out there this morning."

"You think?" We just looked at one another. Then Marta broke out in what sounded all too much like the mad, jagged laughter I'd been fighting off. "Why not?" She squeezed my shoulder. "Let's go."

Morning became afternoon and the afternoon wore on in turn. We passed through flat, featureless brown waters, endless and still. At least there were no winds yet, no storms.

"Jesus Christ!" Marta was staring over the guardrail, she looked sickened and fascinated, all at once. "Have you seen this?"

I looked over the side and felt my stomach perform a slow roll. The boat was cleaving its slow, steady way through a thick, matted brown mass. At first I thought it was sewage, but then I looked more closely and saw the fur. More; I saw paws, tails, tiny faces twisted in a last agonised snarl.

Rats. Thousands, *millions* of drowned rats. They piled up around the bows of the boat and against the sides, rolling back and down into the water. Their legs stuck stiffly out, bellies bloated, huge as if massively pregnant.

Marta turned away, grimacing. The smell was foul. I saw other debris mixed in with them. A broken chair. A tyre. Plastic bottles. Twigs and branches. Clothing, snarled up amongst it.

Clothing?

It was nearly ten minutes later – the boat still forging a path through the matted tangle of corpses – that it hit me.

Where would all the rats have come from? Rats live among people. In a city, someone told me once, you're never more than three metres from a rat.

Please let them have drifted. Let them have drowned somewhere far away.

"Katja?"

Marta was pointing out to starboard. I looked.

The dead rats spread out for metres on all sides of the boat. The surface was lumpy and irregular. But there was something under it, where she was pointing.

Two somethings, to be precise.

Two somethings that glowed green.

As I watched, the surface broke. Rats and water streamed and tumbled away from something dark with glowing eyes.

Then another appeared, and another. I whirled, stared down the side, towards the stern. A head bobbed in the stretch of dead water behind us. Two others rose behind it.

"Shit." Marta was looking portwards now. "They're over there as well."

She had Derek's automatic; I had my gun. "Marta?"

"Yes?" She was still looking to port, hypnotised. I caught her arm. She started, turned and stared at me, face white.

"Get the shotguns," I said. "And spare ammunition." To port and starboard I could see dozens of the dead things now, rising all around us, watching – just watching, for now. "Plenty of it."

The sea of dead rats never seemed to end. We had to be over a population centre. A good-sized town, at least. I hoped that was all it was. At best, it meant hundreds of the dead things; at worst, thousands. But if we were over a city...

I stayed on the tiller, the shotgun slung across my back. Marta had climbed up on the cabin roof to scan for danger ahead.

The engine growled, the only sound. And all around there were heads in the water. None of them moved, other than bobbing up and down. Treading water. And watching.

They weren't mindless. They might look it, but they weren't. It might just be an animal cunning, but that was dangerous enough; they had huge superiority in numbers, after all.

They seemed to prefer it in the water. They ventured out of it only when they had to. And they seemed to know when their victims were helpless. I remembered Derek shooting the dead thing that swam after us; the others had retreated. Staying in their territory. Back at the brothel, when I'd killed a couple of them – was killing the word, when they were already dead? – the others had retreated. They'd killed everyone else, the unarmed ones, but left us alone.

Briefly. Then they'd come back, attacking in force.

At least with the boat, we had the advantage of being mobile. The swimming ones had let us go; once we'd left their territory, we were of no interest. Which meant that –

"Katja!" I looked up. Marta was grinning over the edge of the cabin roof. "It's clearing up ahead! I can see it!"

I craned my neck to see ahead. Marta was right. Perhaps another twenty or thirty metres, and the drifting mass of rats came to an end. The open waters beyond seemed empty. *Seemed.* It could be a trap.

How much intelligence are you crediting them with, Katja?

I didn't know. But better to be cautious than otherwise. Would we be any safer when we reached land, or would we have just painted ourselves into a corner? But Derek had said himself, there was only so much fuel. Sooner or later, we would have to stop for good.

But for now, we were moving, and the dead things weren't. They were just watching. And soon we'd be clear of them, I hoped, and then –

The dead things were shifting in the water. I wasn't sure, but I thought their eyes had brightened.

The engine. Its steady puttering growl had begun to falter and cough.

I looked at Marta. Her face had gone white, the blood draining.

The *Rosalind* jerked in time with a couple of particularly violent coughs from the engine. No more than twenty metres left to go. They were up ahead, but moved aside as the boat passed. Shouldered aside by the bow wave. Behind us, they were moving too; closing in to fill the gap the boat had made in their ranks.

The engine whined. And died.

The boat jerked and jolted once, and then stalled. It cruised forward under its own momentum a little further, but it wasn't enough. Not enough to take us clear.

We were between ten and fifteen metres from the clear water. With the motor gone, the only noise was the slap of waves against the boat's sides. The world was so silent now.

I unslung the shotgun. "Marta?"

"Yes?"

"Get in. Shut yourself in a cabin."

"What about you?"

"Do as you're told!"

Careful, Katja; don't panic. Remember, panic –

Panic is a choice. Yes Papa. I heard you the first time.

"What are you going to do?"

I pumped a round into the shotgun. "Hold them off."

Marta pulled back the 'pigeon box' on the roof and dropped in through the skylight. I didn't like giving her a gun. Perhaps, after this, I'd show her how to use one. The heads just watched me. The blue, bloated faces of the lately drowned, the oozing, rotted ones of those longer dead.

A muffled thumping came from forward. The bows.

I scrambled up onto the cabin roof and ran. It was the best place to be. Exposed and vulnerable, but it gave the best vantage.

Three of the dead things were clinging to the bow. Their hands thumped on he hull as they clutched for a hold. One was hauling itself over the gunnels. I aimed down and fired.

A shotgun isn't a marksman's weapon, but it didn't need to be at that range. The full charge hit the back of the dead thing's head and blasted a gaping hole in the skull. It teetered and then flopped forward across the gunnels. The second of the three was heaving itself up, mouth agape. A low hiss escaped, like gas from a punctured, bloated corpse. I pumped the slide and fired again, blowing away everything from the eyes upwards.

The last one looked from the second thing's body in the water to the first's draped over the gunnels, then back up at me. I pumped the slide again. Hissing, it let go and slid back into the water.

I stepped back, looked around. The heads in the water had closed in around the *Rosalind*. They were all staring at me.

Reload while you can, Katja.

Yes, Papa.

I was wearing an old coat of Derek's, pockets stuffed with shotgun shells. I pushed two fresh ones into the gun.

Marta, down below. Derek's death had done something to her, hardened her somehow. Whether this was a good or a bad thing, I couldn't decide. Should I have kept her with me? Had I underrated her? But she was still just a child. She should be still in school, getting her first boyfriend, swapping kisses and gropes in sweet secrecy. Not this.

And I should be teaching English. And the ground should still be above the water. And the world should be fair.

None of them were making any move to attack yet, but it was surely just a matter of time.

Bows, stern, starboard. I could cover all three at once. Nothing moving. Nothing moving –

Thump.

Behind me. The port side.

I whirled, but I was too slow. Rotting hands grabbed hold of the shotgun. I fired, the blast smashing into the dead thing's side, blowing it back off the cabin roof. It tore the shotgun out of my hands. But the gun was still slung around me. I crashed flat on the roof, sliding forward. The dead thing hissed. The parts of its face that hadn't been eaten were blue and mottled with decay. It wore a baggy top and tracksuit bottoms and its hair was a slimed mess; I had no idea if it had been male or female. It reached up for my face. Two others were clutching at the gunnels below.

The revolver; the revolver was in the back of my waistband. I pulled it out, pressed it to the rotting forehead and pulled the trigger. For a horrible moment I thought it wouldn't let go of the shotgun and I'd be pulled out after it, but then its hands opened and it fell away. I shot another dead thing as it climbed; I fired too fast, without aiming properly, and caught it only in the chest, but the impact knocked it back into the water. The third one I got in the forehead.

"Katja!"

The second shotgun roared. I scrambled over and dropped into the stern. Marta was clambering up the steps from the boatman's cabin. The shotgun's recoil had thrown her back down them. A dead thing bobbed in the water off the stern. Four more were clambering over. I fired the shotgun again and again till it was empty. No sooner had they fallen but another pair of hands began clutching at the bottom of the guardrail.

"Back!" I grabbed Marta and dragged her inside the boat, slamming the door shut behind us and locking it. Hands began pounding on the wood. Through one of the windows, behind the net curtains, I saw another body drag itself up into the starboard gunnels. Its free hand pounded against the window.

Thumping came from the port side too, and from the windows forward.

"Oh Jesus," Marta was whispering. "Jesus, Jesus, Jesus..."

"Reload," I said, pushing shells into the shotgun. She was wearing one of Derek's coats against the cold. She looked tiny in it, more of a child now than ever in her fright. "Marta! Reload your gun! Now!"

She dug out shells and thumbed them in. I broke open the revolver and replaced the empty shells.

A blow rattled a window. Marta turned, raising the gun, but I caught her arm. "Don't. If you shoot out the glass, it's easier for them to come through."

"So what do we do?"

"We wait until they start breaking in before we open fire." I thought for a minute. "You go forward. Cover the galley. I'll deal with them here."

"OK."

"And remember, if it goes quiet –"

"Then reload. I know."

"Good girl."

"Don't be so bloody patronising."

I had to smile, although I didn't let her see it. A teenager is still a teenager. "OK. I'm sorry."

Up at the bow end, glass shattered.

"It's alright," said Marta. "Oh God. Oh God." But she walked towards it.

The banging on the stern door, now savage and loud. The port window smashed, a hand lunging through, sliced bloodlessly by the glass. I wheeled and fired. In the confined space the explosion reminded me of an old cartoon I'd seen, where a character's head is slammed between two cymbals. It was less a sound than an impact on the ears. After it, a long bell-tone sounded. The dead thing flew back, headless.

I chambered another round. Marta fired.

Glass breaking – the galley.

A dead thing climbing through the window. The recoil slammed me against the doorframe when I fired; its head evaporated across the walls and ceiling. The bell-tone rang in my ears. What if I couldn't hear where they were coming from next?

Marta kicked in the bathroom door and fired. The recoil drove her back into the far wall. She pumped the slide, stepped through the doorway. A dead thing hung in the window frame, half-in half-out, one arm dangling limply and half-severed. She aimed at its head, keeping her feet wide apart, bracing herself for the kickback, and fired straight into its head.

Wood splintering. The stern door. I ran towards it, working the slide. Behind me more glass broke – the galley again. But no time. "Marta!"

I heard the shotgun fire behind me and shouldered my own gun, aiming at the door. It splintered in the middle from the blows. A hand reached through, skin hanging off it like rotten wallpaper, and groped for the lock.

Marta shouting behind me. I could hardly hear it over the bell-tone and my heart's pounding. To my right – I wheeled towards the port windows and fired.

Marta screaming.

I turned, ran aft. A dead thing scrambling through the galley window. Marta's shotgun on the floor. Reaching for her pistol as she backed away.

Another dead thing lurched between us, grabbed at me. The shotgun was useless at that range. Too close. I let it go, pulled out the automatic. The dead thing still had both its eyes; they were clouded and lit from within, like misted lightbulbs.

Marta screamed again. This time it was different. The thing had grabbed her left forearm and sank its teeth into the flesh. Its head shook side to side.

The dead thing forced me back against the doorframe, hands clutching at my throat and shoulders. I fired into its chest, twice. It stumbled back into the galley. I shot it in the head.

Marta screaming.

Aim two-handed. Steady. A breath. Then fire.

The top of the dead thing's head blew apart, and it slumped. Marta screaming and sobbing as she tore her arm free of it. The ragged bite wound gaped in her slender arm, marring the child's flesh. Blood poured down in a slick. She grabbed the shotgun off the floor and blasted the corpse.

There was a crash as the stern door gave way. I shouted. No words, inarticulate. All I had time and space for. Ran astern. The door hung off one hinge, splintered and smashed almost in two. A nightmare thing staggering through, its face half-eaten, the rest discoloured, its scalp reduced to mangy patches by scavengers. One eye a gaping, glowing socket, the other clouded and glowing.

Aim and fire. Watch it fall. Pivot left, shoot again. Then right. Marta not at the port windows. Scream for her. Seeing her out of the corner of my eye, stumbling and firing.

I can't remember the next few moments with any clarity. It couldn't have been much longer than a handful of minutes, but the fight seemed endless.

The shotgun emptied and there was no time to reload. I let it hang on its sling, relied on the automatic.

We tried to get them as they crawled through the windows. We left them where they died; if they were blocking the windows, it took that much longer for the next dead thing to drag the carcass out of the way.

I felt small, hard things crunching underfoot. I could hear the sound of them faintly, through heart-thunder, screaming – Marta's and mine – and the bell-tone. When I looked down – during a brief second where nothing seemed to be trying to break in – empty cartridge cases littered the floor. Shotgun shells. Pistol cartridges. Surely I couldn't have fired so many? I didn't remember reloading. But when I checked my pockets, one of the three spare magazines were gone. One lay empty on the floor.

There were two shots from Marta, then silence. I watched the windows and the shattered doorway. Nothing. I safetied the pistol, shoved it through my belt, then unslung the shotgun and started thrusting fresh shells into it.

Something fell against the stern doorframe, lurched into view. Derek.

His clouded eyes glowed dully. The top of his head flowered

open; something clotted seethed in the ragged, gaping wound. A flap of torn flesh hung down under his chin from where the bullet had gone in.

I'd thought by shooting him through the head I'd spare him this. I thought I'd owed him that, if nothing else. But I hadn't spared him anything.

He let out an almost plaintive moan and shambled forward, hands clutching at the doorframe. Did he know? Did some vestige of memory remain, to tell him this had been his home? That I wasn't just food, but his killer?

I didn't bother asking. I shot him between the eyes.

He toppled backwards, crashed against the tiller, and slumped down.

And after that, finally, there was silence.

"Katja?" I heard Marta's voice through the bell-tone. My heart was no longer thumping quite as hard as it had been. "Katja, are you alright?"

I looked at Derek's body, nodded without speaking.

"Katja?"

"Yes."

"Glad to hear it," she said. "I'm not. How about some help?"

I turned. She was sagging in the galley door, face less white than grey, blood puddling under her torn, dangling arm.

I caught her just before she fell.

The attack had stopped, for now. The only dead things in sight were truly dead now. At least, I hoped so. I'd thought Derek was, but...

I tried not to think about it as I cleaned the ugly, ragged hole in Marta's arm. She whimpered as I sponged the raw flesh with antiseptic. I made no comment. She'd earned the right to whimper at least once. Besides, a teenager is a teenager...

Once I'd done all I thought I could, I bound a gauze pad over the wound and bandaged it tightly, but I was still thinking about the bodies scattered around the boat. Was the headshot only a temporary stopper? Were they all going to come back anyway?

They showed no sign of doing so, but how long had it taken for Derek to wake up again? We'd voyaged some way from where we'd dumped him. That was it; he must have followed the narrowboat. He'd said they tended to stay where they'd died. Their homes, their familiar surroundings. But then, it had been different for him; the *Rosalind* had *been* his home.

I fought back that crazy, jagged laughter again.

So he must have revived quickly, to catch up with us. I looked at the dead things; they remained still. Perhaps they were truly dead after all.

"Can you move your fingers?" I asked Marta. She waggled them.

"There's that at least," I said. "As long as we can keep it clean of infection, it should heal up OK."

I hoped I sounded more convinced than I felt.

I gave Marta some painkillers and went astern to try the engine. It sputtered and coughed, but it didn't start.

I lifted the hatch near the tiller. The propeller shaft was almost lost to sight amongst chopped, crushed flesh and bone. Twisted and bent, the fingers of a human hand stuck up when the hatch rose. They moved. An accident? Or deliberate? How much intelligence should I credit them with?

There would be another attack. Just as there'd been at the brothel. We'd killed some of them, and the rest had retreated. But before long, they'd come back.

As for the propeller, I wouldn't know where to start.

I went back to Marta.

"It's fucked, isn't it?" she said.

I nodded and sat beside her on the couch.

"We're fucked then, too."

I didn't answer. I wanted to tell her no. But I couldn't.

Marta took the gun from her belt. At first I didn't realise what she was doing, until she brought the pistol up to her head.

"No!" I grabbed the barrel.

She glared at me. "I won't let that happen to me, Katja! I'm not going to let them eat me. Like they did to Marianna. I don't want to die like that."

"You won't. Marta, you won't."

"Of course I bloody will! They're going to come back again! And then again, and again, and again! Even if they don't get us next time, they will the next, or the one after that. Don't you get it? They aren't going to give up."

What could I say to her? The boat wasn't going anywhere. And it wasn't like there was another –

"Marta?"

"What?"

I let go of the gun. "I've got an idea."

We fetched the fuel cans from the locker. Most were full. Next we pumped up the dinghy – or I did while Marta kept watch. She fetched bottled water and provisions when I took my turn on lookout. The open water seemed hardly any distance at all. Ten, fifteen metres. The kind of distance that can be tiny, or huge.

A head broke the surface, eyes glowing. Then another. And another.

It wouldn't be long now.

I uncapped a fuel can and poured it over the port side.

Marta came back up. "I brought the first aid kit too."

"Good thinking." We were also taking one shotgun, the rifle, plus the two automatics. There wasn't room for more.

Marta poured a can over the starboard side. We poured some over the stern too. Can after can, very quickly, before it could evaporate. Everywhere except over the bow.

When the fuel was gone, I lit the first spill. We'd made them from the pages of a book we found in Derek's cabin. I threw it over the stern rail. For a second, nothing happened. And then the fuel caught.

Whumph.

Blue and orange flames rushed outwards. There were muffled explosions as the bloated bellies of the rats burst.

The water churned and splashed. The dead things were flailing about. They were retreating from the flames.

"It's working!" I shouted. Marta threw a spill overboard.

I threw another off to port. Then ran back through the narrowboat to the bow.

The water frothed and churned as the dead things retreated. Heads vanished under the surface.

"Now. Quickly."

Marta nodded. She was pale; sweat studded her forehead. I'd give her more painkillers later. When it was safe.

A narrow strip of clear water led off from the prow. We lowered the dinghy over the side. I climbed down, crouched there and reached out for Marta. She flopped into the dinghy and it almost capsized.

I grabbed the oars. I felt hairs shrivel on my arms. The heat. The dinghy would start to burn soon as well.

I rowed and kept rowing, hauling on the oars. I was in the bow, facing the boat, my back to whatever was coming up ahead. Marta sat in the stern, her automatic in her lap.

I felt the solid mass of rats fouling and clotting the oars. At any moment I expected something to seize one or other of the oars and tear it out of my hands. But nothing did.

"We're almost there!" Marta's voice was high. Spots of colour stood out now in her pale cheeks. I took it as a good sign.

Where would we go after this? How long would our supplies last? What chance did we have?

More than we did here. Here, we had none at all. Perhaps, like this, we'd be too small to be noticed. Perhaps.

The oars suddenly moved more easily. I looked down. No rats.

I rowed fast and hard. Would they come after us? I could see their heads emerging from the waters now – from the clear waters around the boat. Their eyes glowed. They watched us. Were they going to follow?

Marta managed to shift herself round in the dinghy. She held her gun ready in both hands.

But they didn't follow. One by one, the heads disappeared below the surface. I kept rowing. Nothing happened to us. The boat receded into the distance; by now it was on fire. There was a muffled bang from aboard it, and flames spurted out.

It didn't sink, not that I saw. Just burned. It receded as I rowed, slowly. Gradually the faint mist thickened around it, and it was gone.

CHAPTER NINE

We'd been rowing for about an hour before I dropped the oars and let out something between a gasp and a cry.

Derek had had a compass. And I'd forgotten it. The most obvious thing of all. It'd probably been in his pocket when I'd put him over the side. Might still have been when he'd come back. With it, we could have got a bearing on the land I thought I'd sighted. With it, we'd have known which way to go, and if we were still going there. A forlorn, threadbare hope, perhaps, but better than this.

There were no landmarks; only the bare, spreading water which in any case was disappearing into the encroaching mist. All I could do now was to keep rowing, and hope we were still pointing the right way.

I would have suggested that Marta and I take turns rowing. But it's not easy to change positions in a dinghy. If we capsized, then even if the dead things didn't take us, we'd lose our supplies of food and water, maybe the guns too. To say nothing of the risk if the filthy water got into an open cut.

And in any case, Marta was in no fit state to row.

She'd grown pale, and groggy. When I gasped, she stirred and forced her eyes open.

"Katja?"

"What is it?"

"I don't feel well at all. I feel... I think I'm going to be sick."

"Aim over the side."

"What if there are... things in the water?"

"I don't think they'll be interested in vomit," I said, trying to smile. She tried too. I don't think either of us made a very good job of it.

The water slapped against the dinghy. It rocked and bobbed. Marta gave a faint moan; the dinghy listed badly as she leant over the side. I looked away as she threw up.

Maybe it was just seasickness. She'd been ill on board the *Rosalind*, at first. On the heels of that came a second thought; what if we met another storm? We wouldn't stand a chance in an inflatable.

I didn't let myself think about it. Or how easy it would be, in the mist, to row straight past the land I'd seen. If it had been real.

If we were heading the right way.

All I could do was row.

Out of the frying pan. Into the fire.

"Katja?"

"Yes, little one?" I spoke gently. She was white now, dark rings around her eyes, swaying slightly.

"I feel horrible. I need to lie down."

"OK." I stopped rowing. "Careful now."

She nodded weakly and wriggled round. She rested her head in my lap and propped her feet over the edge of the stern. I tried not to think about dead hands lunging up to grab them. Her forehead was burning not.

I gave her some water and painkillers, hoping they'd take the temperature down. Were there any antibiotics in the first aid kit? I needed to stop and look properly. I needed some solid ground under us. But there wasn't any.

Something scraped the dinghy's hull, rocking it. I let out a yelp. Marta moaned in fear. Then I looked astern and saw thin, limp twigs and drooping leaves, just breaking the surface. A tree.

A tree.

"Higher ground," I whispered.

"What?" Marta's voice was a croak. I held the water bottle to her lips. "Not too much," I whispered. Supplies were finite. If we had to drink the muck around us, the dead things might offer a quicker death.

"It was a tree. We might be close to somewhere. Land. There might even be other people."

Perhaps even a doctor. I didn't dare say it aloud. This wasn't seasickness. The fever, the nausea, the weakness: they all spelt one thing.

Infection.

The dressing on Marta's arm was still relatively clean, but that was no indication of what might be under it. I didn't want to look, not yet.

The first aid kit lay next to my left knee. I picked it up and opened it. Antiseptic creams, TCP. More painkillers. Plasters and bandages. Surgical tape. No antibiotics. "Katja?"

I touched her hot cheek.

"I'm scared."

So was I. "Just hold on, baby." My voice wouldn't stay steady. "We'll get to land. We'll get you help. Just hold on."

I began to row again.

I kept on for another hour, with brief pauses. Finally I had to stop. My arms were throbbing. Marta's eyes were closed, and her breathing was shallow. I looked at her arm.

My breath caught. The bandage was stained an ugly yellowish-green. The flesh on either side of it was livid and swollen.

The kit held a small pair of scissors. Marta let out a faint moan as I snipped at the bandage, and I stopped, but her eyes didn't open.

I peeled back the bandages. The gauze pad was stained and wet, and the thick green smell of the wound was nauseating. I'd smelt something similar once. A staphylococcal infection. But I'd never seen one develop so *quickly*.

The wound itself was thick and oozing pus, but the flesh around it was, if anything, worse. It was black and green. Like something rotten.

I threw the stained bandages over the side, poured TCP onto a cotton-wool pad and pressed it to the wound. It was all I could think of to do.

Marta's faint, sick cry was worse than a shriek. Either she was too weak to even give proper voice to the pain, or the damage was already so bad she had almost no feeling there.

Antibiotics. We needed antibiotics. Nothing else would give her even a chance of survival.

This was how it began, I realised. The second wave of deaths. After the flooding, after the dead things. Deaths from lack of clean water. Lack of food. Lack of medicines. Deaths inconceivable only the day before. That is how quickly it can go – how quickly it *had* gone.

Even Ilir, if Marta had been this ill, would at least have called a doctor. He might dispose of her if she'd suffered something too expensive or troublesome to treat, but antibiotics wouldn't have been a problem. But now even the water was a precious, limited reserve. I rinsed my hands with some of it, and rubbed antiseptic cream into the wound. Then I gauzed and bandaged it, and secured it tightly with surgical tape.

That was all I could do.

I could see the blue tracery of veins on Marta's eyelids. Her lips were parted and dry, already starting to crack, her breathing hoarse and shallow. Soon, she would be thirsty. When she woke – *if* she woke – she'd have to drink.

And there was only so much water.

It might be better if she never woke up.

If it's just you, there's less weight. You'll go further. If it's just you, there's more water. You'll live longer. If it's just you, there's more food. You'll be stronger.

The worst thing about the voice that said all this? It was my father's.

Marta was my friend. More than that. She was a younger sister, or a child. The difference in ages was such she could have been either. And she looked so like my mother.

Marta was all the family I had.

And she is dying, said Papa.

No. We could get help.

What help? The authorities are either in hiding or they've been wiped out too. Even if they had any intention of providing help, do you think they'll have the means?

But a village, high on a hill. We might find that. There might be a doctor's surgery there. They would have medical supplies.

Perhaps. And if they do, why should they give them to you? It is survival now, Katja. The others who've lived through this may even now be fighting amongst themselves for dominance and control of resources.

If they were divided, it would be so much the easier to take them.

But you will be on your own. What then? How will you establish yourself in such a community, if you find one? Why should they share what they have with a stranger?

I have food and water. I have guns and ammunition.

Without which, you are dead.

I have my body.

Hours after killing Derek for what he'd forced me into, swearing I would never do such things again, I thought this quite calmly.

I have my body.

And if you offer that, what then? They'll expect more such favours. And when you give yourself to them, how will you stop them overpowering you, taking your guns? You will be where you were before the floods came. And Katja – Katja, look at her. She is beyond help. This infection has taken hold so swiftly and savagely. She will be dead before you reach land.

"No!"

Marta moaned at the shout. So, this was it. Madness at last. Drifting in a boat with a dying girl, arguing with a ghost. No, not a ghost. A figment of my imagination.

Katja, you admit yourself that she is dying. There is no choice here.

"No."

Triage, Katja. Advanced triage. You know what that means.

And I did. Triage was how you graded the severity of injuries – decided who would cope with little or no treatment, whose treatment could be delayed, whose treatment was required now?

But advanced triage...

Oh Papa, you've taught me too well. I don't need these things in my head.

Without them, Katja, you'd already be dead.

And now I was conversing with a ghost in rhyme. Final proof of madness.

That crazy, jagged laughter, climbing in my throat again.

Advanced triage.

In advanced triage, patients with no or small chance of survival may not receive advanced treatment. Painkillers, nothing more. At most.

I didn't have much more than painkillers anyway.

But the rationale – where there aren't the resources to spare, where there's no chance, you let them die.

I looked down at Marta.

She is dying, Katja. You cannot help her. Anything else is a delusion.

I shook my head. Dimly I became aware that I was crying. Tears splashed Marta's pale face, like tiny drops of rain.

You were ready to kill her before, at the brothel. When the alternative was an agonising death, you were ready to kill her quickly to spare her. Do you want to see her die in such agony now?

I shook my head. "Shut up," I whispered through my teeth.

Katja –

I grabbed the oars and jerked them savagely, smashing the

surface of the water into froth. A petulant child, throwing a tantrum in response to a truth she wouldn't accept. "Shut up! Shut up! *Shut up!*"

Marta moaned and opened her eyes. Her lips were bloodless. "Katja?"

"It's alright, darling." I touched her cheek, bent to kiss her forehead. Both burned to the touch. "It's alright. We'll soon be there."

"You've... found somewhere?"

"Not yet, little one. But we will. It's close. I can feel it."

I grabbed the oars again and began rowing. Her eyes closed again.

Stop crying, my father said. *Stop crying.*

"I'm not crying."

You are. Stop crying. You have to be strong, Katja. You have to be strong.

But it was so hard to be strong, watching this.

My father's voice faded as I went. I never heard it again.

One other loss, amongst so many.

My arms ached terribly. I took two of the painkillers at long last. I had to keep going. Had to. There was no alternative.

Had to find land. Had to find land.

A dank, chilling mist lay thick around us, reducing visibility to a few metres. The redness had spread up to Marta's shoulder now. Her hand was a bloated claw. Around the edges of the bandage there was a thin rime of black, green-tinged flesh. The veins on the arm around the wound were visible. They too were black.

So much easier to kill her. To finish her before it got worse.

It would be bad. I knew that. It would be bad. But I could do it.

But that would not be the worst.

Because even if I killed her with a bullet to the head, even then –

She would come back. She would come back and *I would have*

to do it again. And I could not do that. *I could not do that.*

But if she died anyway, died of the infection –

If that happened she would come after me anyway. And it would be kill or be killed.

So it was very simple. Marta was not going to die. She *could not* die. It could not be allowed to happen. Could not be countenanced. It became my mantra, as I rowed. I may have mumbled, or spoken, or screamed it aloud. Marta could not, must not, die.

It was as simple as that.

I had to stop at last. Gathering my breath. Painkillers or not, my arms were throbbing.

Marta's face was grey. Shallow breaths hissed in and out through her lips. Her forearm was black from elbow to wrist. Her small, swollen hand had gone green; so had about half of her upper arm. The bandage I'd secured was already sodden.

She's dying.

No. No.

I took the oars up again. It felt like I was trying to lift and move tree-trunks.

Something hit the side of the boat. I yelped, released the oars and grabbed my pistol.

Something in the water.

I actually had the gun aimed at it, finger tightening on the trigger, before I realised what it was.

A treetop. Beyond it there were more, vanishing into the mist. And then I saw the roof of a white, half-submerged house. Another building beyond it. A chimney.

I looked around. A dark mass to starboard. *Land.* A wind began to rise, thinning the mist. Up ahead, I saw a bridge. Something else. Through it all. I heard voices. I was sure of it.

I looked to port. A road rose up out of the water, bordered by a stone wall and half-submerged tree. The road rose to the bridge. I thought I saw a rooftop – up on the dry land.

I rowed the dinghy past the white house. We passed a window; through it I could see the bedroom. A figure stood, its back to me. It started to turn.

As the mist dispersed I saw peaks. Hills. All around us. I hadn't seen them in the mist. And my frenzy to keep moving. Because I'd never really believed we'd reach land. I'd hoped. I'd *had* to believe. But deep down, I'd known. We were fucked.

I twisted slowly round and looked aft.

Rooftops. Hills. One in particular, tall, wide and sheer, rising to a steep crest. It looked like a huge wave. But it was made of rock and earth. A sheep's bleat drifted towards me.

"Marta?" I whispered. "Marta, we've done it. We're here. I can see land. It's right there. People."

She didn't answer. I turned, put my hand on her shoulder. Stopped.

Her face so grey.

No sound of breathing.

"Marta?" I shook her. "Marta!"

No. Nothing. No. No. No.

I kept shaking her, till finally her head lolled sideways, lips slack.

I felt her throat for a pulse. There was nothing. I kept trying. This time there would be something. This time. But there wasn't.

I blew air into her lungs, spat out the sour taste of her dead mouth. I pushed down on her chest, tried to pound her heart back into life. The dinghy rocked and tipped, nearly throwing us both out.

Nothing.

I don't know how long it was before I gave up. I slumped back, away from her. Nothing. All for nothing.

I sat there. Again, I have no idea for how long. Time was meaningless now. Marta was dead. The last of my little family was gone.

The swelling was going down, I noticed, and let out a wave of that jagged laughter. Her arm, paling, was regaining its normal size and shape almost as I watched. I couldn't stop laughing. All this way, and for nothing. A hundred metres from land and any point to continuing was gone.

Except it wasn't. *I* wasn't dead. There was one thing I could still do for Marta: get to land. Try to survive.

And if she rose, put her back down into the earth.

I forced myself to pick up those heavy, heavy oars.

And rowed.

Her head was still in my lap. I looked down at her face; I'd turned her head back upwards so I looked down into it.

Suddenly, there was movement. Had something hit the dinghy? No. The movement was coming from within it.

From Marta.

The infected hand was twitching. The arm shuddered. The small, delicate fingers flexed, opened and closed. A leg kicked.

I knew what it must be. How could I not? But if we excel at one thing, it's self-deception. For one, precious moment, I thought I was wrong, that she wasn't dead, that she was coming back...

And then I saw her eyes.

Through her eyelids, I saw a flickering, greenish glow.

Oh God, oh no, oh fuck...

Dim at first,the glow was strengthening, flickering, pulsing.

Brightening.

And finally blazing.

Her arms thrust outwards, fingers hooked and clawed, shuddering. Her legs kicked and shook. Her lips peeled back from bared, snarling teeth. Thin spit jumped through them. An eye burst; warm, thick fluid spattered my face. I screamed then.

The other eye opened, the eyeball clouded over, glowing from within. The empty socket blazed. With a gagging, choking noise, Marta's jaws yawned open. A hissing, croaking howl escaped her dead lungs.

The boat rocked, water splashing over the gunnels.

Her head rocked side to side. Then stopped. She stared up at me, the burst eye congealing like wax on her cheek. And lunged up at my face. I tried to pull back and overbalanced, toppling into the water.

The shock... I'd heard the shock of icy water could stop a heart. In that second, I believed it.

Marta sat hissing in the dinghy, a vaguely baffled expression on her slack, empty face.

And when I'd killed the blue woman, I'd mourned the loss of

an enemy whose face I knew...

There could be more in the water. The road was near. I struck out for it and Marta lunged after me.

Kill her, Katja.

Was that a last fading echo of my father's voice? I didn't think so. It was my own. Perhaps it always had been.

Kill her. If you care for her, finish it. This is not Marta, just a dead thing that looks like her. A puppet made of her body by something vile. An obscenity. An insult to Marta, and you. Destroy it.

And give her rest.

But I couldn't, because it *was* still Marta, and if I pulled the trigger, I'd be killing her. Again. As I already had, by not reaching land in time.

You did everything you could.

But it hadn't been enough.

She swam closer, eyes glowing above the waterline.

I reached the road's edge. Clutched at the wall. Pulled myself clear. So heavy, so slow. She'd grab me any second. I flopped over, onto the tarmac. My feet slid but I was on dry land at last.

When I looked back, Marta was scrabbling over the wall, a thin arm reaching out, eyes blazing in the fading light, hair matted and straggling, face grey and slack and full of hunger. She slithered and fell in the mud.

I began to run. Hills rose through the mist. A big grey building. A sign on it: The Pendle Inn. A row of houses.

The wet splat and slap behind me of her feet.

Kill her or she kills you.

It wasn't her anymore.

Turn around, look into her eyes – they weren't really her eyes now anyway – and blow her brains out. End it for her. Kill a part of me too, of course, but...

I reached into my waistband for my gun.

It was gone. I must have lost it in the water.

Marta suddenly flying forward, in a manic, thrashing burst of motion.

I went backwards, tripped. Fell.

The bullets hit her with a wet, sickening thud. Holes exploded in her chest and stomach; pieces of meat, cloth, bone and clotted blood flew out of her back. More bullets whipped past with an angry hornet's buzz. They cracked and whined as they hit stone.

Marta stumbled, but didn't fall. She stared up to my left, and hissed with a kind of drunken, baffled rage.

Her right hand – so tiny, so delicate – flailed through the air. A bullet, or bullets hit it and blew it apart. A forefinger and a thumb remained, twitching.

Another half-dozen hit her torso. One must have shattered her spine; she dropped to the ground and lay hissing and thrashing.

And still the bullets came. One whipped past me; two more hit the ground centimetres away. I think I screamed.

"Cease fire! *Cease fire!*"

A man ran down the road.

"*Cease fucking fire!*"

Tall, reddish hair, a soldier's lean hard build. A military uniform and a pistol in one hand, pointed at the ground away from his feet.

He brought the gun up, two-handed and aimed past me, to where Marta lay. He fired once.

The hissing and snarling and the drumming sound of thrashing limbs on the ground stopped. A long, rattling sigh from Marta. And then silence.

The solider pivoted, and pointed the gun at my face.

The muzzle of a gun looks so small.

Except when it is pointed at your face.

For a second I thought my bowels would fail, but I held onto that shred of dignity at least, although when he shot me they would open anyway. Like Derek's had when he'd died.

Then he stepped in closer, gun still aimed. "Were you bitten?"

He had a harsh accent I hadn't heard before. "Answer me! *Did she bite you?*"

I shook my head. "No," I said at last. "No."

He looked me over – in case I was lying, in case there were any wounds a casual glance might have missed – then nodded, stepped back, pointed the gun upwards and shouted "Clear!"

Other voices echoed the cry. "Clear... Clear... Clear..."

The soldier uncocked and safetied his pistol, then holstered it. He held out a hand. "I'll no hurt you. Come on."

I took his hand; he helped me to my feet. "Don't look back," he said. But of course I did. Marta was a stained, ragged bundle of cloth. I pulled free of him and went to her.

I didn't cry. I just stood there, looking down. There was nothing I could do. I didn't want him to see a frightened woman. I was more than that. I had strength. I knew that now. It had its limits like everything else. But I was still alive, and I wouldn't have been otherwise.

If I could have, I told her silently, *I would have saved you too.*

Her mouth hung slackly open; her clouded eye and empty socket – both now lightless – gazed blindly upwards. A neat hole starred her forehead; fragments of skull, scalp and brain littered the road behind her. I'd get no answers there. Neither accusation nor forgiveness. If Marta was anywhere now, it wasn't here.

The soldier came up behind me. I turned sharply; I don't like it when people do that. Never have. "You can do nothing for her," he said. His voice was as close to gentle as he could make it.

At last, I nodded. He nodded back. He motioned me forward and I followed him up the road. I kept my back straight, tried to show nothing with my face. No weakness. No fear. No helpless woman. I vowed as I followed him that I would never be helpless again.

PART TWO

Storm's Eye – Floodland

None wears the face you knew.
Great Death hath made all his forevermore.

Charles Hamilton Sorley, 1895-1915.

CHAPTER TEN

McTarn

The time: approximately 06:00 hours, November 7th. That day of all days. If there is someone up there, He, She or It really has a twisted fucking sense of humour.

The place: a briefing room at Fullwood Army Base, Lancashire. Eleven soldiers, including me, plus one RAF commissioned orifice – sorry, officer.

Outside, the rain beating down, and a gathering storm. Inside, Squadron Leader Tidyman telling us it was the end of the world. And worse.

I couldn't sleep that morning anyway. My first clear memory is shambling fully dressed round my home just before dawn.

Home was a small detached house just outside Preston, Lancashire. Rented, obviously. Since leaving the service I'd bounced between security jobs and the dole queue. Doesn't make bank managers reach for the mortgage applications.

I finished up in the front room. Threadbare carpet. An old sofa, a pair of armchairs – one leaking stuffing – and a vintage '70s coffee table with heel marks where I'd put my feet up. Kept forgetting to clean my trainers when I came back from a run.

I didn't bother switching the lights on. Grey pre-dawn light played on the wall, shaped by the rain trickling down the front-room window.

I paced. Flopped onto the sofa. Tried not to think of the six-pack of McEwan's in the fridge. From outside, a soft hiss; the rain. It'd been pissing down for the past week, non-stop.

For the first time in over a week, I switched on the TV. Flooded streets. Houses half-underwater. Odd words came out of the babble: *emergency; death toll; evacuation; army.*

Army. Teams of squaddies – not even remotely blending into the landscape in their camo gear – piled up sandbags, got old dears out of flooded houses, wheeled in food and blankets for all.

See the nice soldiers. Here to protect you.

Sand blowing across a dirt road. Blood on my hands. Blood on my face.

I switched it off. I looked at my hands. They shook.

Outside, dawn breaking. What the fuck. Sun was over the yardarm somewhere. I fetched a can of McEwan's and popped the tab.

These days, this was as good as it got for me. I wasn't complaining.

I deserved a lot worse.

I took a deep breath, and then a sip.

Someone knocked on the door.

Churchill said you're in a free country if, when there's a knock on the door at five a.m., you know it's just the milkman.

But I got my milk from the corner shop.

I turned, looked at the door. They knocked again.

I parted the curtains. Two men in combats stood outside. Red-caps. Big. Pig-faced. Pig-eyed. Shaving rashes. Practically fucking clones.

One had a moustache, one didn't. Tweedledum and Twee-dledee.

I opened the door. No security chain. I'd been meaning to get round to that.

"Robert McTarn?" said the one with no 'tache. Tweedledum.

"No, pal, I'm the fucking Tooth Fairy."

He didn't like that. He tried to push in through the front door. I didn't budge.

"Fucksake," said Tweedledee.

"Are you Robert McTarn?" Tweedledum asked. He was very pale. Looked ragged round the edges. Something was very fucking wrong. Something clenched and curled in my guts like a cold worm. I think they call it dread.

"Aye, that's me. What do you want?"

Tweedledum took a deep breath and pointed to the Jeep parked outside. "Need you to come with us, Robert."

Old habits die hard. Despite it all, I nearly did as I was told. *Nearly.*

"You can get to fuck," I said, and shut the door.

On his foot.

Tweedledum just looked at me.

"In case you hadn't heard, I was discharged. I am no longer a serving soldier in the Armed Forces. So with respect, fuck off."

"You're still on reserve list B, Sergeant McTarn. They've called you up." I wondered how many of his teeth I could knock out with one punch. "So please, come on. Let's not make this difficult, eh?"

I wondered just how difficult these two grebs thought they could make it for me. "If I've been called up, where's the tele-gram?"

They always do that – I don't know any other buggers who even send telegrams anymore. Except HRH, of course, when you make the century.

"Telegram?" Tweedledum looked at Tweedledee, who shook his head. "Have you *watched* the fucking news lately, mate?"

"No. It just depresses me."

He pulled something from his pocket and shoved it at me. "*There.* OK?"

I opened it. Read. *Bollocks.*

"Now will you get a bloody shift on please, Sergeant? We have a national emergency. *International.* And you're needed. So – *please* – while I'm still in a good mood, stop dicking us around and get your fucking coat."

"Gonna tell me what it's for?"

"You'll be fully briefed at base."

"You mean you don't know either."

His eyes narrowed; his mouth compressed. "Sergeant, I am not going to ask again."

Jesus. That was it. I'd been trying to pin down the look in his eyes. He was scared. Both of them were.

No-one likes the redcaps; they have a habit of turning up and spoiling the fun while you're beating up your platoon commander. But they're not complete girl's blouses. *International emergency.* The cold worm writhed in my guts again. I was thinking *crisis*, I was thinking *war*, I was thinking *fucking mushroom clouds over Britain.*

"Alright."

"Good boy."

Driving fast. Avoiding certain main roads. Sandbags stacked at the roadside. A huge wash of water blown outwards by the wheels as we passed. The wipers beating hard to clear the view ahead.

I sat in the back. Tweedledee looked back at me, offered a cigarette. I took it with a grunt. He lit one up. So did Tweedledum.

"Don't know the details," Tweedledee said. "But there's a major crisis on and they needed to put together a reinforced section PDQ. Someone's got you down as a good section commander. Any truth in that?"

"Used to be."

Translation into plain English for non Army-speakers: a section is eight men. A reinforced section is ten men.

"There's a Chinook coming in from the Sneaky Beakies to lift you out. You'll get the full brief on arrival."

Sneaky Beakies: Special Ops squadrons.

"'Fraid that's all I know."

"Thanks," I said at last.

"Mention it." He turned to view the road. Brought the cigarette to his mouth. Hand shaking as he did.

I finished mine. Stretched across the backseat. Closed my eyes. Might as well put the time to good use.

I dreamed of the desert road. When they woke me on arrival, I was glad of it.

"Sergeant McTarn?"

RAF uniform, shoulder pips. Thin. Pale. Clipped moustache. Old reflexes; I snapped to attention, Tweedledum and Tweedledee on each side of me. "Sir."

"Squadron Leader Tidyman." Sweat on his brow. "This way. We haven't much time."

"Sir?" Tweedledum. "Beg pardon, sir, but what do we do now?"

Tidyman looked back at him. "Make whatever preparations you think best for yourselves." He turned away.

I looked at the redcaps. They'd both gone white.

Poor bastards.

"Good luck," I said and turned away before they could react. I've no idea what happened to them.

"There's a set of combats for you in there. If you can change into them during the briefing I'd be obliged."

"Sir."

"We're loading the remaining kit aboard the transport. I'm in overall command, but on the ground you're in charge. Under-stood?"

"Sir."

"Good." He opened a door. "After you."

Ten chairs, all but one of them occupied. Lights off. Heads turned our way. They were in uniform, but some had bundles of civvy clothes at their feet. A plasma screen on one wall, a laptop on a table. Thick, stale air; cigarette smoke, sweat.

"This is Sergeant McTarn. He'll be this section's ground commander."

"Robbie?"

A wiry little man with a corporal's stripes, grey hair and a leathery monkey's face. "Chas?"

"Good to see you."

Chas Nixon. We'd served together.

The girl turning back to look at us. The look on her face. Incomprehension and grief.

"We need to start." Tidyman waved me to my seat. On it, folded combats and a pair of boots. I sat. I didn't want to touch them. And yet I did. I touched the fabric, felt the coarse weave.

Fuck. And they wanted me to lead these men? Didn't they know? I couldn't do this, not anymore. A wave of anger and resentment. Stupid bastards. They'd get them all killed. *I'd* get them all killed.

"You OK, Rob?" whispered Chas. I nodded.

"Alright," said Tidyman. "We'll come to the mission details in a moment, but first..."

I spotted someone else I knew: forty-something, six foot tall, still a private. Alf Mason. Not the brightest, but good at your back in a fight. We exchanged nods.

The plasma screen came on.

"This footage was shot in London earlier this morning."

Not much earlier. It's the same grey half-light I was wandering about in before dawn. They put this together fast.

Filming from a helicopter. The buildings nearest the Embankment are *gone*. Aerials and chimney pots, the occasional roof – nothing else stands clear.

The streets are awash. The water looks like stewed tea. But you wouldn't be drinking this. Sediment from the river bed, maybe raw sewage as well.

Further out, buildings are only half-submerged. Abandoned

buses and lorries are visible on the roads, roofs just above water.

Fuck, it's bad. I look around the room, at people's faces. I see the same looks on theirs too.

Still, least it doesn't look like nukes.

The screen changes. Satellite pictures. I could tell that much; see the banks of shifting cloud and the shapes of sea and land through them. Beyond that, they meant nothing.

"Anything you've seen on the news in the last week is just the tip of the iceberg." Tidyman smirked. "No pun intended."

"Dicksplash," Chas Nixon coughed into his hand.

I suppressed a grin. Tidyman ignored him, a flush rising up his neck. "There's been a media blackout. Here's why. These pictures were also taken this morning. This is the Greenland icecap. This," the picture changed, "is the Antarctic." Tidyman looked round to make sure he hadn't blinded any of us with science yet.

I unbuttoned my shirt.

"What you've been seeing on the news isn't restricted to the UK. It's global. Virtually every country on the planet is experiencing, or about to experience, flooding on a catastrophic scale."

"Good news for the Africans," said a goatee-bearded soldier with a Liverpool accent. The one black soldier in the room – Akinbode – gave the speaker a killing look.

"Parfitt," snapped Tidyman.

"Sorry, sir."

Tidyman carried on. "We have no idea what's caused the rapid melting of the ice-caps."

"Not global warming, sir?" Akinbode.

"Unlikely. No predictions concerning global warming have suggested anything happening at this speed. If the current rate of meltdown continues, we're looking at a rise in sea level to 720 feet within a matter of *days*."

No-one looked any the wiser. I could almost hear Tidyman reminding himself he was briefing a gathering of thick-headed squaddies.

"If that happens, almost the entire British Isles will be underwater."

Gasps, cries of "What?" Somebody even said "The *fuck*?" and then ducked down – a small, wiry soldier of about twenty with cropped, light-brown hair. I read his tag – Mleczko. Trying to pronounce that was going to be fun.

"Multiple storm fronts are also appearing. The first storm surge is expected to hit London within the hour. Another five, possibly six, are expected by the end of today, all over the coast. And that'll just be the start."

My stomach hollowed out; nothing inside my ribcage but echoing space. Looked like I'd never be going home now. I didn't have much there – books, a few souvenirs. But what was there was mine.

But there were photos. Mam. Me and Jeannie. Aw Christ, I didn't have any with me.

Focus, Robbie. Couldn't do anything about that now. The Army had been my family. Like it or not, I was back in. *These men depend on you, Robbie. Focus on that.*

Shirt off. Trousers and shoes off. I dressed without looking.

"We have contingency plans for incidents like this."

Grab all the top wankers and put them somewhere safe.

"The central government has already been evacuated from London. The capital's flood defences have already failed. We're broadcasting what information we can to the public, but the harsh truth is it's hopelessly inadequate to the task. Nothing on this scale was ever anticipated. There's virtually nothing we can do for the bulk of the population. We don't have the resources."

They never do.

"Central government will hand over power to regional control centres, as they would in the event of nuclear attack. They will do what they can to control the situation."

Probably fuck-all except sit tight.

"Teams such as yours are being sent to retrieve key personnel to secure locations."

Like I said, grab all the top wankers.

"Because of the nature of the crisis, I'm afraid we've been caught somewhat on the back foot. So some teams – like this one – have been put together at short notice. We've had to pull in people from the reserve lists." Another smirk. "Sorry for any inconvenience."

"Wankstain," Chas coughed. Sniggers broke the tension.

"Nasty cough, Corporal Nixon."

"Sorry, sir."

"I know this is a lot to take in, but I'm afraid there's more." Tidyman licked his lips. What could worry him worse than the floods? "We'll get to your mission in a moment. But first, I'm going to show footage shot by a team sent in to investigate reports from London earlier this morning. It was emailed over in the last hour." Deep breath. "This is the part we've *really* kept the lid on, men. It's easiest if you see for yourselves."

An office block. Bottom floors submerged, but the top two are clear. The 'copter hovers, then descends.

It touches down. Soldiers de-bus across the flat roof. Moving fast, keeping low. M-16 carbines. SAS issue. The cameraman follows.

A door on the roof opens onto a stairwell. A soldier aims down, shouts "Clear." Another soldier runs down the steps. The cameraman moves to the door. The steps are dimly-lit – the power's out.

"Clear."

The rest of the squad shoulder past the cameraman. The picture bounces. Then down into the dark.

Out into a corridor. Torches clipped to the rifle barrels pick out bloody handprints on the walls. Thick muddy stains on the carpet. Dripping red arcs on the walls: arterial spray. On the ground – a handbag, a shoe. Dark lumps, mercifully not identifiable.

A hand.

Fuck.

(Tidyman's not looking at the screen. Seen it already. He wipes his mouth with the back of his hand. It's shaking.)

The hand is female. Slender, rings, painted nails. Not cleanly severed; strings of torn meat trail from the stump, and a jagged end of bone.

They move on. Open doorways. Empty offices. Overturned desks and tables. Blood on windows.

Then down the stairs.

Two flights down the stairs vanish into murky, lapping water. Torch-beams play over the surface. An empty drinks can, twigs and leaves, a dead rat.

Voices:

"The fuck?"

"See that?"

"Where?"

"There. *There.*"

The beam plays over the water again.

"*There.*" And clicks off. Now we can see it. The camera zooms in.

Beneath the surface, glowing through it – two green lights. Like eyes –

They brighten. I realise they're moving up just before the head bursts out of the surface.

("Shit!" Half a dozen people yelp it together, in the film and in the briefing room. Nervous laughter, choked off before Tidyman says a word, as –)

The head's rotten. Greenish skin. Sunken cheeks, with holes showing the grinning teeth beneath. The eyes are two ragged holes. They glow.

A hand rises from the water. Skin hangs down in flaps. Bones and ligaments work inside. It slaps on the wall, scrabbles. The rest of the body rises after it. It sways and lurches, like a drunk. The hair is a collapsed, bedraggled mess.

A second one rises. A woman, in her twenties. Skirt, suit jacket, smart blouse. This one is fresher, hardly looks dead at all. Apart from the wounds. A chunk of her neck's missing. The wound's open and raw, but doesn't bleed.

They lurch forward; behind them a third nightmare bursts out of the water.

Someone fires. Full-auto. In a confined space, not very clever. The water erupts into spray. The three figures jerk and stagger. Pulped bone and meat hit the walls behind them. The rotted one and the third nightmare – a skeleton hung with rags of skin – fly back into the water. The woman's hit in the arm and falls against the wall, but doesn't show any pain.

Someone steps into shot, aiming at her. He blocks her from view, so we can't see what happens, but suddenly she's on him, clawing at his face. He screams, fires. She's thrown back into the water. The gunner doubles over, clutching his face.

The other two nightmares burst out of the water and seize him. The woman's up too – her blouse gapes open. Her breasts are out; one's been torn apart by the bullets.

She throws herself on the gunner too, and before anyone can shoot, they all crash into the water together.

Bullets blast the water into froth. The water's red.

And suddenly also full of all these pairs of glowing green eyes...

Something screaming in the water. An arm flails, missing a hand and spurting blood. The nightmares don't bleed. The gunner. Must be, but I can't be sure. He's got no face.

"Pull back! Pull back!"

The camera's all over the place, catching random glimpses – steps, walls, ceiling, soldiers running back up, one firing a burst from his carbine till someone screams at him and he runs too.

Up the stairs. Back into the corridor. Shouts. Turning back. Drunk-looking figures lurch into the corridor. Dim light – it's a dull day out, with all the rain. Can't make out much. Shadows. Silhouettes. The glowing eyes stand out. They lurch forward. Slow, clumsy, but relentless as machines.

Half a dozen automatic weapons fire. It sounds like a single blast, an explosion lasting five seconds. The nightmares dance back, trying to keep their balance, hit the walls and drop, but then they get up and lurch forward. More come shambling into the corridor.

Then it happens. I don't know if it's luck or deliberate, but one of the nightmares – I think it's wearing a skirt, I think it could be the woman – takes a headshot. Head snaps up and back. Dark stuff flies up and out from it.

It drops to its knees.

Its eyes stop glowing.

And it falls.

Doesn't get up again.

The other nightmares stop. Look down at it. Look back up.

Someone shouts: "Go for the head." More gunfire. Two more nightmares go down. The others – they blunder back through the doors, and they're gone.

Nobody goes after them.

They go over to the woman. She's face down. The back of her head is just a hole.

Kicked in the side. She doesn't move. They flip her over. Yup, it's her. She definitely looks dead. Then again, she did when she was still moving.

"Let's go. Go, go, go!"

And cut.

(The screen goes blank except for the DVD logo. No-one says a fucking word. Just dead silence, except for the hiss of rain outside, bringing all our deaths closer.)

The silence stretches on and on, till Tidyman breaks it.

"Before anyone asks, yes. It's exactly what it looks like. They're dead. But they're moving. They kill and eat the living. And the only way to put them down is to destroy the brain. Questions?"

The medic's hand went up – a young Asian guy, tall and wide-shouldered. Hassan.

"Other than what's causing it."

Hassan's hand went down. A few people laughed.

A klaxon blared. Tidyman shouted over it.

"Your destination will be north-east Lancashire –"

The briefing room door burst open. A Flying Officer, forty-something, stocky and bald on top. He looked scared. He opened his mouth to speak.

"Knock before entering!"

"Sorry sir."

"Well?"

"Floodwaters entering the compound, sir."

Tidyman took a deep breath. "Alright. Let's wrap it up."

"Probably got about ten minutes, sir."

"*Thank you*, Cannock." The airman ducked back. Distant shouting, feet thudding. Splashing. In water.

A man's face flashed up on the plasma screen. Long black straggly hair, streaked grey. Thick beard. Gaunt face, deeply lined. Reddened, bleary, staring eyes.

"Your target," Tidyman said. "Dr Benjamin Stiles."

"Fuck's he gonna tell us?" muttered Chas. "Apart from the best brand of White Lightning to get your brains fucked on, I mean."

"Pack it in, Chas."

"Alright, Sarge. But you must admit."

I knew what he meant. The poor bastard looked a total train wreck.

Still, I didn't have anything better do, so I sat back and listened.

CHAPTER ELEVEN

Fullwood Army Base, 06:30 hours approx, November 7th.

Outside the building, wet spray hit my face. On the airstrip, a Chinook HC2 transport helicopter. A Flight-Sergeant stood at the back-end, beasting the ground crew as they backed a short-wheelbase Landrover aboard. The heavy rotors at each end were whirling, whipping up the water on the tarmac. It was already ankle-deep.

Stupid thought number one:

Fuck me, they weren't kidding.

Dr Benjamin Stiles. Ben to his friends. Assuming he had any left. When they think you're a mentalist, the friendships tend to dry up.

From the photo, I'd've put his age around fifty.

He was, according to Tidyman, thirty-six.

Stiles' area was marine biology. Five years ago, he'd been in a diving accident. Tidyman skimmed the details, but in a nutshell the poor bastard was physically fucked and in constant pain. And naturally, he could forget about diving again.

His career had fallen apart. The drinking hadn't helped. Probably to deaden the pain. Alcohol's good at that. But there was more. Obviously.

He'd started spouting doomsday predictions. Oceans rising, floods, the end of the world.

Not that unusual. Not enough to end a career.

That'd come when he'd started predicting the rising of the dead.

Tidyman skipped the details there too. Not relevant. What it boiled down to:

The powers that be wanted to pick whatever brains Stiles had left.

Location: A village called Barley. North-east Lancashire.

We ran across the strip. They were trying to shore the sandbags by the main gates but already the water was gushing through the gaps and they gave way as I reached the chopper. Akinbode and Mleczko went sprawling in the surge of brown water that rushed across the compound towards the strip like a breaker from a dirty sea.

"Move it! *Move* it!"

Back five minutes and it was like I'd never been away. Akinbode pulled Mleczko to his feet and they scrambled aboard. The water washed shin-deep. Shouts and screams.

I jogged up to the Flight-Sergeant. He turned around and we eyed each other up. Any transport 'copter – Sneaky Beaky or otherwise – has a loadmaster. The pilots decided where we flew, but just as I was in charge when we hit the ground, the Loadie was God when it came to deciding what went on or off the chopper. "McTarn."

"Lomax."

"Anything I can do to help, Loadie?"

He shook his head. "Just get your arse in there before you

drown."

I didn't need telling twice with it pissing down like that. Cannock was at the controls. The co-pilot, a thin droopy-moustached type called Hendry who looked as if his cat'd just been run over, stood in the cockpit doorway, staring out. "That everyone?"

I looked out of the main doors. The rain was rods and bolts, the sky black. Two last runners coming in: Nixon and Tidyman. "Couple more."

"Tell 'em to get a shift on, or we'll be flying underwater."

"Move your fucking arse, Nixon!"

I wasn't beasting an officer. I'm not *that* stupid.

Chas put on a burst of speed and jumped for it – pretty limber for a man near fifty. "Nice to have you back, Jock."

"*Sergeant* Jock to you, grotbag."

An old joke, but still a good one.

"That's the lot!" Lomax shouted. The loading ramp at the back closed up and he dropped into a seat.

"Everybody sit down and buckle up!" That was the co-pilot. "If we're going, it's fucking well now."

"Room for one more, I hope." Tidyman climbed in.

The co-pilot went red. "Sir."

Tidyman pulled the door shut. "Whenever you're ready."

I looked Tidyman over as I strapped myself into my seat. The Chinook lifted, rocking in the wind. Tidyman seemed at ease. In his comfort zone now.

My old CO, Lieutenant Alderson – he'd seemed decent enough as officers went. But the orders he'd given me...

I hoped Tidyman didn't give me orders like that.

Because I couldn't obey those orders again. I could not. Fuck.

Why put me in charge, you stupid bastards? Why? I'm not fit for it. Not anymore.

I look out of the porthole. The waters were flooding the compound now. The men ran back and forth. Like ants.

Had they been told they'd be evacuated too? Must have been, to stay at their posts like that. Or maybe it was duty. I used to believe in that.

"Everybody hang on," Cannock shouted. "Winds up here are

a nightmare."

Nightmares in the water, nightmares in the sky, and the ground all washing away...

So who the fuck am I?

Robert James McTarn. Born and bred: Easterhouse, Glasgow. Age thirty-six. Only child of:

Rose Frances McTarn. Wife, mother, drudge, part-time cleaner and full-time punching bag for:

Douglas Robert McTarn.

My father. Six-foot-three, equal parts lard, muscle and bone. Very little brain. A dozen tattoos, one professionally executed – the Red Hand of Ulster, on his chest – the rest homemade: RANGERS FC, NO SURRENDER. He kept vowing to get a full-scale depiction of the Battle of the Boyne emblazoned across his back but never, to my knowledge, fulfilled it. Too busy pissing the weekly wages from his builder's job up the wall. He worked like a bastard, I'll give him that.

He battered my Ma, and he battered me. No plea for sympathy here. Just a simple statement of fact. That stopped at seventeen; I blocked one of his punches and dealt a few back. Not many. Not enough. He was down on the floor spitting blood and teeth and still it wasn't enough.

And my Mam, pounding my back with her fists, scratching my face, screaming at me to 'get away from her man'.

I went out the door and kept on walking. I didn't stop till I'd reached the recruiting office. Too young to drink, too young to vote – Christ, I wasn't even old enough to put my name on a direct fucking debit. But old enough to sign my life away.

I armed myself up, built muscles and combat skills. None of it kept out the real pain. My father might be a bastard (and was), but he was the only one I had. My mother might've tried to scratch my eyes out, but she was still my Mam. If you don't like it, go take a long hard look at your family, and then come back and start preaching.

I came back home exactly once, for Mam's funeral. We'd exchanged a few awkward letters in the decade since I left. Never talked about it. Never would now.

As the chopper flew north-east, I hoped she was too long-dead and rotted away, to ever come back for me.

The winds picked up as we flew. The pilot kept us above the cloud cover wherever he could, for why I don't know. Not as if we had any enemy aircraft to worry about, not unless the nightmares could fly Harrier jumpjets.

I wasn't even going to *think* about that.

We tooled up in mid-flight.

Tidyman, Cannock, Hendry and Lomax all carried pistols – Sig-Sauer P226s, with the extended twenty-round clips.

Most of us 'other ranks' carried Army-standard SA80A2 rifles. I picked one up and it felt like coming home. Some put their faith in Jesus, and that's well and good, but he can't deliver 610 rounds per minute on request. We had a reinforced section, which in our case meant three snipers. There was Akinbode, who I'd met already; the other two were called Andrews and Levene. All three carried Parker-Hale L96 rifles. High-quality, bolt action. Lovely bit of kit. Andrews was thirtyish with short dark-brown hair and a goatee; Levene was a few years older with dark, grey-flecked hair and a droopy walrus moustache, and seemed permanently half-asleep. Neither said much, but snipers can be a funny bunch.

We were also issued with two Minimi M249 light machine guns – box magazine or belt-fed – as support weapons – along with a GPMG (general purpose machine gun), and a blooper (Mk19 grenade launcher.) All that and two Landrovers to mount them on.

They'd also issued us with combat knives, although quite frankly if the nightmares were *that* close in we really were fucked.

Still, in for a penny...

For all I know, my dad's still alive. Only the good die young. He was at the funeral. I was pretty sure I'd given him the cauliflower ear. Maybe the skewed nose too. Although Dad was never shy of battle scars.

We didn't speak or approach each other. A truce. Neutral territory. He stayed with his cronies and I stayed on my side of the church, in my lonely pew. I waited till they were all gone from the Crematorium, him and his pals from the boozer and the football terraces. Someone brayed a laugh as they went, I'm pretty sure it was him.

I never saw him again. If I had, I might have killed him. Mam was the only thing that might have stopped me.

I'd barely made it to the funeral in time. The flowers were from the corner shop down the road. I left them in the Garden of Rest and the rest of my leave and what money I had in London drinking, whoring and punching out any bastard who could stand in for my father for long enough.

In between leaving home and coming back, of course, I'd seen action. It saved me from thinking. When I wasn't doing that, there were always boozing sessions with the lads and trips to the red light district. That last one stopped when I met Jeannie.

More or less.

There'd be nights before a mission. The kind I mightn't come back from. All the boozed-up camaraderie can't help with that, but a woman can. And Jeannie might not be in reach on nights like that.

I wasn't the only one. I never told her. She never asked. She was an army wife. She understood these things.

She did.

That wasn't what broke us up, anyway.

That came later.

Maybe it'd been building up for a while. All the things I'd done for Queen and Country, never asking, never questioning. Maybe it was only a matter of time. The invasion just brought it to a head.

The Army had been my new family. The invasion was where that ended.

121

Lightning flashed through the portholes. The thundercrack followed seconds later.

I glimpsed the ground through rain and clouds. Streets turned into rivers. People huddled on rooftops. Waiting for help. Maybe they heard the Chinook over the storm, thought it was coming for them. Poor bastards if they did.

Only glimpsed them; no time to interpret. To see if anyone was looking up. Screaming for help or deliverance. Held up children like we were a friendly eagle come to snatch them away. Screamed in terror because they'd seen eyes glowing down in the water or their owners crawling out.

Imagination's a curse for a soldier. Never thought I'd had one. Probably got it around the same time as a conscience, and a mind of my own.

The woman screaming at us. Bastards, murderers – I could tell the meaning without knowing a word of her tongue...

Blood on my hands, blood on my face, blood I could never wash clean...

"You OK, mate?"

Chas, sat next to me, leather face furrowed. "Fine, Corp."

"You look stressed." The look in his eyes said: *Talk to me.*

I lowered my voice. "Don't know if I can do this, Chas. The fuck were they thinking?"

"That you were a fucking good section commander. That's what. You've done this before."

"That was before –" Before the desert road. Before all that.

"Yeah, I know, mate. But you did it once, you can do it again. It's not like then. Not now. You've gotta do it. For the lads."

"I know. I know."

"I've got your back, Robbie. You need help, you got me. Alright?"

I nodded, bumped his shoulder. "Thanks, Chas."

"No probs."

We managed to stay above the storms. To stop myself thinking about how much I fucking hated flying, I started matching names to faces. Well, you want to know what to call the soldier you're commanding, don't you?

Chas, Alf, Mleczko, Akinbode, Parfitt, Hassan, Andrews, Levene – I knew them already. That left two. There was one with greying hair, but who couldn't have turned thirty yet – that was Joyce. And the other one, a skinny girl with short blonde hair who barely looked old enough to join up – that was Parkes, the 'Sparky' (radio op in plain English.) Chas, the Corporal, was section leader, with Joyce, carrying a Lance-Corporal's stripe, as 2IC. I ran the names through my head as we flew.

When Cannock finally took us down, closer to the surface, almost all we could see was open water. Sea. It looked close enough to touch.

The water was mostly empty, stewed-tea brown, churning sluggishly as it poured further inland. Further ahead, as the ground rose, the roofs of houses were visible. Telegraph poles. Treetops. Street lamps. Debris clotted in thick swirling clusters on the surface. I looked out towards the horizon. Rain spattered against the porthole. The sea looked calm.

"Any idea how much further, sir?" I felt like a kid asking *are we there yet?*, but couldn't help it.

Tidyman shrugged. "Weather's been slowing us down, but I think the worst of it's behind us. At a guess, we're about halfway."

Only half?

Tidyman seemed to read my thoughts. "Don't worry too much, Sergeant. Making better time now. Should be there within the hour."

"Thank God."

Tidyman smiled, but it looked fixed. Sweat glittered on his forehead. Well, we were all wound tightly at the minute. I felt like the last man who should be in charge when we hit the ground. I wasn't sure if I still had the skills, or if I'd want them back. What would being a soldier again do to me?

All the same, I'd seen men look like that before. It was never a good sign.

Further north, the ground rose higher, and land broke the surface. Just hilltops at first. Little islands, some with a few be-draggled sheep grazing. I wondered what they made of it. My knowledge of sheep psychology was a little vague.

Hendry had taken over; he flew in low and at low speed.

A larger hilltop. A farmhouse near the water's edge. A man, a woman, a couple of kids ran out. Waved up at us.

I felt like flinging open the door and screaming, *we're not here for you, we never were*. But didn't.

Same old shite. The powers that be give the orders, move the chess pieces. Poor bastards on the ground suffer and die.

This trip brought all the memories back. But it's like the end of a marriage. All sorts of things aren't the same. First kiss, the first time you said *I love you* – they're all tainted by it being over now. The pain of that.

The same here. The camaraderie, being among men who under-stood what it was to be a soldier. I'd missed that. But I couldn't love it as I used to.

Whatever. Truth was, I was a fucking Sergeant again. Like it or lump it. And lumping it wasn't an option. I was responsible for my men.

Hills, rising clear of the water. The Chinook wove between them.

"There it is," Hendry called out.

A road came up out of the water. There was low ground on either side of it, flooded and overflowing it. The top storey of a large white house stuck up above it to the right, and ahead of that a tall chimney and the upper story of what I guessed to be a converted mill. On the left were only the tops of trees.

"Barley Road," said Tidyman. "The village should be dead ahead."

And it was, perched on the edge of the floodland, where the road branched off into a Y-junction. The one on the left led higher up the neighbouring fell; the one on the right led through a short row of houses before curving off into the distance.

"That's Barley, there," Tidyman said. "Stiles' last known loca-tion."

One street. A pub. Fields. Meadows. Farm buildings further out, as the ground rose, sloping steadily up towards a big, wide hill like the fin of the biggest fucking shark in the known universe. For a second, it looked like a huge wave coming in at us.

I got a good long look at it, as the Chinook wheeled about.

"Pendle Hill," said Tidyman.

Cannock took us over the village, found a flattish field on the lower slopes, began to descend. The grass flattened out from the downdraft.

"Sarge?" Chas Nixon waved me over to his porthole.

I looked. A dozen stick figures were clambering over the dry-stone walls and into the field. They didn't have the staggery, drunken walk of the nightmares in the video. That was a plus. On the other hand, they were all holding shotguns and rifles.

"This could get interesting," I murmured at last.

"You're not wrong, Jock," Chas murmured back.

"Sergeant to you," I murmured back, "grotbag."

CHAPTER TWELVE

The Chinook's wheels bumped the ground. The chopper rocked, finally settled. The rotors wound down. As the rotors fell silent, the whistle and howl of the wind came, and the patter of rain on glass.

I got to my feet: "De-bus!"

First order given. That was easy enough.

Doors open – the wind's bitter bite came through. The men baled out. They moved fast, forming a circle round the Chinook, dropping to one knee, guns aimed out. Lomax leant against a bulkhead and watched with folded arms, giving every appearance of being deeply unimpressed.

"Stand by for take off at short notice," Tidyman, unbuckling. "We're not bloody stopping for long."

"With respect sir, we might have to," said Cannock. "Looks like there might be another storm coming in." He pointed. Out to 'sea', a black stain was sweeping in across the sky. "Flying in that'd be suicide."

"I'll be judge of that, Cannock." Tidyman's voice rose; his face was very white. "Just remember who's in command here."

"Sir."

"Best get a move on, either way," I chipped in. "Take it I'm clear to go, sir?"

Tidyman nodded irritably. I decided to leave them to it and hopped out, then turned back. "Sir?"

Tidyman stuck his head out of the cockpit. "Sergeant?"

"Where do we find Dr Stiles, sir?"

"We don't have an exact address. He sort of dropped off the grid."

Off the grid. So, not a private house, then. A squat – some tumbledown cottage or barn? A tent? A static caravan, maybe...

"Sarge?" Chas pointed at the group of men moving in on the chopper. "What about them?"

"Fire on them, man!" shouted Tidyman.

"Beg pardon, sir, I'm pretty sure they're civvies."

"So am I," Tidyman said. "I'm also sure we've got a military helicopter, along with weapons, medical supplies, and food. Which they'll want. This isn't a relief mission. We're here to locate Dr Stiles and get him out. Nothing more. That is our priority. Nothing can be allowed to stand in the way of it." Flecks of spittle had gathered at the corners of his mouth.

I felt my hand drop to the butt of the SA80. I'd been somewhere very like this before. Some orders must not be obeyed.

Luckily, Chas Nixon stuck his head back in through the doorway before I did something stupid. "With respect, sir, they're not showing any hostile intent. No sense in starting a fight yet if we don't have to, is there?"

I stepped in. "He's right, sir. You said yourself I was in charge once we were on the ground."

"But I retain overall command, Sergeant."

"Not in dispute, sir –"

"Better not be!"

Sent to retrieve a fucking mentalist, and now it turns out the CO's one too. Any chance of some sanity round here?

Looked like I was the best bet for it. God help us all.

Pull it together, Robbie. You're not at home now. No time to go on your fucking guilt trip.

"Actually, sir, I was thinking of asking them where Stiles is. Sooner we know, faster we can finish, right?"

Tidyman's mouth twitched violently. "Very well. But the first sign of hostilities..."

"Sir."

Our lads were watching the locals and the locals were watching us. Nobody actually pointing their guns at anyone yet, thank Christ.

"Thanks, Chas."

"No probs."

"Keep an eye on Tidyman. Don't for fucksake let him kick anything off."

"Will do, Sarge."

A thought occurred to me. "Sir?" Tidyman leant out of the chopper. "You have a photo of Stiles?"

"What? Oh. Yes. Think so."

He disappeared back inside the Chinook, emerged a moment later with an eight by ten glossy. The same shot we'd seen in the briefing room.

"Thank you, sir." I turned to Chas. "I'm going to have a chat with the natives. Watch my back."

"Will do."

I slung the rifle across my back and started walking, hands out from my sides.

The apparent leader was a tall wide-shouldered man in his late fifties, maybe early sixties. He had a thick full grey beard and wore a heavy coat with the hood pulled up. The rest were a mixed bag, aged between eighteen and fifty.

The big man had a shotgun. A Franchi SPAS-12. More of a combat gun than something you'd use to clear the rooks off the cornfield, but oh yes, very, very nice. I felt a twinge of Shiny Kit Syndrome. Every soldier gets that when they see a nice-looking bit of equipment. If it'd been loose, I'd've tried swiping it for myself. Unfortunately, the big man was holding it.

He looked me over. His eyes were pale and cool. Wolf's eyes.

Rain spat down between us. The ground squelched underfoot.

I closed the distance and nodded at the other men. I didn't get any responses. They looked surly more than anything else.

I held out the picture. "We're looking for him."

The big man looked down. His bald crown gleamed in the rain. "What you want him for?" A Lancashire burr ran the words together.

"We're not after giving him any trouble."

"What'd he do, you're coming out for him in all this? Did he start it all off or summat?"

For all I knew, he had. "We need his help. Believe it or not, he's a scientist."

"Bugger can barely tie his own shoelaces."

I'd known men like him before. Mam had had family in the countryside, farming folk. Used to long hard hours of back-breaking work and nothing but scorn from the 'townies' who'd have starved to death without them. They'd been hard folk, tough, giving little away. The kind of men I'd want on-side in a fight. What would Stiles have been to him? Pitiable? Ridiculous? Both?

He shrugged, pointed out towards the Hill. "Lives out near there. Caravan in the field. Foot of the Hill."

"Any chance you could show us?"

He shrugged. "Aye."

"Good."

I glanced at the shotgun. Lovely bit of kit there; take a nightmare's head off like a fucking dream. "Bring that with you."

"I was going to, lad."

We took the Landrover with the mounted GPMG and got it onto the main street in Barley, Pendle Row – no way of driving straight up from where we'd landed. From there it was a short journey up the hill-roads to the base of Pendle itself. Alf Mason took the wheel; Mleczko crouched behind the Gimpy in case any large numbers of nightmares showed up. Akinbode sat in the back with his rifle. The big man sat in the back with us, the

SPAS-12 across his knees. He only spoke to give us directions.

We went round the back of the Hill. The floodwaters had come in pretty close at that side too. Alf parked as close to the base of the Hill itself as we could get; we left him with the Landrover and sprinted round to the Barley-facing side. The big man loped along without breaking a sweat, while Mleczko, on point, was outright bounding ahead. Me, I was feeling the effects of letting myself go. I was still in halfway good shape, but too many beers, too many takeaways and too many cigarettes were taking their revenge on me now. Still, at least overindulging in them wasn't too likely to be a problem in the immediate future.

Akinbode brought up the rear, making sure we weren't followed. Thank fuck, there was no sign of the nightmares.

The farmhouse was a big, solid-looking square building, built from blocks of yellow-brown stone. Shapes moved behind the windows. I glimpsed a gun. Shotgun or rifle, again. Probably no threat, more scared of us than anything else. But fear could be bloody dangerous. You never assumed anywhere was safe.

Behind us was the Hill. A flight of steps made from biscuit-coloured rock led up a side that was as close to vertical as you could get without needing ropes and climbing irons. Thank fuck we didn't have to climb *that*. You see, there's always a silver lining, if you look hard enough.

"What now, Sarge?" Mleczko looked flushed and almost happy from the run. I felt like giving the little sod ten laps around the Hill on general principle.

"Check the house, front and back. The rest of you, with me."

Another drystone wall marked out their front garden. I cut round it, keeping low, till I had the meadow in plain sight.

They'd left it lying fallow. Thick tufts of grass and weed sprouted up. Good cover for the approach, but the ground could be uneven. The caravan was tucked away at the far side, close to a thick hedge and under a heavy tree shedding leaves all over its roof. The caravan had to be twenty, thirty years old, the kind you saw on the roads when I was a kid – short and rounded at the ends with a set of wheels in the middle. I stopped at the wall's edge and lifted a hand as the others came up behind me.

I looked at the others. Mleczko jogged up. "Clear, Sarge."

"Good work. Alright; Akinbode, you cover us. Mleczko, you're with me. Spread out across the meadow. Stay low, use the cover. Clear?"

"Clear, Sarge."

"Sarge?"

I glanced at Akinbode. He had a narrow face and quick eyes. Looked like he might have a brain. Always handy. "What?"

"Thought this guy was a friendly."

"Briefing said psychiatric problems. We don't know his mental state, and for all we know he's armed. So we take no chances. Questions?"

"If he does fire on us?"

"How good are you?"

"Good enough, Sarge."

"We want him alive, so if you do have to, shoot to wound."

He nodded. Christ. Almost sounded like I knew what I was doing. Step back. Assess the situation. Take action. Keep it simple. Forget whatever memories it threatens to bring back.

"Any more questions?"

Akinbode shook his head. Mleczko'd never had any to begin with. The big man said nothing. "You stay here with Akinbode," I told him. "Watch his back in case anything tries sneaking up."

He grunted.

We spread out from the wall, into the low grass, Akinbode spreading himself prone on the ground by the gate and aiming on the caravan.

"Remember to spread out, Mleczko."

"Copy, Sarge."

"Go!"

I ran in a crouch with my head down, picturing Stiles in there pointing a Kalashnikov through the window.

No gunfire. Reached the caravan. Mleczko appeared in the grasses at the far end. I belly-crawled to the door. Reached up and knocked on it. Ducked back, expecting bullets to punch through it. Nothing.

"Dr Stiles?"

No answer.

"Dr Stiles?"

Still nothing. Fuck.

"We go in," I said. I motioned Mleczko to get the door, moving back to cover him.

Mleczko pulled the door wide. The stink washed out; I smelt piss, shit, stale sweat, rotten food.

"Stiles?"

Still no answer. I leant in through the door. This end held a kitchenette. Filthy 1970s lino with old food smeared and trodden in. A sink piled high with filthy pots. I climbed up and stood.

Bathroom at the end, door ajar. Stench making me gag. A faint buzz of flies.

In between the two, the main room. An old TV set in one corner, the screen smashed. A couple of chairs. A small table lying on its side. Threadbare carpet with scattered ash from the table, plus old beer cans, dirty plates, pizza boxes and the like. And a divan.

A man was sprawled on it, on grimy sheets. Even in the grey light coming through the curtains, I could see they were dark and wet.

"Fuck!"

I moved forward.

"Sarge?"

"Stay put."

I went to the divan. The man was Stiles alright. Eyes shut. Face grey. An empty whisky bottle in one hand, a knife in the other. The dark stains were round the hand with the bottle. He'd cut the wrist, but clumsily – gone across, not up the vein.

Stiles' wrist was still oozing blood. Still alive, then. Small mercies. I pulled out a field dressing, bound up the wrist. He let out a weak moan, then coughed and puked out a thin stream of bile.

"Mleczko, get in here!"

We drove back fast. Stiles lolled in the back, head propped up on a blanket roll. He threw up twice more. Joy of fucking joys.

The wind blew harder as we went, and the spray of rain was heavier. When I looked up, the sky was black overhead. Lightning flashed. Thunder rolled in with deafening cracks.

Some of the locals were still in the meadow, huddled by the nearest drystone wall. Keeping watch. If it came to an all-out fight I doubted they'd stand a chance. Then again, they could take a few of us with them. Chas still had the rest of the men around the Chinook.

And the rain poured down, and the wind flicked the long coarse grasses of the meadow to and fro.

The storm hit full-force as we reached the Chinook, displaying some truly perfect timing. There were two, three strokes of lightning, almost directly overhead, and the rain became industrial in force, hammering into us like machine gun fire. When it drove into your face, you were practically blind.

"Medic! Medic!"

"Jesus Christ!" Tidyman jumped down from the helicopter as we ran up. "What the hell did you do to him?"

Hassan leant out of the helicopter and looked down at the limp body. "What happened?"

"Found him like this. He cut his wrist."

"Just the one?"

"Aye. He'd put a lot of whisky away, too."

Hassan shook his head sadly. "Get him in here."

Mleczko and the others bundled Stiles inside. Tidyman clambered back into the Chinook, and I went after him. Hassan was spreading a blanket out on the floor. "Put him down here."

He checked the throat pulse and airways, unwrapped the dressing on the wrist wound. "Will he be alright?" Tidyman demanded.

The medic didn't look up. "Can't say for sure just yet, sir. Give you a sitrep soon as I can."

The wind picked up into a roar and the Chinook rattled from the force of it. Muffled curses came from the men outside. "Let's get airborne," Tidyman shouted over the tumult. "Get out while we can. We can get him better attention at a secure location."

"Beg pardon, sir." It was Cannock. He stepped out of the cockpit. "We can't fly in this. Just look at it."

Tidyman didn't. I'd already seen it. Even without looking, I could hear the rain hitting the bodywork. It sounded like a platoon of drummers going flat out. Like machinery. Like machine guns, all firing together.

"Stop contradicting me," said Tidyman. His eyes had a fixed, unblinking look to them now, and he spoke through his teeth. They were bared, like an animal's.

"Sir, we have to wait out the storm. It's all we can do."

Tidyman's gun was in his hand. I hadn't expected him to move so fast. The Sig-Sauer was lined up with Cannock's face before either of us knew what'd happened. All of a sudden, Tidyman looked very calm.

"You can take the bird up yourself," he said. "Or I shall do it for you. I'm quite capable, you know." I don't know if he meant flying the Chinook or blowing the pilot's brains out. I guessed at both. "Now which is it to be?"

"Sir, if we try taking it up in that –"

Tidyman cocked the Sig-Sauer. "Is that your final answer?"

"Sir!" Lomax called out, but he was frozen. His eyes met mine. The same thought passed between us both: *Fuck.*

I leaned in. Reason wouldn't work. Use a language he'd understand. "Sir, I understand we have to complete the mission. I know. But if we attempt to fly in that, the chopper will go down. If that happens, we die. You die. And most of all, so does Dr Stiles. And the mission will have failed."

A bead of sweat – or it might have been rain – ran down Tidyman's temple. His eyes flicked over to me. I had his attention anyway. "But if we wait out the storm, sir, we can fly out when it's clear. We get Stiles where he needs to go, and the job's done."

After a moment, he nodded, and lowered the Sig. "Alright," he said. "Carry on, Cannock."

Cannock swallowed hard, looked at me, then back to Tidyman. He nodded quickly and went back into the cockpit. His hand hesitated on the door as if to pull it closed. I wasn't surprised if he wanted to, but then maybe that would set Tidyman off again.

I looked at Hassan and the others; they were all staring at us. They quickly looked away again.

"Sergeant?" I turned back to Tidyman. "Alright. If we're staying here, here's what we do. I want you to send the men out and confiscate all firearms."

That weight in the belly. Something dropping away.

This is the moment. The order I cannot obey. I just know it. "Sir?"

"*All* firearms, Sergeant. This is a potentially hostile situation. Leaving them armed is insanity."

I fought to keep my voice level. "How are they supposed to defend themselves if those things attack, sir?"

"That's not our problem, Sergeant. Anyway, as long as we're here, they don't have to worry, do they?"

"We'll be returning them on departure, sir?"

He stared at me and his mouth opened, twisting into an aborted laugh. "Don't be ridiculous, Sergeant. We'll be abandoning them to those things. If they have weapons, you can guarantee they'll fire on us. It only takes one lucky shot."

The man shouting, holding out his hands. The pleas. But I'd had my orders. Hands reaching out. The shot.

He had a point, perhaps. There might be a good reason. Just as with the plans to pull all the key players back and leave the common herd to drown. There might be a good reason, but guess what?

There is *always* a good fucking reason. Whoever gets left to die, whoever gets the bombs dropped on them. Someone, somewhere, always has a good reason why that has to be done.

Tidyman was carrying on. "We will confiscate the firearms and we will take them with us."

Watching them walk away down the road, through the plumes of sand blowing across. Carrying their dead. Trying to call them back, screaming it, but they kept going.

"If we do that, sir, these people will have no chance of survival." I tried to keep my voice level.

Tidyman leant close. His breath was sour and rank. "For the last time, Sergeant, *that is not our problem.* We have our priorities. Civilian rescue is not one of them. I will not put the mission in jeopardy over a few minor qualms about a handful of surly yokels."

"You are sentencing these people to death, sir." My voice sounded hard and flat. I said it without thinking. Sometimes something kicks in, some override. Emotion. Something. Makes you helpless. Your actions seem to belong to somebody else. You hear your voice, see your body move, but they belong to someone else. That was happening now.

Tidyman's face was white with rage. "I am giving you an order, Sergeant. Now get out there and take those guns off those people if you have to shoot every single one of them to do it."

"No, sir."

For a blissful second, I thought Tidyman was about to give himself a stroke and save us all the trouble. "What did you say?"

"I said, I will not obey that order. Sir. They're giving us no trouble and we can cross that bridge when we come to it if they do. We can't fly yet and we may face attack from those things. If that happens, they have weapons and they have local knowledge which will come in pretty damned handy."

"I am in command here!"

"And I am in charge on the ground, sir."

"*Were.*" His head swivelled. "Corporal Nixon –"

I stepped in close. "The Chinook has the carrying capacity to take most 'if not all' of the local residents with us sir, and no hassle. Doing so will not jeopardise the mission in any way, shape or form. And I'll be quite happy to tell them that, not to mention your little plan of leaving them behind to be eaten alive. *Sir.*"

His mouth snapped open. Sound came out. A sort of screeching. He might have been planning for it to turn into words, but there was no time to find out. The gun was out of its holster again, and coming up.

I caught his wrist and twisted. Tidyman screamed and dropped the Sig. Then kicked out at me. It caught me on the thigh. I blocked a punch, then caught his hand as he tried to scratch my face and nutted him as hard as I could.

Another thing I hadn't done in a while, but it wasn't a bad job. A good Glasgow Kiss is supposed to hurt the other guy more than you. On those grounds, I did pretty well. My forehead smarted a little, but Tidyman's nose crunched under the blow and warm blood splashed my face.

Blood on my face, blood on my hands. Grained into the skin. Still there. Still there now. Impossible to shift. Always carried with me. The blood. The guilt. My guilt.

His head snapped back. His eyes crossed and rolled up and the weight of him sagged. I lowered him to the ground. He let out a weak groan.

Everyone was staring. Hassan, Mleczko and the rest had all frozen over Stiles, and Cannock and Hendry were in the cockpit door. Chas was at the main door of the craft, looking in. He looked down at Tidyman and then up at me.

Shit.

We looked at each other for a few seconds that lasted a lot longer for me. Chas had been there too, that day in the desert, outside the city. He'd seen what I'd seen, been part of what I'd been part of. He understood. But at the same time, he'd stayed in when I'd left. Maybe he was just a tougher nut than I'd been, I don't know. Or maybe it was just that he'd been in too long; had nowhere else to go.

After a moment, he nodded and turned away.

Lomax stood there watching, about as easy to read as the fucking Sphinx. After a moment, though, he nodded too. I breathed out. Then I picked up the P226 and unbuckled Tidyman's gunbelt, strapped it round my own waist. Well, he wasn't going to need it now. Shiny Kit Syndrome again..

Cannock looked from me to Tidyman and back again. "Thanks for before," he finally said.

"Mention it. Chas?"

"Sarge?"

"See to the Squadron Leader, if you would. Get Hassan to look him over once he's finished with Stiles. In the meantime, better place him under restraint."

"Copy that. What about the men?"

I wiped my face. It felt cleaner, but traces of blood were still on my hand. "Stand them down for now. We're in the same boat as the locals. Better off pooling resources."

"Makes sense."

I stepped out into the rain and looked across at the farmers as Chas barked out orders. The big man with the shotgun gave a slight smile and nodded. I nodded back. Finally a response. I wondered how much he'd seen.

Chas drifted up. "He's in cuffs for his own good, but he's still conscious and he's coming round. My guess is he'll be breathing hellfire and damnation. Want me to give him a little tap on the head?"

Tempting, but perhaps not. "Maybe later, Corp."

"If you say so."

"I do. Want to see how Hassan's doing with Stiles?"

"Not particularly," sighed Chas. He half-turned away, then turned back. "You know, Sarge, you probably could've disarmed him without smashing his hooter like that."

"What's your point?"

Chas grinned. "Good to have you back, Robbie," he said, and moved off.

Time to talk with the natives again.

I made my way over. Most of them had drifted away by now, but the big man was still there.

"Looks like we'll be staying here for a while," I said at last.

He grunted. "I could have told you that, lad."

"Aye, well. We'll not be a bother to you."

"Come in handy, having you lot around. If those bloody things come back."

"Things?"

"Don't piss about, lad. You know what I'm talking about."

I nodded. "We're better off co-operating."

"What I thought. You want to get your lads in out of this?"

"Where did you have in mind?"

He gestured. "Pub's down at the end of Pendle Row. They can still pull a decent pint, even in this. Might be the last chance to get one in for a while."

I nodded. "Just keep 'em away from the optics to be going on with."

"We'll manage, I'm sure." He offered his hand. "Ged Wynn."

"Robbie McTarn."

I headed back to the chopper. "Chas? Move the men into the pub. Just leave whoever we need to keep watch on this." I gestured to the Chinook.

"You mean Tidyman."

"I mean both." I climbed aboard. Stiles was still out. Tidyman too. "Thought he was waking up again."

"Had a bit of a dizzy spell," said Chas. One thing about Chas Nixon, he could always keep his face admirably blank if he wanted.

"That'll give us some peace." I pushed through into the cockpit. "Sir?"

Cannock and Hendry looked up. "Either of you know where it is we're supposed to be going?"

Cannock shook his head. "Not exactly."

"Not *exactly*?"

Hendry chipped in. "It's in the Cotswolds somewhere, Sergeant. That's all we were told. The only one with the exact location is Squadron Leader Tidyman."

I took a deep breath. "Please tell me we have a contact frequency."

"Yes. And a call sign for them. Windhoven. Twice a day – oh-nine-hundred and twenty-one-hundred."

And we were nowhere near either. Fuck.

"I suggest we get on the radio, and see if we can raise anyone else – army base, airfield, anything."

"Good thinking."

"Aye. Parkes!"

"Sir." Parkes showed her face at the doorway. She looked terrified.

"Work with the pilots. See if you can raise anyone who can point us in the right direction." I looked over at Cannock. "Do you want to see if you can get anything helpful out of Tidyman when he's a bit more awake?"

Cannock nodded. "Will do."

"Sergeant?"

Lomax. "Aye?"

"We'll need to secure the chopper. I mean *physically* secure it, in this storm. There's some tarps and guyropes in back. Am I OK borrowing a few of yours?"

"I'll see to it."

"Thanks."

I clapped Chas on the shoulder and we stepped down. Ged Wynn was still standing by the drystone as we approached, the broken shotgun over one arm.

"Haul three of the lads in to help Lomax. Get the chopper secured and then all we've got to do is sit tight till the storm clears."

"What about Tidyman?"

"Think the aircrew'll back me up. Frankly, Chas, as long as we're not leaving these poor sods completely fucking helpless I'll be happy facing the music. Worst comes to the worst, you just followed my orders."

He grinned. "Might be a plan securing a perimeter out here."

"Could be right. But we're not near a major population centre. Bit of luck, all we need to do is sit out the storm."

"Ged! *Ged!*"

Someone was running up the footpath.

I felt my hands moving of their own accord to slip the SA80 from behind my back, closing round the barrel and pistol grip. My thumb was on the safety catch.

Ged ran towards the newcomer, catching him as he almost fell. We reached them a few seconds later.

"Billy!" Ged shook the lad by the shoulders. "What's up?"

The lad was about nineteen, at a guess, with a round pallid face. He looked from face to face, like a scared kid half his age. "They're coming," he said. His voice sounded thick, slurred, as if something was wrong with his mouth. "They're fucking coming."

"You were saying, Sarge?" muttered Chas.

"Chas?"

"Yes, Sarge?"
"Shut up."
"Yes, Sarge."

CHAPTER THIRTEEN

Crouched in the doorway of the Tea Rooms, halfway down Pendle Row with Ged and Chas; dozens of the nightmares massing already at the Y-junction at the bottom of the road, all facing our way. Slack, empty faces; glowing eyes. All I saw at first. But looking closer, the details sprang out – clothes, hairstyles. Men, women, and – *aw Christ* – children. Some as young as five. A woman held a baby to her breast, its arm waving. It couldn't be alive. It couldn't be.

If it didn't have teeth, maybe I wouldn't have to shoot it.

The child kneeling in the dust. Baba. Baba.

Ged stared past me at them, lips pressed together white, breathing deep, eyes wide and bright. Billy was across the road behind a parked car, rocking slightly, humming faintly. Pale. His lips twitched. Poor bastard looked ready to piss his pants. What was his mental age? Eleven, twelve? If that, from what I'd seen of him; he'd lolloped back down to Pendle Row with us like a kid off to play soldiers. Retarded or not, though, they'd given him a

12-bore over-and-under shotgun. Please God, they'd taught him to use the damn thing properly.

Up ahead a stocky, short-haired woman in her forties knelt behind a 4X4, aiming a deer rifle at the nightmares.

"Some of them came out before," Ged's voice wasn't completely steady.

"Yeah?"

"Aye. 'Bout an hour or so before you got here."

The nightmares stood, watching us. The rest of the locals from the meadow were with us, in doorways or behind walls or parked vehicles. Everyone else was scrambling for the higher ground.

"Chas!"

"Sarge?"

"Get Joyce and Mleczko down here." I looked around. There was high ground each side of Pendle Row, one to our right, behind the farm opposite the Tea Rooms to our left, the other near the junction with Barley Road. I pointed there first. "I want Mason up there with the Minimi, Andrews and Levene up there." Behind the farm. "You and Akinbode get the blooper round the other side of the Hill just in case."

"Copy that."

"Get as high up as you can. They might come from more than one side. Keep the rest of the lads on standby with the other Dinky. Copy?"

"Copy."

"And Chas? Headshots only, single rounds or short bursts. No wasting ammo."

"Got it."

Water sluiced over my boots. The stream running down from the Hill had overflowed. My feet were cold.

"Been pissing down all week." I looked at Ged. His breath puffed out white as he spoke. "Just thought it were more of the same. Flood warnings on telly. We rounded the sheep up. Stayed in. Didn't want to get caught out in this.

"Then telly went off-air. Then the radio. Then the electricity went. Nowt we could do but wait it out. Then..." He pointed down at the Row. "We just saw it pouring into the valley. Heard folk screaming, but there was nowt we could do. What's been bloody happening out there?"

I told him. Classified, of course, but I was past caring.

"Dear Christ." He shook his head. "We knew it was bad, but... so it's everywhere?"

"'Fraid so."

"Bugger." He nodded down the street. "Should've guessed when those things bloody turned up. There were only a dozen or so that first time. Shot a couple. Rest just fell back."

I nodded. Retreat and regroup, then attack again. "Looks like they've brought friends this time."

Ged gripped his shotgun. "Hard to tell, state they're in now, but... that one there – think that's a bloke called Hargrave. Runs a farm about half a mile down the road. And that one... looks like..."

He stopped. I decided not to push it. At least I wasn't likely to meet anyone I knew. Although I wouldn't put it past Dad to swim down just to take a chunk out of me. Vindictive old bastard.

The young woman holding the baby might have been pretty once. She had dark blonde hair, bedraggled and rat's-tailed. Her eyes were clouded and glowing green. Something had bitten a chunk out of her face. The baby was in a romper suit, a small hand beating the air.

I pulled back the bolt on the SA80.

Beside her stood a tall man, long hair hanging limp and wet. Goatee beard, pasty skin; he would have looked satanic even alive, with or without the Slayer T-shirt under his open cardigan. If you wanted a poster boy for the carnivorous walking dead, here it was.

Behind them was another man, taller still, at least six-three and built to match. Another long-hair. Thick full beard. Looked like a Viking. They seemed to be sticking together. Maybe they'd been friends.

Don't focus on any of them like that. Don't see the people they used to be. See the target. The enemy. The monster.

For once, at least, there was no thought at the back of my mind about the enemy being some mother's son.

It didn't help.

Levene and Andrews were in position. Alf ran past, down one of the little yards branching off the Row, hopping the fence at the end and scrambling for the top.

"Alright, everybody. Don't panic. Remember you need a head-shot."

"Sarge." Mleczko didn't look like a joker any more. His face was hard and tight.

I spoke into my personal communicator. "Levene, Andrews, make sure none of them get past you, and keep them out of the buildings."

"Copy, Sarge."

"Alf – what's Barley Road looking like?"

"Chocka, Sarge."

"Alright. They start moving, aim for the head. Sweep across, try and whittle them down before they get here."

"Copy that."

I turned to Ged. "If I were you, I'd get behind us. We've got more range. Your shotguns'll be handier if they get in close."

Ged shrugged. "You want to put yourself between them and us, you're more than bloody welcome."

I moved towards the riflewoman. "You want to move back too?"

She glanced at me. A wide, impassive face; a small gold ring in each ear. "Not particularly." She turned back to watch the nightmares.

"This is gonna kick off any minute, hen."

"Why do you think I'm here? And don't call me hen."

"Fair enough. Can you can shoot straight?"

"Just watch me."

I studied the back of her cropped head. "Were you in the army?"

"No. Why?"

"Should've been."

She glanced back, grinned.

"Sarge!" Joyce. "They're moving!"

I shouldered my rifle. "Pick a target, lads. Fire on my mark, not before."

They lurched drunkenly along Pendle Row, dressed in a sodden array of coats and colours. Farmers in their Barbour jackets. Hikers in boots and cagoules, some still wearing backpacks. Caught out on the fells, trapped in their cars, up to tour the Witch country.

I sighted on the blonde girl. I didn't want her to get closer. I might see the child properly.

Her eyes glowed. I was looking right into them. That strange glow. It was fascinating. You could look at them all day long, somehow, wondering how they worked.

Keep staring at them right up until –

"Pick your targets and... fire for effect!" I yelled, and pulled the trigger.

Even when you think you're a hardened bastard, however many times you've killed, some deaths stay with you, and always will.

The rifle butt driving back into my shoulder. The bolt snapping backwards. Smoke darting from muzzle and breech, brass cartridge cases jumping out and to the side. A perfect three-round burst.

The woman's head snapping backwards as a shot took her through the left eye, rat's-tailed hair flying wild as the bullet exited the back of the head, tearing the ear loose to dangle from a skin flap.

She dropped forward and lay still. I let out the breath I'd been holding and snapped back into the real world.

The noise crashed in on me first, gunfire erupting left and right. I'd almost forgotten just how fucking *loud* a gunshot is. Falling shellcases tinkled on the wet ground, hissing as they hit the water. Eight nightmares down. A couple staggered – hit in the neck, scalp wounds – but kept coming.

I aimed for the satanic-looking one.

And then the nightmares *charged*. A sudden scuttling burst of motion, jerky but fast, like a bunch of horrible wind-up toys.

"Fuck!"

Focus, Robbie.

Satan-boy was weaving. Not intentionally, at least I didn't think so – just the convulsive, flailing way they moved. I fired and missed, catching the Viking in the shoulder. Didn't slow him for a second.

I fired at Satan-boy again, but he was almost on top of me. A bullet tore off an ear, but he kept coming.

I jumped back, fired again. This one hit him in the face. The Viking knocked him aside as he fell, lunging for my throat.

I got the rifle up to block him and we went down together. I shoved the barrel crossways into his mouth. His teeth gnashed at it, eyes blazing inches from my face.

"Shiiiit!"

The chattering of an automatic weapon.

"Control your fire!" I roared out. A villager ran in to help, but one of the nightmares leapt on him. He staggered, screaming, and two, three more fell upon him. Blood sprayed up.

The Viking hissed and snarled round the metal of the gun, pushing me down. Beyond him, more nightmares were lurching forward. But a heap of them were on the ground too.

A gun butt smashed in to the side of the nightmare's head. It juddered and collapsed as Alf Mason stood over me, put the Minimi to his shoulder and fired another automatic burst, sweeping left to right at head height. Almost the whole front row of nightmares went down, and most of the ones behind. Behind us, another volley of gunfire rang out. Two more nightmares, nearly on top of me now, jerked and dropped.

I rolled the dead nightmare off me; Alf helping me up. "You OK, Robbie?"

"Thought I told you to get the bastards on the road."

"They've stopped coming out of the water. You seemed to need the back-up more."

"Alf!" Another nightmare seized his arm and sank its teeth in. Alf bellowed. I shot it through the top of the head.

Four of them were still snarling and tearing at the fallen villager. He wasn't screaming anymore. The woman ran forward, shot one in the head, swung the rifle to crush another's skull, but the third seized the weapon and grappled for it. Then Mleczko was there, Billy stumbling in his wake, and blew its brains across the nearest wall. The fourth nightmare lunging towards him – he swung back and shot it. Billy fired first one barrel, then another, flinching back from the fire and smoke; another nightmare fell. Then he was falling back with Mleczko and the woman.

Maybe twenty nightmares remained, staring at us with those glowing eyes. I put the rifle to my shoulder and aimed.

Then one by one, they turned and started walking away. One by one, they walked back down Barley Road towards the deep water.

Alf had slumped to his knees, cursing and groaning. I made for the fallen villager. Blood splashed out around him, steaming. Chunks of flesh and organs lay in it. I walked on, pleading to the God I didn't believe in that the poor bastard *was* dead. He was. One prayer answered today.

Something was wriggling out from under the blonde woman's corpse. Something small, wearing a romper suit. It hissed. The small cowled head turned. I glimpsed a tiny, snarling face, two empty sockets blazing with green light.

Oh Jesus, no.

A thundery, rolling *boom* and its head exploded. The rest of the body, torn and mangled by the shot, twitched and was still.

Ged pumped the shotgun slide. The cartridge case clattered on the ground. His hands shook. He dragged a sleeve across his eyes, then turned away without a word.

Alf's face was grey. Mleczko wrapped a field dressing round the wounded arm. "Get him to Hassan," I said.

Billy stood staring down at them. "D'you want any help?"

"Er, yeah." Mleczko took Alf's bad arm. "Giz a hand here, yeah?"

"Yeah. Yeah." Billy was nodding as he looped the other arm about his shoulders. "Upsi-daisy!" He grinned.

The woman clapped Mleczko's shoulder. "Cheers for before."

"No worries." Mleczko and Billy marched Alf off, almost dragging him.

Past them, Ged was trudging up the Row, head down. "Is he OK?" I asked the woman.

She looked savage. "What do you think?"

Ask a stupid question.

She let out a long breath, closed her eyes, pointed at the dead girl. "See that?"

"Yeah."

"That was his daughter. Clare, her name was. Nice kid."

I looked at the bloodied rag doll beside her. "Was that..?"

"Yeah."

"Fuck."

"He'll be OK." I looked at her. "Well, not OK. But he'll cope."

"What I thought."

She cleaned her rifle butt on Satan-boy's T-shirt, then offered a hand. "Jo."

"Robert. Thanks for your help. You did a good job."

She half-grinned. "Cheers mate. You weren't so bad yourself."

She offered me a cigarette, lit her own, leant back against the 4X4.

Inside the Chinook, Stiles lay on a blanket with another pulled over him. Tidyman likewise, only cuffed. Hassan had splinted his nose and secured it with a bandage across the face. Sadly he was conscious now.

"What happened?" he demanded. I ignored him. "Sergeant?"

Hassan unwound the dressing from Alf's arm. Electric lamps inside the helicopter shed a cold, antiseptic glow. "Shit. That's a mess."

Hassan started cleaning the wound. Alf bellowed. "Fucking twat!"

"Sounds more like it," I said, and managed a grin. But Alf was crying with pain. Shit.

"I'll give him a shot." Hassan swabbed Alf's forearm and jabbed a morphine ampoule in. Alf grunted, closed his eyes.

Hassan inspected the damage. "There's a whole chunk missing. Best I can do is pack the wound. What happened?"

"What do you fucking think? One of those bloody things bit a piece out of him."

"He was bitten?" I looked round. Tidyman was sitting up, staring at me. He had a brace of beautiful black eyes too, I noticed. A Glasgow kiss can do that. "Sergeant, you have to listen to me. Was he bitten?"

"Yes. OK? He was bitten. *Sir.*"

"You have to kill him."

"You fucking what?" I scrambled over, shoved Tidyman up against the bulkhead. "What did you fucking say, you arsehole?"

"You've got to kill him!" Tidyman screamed it, all composure gone. "You don't understand. You have to kill him."

Focus, Robbie. Get control. Breathe in, count to four; breathe out, count to four. "Why?"

"The bite. It's poisonous. Everyone bitten by those things dies. Every one of them. There's no cure. Antibiotics won't stop it. Nothing will. And when they die, they come back as one of them."

"Fuck off."

"It's true. Why should I lie about it?"

Good point. "Then why didn't you tell us?"

"There wasn't time."

"Lying bastard."

Tidyman tried to wriggle away from me. "It wasn't my choice. It was decided that if the men knew, they'd be less likely to get the job done."

"You fuckers. You fucking fuckers."

I let him go and turned away.

"You've got to kill him, Sergeant. It's the most merciful thing you can do."

Alf was out for the count, by the look. Thank heaven for small fucking mercies.

"Flying Officer Cannock?"

The pilot didn't answer. "Cannock?" Tidyman demanded again.

"Sir?"

"Can we take off yet?"

Cannock looked at me.

"Flying Officer Cannock? Why are you looking at that man? He is not an officer in Her Majesty's Royal Air Force. I am. I am your *commanding* officer. Answer my question. Can we take off?"

Cannock cleared his throat. "Not yet, sir. We've secured the Chinook against the weather, but we'll have to wait out the storm."

Tidyman's face worked, but finally he got himself back under control. "Alright, Flying Officer. But I expect to be told the moment we're able to fly. I don't intend to wait here any longer than I have to."

Prick.

"And in the meantime, you can let me out of these cuffs." He held his hands out. "Immediately."

Cannock looked over at me.

"Cannock!" It was a scream. A fleck of spittle hit my face. "Stop looking at that man! He has no authority here! I am your commanding officer and *you will let me out of these cuffs immediately!*"

Cannock didn't move.

"Flying Officer Cannock!"

I moved towards Tidyman. He shrank back. "Sir, I suggest you calm down and be quiet. You're staying as you are."

Tidyman was trying to stay calm. "Alright, Sergeant. Now, I accept you had to do what you did before. I overreacted. But I'm perfectly alright now. So please let me go."

I shook my head. His face whitened with fury. "We have to get out of here. That man is vital."

"Stiles? Why? What is it he knows?"

Tidyman compressed his lips and gave no answer.

"I'll make a deal with you, sir. You tell me why Stiles is so important and I'll consider undoing the cuffs."

He spoke through his teeth. "It's classified."

"So they didn't tell you either. Need to know only, right?"

"Sergeant McTarn. I am giving you a direct order."

"Tell you what," I said. "Give me the location of the Cotswolds base and we'll see."

He blinked at me – he almost looked surprised – then smiled. "I don't think so, Sergeant."

"What about this all-important mission of yours, Sir?"

"I don't trust you to carry it out, McTarn. Anymore than I do to keep your word and let me go. No," he leant back, "I have something to bargain with here, don't I?" An odd smile twisted one corner of his mouth. "We'll see who cracks first."

I turned back to Hassan. "Do what you can, OK?"

He nodded.

"What shape's Stiles in?" I asked. I could almost feel Tidyman's ears pricking up.

"He'll be OK," Hassan said. "My guess would be he decided to kill himself – perhaps because of all this – but had to get drunk to do it." He smiled. "So drunk he passed out before he could cut anything vital."

I had to laugh. "Well, thank fuck for that. Put the bloody tin lid on it if we'd come all this way for nothing."

I left Hassan at the helicopter with Hendry and Tidyman. And Alf. I was trying not to think about what Tidyman had said. I didn't want to believe it.

I stationed Parfitt on Alf's former position with the other Minimi, kept Levene where he was and moved Andrews to an upstairs room at the Pendle Inn. Guard and lookout duty would rotate hourly. I posted Joyce and Akinbode on top of the Hill.

We moved the booze out of the Inn to one of the nearby farmhouses. It was a large place and empty, so it would serve as a billet, meeting place, and if necessary an informal boozer. The Landrovers were stationed outside, ready to be mobilised at a moment's notice. Chas had put the one with the grenade launcher to good use earlier – the nightmares had been coming out of the water on the far side of the Hill towards Clitheroe, but a quick fusillade from the Mk19 had put them to flight.

I allowed myself a small tipple, the Inn had had some decent single malt in. Isle of Jura; not bad at all, though for me it's really got to be one of the Islay malts like Laphroaig or Lagavulin, but I wasn't going to complain. There wasn't much chance of me tasting a good whisky in the future. I tried to remember how far above sea level the Inner Hebrides were.

Besides, the spirits might be a lot more useful for other purposes – Molotov cocktails, not to mention for a steriliser if Hassan needed it.

The rest of the section congregated in the front room, along with a few of the villagers. Lomax leant against the wall and sipped a Coke, surveying the proceedings with a fine disdain. Mleczko perched on the arm of the sofa, with Billy sat on the floor beside him, gazing up with what looked suspiciously like hero worship in his eyes. Jo sat on the sofa next to Chas. They were chattering away nineteen to the dozen; he said something and she not only laughed, but reached out and ruffled his hair. And Chas Nixon – as the God I don't believe in is my judge – actually fucking *blushed*. Now I *knew* it was the end of the world.

"Lads!" Heads turned. "Just wanted to say – well, I think we can safely say no-one else has *ever* had to deal with anything quite like we have today." That got a few grim chuckles. "You all did bloody well. I'm proud of you." The words felt false, like any of this still mattered. "One beer apiece. Everyone takes a turn at watch tonight." Groans. "Corp?" I gestured towards the kitchen. Chas nodded and got up. "Parkes, you too."

"Sorry, Corp," I murmured as we went. "Hate to break up the romance."

"Piss off, Jock."

Ged, Cannock and Hendry were waiting in the kitchen. I took a sip of the Jura, resisting the temptation to gulp it down. Outside the wind howled, dashing rain against the windows.

"Situation's this," I said. "For the time being we're stuck here. Big question is where we go when the storm clears."

Ged was watching me closely. So was Chas.

"According to Tidyman, there's a secure location we're supposed to take Stiles to. Problem is, only he knows where this fabulous place is, and he won't talk unless I let him go. Which I don't fancy."

"He wants to get out of here, doesn't he?" snorted Chas.

I nodded. "Thinks he can wait us out. Meantime, we've a contact frequency for them, and designated times to try them." I turned to Cannock again. "Just how much fuel do we have for the Chinook?"

"Enough to get to the Cotswolds, certainly; even enough to spend some time searching for the base. But from what I understand, Windhoven is an underground bunker, and, obviously, hidden from plain sight. We could search forever and not find it."

I nodded. "So unless we can scavenge further fuel supplies, we've got one shot."

"You got something in mind, Rob?" Chas.

"I have. For the minute, we're going nowhere anyway. We can't fly in this, and we don't know what the national situation is. Parkes?"

The radio-op looked up from a pint of Foster's she didn't look old enough to legally drink. Not that that mattered anymore. "Sarge?"

"Any luck?"

"None, Sarge. But the electrical storm's playing hell with our comms."

"I thought we had top of the line sat-comm equipment."

"We do, Sarge, but it's not much good if you can't connect with the satellite. Again, our best chance will be when it clears."

Pretty much what I'd expected. "So we can't fly, and even if we could, we wouldn't know where to go. On top of that we don't know what Windhoven's status is, or that of the regional control centres. For all we know, those things have overrun them all. So till we know better, we're on our own." I looked over at Ged. "While we're here, we can help organise the defence of the village, search for other groups of survivors. Then, when we do fly out, you're not all left completely in the lurch."

Ged nodded. His face was expressionless, and he had a large brandy – triple or quadruple at the least – on the go. Was making pretty good headway with it, too. I didn't think he'd said a word since the fight on Pendle Row.

"If anyone's got any better ideas, let's hear them."

No-one did.

"Alright. Light 'em if you've got them. Unless anyone has any objection?"

Ged shrugged, the faint memory of a smile curving his lips. "Never liked that fucking smoking ban anyway."

Cannock went to mind the chopper around twenty-one hundred, taking Parkes with him, to try Windhoven again.

The storm was still raging. Fresh cracks of thunder rolled in every few seconds. Ged told me there was a local saying that if you could see Pendle Hill it was about to rain, and if you couldn't, it was already raining, but even by local standards it was fucking well pissing it down.

Then the first shots rang out.

"Oh shit."

I snatched up my rifle, pulled back the bolt. My PC crackled. "McTarn."

"Sarge? Joyce. They're coming out of the water, over."

"Shit. Location?"

More shots. "Just looks like a localised attack. Near the two pools."

The pools were just north-east of the Hill, on a wide flat stretch of open ground beneath a wooded slope.

"On our way," I said.

"Don't think there's any need, Sarge." A few last shots, then silence. "Looks like that was the lot."

I sat back down. "You mean you woke me up just for that?"

Muffled laughter.

"Keep us posted, Joyce."

"Will do, Sarge. Out."

I looked at Chas and grinned.

Then more gunshots. From right outside.

I broke outside, into the pelting rain, Chas at my back. Ged and Mleczko followed, Billy stumbling after.

"Sarge! Sarge!"

Parkes. She ran towards us fast, head down.

"What? What is it?"

"Tidyman, Sarge. Got loose somehow. Knocked Hassan out, maybe killed him. Shot Cannock. And –"

"What?"

"Private Mason, Sarge. He shot him in the head."

"Bastard." I unslung the rifle, passed it to Chas. "That'll be no good where I'm heading." I drew the P226.

"Need any back up?" He asked.

"We start firing rifles at the Chinook, we could fuck our ticket out of here."

"Copy that."

"But we need to keep Tidyman occupied. Get a couple of the lads to the chopper and bang a few off, but for fuck sake aim high."

Chas nodded. "Mleczko?"

"Sarge?"

I thought of how he'd done back on the High Street; a man you'd want with you. "Can you use a pistol?"

"Yeah."

Hendry and Lomax had joined us. "Mind if Mleczko borrows your gun, Sir?"

Hendry, face pale, nodded, and handed it over. "Thank you, Sir. Mleczko, you're with me. Priority's keeping the Chinook in one piece. Tidyman's gone apeshit so if you have to, drop him."

Mleczko nodded. He didn't seem to have a problem with that. If anything, he looked pretty bright-eyed at the prospect. Then again, that could've just been Shiny Kit Syndrome, at getting his hands on the pistol. He handed his rifle to Chas.

"Need another body?" asked Lomax.

"Always handy. You're a good shot?"

"I can hit a barn door."

There was a coughing sound from the Chinook. "Just don't hit anything important. Chas, ready to fire. Mleczko, Lomax, move your arse."

Shots rang out behind us as we ran low across the field. A

bullet whined and buzzed past my ear. Too fucking close. Sparks flew from the cockpit canopy.

"You do know," Lomax huffed as we went, "the Chinook's got two Gimpys mounted in there?"

I did, but I'd been doing my best to forget that. Hopefully Tidyman would content himself with Hassan's rifle.

Something lay in the grass outside the helicopter. It was on fire.

The rotors were turning.

Shit.

But thank fuck, the side door was ajar. I ran faster.

Then the door flung wide. Tidyman stood in it. He was holding a SA80. Probably Hassan's.

Oh shit.

The rifle's muzzle spat flame. I dived. Bullets whined overhead.

I brought up the P226, fired three rounds. Tidyman ducked back.

I got up and ran. Lomax's heavy boots pounded the turf behind me. Tidyman popped back up, fired again. Lomax cried out; a body hit the ground. The rifle arced towards me, but Mleczko fired first; Tidyman screamed and dropped the rifle on the ground.

I was almost at the chopper now. Tidyman was clutching at the door, trying to drag it closed. I fired at his hand as I ran; the bullet spanged off the door, and he scrambled back inside.

I dived through the door as Tidyman fired a pistol at me from the cockpit. Cannock's, I guessed. Blood splattered the inside of the cockpit canopy; Cannock himself slumped forward in his seat.

Tidyman aiming for another shot. I fired twice, a double-tap. More blood splattered outwards across the cockpit canopy. Tidyman fell back across the instrument panel, staring at me, then dropped to his knees and fell forwards.

Alf Mason lay where I'd left him, only with a neat bullet hole behind his right ear and the left eye forced half-out of its socket. Stiles was unmarked, but still unconscious. Hassan was crumpled against one of the bulkheads; alive or dead, I couldn't tell.

The Chinook was rocking. Mleczko scrambled in. "Sarge?"

"I'm fine. Fine. Get Hendry. We need to shut this fucker off."

I went to Tidyman. I put my foot on his Sig-Sauer and slid it away, out of his hand. His head was turned to one side, eyes open and sightless.

Dead, but will he stay that way? Now there's the question.

I checked Cannock. He hadn't been shot; Tidyman had smashed him in the head with the rifle butt. Made no difference in the end – the blow had shattered his skull. I closed his eyes for him.

Then I remembered Hassan. No bullet wounds. Just a lump the size of a chicken's egg behind one ear. I checked the carotid pulse. He'd live.

Stiles too. Still completely dead to the world. Whatever he'd been drinking, I made a mental note to get myself a bottle if the opportunity ever presented itself.

Feet thudded on the grass outside, then clanged on metal. Chas, Mleczko, and Hendry scrambled aboard. Hendry stepped over Tidyman's body and gently moved Cannock's to one side. The coughing roar of the engines died and the rotors quickly wound down.

Lomax sagged against the doorway, clutching his arm. "You OK?" I asked. He was white.

"I've been fucking shot, you Jock dickhead."

He was OK. I inspected the wound. "You're lucky. Just a crease." For the second time that day, I broke out a wound dressing. "Get Hassan to take a look when his brain's unscrambled."

He nodded. Lightning flickered through the cockpit canopy; a roll of thunder followed.

"Fuck," said Mleczko at last. "What a cunt of a day."

We all stared at him for a moment, and then I began to laugh. It was a jagged, wild sound. Chas was laughing too, even Parkes. Only Hendry didn't join in; he just looked at us from over the bodies of his friend and of his CO, and we fell silent.

"Sorry, Sir." I said at last.

He just shook his head and slumped into the vacant seat beside Cannock.

I smelt burning. I remembered what I'd seen outside and suddenly I knew. I leapt outside and stamped on it.

"Fuck. *Fuck!*"

"Sarge?" Mleczko was jumping down, followed by Chas.

"Robbie?" Chas came over. I'd fallen to my knees beside the remnants. "What's up?"

"I'm an idiot," I said. "A total fucking idiot."

"What?"

Despite the rain, only a few charred scraps were left. Paper.

Tidyman's face earlier when I'd asked him about the location. Surprised, as if I should've known. No fucking wonder. "He had this all along. Probably in his pocket. And I didn't even think to look."

Chas seemed to click. "Oh *shit!*"

"What?" Mleczko looked from one of us to the other.

"Windhoven's location. Just my guess, but I'd put money on it. It was right under our noses all the time."

A mad part of me was glad of it. Opt out, drop out, fuck them all off and piss on their chips. But that couldn't be allowed, not now. For better or worse, like it or lump it, I was a soldier again. I was back in command.

There was a groan from inside the Chinook. Stiles sat up, rubbing his head.

"Fuck..." he said faintly. "Anyone got an aspirin?"

"Obviously, Sir, you're in overall command here now." Hendry's fingers fidgeted around the glass. I sat with him, Chas and Ged in the farmhouse kitchen.

"Squadron Leader Tidyman put you in control on the ground, Sergeant. Until we're airborne, I see no reason to change that. Quite frankly, I wouldn't know where to start."

"Thank you, Sir." I turned to Ged. "We can set up barricades on Pendle Row – slow them down if they come back in any numbers. And all around the island," because that was what it was now, "as well."

Ged nodded.

"For the time being, I've posted lookouts, and the Landrovers will make regular sweeps of the area. We'll get stuck in tomorrow. We'll need to evacuate the houses on Pendle Row, move the occupants elsewhere, maybe use some of the farmhouses –"

"Make yourself popular," chuckled Ged.

"I can live with that. Pendle Row's the front line. We'll use the Inn as an OP, put one of the Minimis there. Install a permanent lookout on the Hill – that way we can monitor the whole area for signs of attack. We'll need help from your people too – there's a lot of ground to cover. We'll give you fellas some basic training on the SA80s and Minimis."

"You sure that's wise, Sarge?" Chas's eyes flickered to Ged. "No offence, mate."

Ged shrugged.

"We need any defenders able to use any available weapons. We'll keep the Gimpy and the blooper mounted on the Dinkies –"

"You what?"

"Sorry, Ged. The general purpose machine gun and the grenade launcher mounted on the Landrovers. We keep them in reserve at a central location, so if the shit hits the fan, they can go straight in to do some heavy fucking duty back-up. Make sense?"

Ged nodded. After a beat, so did Chas. Hendry sipped his drink.

We talked a bit more, and that was it. Ged rose, nodded and made for the door. Hendry got up to follow, then hesitated. He waited till the door had closed behind the big man, then glanced from me to Chas. "Er – a word, Sergeant?"

"Sir."

"In private?"

Chas shrugged. "I'll be through there." He went through into the front room.

I turned to Hendry. "Sir?"

"Sergeant... I just wanted to say, my report on what's happened here..."

Fuck.

"I'm going to put in it that Squadron Leader Tidyman was

killed in action. By the creatures."

"Sir." Something more seemed to be called for. "Thank you."

"I don't know if any of his family will have made it. They all lived in London, you see. His wife, their children, both his parents."

"Christ."

"I know he didn't... handle the situation well, but I served with him, and he was a good man. Better than you saw. He deserves to be remembered... well, you know."

"Sir." It wouldn't be the first time a few white lies'd gone in a report. And if it kept me clear of a court-martial, I wasn't complaining. "Appreciated."

Hendry nodded and went out. Chas came back in. "What'd he want?"

I told him. Chas picked up the whisky bottle.

"Go on, then."

He passed me a glass. "You reckon they'll be back?"

"What do you think?"

He pursed his lips and nodded. "I think they'll be back."

"Aye. Me too." We clinked glasses. "So what do you think?"

"I think we can hold out here a while. Till we can get out to Windhoven. Wherever it is."

"And if it's still there."

"That too."

"You don't sound too enthusiastic about it."

"I don't like the idea of leaving the villagers in it."

"Think I do?"

"But you'd do it."

Chas leant forward. "We have a job to do, Robbie. You know that. Like it or not."

"Yeah."

"Look, it's not like... it's not like that time."

Sand blowing across the desert road. The fading echo of the rifle shot.

"No?"

"No. We'll be training them up, maybe even leaving them some kit. They're not gonna be left in the lurch. They'll make out."

"You reckon?"

"Yeah, I do." But he didn't meet my eyes. Then he looked up and grinned. "Did a good job today though, anyway, Jock."

"Sergeant Jock to you, grotb –"

Outside, there was a shout, then a panicked yell, and then a shot.

"Fuck!" I bolted for the door. Behind me, Chas yelled my name, feet thumping on the floor.

I burst outside and nearly cannoned into Hassan. A body lay at his feet, the top of the head gone. It wore combats, although you could barely make them out under the filth.

"The fuck happened here?" I heard Chas yell.

"Just came at me, Corp –"

I flipped the body over. Alf Mason stared back up me with dead, clouded eyes.

We'd buried him in a grave at the far end of the meadow – him, Tidyman and Cannock. But here he was.

The other two had stayed where they'd been put. For them, at least, it was over.

CHAPTER FOURTEEN

The next afternoon.

Parkes had been trying to raise Windhoven on both the contact and distress frequencies, but got only static in response. The sky was thick with dark cloud. The storm had passed for now, but a couple of times lightning flashed far off in the distance, and a faint crack of thunder would roll in.

Stiles was huddled in a corner of the farmhouse's living room with a microwave lasagne, a dismembered bread roll, and a can of Special Brew, avoiding eye contact and rocking to and fro. He hadn't spoken, except to request food or alcohol. If I'd expected a fount of wisdom, I'd be disappointed. But if the powers that be had been convinced about him, they'd have a sent a full platoon, maybe a company. More likely some senior brasshat or MOD bod had thought of him at the last minute.

Still, I did my best. "Dr Stiles?"

He took a gulp of beer.

"Doctor, I need to know what's happening. We were sent to

fetch you. Please. What is it you know?"

He took another gulp of beer.

I kept trying. After a while he started to hum tunelessly. He wrapped his arms around himself and rocked to and fro. Sweat slicked his forehead. When I tried to speak, he hummed louder. I gave up. After a few minutes, he stopped, unwrapped his arms, and drained the can. Then he breathed out, looked into my eyes and said: "Can I have another one, please?"

The food situation wasn't so bad. As well as having stocks of it in the village, we were in farming country, with plenty of sheep, chicken and cows, plus wild rabbits. Most of the animals had survived, so we weren't looking at starvation just yet. On top of that, we had provisions of our own.

For now, though, the locals were using up frozen food before it went off. Result – large amounts of stews and casseroles were being knocked together. So at least it'd be a while before the freeze-dried Army rations came into play. I still had nightmares about the shepherd's pie. In the first Gulf War, the Yanks had called their rations MREs. Officially, it stood for 'Meals Ready to Eat'. The troops preferred 'Meals Rejected by Ethiopians'.

I decided to climb the Hill and scope out the terrain. Tidyman had had a pair of field glasses, which I'd appropriated (Shiny Kit Syndrome again.) Besides, it might be fun.

Jesus fucking Christ!

If I'd thought I was out of condition before, I knew it beyond doubt after making that ascent. The path up the Hill facing Barley was practically vertical.

The climb took me twenty minutes. By the end of it, my leg muscles were howling and my lungs felt sandblasted. I sat down at the top to enjoy not being in agony for a minute or two, then stood and got out the field glasses.

Visibility wasn't great, with a thick mist rising off the water spreading out in all directions. Fells rose clear of the surface, a scattering of islands. How many were populated? I remembered the folk waving to us as we flew in. Did they have guns? Would that be enough?

If I hadn't already killed Tidyman, I would've by now for not warning us about the bites. Alf might not be dead if we'd known that. Taken precautions. At least we knew now.

Still, now we knew it took more than just dying to turn you into a nightmare. It was the bite; the bite or the water.

God knew *what* in the water. I looked down towards the meadows. In the distance, I could see the nearby reservoir. It should be usable. All the same, I'd given instructions that all drinking water be boiled before use.

But what about the water the animals drank?

Not a productive line of thought.

Still, in a way I was starting to enjoy myself. Other people's problems are always easier to deal with than your own.

I looked across the hilltop, saw someone standing by the thick white stubby plinth of the trig point. I was reaching for my P226 before I realised who it was.

I walked over. "Levene."

"Sarge."

"Anything to report?"

"No Sarge." Stupid question; if there had been my PC would've been quacking like Daffy Duck.

I handed him the field glasses. "These might come in handy."

"Thanks, Sarge." He looked out towards the village. "Sarge?"

"Yes?"

"Something to report."

"What?" My hand on the gun again.

"There's a boat out there."

"A fucking what?"

"A boat. There, see?"

He passed me the field glasses. I focussed in. There it was. Small. A dinghy. In the waters off Barley Road. Two occupants. Both women. One was rowing hard, wrenching at the oars, her back to me. Trimly built, chestnut hair in a bob-cut. The other lay slumped across the floor of the dinghy, feet propped on the stern. I couldn't see her face. She was very small, slender. A child?

Also, very still.

The dinghy shifted in the swell, turning side-on. The girl's head lay in the other woman's lap. I zoomed in. Her face was grey. There was a crudely-dressed wound on her arm. Then the other woman was turning the dinghy so her back was to me and the girl's face was hidden once more.

I felt something cold move inside me. "Got your radio?"

"Sarge."

"Alert them down in the village."

By the time I reached Pendle Row, I could hear screaming. As I ran in, gunshots rang out. Fully automatic fire. Parfitt, with the Minimi. Mleczko and Hassan running from the Pendle Inn, Billy in their wake. Andrews and Akinbode ran down the Row – later they told me they hadn't been able to get a clear shot at the girl through the hedgerows along the roadside. I waved them all back.

The dinghy bobbed, abandoned in the water. The woman lay huddled near the top of the road, crying out as bullets ricocheted about her. Behind her, the dead girl thrashed on the tarmac. I yelled up at Parfitt.

"Cease fire! Cease fire! Cease fucking fire!"

I ran in. The dead one was still making sounds. I aimed at her. She stared back, frothing blood, eyes ablaze. She was just a kid. Had been.

One shot. Dead centre in the forehead. Her head snapped back. Her body went still, a last, rattling breath escaping in a sigh.

I remembered the live girl and spun to aim at her. Checked there were no bites. Safetied the gun and helped her up, led her back towards the village.

Not straight away, though; the woman insisted on stopping to look at her friend's body. Never a good plan. Just gives you bad dreams.

Believe me.

We took her back to the farmhouse. Hassan checked her over and pronounced her in reasonable health; Jo sorted her out with a change of clothes.

She wove a little as she went, still cold and shivering, and I reached out to steady her. She shrugged me off. "I'm fine. I'm fine. I don't need any help. Which way is the toilet, please?"

She went off fast, not looking back. There was an outbreak of sniggering from Hassan and Parfitt at the bottom of the stairs, who'd wandered in to cop an eyeful, not to mention Billy, who'd wandered in after Mleczko, gawping and giggling. I ignored them and got some stew reheated for her.

Stiles was still rocking in his corner. Now and again he'd grimace, as if at a twinge of pain, or cock his head as if he'd heard something. He was cradling a bottle of gin and taking nips from it. When not doing that, he'd roll another cigarette from the tobacco tin he'd dug out of his filthy jeans.

When she came down, her face was scrubbed clean and her hair tied back with an old shoelace. She mumbled a thank you when I handed her the stew. Otherwise she didn't speak.

Parfitt and the others were still eyeing her up. "Shouldn't you be at your posts?" I demanded.

"Sarge," said Mleczko.

"Well shift your bloody arses, then. Now."

The door bumped shut in the wind, Katja looked up. Glanced sideways at me, and smiled for a second. I felt a warm flutter in my chest.

"Try to eat something," I said to her quietly. "Keep your strength up. You've been through a lot."

Her head snapped up. "How the hell do you know what I've been through?"

I noted her accent for the first time. Eastern or Central European. I had to admit, I liked it. Her jaw was clenched, her eyes bright, her hand shaking.

I leant back in my chair. "I think we've all been through a lot, last couple of days."

She glared a moment longer, then nodded. "Of course. I'm sorry." She said it awkwardly, looking away, chin up. I thought of a cat, proud and territorial.

"Forget it. I'm Robbie McTarn." I didn't give my rank. Time was, it'd've been second nature. I stuck out my hand.

She saw it and smiled, maybe despite herself, then shook. Her skin was smooth and soft, but her grip stronger than most women I'd known. "Katja Wencewska."

"That Polish?"

Her eyes narrowed. Shit. Maybe she'd been an illegal before the flooding. "Just asking," I said. "One of ours is called Mleczko. Polish family."

"Ah." She nodded. "It's Polish. I grew up in Romania. A long story."

And clearly not one she planned to tell. Fair enough. It hardly mattered now.

She ate. At first she was forcing herself but before long she was doing it with real hunger. I wasn't surprised. I didn't know how long she'd been rowing for when I'd first seen her, but from the speed and fury she'd been putting into it, it must have taken its toll.

There was only silence in the room, except for her eating and the odd little noises from Stiles's corner. So as she ate, I told her my story. Some of it anyway. I didn't tell her about the desert road. I don't tell anyone about that. But I told her about the redcaps coming to my door, why we were here, and what had happened – Tidyman, the nightmares attacking.

Katja put down her fork and looked over at Stiles. "What is it that he knows?"

"Search me, hen. No-one saw fit to tell us, and he's not talking." I felt anger flickering up in me suddenly. "One of my men is dead, plus one pilot –" I didn't mention Tidyman because I couldn't care less about the sod "– and the whole reason for the operation sits on his arse stuffing his face and getting pissed. Isn't that right, Stiles?"

He flinched. He'd been looking in our direction; now he looked away.

"Please don't." I looked at Katja. "It's not his fault," she said. "I know it's difficult, but he didn't ask you to come."

"Difficult? You don't know the half of it, hen."

"I know more than you might think. My father was a soldier. Special forces, yes?"

I nodded.

"So I know something of it."

"And what about you?"

"What about me?" She met my gaze full-on.

"What happened to you?"

She didn't speak for a few seconds. Then she shrugged and forked more food into her mouth. "I survived," she said. "Just me. That's all."

Stiles had stopped fidgeting. He was looking over at us both. At *her*.

As I turned back to Katja, he spoke.

"They're calling me," he said.

"Who?" I asked. He didn't react. He was staring at Katja.

She glanced at me, then back at him.

"Who?" she asked.

"The voices. The souls. All the dead."

He wouldn't say anymore than that. He just stared at her, and her back at him. I don't know what he saw there – more than just a pretty woman, I'm sure of that – or what she saw in him. But after a moment, she went to sit with him. Waiting for him to say more.

Chas slipped in, sat beside me. "All quiet," he murmured.

"Good."

He saw Katja and Stiles. "What's this, then?"

"Fucked if I know."

"Not bad-looking, is she?"

"Shut up, Nixon."

"Robbie?"

I looked at him.

"Don't go falling in love now, for Pete's sake. You're bad enough without getting blue balls."

"Piss off. What about you and Jo?"

He reddened coughed. I stared. "Don't take the piss, Robbie, eh? She's a nice girl."

I shook my head and looked back at Katja and Stiles. I could see Stiles's lips moving, but I couldn't make out what he said, and afterwards, Katja wouldn't tell.

CHAPTER FIFTEEN

"I want to help."

Katja: hands on hips, hair cropped raggedly short, head cocked back to look me in the eye.

Joyce, Parfitt and Akinbode climbing aboard the Chinook. Hendry at the controls, Lomax guarding the entrances like fucking Cerberus. The rest were staying to guard the village.

"If you want to help, see if you can get anything more out of Stiles."

Folding her arms; looking pissed off. "Stiles talks when he wants to. I don't control him."

"No, but he's more likely to want to talk to you than anyone else."

A shrug. "I can do more than that."

"How?"

Nodding towards the Chinook. "Let me come with you."

"What for?"

"You need everyone you can get."

"These men are professional soldiers."

"So was my father. And he taught me a lot."

I still didn't know exactly what she'd gone through, but it couldn't have been easy. I remembered her eyes when I'd first seen her, after the initial terror. They'd been dark and staring somewhere far past me. She'd seen Hell, or something damned close to it, and she'd survived. She'd kept her head.

"Can you handle an automatic weapon?" I asked her.

"Give me my rifle and I'll show you."

I looked into her eyes; she didn't flinch.

Some things break under pressure. Others grow stronger.

"OK."

Our third day at Pendle.

We'd hooked up with the occupants of the other hamlets immediately around the Hill; Newchurch-in-Pendle, Sabden, Spen Brook. No further attacks. Nothing on the radio.

Too fucking quiet for safety. We were soldiers. Needed to be doing something.

Needed to see what was out there.

The rotors chopping at the air. The sound beating through the hull. The sky outside still dark. Rain peppering the cockpit canopy. Least they'd managed to scrub Cannock and Tidyman's brains off it.

Katja sat, rifle across her lap, in a spare army jacket two sizes too big. It, and the Browning pistol in her belt, had still been in the dinghy. The pistol had been Marta's – I'd got her friend's name from her, though nothing else. The rifle was an old US Army M-14, firing 7.62mm NATO rounds. They packed a punch. The 5.56mm rounds in our SA80s wouldn't even slow a nightmare down unless it was a headshot, but a 7.62 would knock it flat, dead or not.

The men huddled in their seats, smirking. Probably thought I was cunt-struck. But the smirking stopped if she looked their way. There was nothing comic about her, outsize jacket or no. Her face was hard, expressionless, her jaw set.

We touched down on the fell we'd passed on our first approach, a broad shoulder of grass and rock. The men de-bussed, surrounding the chopper. Katja went with them and fell into place, gun held ready.

"Akinbode, stay with the chopper. You and Lomax man the guns."

"Sarge."

"Rest of you, with me."

The farmhouse was near the water's edge. No-one in. The only other life visible on the fell were a dozen or so sheep, cropping the grass.

The rotors wound down and fell silent. A thin wind keened across the fells and the sea. I heard the faint lap and suck of waves on shore. A sea sound. It didn't belong here.

A sea.

Sometimes it takes that one final detail to bring it home. To make it real. It was all gone. Waterstone's and Starbucks, Tesco's and the Co-Op, Boots the chemist, multiplex cinemas, McDonalds, Burger King, KFC, Pizza Hut. All the totems and trademarks of the world we'd lived in. All gone.

Glasgow. The street I'd grown up in. The house I was born in. Gone.

London, Manchester, Birmingham, Paris, Berlin, New York, Washington, Pretoria, Harare, Brisbane, Melbourne...

Gone.

This huge sea, in place of them all.

Focus.

There are different kinds of silence. The kind that's all charged up with something about to happen. The hush before something breaks.

Or the kind that says nobody's home. When you walk into the married quarters and you know she's gone. There's more space in the house suddenly.

This was the second kind of silence.

A sheep bleated. An ordinary countryside sound. Like the lapping of the water, it made the loss more real.

It would be so easy just to stand here and try taking in the scale of it. The people we knew who'd be dead by now. That we *couldn't* believe might have survived, because the one thing worse than certain death was false hope.

So easy.

Mustn't let it happen.

"Parfitt?"

"Sarge?"

"Round up the sheep."

"Sarge?" He looked like I'd just told him to piss out his ear.

"Round them up. We could use the meat."

"Fucksake."

"What was that?"

"Yes, Sarge."

I grinned as he scooted off. Lomax would probably say a damn sight worse when we started herding old McDonald's farm aboard the Chinook.

"What if there's still someone here?" whispered Katja.

"That's the big question, isn't it? Joyce?"

"Sarge."

"Check round the back." Joyce nodded and moved off. I turned to Katja.

"Alright, hen. I'm going in."

She covered me as I went down the slope. The door had been smashed in. Most of the windows were gone as well.

Joyce moved round from the other side of the building, keeping out of Katja's line of fire. "Clear, Sarge."

"OK." I motioned to Katja and she followed us in.

Chairs knocked over. An old child's Peter Rabbit mug – probably the mum or dad's, handed down – on the table. A congealed, half-eaten plateful of bangers and mash with listless-looking flies crawling on it. Potted herbs on the windowsill. A Welsh dresser surrounded by broken crockery.

Spent shotgun shells on the floor. Buckshot spatters on the walls.

Three bodies, the waxy remains of their eyeballs crusted on

their cheeks below the empty sockets. Nightmares. They'd each been blasted in the head.

Another nightmare lay in the hallway by the smashed front door, head gone above the eyebrows. Arcs of blood on the walls. Arterial spray.

When had it happened? During the storm, maybe, when the nightmares had attacked Barley. I hoped so. Because then we couldn't have saved them. It wouldn't be my fault. No need to feel guilty.

Only, I did.

The bodies in the sand, staining it with blood. The women and children, carrying the dead away. The girl looking back.

I shook my head.

Focus, you prick.

The dining room. Untouched. The battle had never spread there. The table was set for some special occasion that'd never arrived. It could come and pass unmarked now, with no-one to observe it or even know what it was.

The living room.

Katja went in first.

There were bloodstains on the living room carpet. Chunks of shrivelled flesh. A couple of severed fingers. A hole blasted in the ceiling. Shotgun.

I found the shotgun itself in the corner, broken open. A shell loaded into one barrel, the other empty. An unfired shell on the carpet. Like a painting – the composition tells the whole story. I picked it up, pocketed the shells.

Katja was staring at a photograph she'd found. When she saw me looking, she put it face down on the mantelpiece and moved away. I lifted the picture; a husband and wife, three kids, the youngest not much more than a toddler.

We checked upstairs and in the cellar. There was no-one else, dead, alive or anywhere in between. There was blood in one of the bedrooms. A child's nursery. Arterial spray on walls and ceiling.

Messy eaters.

There were cured hams and flitches of bacon stored in the

pantry. Cans. Jars. Some fresh. Cabbages and lettuces. Boxes of shotgun shells. We took them all.

Parfitt had herded the sheep onto the Chinook. Lomax didn't look happy about it. Neither did Parfitt. Or the sheep, come to that. When not thrashing or nipping, the sheep retaliated by shitting everywhere.

Akinbode seemed to think it was hilarious. If looks could have killed, the one on Parfitt's face would have finished him on the spot. Meantime I told them to help Joyce load the provisions.

Katja and I picked up the last load. We were about ten yards up from the farmhouse when Akinbode pointed down the slope and shouted.

They stood in the shallows below the farmhouse. It lapped around the knees of the two adults and the waists of the two older children. The toddler clung to the mother. They stared up at us with their slack, empty faces and glowing eyes, but they didn't move.

"Shit!" I dropped the cans and fumbled for the rifle. Katja was already on one knee, the M-14 shouldered.

I don't know why we didn't fire straight off. But we didn't. The father turned his head to stare at the farmhouse; he cocked it to one side, as if trying to recognise it. The children stayed close to their mother, who clung to the toddler. All of them staring up at us.

"They're all around us, Sarge," Akinbode shouted. I managed to look away from the family. Heads broke the surface here and there. Not many. After the other day, there couldn't be that many left in the area. But they were in the water around us, watching.

"Fall back to the Chinook," I shouted, "and fast."

I walked backwards. They didn't move. Maybe they could tell they were outgunned. There weren't enough of them to rush us.

Not yet.

The doors slammed. The rotors churned. The chopper lifted.

I peered out of the window. The family stood where they'd first appeared, watching us go – except for the father, who still stared towards what had been his home.

Katja was looking down at them too. I touched her arm; she whipped round.

"You did good back there," I said.

"I know," she said.

But a small, crooked smile touched her lips.

Back at the farmhouse, we opened a few tins in the front room. Stiles was in his usual corner with another bottle of gin. His eyes brightened when he saw Katja. She went over and sat beside him.

The rest of us sat on the far side of the room, drinking in silence. It was Parfitt, in the end, who said it.

"You reckon they remember anything, Sarge?"

"What?"

"Those fucking things."

"Why should they?" Akinbode's fingers brushed the small cross at his throat. "They are dead. They are just... corpses. Things made to walk around. What could they remember?"

"The fuck should I know?" There was an edge in Parfitt's voice; Stiles and Katja both looked up. He glanced at them, took a deep breath, calmed himself down. "I mean... come on, Aki, you saw them too. You and all, Sarge. It was like they knew the place. Like they remembered it'd been –"

"Shut up," said Akinbode. "Just shut up, Mark."

But I knew he had a point. We all did, even Akinbode; he just didn't want to accept it.

When they were just nightmares it was easy enough. They were monsters. They weren't human. You pointed a gun and you shot and their brains flew out and they were dead. Like they should've been to begin with.

But the way they'd stood in the shallows. The way the father had looked up at his old house. The way the dead mother held her dead baby...

I'd felt fear, yes. But something else. Almost... pity.

"Doesn't matter," I said. "Doesn't change anything. We've seen what –"

"They don't remember," said Stiles.

We all turned around and looked at him. Even Katja was staring at him. I looked at his drawn, prematurely aged face, the bleary, reddened eyes.

"They don't remember," he said, "but the Deep Brain does."

"What the fuck is the Deep Brain?" I asked.

His face tightened in pain, and he looked down.

"Stiles? Stiles, what's the Deep Brain?"

He didn't answer. Katja laid a hand on his arm, looked up at me and shook her head. She leaned in closer to him and spoke softly, but his head kept shaking, although after a while, I heard murmuring too. I shrugged and turned back to my beer.

We finished our drinks and the others went off, they all had work to do. So did I, but fuck that for now.

Stiles had slumped over in the corner. Katja looked up. "Passed out. Can you help me get him back?"

"He was lucky to survive," she said back at the caravan, looking down at him sprawled on the filthy divan. "He was in agony, after the accident. Still is. Not as bad, but he's still in constant pain."

Just for a second or two, the hard mask slipped, and I saw – something. Sorrow, perhaps.

"Poor bastard. But it's not much use to us. No fucking relevance at all that I can see."

Katja put her finger to her lips. "I think there *is* a link," she said outside. "But I don't know what. I also think he wants to tell us. Or me, at least."

"Did he say anything useful?"

She shook her head again. "Odd words and phrases. The Deep Brain, the voices, the souls. They're calling him. Over and over again."

"Word salads."

She gave a short laugh. "That's a good phrase. I like it. Otherwise, he talks about his childhood, his adolescence, his first girlfriend, university, going diving. He wants to make sense. But he can't. It's like..."

"What?" We started walking back down, close, almost touching. Not a date, exactly. But a man could always hope.

"He's afraid."

"He can join the fucking club."

"Do you have to swear so much, Robert?"

I was tempted to say *aw fuck off*, just for the hell of it, but that was lost in the realisation she'd just called me by my first name. For that, I'd even sign the pledge.

Well, hang on. Maybe not that far. I'm not fucking *demented*.

"Sorry."

She shrugged. "No. I am. Stupid really, with everything that's happened."

I didn't say anything. Sometimes women want you to agree with them and sometimes not. Buggered if I ever know which it is.

Probably why I know what a married quarters feels like when you go in and you know it's empty, and she's gone.

Jeannie.

Christ. Don't start thinking about her, Robbie.

The blood in the sand, the bodies, the women walking away.

No, she wasn't there. But she was part of the casualty list, even so. Part of the fallout.

Death, murder... the cost is limitless. Like ripples from a rock. The damage it does knocks on, in ways you never expected. It can come back and damage the murderers too.

No more than I deserved.

But still it fucking hurt.

"You said he was afraid. Stiles, I mean. What's he afraid of?"

"I think..." She looked up at the hillside, bit her lip and shook her head, then looked over at me. She really had beautiful eyes. Big and dark.

Christ, Robbie, you're falling. Don't fucking do it. Just don't.

"I think he's afraid that if he talks about it – whatever it is he's so scared of, this Deep Brain thing... he's afraid it will know and come for him."

"What the fuck is the Deep Brain, when it's at home?"

She didn't tick me off over my language this time. "At a guess, whatever controls the dead things."

"Controls them?" That would make sense. I mean, there had to be a reason that the dead started waking up. Didn't there?

"The 'Brain' part would suggest a controlling intelligence, yes? But what it is, and where..."

"That's what we need to know." The thought of the 'Deep Brain' made things better and worse at once. Worse because it was bad enough when the nightmares were just shambling flesh-eaters. The idea of something directing them...

But if there was such a thing, it could be found. Perhaps destroyed, if there were some submarines left. Torpedoes punching through soft grey brain tissue and exploding, blowing it into scraps of fish food. The nightmares keeling over, the lights going out in their eyes.

Give me an enemy I can fight, and I'm a happy man.

"We're so in the dark, with this." Katja sat on a drystone wall. "We don't even know what his theories *were*. He could be insane. Or only half-right. Which could be just as disastrous."

"Well, keep trying. You're the only one he seems to talk to. Maybe he's in love."

She didn't answer.

"Sorry," I said.

"What for?"

"I shouldn't – I mean, I wasn't – I didn't mean to take the piss."

"You think you can offend me?" She looked up."You will have to try harder than that. Do you know that there are mornings when I give thanks for the flood, even for the dead things? Do you know what I was, before this? What was done to me? I was fucked by a dozen, twenty men a day. Sometimes so sore I *bled*. Fucked in the arse so I could barely *walk*. Treated as a piece of *meat*. You think a *joke* will hurt me?"

My face was burning.

"But," she carried on, "you could be right."

"What?"

"Stiles. Perhaps I remind him of someone. Perhaps I'm just

the first pretty girl who doesn't laugh at him or look at him in disgust. Either way. He wants to make contact with me. He just doesn't know how. And I don't know how to help him."

I looked at her and I wanted to kiss her. I wanted to ask if I could kiss her. Been a long time since I've done that. I've slept with hookers. But Katja wasn't one, not anymore, and God help any man who treated her as one. And even then –

I didn't just want her. I wanted her to want me.

I had no idea where to start with *that*.

"When are you next going out?" she asked.

"Tomorrow. We'll scout west."

"Can I come?"

"Aye."

"Thank you."

"Just be careful."

No-one else could get shit-all out of Stiles. If she died, we'd know nothing. Always assuming there was anything to know in the first place.

If I was honest, that was why I didn't like him – apart from the obvious one of him being mad. I'm not comfortable around mental illness, can't handle the idea of it finding a home in me. I laugh at nutters out of fear – fear I might become one of them. Because I've come too close to it. So I laugh, because I'm still on the rails and they're not. Ugly but true.

But it wasn't just that.

It was Katja.

I was jealous.

We found survivors in nearby villages that had survived the flooding – Blacko, Roughlee, Downham. More often than not, we'd see the nightmares, lurking in the shallows. They didn't attack, just watched. We never had to fire a shot.

For the first time, an uneasy hope began to blossom. Perhaps they'd leave us alone.

After all, they were dead. And dead flesh rots. Tendons and ligaments parting, the skeleton falling apart. And bodies in water, salt water most of all, rot away fast.

If we could just wait them out. If we could just hold on long enough, then nature would do the job for us.

About a week after that first flight out, I was in the farmhouse front room, drinking with Mleczko and Chas. Billy sat by Mleczko – there was no shaking him, which got Mleczko ribbed unmercifully – while Jo and Chas sat together on the sofa, holding hands like a couple of kids. Nobody took the piss, and not only because Chas'd make their lives hell if they did. It was – never thought I'd say this about Chas Nixon – sweet. Good to see something going right.

Katja and Stiles were talking in their corner. I took a large swallow. Stupid to be jealous of Stiles anyway. She wasn't with him out of love.

Katja got up, left the room.

Mleczko nudged me. Stiles was coming over, hunched and moving stiffly, grimacing at the pain each movement brought. Poor bastard.

He had Katja. Lucky bastard.

Stop snivelling, Robbie.

"It isn't over."

I looked up at him. "What?"

He gestured round with a free hand. "You think it's all over. Don't you?"

"They think it's all over," Billy sniggered. "It is now."

I ignored him, and so did Stiles. He just stared at me. His eyes were incredibly bloodshot, the irises snared in red webs of tiny broken veins. Dad'd had had eyes like that.

"It hasn't started yet," said Stiles. "The Deep Brain. It's watching and waiting. The ocean. The voices. The souls. It's coming."

"What is?" I asked.

Stiles' eyes screwed shut, as if against a sudden jab of pain, lips peeling back from his clenched, yellowed teeth. Then he sucked in a breath and opened his eyes again. "It's coming, Sergeant," he said again, and then turned and limped back to his corner.

"What is?" I asked. He didn't answer. I stood up and shouted. "What fucking is?"

The whole room was silent. Movement at the corner of my eye; Katja, stood in the doorway, watching.

Stiles did not turn around. "Death," he said. "Death is coming."

Then he sat back down, picked up the bottle he'd been working on, and said no more.

Katja went over to him. I sat back down.

"Fucking lunatic," muttered Chas. Jo huddled closer to him, as if for warmth. It was the closest to frightened I'd seen her.

"Apeshit," Mleczko agreed.

"Yeah," Billy echoed, "apeshit."

"Yeah." I grunted.

I saw them sat together. I wanted to look away, but didn't.

He was holding her hand. And Katja... Katja wasn't just *letting* him hold her hand. Do you understand? She was squeezing his hand back, stroking the knuckles with her thumb. She was responding. Of course, it could have just been like a whore's kisses – faking it to please the customer.

But I could see how she looked at him. I could've handled pity. Even lust, hard to imagine though that was.

But this was something else. This was the look I'd wanted to see in her eyes when she looked at me.

She realised she was being watched. She looked up. I turned away before she met my eyes.

"I need some fucking air," I said, standing.

I went outside.

"You OK, Robbie?"

"Aye."

"Rob –"

"Chas, I'm fine."

I felt the cold wind on my face, breathed out. The clouds had broken briefly, letting moonlight gleam on the dark waters beyond. Scratching the surface, shedding no light on the depths. And all I could think was:

Death, Sergeant.

Death is coming.

CHAPTER SIXTEEN

The nightmares made a brief, vicious attack on Blacko a few days later. They struck in numbers, but they were driven off. If something was controlling them, it was new and slow when it came to tactics. Humans have been killing each other for years, on the other hand, so that gave us an advantage.

Almost too easy. Almost like a testing of our defences.

Parkes and Hendry tried, every day, almost religiously, to contact Windhoven, but there was only ever the hiss of static. I had to believe they were still out there. Had to.

Katja had been staying with Ged. He never put a foot wrong with her, she assured me. A widower. Better things to do. He'd sit up late into the night, cradling a photograph of his daughter, her boyfriend and their kid. She reckoned he liked having her round. Reminded her of his daughter. For some reason I didn't understand at the time, she didn't seem to like that.

Anyway, she moved in with Stiles. That's right. Into that filthy hole of a caravan. Not that it stayed filthy for very long. When she was done, the caravan was unrecognisable. Scrubbed clean.

And yes, I have to admit, that burned. But I turned away, blanked it out. And got on with my job. At such times, I was glad to be a soldier again.

"There's a location not far from here," said Hendry. "An army base, pretty new, but with landing facilities and some fuel supplies. We were told we could use it as a temporary stopover if we couldn't fly straight out to Windhoven."

"You didn't mention this before, Sir."

"We tried contacting them just before we flew out, but..."

"What?"

"They were being overrun. God knows how – they were on high ground, well-defended – they should've been able to hold off any attack, especially in the early stages."

"But they didn't?"

Hendry spread his hands helplessly. "I don't know the details. We got a few garbled messages, enough to tell us what was happening without saying how and why. Right then it didn't seem particularly important."

I nodded. "But the base itself?"

"Should be intact."

"And those things?"

"Again, no way to tell. All we can do is... go and take a look."

"What kind of supplies are we talking about?"

"Avgas for the Chinook. Plus army rations, medical supplies, weapons, ammunition..."

"Christmas come early, you mean."

"It's not far off, anyway," Lomax put in. "Christmas."

Jesus, he was right. Well, at least if I lived that long, I wouldn't be spending Christmas alone. I could thank the nightmares for that, if nothing else.

"What?" said Lomax.

I realised I was smiling. "Doesn't matter. Alright then. Let's go take a look."

The Chinook flew over Nelson; as we went we could see what was left of the town, the tops of taller buildings and a few of the higher-up streets poking clear of the water.

Another thing I noticed as we flew.

The waters were clearer.

They'd lost that shitten, stewed-tea look they'd had. Under them, we could see houses, buses and cars, streets.

It was, for the record, a weird fucking sight.

I was glad when the chopper veered away from it and homed in on a flat-topped hill nearby.

High fencing ringed the base. A watchtower. At one end the perimeter was partly submerged.

The compound itself was a cluster of unremarkable prefab buildings on a concrete floor. Probably still in its early stages.

We flew over a couple of times. No sign of life. On the other hand, if we kept flapping around overhead, then anything lurking in the water might notice. And I wasn't keen on having a welcoming committee when we touched down.

"What do you think?" asked Hendry.

I took a breath. "Let's chance it."

On board we had Joyce, Hassan, Parfitt and Akinbode, along with Lomax and Katja. Also a couple of villagers, Neil and Steve. 'Villagers' was probably the wrong term – they were both tourists who'd been trapped in Barley by the floods. Steve was in his forties and had had a potbelly, which had disappeared in the two weeks they'd been with us. He and his wife had been celebrating their anniversary with a hiking tour of the fells. Neil was in his late twenties, rangy and outdoorsy-looking. He'd been down for 'a spot of bird-watching'. Both could handle a gun, and carried hunting rifles.

"Alright," I said. "Our main priority's the Avgas, followed by medical supplies. We've already got guns and food, though extra supplies would be useful. We go after them later, if we've time and room. Clear?"

"Sarge."

Lomax pointed at one of the buildings. "That'll be the QM store. Pretty much everything we're looking for should be in there."

And what else, I wondered?

"Akinbode, you're on lookout. Lomax, Joyce – take the Gimpys. Neil, Katja, Steve – we're looking for fuel. Hassan, Parfitt – find the medical gear. Any sign of trouble, raise the alarm and fall back. Do not, repeat, *not*, engage unless absolutely necessary. I'll decide if we start a shooting match or not. Any questions?"

There were none.

"Right. Let's go."

Exactly what purpose the base'd been meant to serve even Hendry didn't know. A support base for the regional control centres, perhaps, although the floods hadn't been recognised as a major threat till only a few days before November 7th. This hadn't been built *that* quickly. Of course, there were any number of dangers the authorities could've had in mind, not least its own citizens.

We landed the Chinook broadside-on to the storehouse. Joyce manned the Gimpy in the rear doorway, aiming at the half-submerged end; Lomax covered the side of the compound opposite the storehouse with the other one. Akinbode stood by the cockpit with a Minimi, watching the far end.

The rest of us de-bussed, formed a perimeter. Neil and Steve'd been briefed on what to do, and they fell into step pretty well for civvies.

Wind moaned across the concrete.

"Sarge?" asked Parfitt.

"Go."

The door wasn't locked. I stepped back, rifle shouldered. Katja, Hassan and Parfitt followed suit. I motioned to Neil and Steve to pull the doors open.

Inside was dark silence. I moved forward to the doorway, sighting left and right, quarter-turning the sight to activate the night vision.

Rows of steel shelving and a big central aisle. Nothing moving.

"Clear. Parfitt, Katja – go."

They moved forward, rifles aimed. "Clear."

"OK. Get looking."

The Avgas was near the back; behind it was –

"Sarge! Check this out!"

Two more Landrovers. "Very nice, Parfitt. Shouldn't you be looking for the medical supplies?"

"Sorry, Sarge."

He found them; luckily they were very portable. Which freed him and Hassan up quickly for the next job – rolling drums of JP-4 Avgas on board the Chinook.

"Alright. Let's move."

"What about the other stuff, Sarge?"

There'd been Gimpys, SA80s, Minimis and a shedload of ammunition back there, not to mention that Landrover and at least one Mk19. "No room for it. We'll come back."

When we returned, everything seemed as we left it. A good sign.

The weapons were crated up, so we moved them out fast. Just as planned. All running smoothly. *Thank you, oh God I don't believe in.* Not a hitch.

"Sarge!" yelled Joyce.

Fuck.

Just outside the perimeter fence, up to its thighs in foul water, was one of the nightmares.

I threw the rifle to my shoulder and sighted. It didn't move. From the chopper I heard Joyce cocking the Gimpy. "Hold fire!" I yelled. If there were more, a shot could open up a whole new world of grief.

It wore the remains of an Army uniform; much of its face was eaten away. The jawbone yawned, almost unsupported, the cheeks hung like tattered flags, and half its nose was gone. But there was still flesh on its limbs, and the empty sockets of its eyes blazed green.

"Shit," I heard from behind me, followed by a rifle bolt snapping back.

"Hold fire, Parfitt."

As I watched, the water beside the first nightmare stirred and broke. A fretted scalp, clumps of skin and hair still clinging to the skull, broke the surface. Its face was greenish coloured – there seemed to be something furring it up – but otherwise more or less intact. Its eyes were whole, glowing like dusty bulbs, and I could even make out a moustache. It stood beside the first nightmare, a few short yards away, and watched us.

Another rose beside that, upper half canted sideways. Its face was badly torn, hanging loose off the bone on one side. It straightened up as it neared the fence. They all wore Army uniforms.

"Another round here!" Katja was aiming her M-14 round the side of the store. "In the water."

"I've got some too," Lomax called. "By the fence."

"Hold fire!" I shouted again.

"What the fuck?" said Parfitt.

I looked back at the three nightmares. Their eyes were... pulsing. The glow brightened to an unwavering blaze, faded, then brightened again. All in perfect sync.

"I've never seen this before," Katja called. "But I don't think it's good."

When was it ever? "Hold your fire!"

They stood there, eyes pulsing. Then it stopped.

A few seconds later they turned and sank back down into the water.

"Sarge?" Parfitt again. "What the fuck was that?"

"Fucked if I know," I said. "Let's get out of here."

Back at the farmhouse.

"We saw maybe a dozen, Chas. Not exactly an army."

"Yeah. But what if they've started inviting their mates?"

"Aye, I know. There's the rub."

But the Landrovers, more weapons... that grenade launcher, which we'd forgotten in the rush...

Chas shrugged. "No point doing the job if you *don't* take a risk now and then, is there?"

This time we circled the base twice, and saw nothing. Everything exactly as we left it.

"OK, let's move." Lomax and Joyce manning the Gimpys again. The rest of us were heading straight for the store.

"Let's go, let's go. Get the doors open."

Steve and Neil pulling the doors open. The darkness within.

The stench rushes out to meet us, and the green glow of eyes in the darkness.

And the dozens of leering, rotted faces.

And their outstretched, rotting hands.

Death, Sergeant.

Death is coming.

Parfitt's closest, doesn't stand a chance. Gets off one scream as they lunge forward, one biting into his face, two, three others falling on top. Can't get a clear shot. He's screaming. Blood spews out in a jet. The screaming stops.

Fall back and fire – me, Katja. Steve and Neil already hightailing it back to the chopper. A few go down.

"Go!"

Akinbode's Minimi firing, more of them coming out of the other buildings in the compound. They're fucking *everywhere*.

The Gimpys hammering. They're in the water at the far end.

Thinking as I run: *they were waiting for us. They were fucking waiting for us.*

A trap.

They set a fucking trap.

"Akinbode! Move your arse you bastard, now!"

Akinbode frozen, seeing the nightmares rushing in on our tail. Then he blinks and runs for the side door.

Too slow. One leaps on his back – two more throw themselves in.

Akinbode screaming.

Drawing the pistol. Firing. Three headshots. Three down. Akinbode scrambling up as –

"Down!"

Lomax, running in, firing his Sig-Sauer over my head. "Come on!"

More nightmares rushing inwards, teeth bared and arms reaching out. I blow the face off one, then I'm backpedalling.

"Akinbode! Get on the fucking Gimpy! We're leaving!"

He scrambles aboard the Chinook.

"Sarge!"

More of them rushing in, no time to aim, oh fuck –

Rat-a-tat-a-tat-a-tat.

Joyce on the tail GPMG, raking the submerged end of the compound and the dead figures coming out of it. Three, four go down. Akinbode firing the door gun.

"*Move move move! We are leaving! We are very fucking leaving!*"

And then the kind of scream I never want to hear again.

"*McTarn!*"

Lomax on the ground. Pinned flat. Still alive, but already they've started eating him, tearing chunks off his hands, arms, legs, face. The look in his eyes, the fucking horror in his eyes.

I aim at Lomax. I see his eyes close.

And I fire.

"Robert!" Katja. "Come on!"

I run for the chopper. I look back.

Bad idea. Just ask Lot's wife.

The nightmares are still coming.

And shouldering through the crowd, a fresh one. Mangled, bloody. A hand, reaching out towards me. Two fingers missing.

The torn, ruined face, slack in death. The eye sockets empty and glowing. Clumsy. Shambling. Parfitt's jaws gape open. And he gives out the hissing snarl I've come to know so well.

"Aw fuck."

A hole appears in his forehead and the back of his head blows out.

Katja, lowering the M-14. "Come on!"

The Chinook's rotors thundering, beating at the air. Hands pull me aboard. We're lifting. Not even time to close the door.

The nightmares are running for the chopper. One jumps. In through the fucking door. Lands on its feet, rocking and swaying for balance.

Scrambling back on my arse, fumbling for the P226, knowing there's no time, it's glaring down at me –

Claws reaching down –

The side of its head blows out and it falls sideways onto the deck.

Katja lowers her pistol.

I am really fucking glad, for the record, that I let her tag along.

Airborne. Looking down. The nightmares gathering below, glaring up.

All across the compound, glaring up.

And as we fly out, I see more of them.

They're swimming up through the waters, towards the surface.

Heads breaking water. Staring up. And they're moving.

They're moving after us.

But we're faster. We're leaving them behind. Not fast enough for me, though. Never fast enough.

Joyce moves to the dead nightmare, face white. He grabs its ankles to drag it clear. Dump it.

"No," I tell him. He stares at me. "No."

I'm looking at it, and something is different; something is definitely different. I need to know, we need to know, *what*.

"We're taking it with us," I say. "Time we got a proper look at one of these things."

"Oh, God!"

Akinbode.

He's cradling his left arm. He's staring at it.

Oh shit.

Even from there I can see the wound in his forearm. I can see it very clearly, because there is white bone gleaming through the mess.

But worse.

Oh, worse.

Far worse.

His hand is swollen. Horribly swollen. He's cut the sleeve open with his knife. The flesh all around the wound is already black and green.

"Oh no. Oh fucking no."

Feeling my hand drift towards the P226 at my belt.

And Akinbode's suddenly on his feet in the doorway, holding his rifle one-handed, and the muzzle whips towards my face, then away, towards Katja's.

And then he puts the barrel in his mouth.

"Akinbode!" I yell.

He pulls the trigger.

He drops down into space.

He hits the water below, and we watch it churn into a bloody froth.

It recedes fast, into a pale, fading spot on the water.

Until Katja stumbles over and pulls the door shut.

Click.

Hassan had set up a temporary hospital in a barn. A trestle table rigged up; the dead nightmare laid out on it. He didn't have much else to do. That was one thing about fighting the nightmares – there wasn't much middle ground. You were either unscathed or you were dead.

"Sarge." He looked up as I trudged in. Tired, gaunt. Dark rings around his eyes. Stubble thickening on his cheeks.

"Hassan. You OK?"

He nodded. "Not enough sleep, that's all."

"What can you tell me?"

"I'm just a medic, Sarge, not a pathologist."

"Give me your best guess."

"The body's not bloated. And the skin... I'm not sure what that green stuff is. Some kind of algae, or mould. If I had to guess, I'd say it's protecting the skin somehow."

"Protecting?"

"From the water, Sergeant. Bodies in seawater decompose very quickly."

"But this hasn't."

"No."

It hasn't started yet.

"So when we hoped they were just going to rot away..."

Hassan nodded. "I don't think they're gonna, Sarge." He rubbed his face. "I don't understand how it works. I mean, the water must get into body cavities, in through the mouth. It should rot them from the inside out. Unless it coats them on the inside too. But then..." he trailed off.

"Like you said, you're not a pathologist. But there is one thing you might want to consider."

"What's that?"

"We're dealing with something that makes the dead get up and walk. That's against pretty much every fucking law of nature I ever heard of. If it can do that, rustproofing the bastards shouldn't be much of a challenge."

It.

The Deep Brain.

Neither of us could add much to that. I didn't know what he was thinking as I trudged back out into the night, but I could guess.

Death, Sergeant. Death is coming.

I sat in silence in the bar of the farmhouse kitchen.

Alone. Unless you counted that bottle of Isle of Jura.

I didn't want anyone to approach me. No-one did. Maybe they knew how I felt and respected it. Or maybe they just wanted to keep away from me. Blamed me for it. My fault.

Death is coming.

Parfitt going down under a rush of nightmares. Parfitt, now

a nightmare himself, staggering forward. Parfitt falling, brains blown out.

Akinbode. The terror and the despair on his face. His arm rotten and necrotic in fucking *minutes*. The gun in his mouth. The eyes popping out of their sockets as he blew off the top of his own skull. Dropping back out of sight. And gone.

Akinbode's arm. Alf Mason had quickly fallen ill, had passed out. Katja's friend, Marta – the bite had taken time to kill her. In a rare moment of openness, Katja had described the state of the girl's arm, but it had taken hours to get to that state. Akinbode's had been turning green and black in the time he'd been taken on board the helicopter and into the sky.

It's working faster. Getting more poisonous.

I poured myself another shot.

"Robert. How are you?"

I looked up.

"Can I join you?" asked Katja.

I shrugged. "Free country."

"Is it still?" She gave a thin, tight smile. Good point. God knew what kind of country it was anymore. Whatever was left of it.

She sat. I lifted the bottle. She nodded. I poured a shot.

"Are you OK?" she asked.

"No. I'm not."

"I didn't think you would be." Her eyes were very dark, very frank. "There's nothing you can say, is there?"

"Not really, no."

"When Marta died. I was responsible for her. I felt like I'd failed her. For a while I felt as though I shouldn't be alive."

"Still feel that way?"

"No." A small shake of her head. "But it still hurts. I don't let myself think of it often. One day, I'll be able to. It'll never *not* hurt. But it will be bearable."

"In time."

"Yes."

"That what you came to tell me?" My voice sounded sharper than I meant it to. She drew back a little. When she spoke again, her voice was more clipped. "No." She looked at me. "Stiles wants to see you."

I stared at her. "He does?"

She nodded.

"That's a switch."

"I don't think it's good news."

"When is it ever?"

"Just go easy on him, OK?"

We walked up towards the Hill.

"I've been going easy on him ever since we got here, hen," I said. "I can't afford to anymore. He said death was coming. Remember?"

"Yes."

"Has he said anything to you?"

She nodded, her eyes lowered.

"What?"

"Something happened last night," she said. "How much do you know about him?"

"Got a basic bio before the mission. I don't know his shoe size or anything."

"Size eight English, forty-two European. I read it on the label." She smiled crookedly. I couldn't keep away a little pang of jealousy.

She knows his shoe size, if he snores or talks in his sleep. All those little things lovers know.

Focus, Robbie.

"Does the name Ellen Vannin mean anything to you?" she asked.

I ran back through the briefing in my head. "No. Why?"

"He woke up screaming it."

"Oh." Maybe a nightmare that *didn't* relate to this? It could still happen. Maybe.

"Early hours of this morning. He woke up screaming her name. All he said was 'It's Ellen. Ellen Vannin. She's found me.'"

Tears gleamed in her eyelashes. I put my hands in my pockets, because all I wanted was to reach out and touch her. "You love him. Don't you?"

"Yes." A whisper.

"I'm sorry."

"I'm not. I'm not sorry I love him. But..."

"What?"

"He cries, you know? He looks at me sometimes, and... he just... cries. I think... I think it's that he knows I'm going to die soon. We all are. That's why I'm crying, Robert. I don't want to die."

"None of us do."

"Stiles... he said that we all die alone. And he's right, isn't he? However you die. Whoever you're with. In the end, it's always alone."

I nodded. "Yes." I'd seen men die often enough. I knew it was true.

"And I don't want to. Do you know what the strangest thing is? I'm happy here. Meeting him has been the best thing to happen to me since I lost my parents. And it wouldn't have happened without this. Do you ever think that perhaps there is a God, and that he has a very cruel sense of humour?"

"Only explanation that ever made sense as far as I'm concerned."

Katja began to laugh, and she wiped her eyes. She looked around at the fells, the meadows, the woodlands, even the sea that surrounded us, and seemed to see it, really see it, for the first time. "It is very sweet, isn't it?"

"What is?"

"Being alive."

And it was. And to be savoured and treasured and lived, and all of that. And if this had been a movie I would have swept her into my arms and kissed her then and there, rather than go my grave not knowing it. But I didn't. It would have been wrong.

But she took my arm as we walked the rest of the way to the caravan, and I savoured every minute of that. It was as close to her as I was ever going to come.

"Thanks for coming," Stiles said, forcing a smile.

Even for Stiles, he looked pretty ghastly – pale, sunken-eyed, his hands shaking. Two bottles of own-brand vodka stood by the rickety chair he perched on.

Katja sat on the divan, her knees pulled up to her chest. Stiles was breathing, fast and shallow.

"Sorry," he said. "Just... some pain. That's all."

I sat on the other divan. I kept still and didn't speak. I could see the effort he was making, and finally started to realise what he was up against. But I mustn't speak. Mustn't give him the chance to back out. He needed to talk and I needed to listen. Silence was the only help I could give him.

"I know... you came here to find me," he said. "And I know that you don't really know why. And you've a right to know. I'm afraid, though... it won't make much difference."

I felt my stomach hollow and tighten.

"The thing is... the Deep Brain... whenever I think about it... I can always hear it, you see. The voices. The souls. I can always hear them. It's like a screaming in my head, a roaring. Drowning out my thoughts. It's always in my head, Sergeant – never far away. But when I think about it, *talk* about it..." His voice had risen. His fingertips touched his forehead.

"Ben –" Katja, a hand outstretched. I touched her wrist. Wordlessly, I shook my head.

For an instant, there was fury in Stiles's face. Then it cleared. He straightened up and nodded. He uncapped one of the bottles and took a big gulp. He leant back in the chair, face screwing up, tightening, flushing a violent red, and let out a long, explosive breath. After a few seconds, he opened his eyes again. Forced a smile.

"Takes away the pain, a little."

Swaying slightly, he leant forward again, breathing quick and ragged. He swallowed hard.

"As I said... when I talk about it, the pain gets worse. I'm still not sure... not even now... if it's trying to silence me, or... if it just becomes more aware of me at those times."

I waited.

"Would it surprise you to learn, Sergeant, that I was predicting what's happened as long as five years ago?"

"No," I said at last.

"I suppose not. You're not stupid, after all." He gave a sudden, almost boyish grin. "Not a Nobel prizewinner or anything, but you're not stupid."

"Was that a compliment?" I asked, feeling my eyebrows go up.

Stiles grinned again. "After a fashion."

After a moment, I grinned back.

"Ben." Katja, cutting in on the male bonding. "There isn't much time."

Stiles nodded wearily. "The alcohol's just a temporary aid," he said, "and it's getting less and less effective. The Deep Brain is the only name I've got for what we're facing. I've been aware of it for several years now."

"Since the diving accident?"

"Yes." He pulled a sheaf of stained, rumpled papers out from under the divan. "It's all here. I've managed to write it down, just about. Katja will tell you – I've been up late writing these past few nights. Mostly drunk out of my skull."

I looked at Katja. She nodded. Stiles reached out and took her hand. "Only way I could manage it. Very difficult. Painful. But, this will give you some idea of why you were sent... but as I say, I don't there's anything we can do to stop it."

"That bad?" I asked. Stupid question.

"How do you fight the sea, Sergeant? Men have been trying for millions of years. And it's always won. And now it's starting to move against us in earnest."

A chill ran over my skin. Pretty much what I'd suspected, but now it was confirmed in black and white, so to speak.

"I don't think there's much you can do with the information, to be honest. But I thought you had a right to know."

I nodded my thanks.

"The dead rising was only the beginning. When it had enough control, enough strength, it found ways to preserve the bodies it controls. Also, the waters were thick with silt after the floods. Impossible to see very far. The walking dead are the Deep

Brain's eyes and ears. It's split itself apart, a tiny fragment of its consciousness in each reanimated corpse, each independent but linked into a greater whole. It can't keep track of them all at once – imagine having a billion eyes, each moving independently – but it gathers information steadily. And now, with the water clear, it can move in search of survivors."

"Why didn't you warn us when we went to the army base?"

"Would you have listened? Besides, you might have escaped without incident. And it was inevitable we'd need supplies. The same with any other group of survivors. Sooner or later there'd have to be a clash."

"Clash?" What he was describing sounded more like genocide to me.

Stiles sagged, deflated. "It's a word for it. Not a very good one, perhaps. Anyway..." He took another gulp of vodka, his throat working. Squeezed his face tight as the booze hit; he flushed again. "I'm afraid we may be at a particular disadvantage, because I'm here. It wants *me*, Sergeant, most particularly."

"Why?

"It's all in my notes. Perhaps if you killed me, you might have a better chance."

"Ben!"

"It's true, Katja. On the other hand, it might attack even harder out of rage. Or you could fly me out, far away from here, abandon me on some far-off scrap of land."

"Ben, don't talk like this."

"If it gives the rest of you a chance of survival, Katja, then it has to be done. I'm tired of hiding. I'm tired of being a coward."

"You're not, Ben."

Stiles turned to me. "I've told you pretty much all I can. I don't know any way to fight it, or destroy it. I'm sorry, Sergeant."

"So am I." I got up. There really wasn't much more to say. Stiles wasn't looking at me, but Katja was. Her eyes were bright."You're tougher than you look, Stiles. I'll say that for you."

He looked up and forced a smile. "Was that a compliment, Sergeant?"

I forced a smile back. "After a fashion."

Katja walked part of the way back with me. Stiles had said he wanted to be alone for a while. The fields and the meadows spread out before us; beyond them the glitter of the water that would bring all our deaths.

A thought occurred to me. "You don't think..."

"What?"

"Stiles. You don't think he might do something stupid?"

A moment's unease, then she shook her head. "I don't think so. Not yet. I think he'll wait until the end. When he's sure there's no hope. It'd be stupid – wouldn't it – to kill yourself only to find out you were wrong?"

"You think he is?"

"I wish I did."

So did I.

"What about you?"

"Me? I think, yes, I'll kill myself, rather than let them take me. I don't want to die like that. And I don't want to be one of them. But I've been here before."

I waited. She told me how it had begun for her. Trapped on the brothel's roof with Marta.

"I fought as long as I could, until I was sure there was no more hope. Then I was going to kill myself. Marta too. But we were rescued." She told me the rest then. Her voice faltered once or twice, when she talked about what had happened on the narrowboat. "We went through all of that, just to die here. Hardly seems fair, does it?"

"Life isn't fair."

"I knew that," she said. Of course she did. Even before the floods, she'd known that. "But still..." She shrugged. "Well, I'll do the same. Hold out until I'm sure there's no more hope. Until then..."

She shrugged, looking off into the distance, towards the sea.

"Katja?" She looked at me. "I don't want to die either."

She smiled. Then leant forward, put her hands on my shoulders, and kissed me once, very softly, on the lips. I tried to respond, but she pushed me back, shook her head. "To remember spond, but she pushed me back, shook her head. "To remember me by," she said. Then she looked away. "I'd better get back."

I watched her walking back up to the farmhouse, to Stiles' caravan. The kiss still tingled on my lips. It lifted me, a little, but there was a cold hard weight in my stomach, and it wouldn't go away. I thought they called it doom.

I've read Stiles' notes. Not an easy task. His handwriting's not brilliant, and the pages are a mess; creased, crumpled, stained – spilt booze, spilt coffee. And what he's got to say is pretty wild. Craziness on craziness. Except that I can't say it doesn't make sense.

It gives me some idea of what's coming, and why. But it doesn't help.

I've been writing this last thing at night, first thing in the mornings. I know Katja's done something similar. Seemed right to leave a sort of record, for the future.

Except there isn't one. Not for any of us.

I was called away. We've just heard.

Dear God. Already.

It's started.

CHAPTER SEVENTEEN

We'd left a radio with each of the groups of survivors we'd found. Each morning, Parkes hailed them to check their status.

That morning, the survivors at Roughlee didn't reply.

Hendry, Parkes, Mleczko and Joyce flew over in the Chinook. Doors stood open. There was only silence. No-one came out to greet them.

They made a landing, Parkes handling the Gimpy while Mleczko and Joyce searched the houses.

All empty. Blood on the walls. Torn flesh. Fragments of bone.

They'd hit, and hit hard. No warning, no alarm raised. And everybody gone.

No defence is total.

And for all the advantages of technology, training and equipment give you, numbers always win in the end.

In the evening, just before the light failed, Parkes got a transmission from the survivors at Blacko, nearby. The nightmares were gathering in the waters around the village – dozens, scores, finally hundreds. Standing in silence, with their glowing green eyes.

They were massing, but had made no hostile move. Yet. If I sent the Chinook for them, would that trigger an attack? Unknown. But if we waited till they *did* attack, we'd never reach them in time.

I sent the Chinook, with Mleczko and Parkes. Just them. We weren't there to fight. It was an evacuation, pure and simple.

The Chinook returned just before dawn. The villagers disembarked, pale and shaken and out of place; people with nowhere to go, reliant on the kindness of strangers. The shell-shocked look of people who'd had what security, what stability, what home they'd had, snatched away. I'd done some peacekeeping duties in the former Yugoslavia; I knew that look. Refugees.

No violence. None of the nightmares had emerged from the water or attacked.

Mleczko stepped off the Chinook and came over; he looked grim. "They were in the water," he muttered.

"We know that."

"Not around Blacko. As we flew back here. Sarge, I think they were on the move."

As dawn came and light stole across the landscape, Parkes' radio came to life again.

Hendry flew out to the other communities. As before, it was an evacuation, not a fight. Any food, fuel or weapons available were cleared out and brought back.

As Hendry flew in, the Chinook wobbled in its flight, the engine sounded an irregular, coughing and spluttering note. The rotors were skipping beats.

He brought it down in the meadow near the Hill, where Stiles' caravan stood. He came out to meet me as Parkes and Mleczko shepherded the evacuees clear, the rotors winding down.

His face was pale, lips moving without sound.

I said it for him. "It's fucked, isn't it?"

He nodded.

"Can you fix it?"

"I don't know."

"Shit!"

"I can try, Sergeant. That's all I can say. We'd never be able to move everyone, anyway."

"We could at least get some of them clear."

"Where to?"

"Right now, anywhere but here would probably be good." We looked at each other. "Just do whatever you can, Sir."

A few minutes later, my PC crackled; the first of the nightmares had been sighted in the waters round Pendle.

In the farmhouse, we held a brief council of war.

Joyce was in charge of the men while we talked. Jo was working with him to co-ordinate with the villagers. Katja, meanwhile, I'd put in charge of the refugees – we had close on a hundred of them. She was finding places for them to stay – hunting up tents or anything that could be used to jerry-rig them, spare rooms in farmhouses, abandoned buildings – while at the same time trying to pick out potential fighters. We needed to mobilise everybody capable of using a gun.

Round the table: me, Chas, Ged and Hendry. Parkes was on the Chinook's radio, trying desperately to hail Windhoven.

Hassan was clearing space in the abandoned barn, a couple of local women as impromptu nurses. Not much he could do for anyone bitten, but there was still the risk of injury from shrapnel, stray bullets, falls.

The sky was darkening. A thin, mizzling rain had started to fall.

"Focusing," I said.

"What?" asked Hendry.

"What Stiles said. Imagine having a billion eyes, all working independently. You couldn't keep track of it all. Drive anybody mad." An insane controlling intelligence? Fucking hell, it just kept getting better. "But as it becomes aware of survivors, it focuses on them, one by one. And it gathers its forces... and marches."

"And keeps attacking till they're all gone," said Chas.

"I think so."

"Lovely. Got a cig?"

I threw him my packet. "The attack this morning... testing its strength. Seeing how we'd respond."

"Are you trying to say they're using tactics?" Hendry looked at me as if I'd just dribbled on my shirt.

"I know how it sounds, Sir. But according to Stiles, there's a controlling intelligence. Primitive, only recently conscious. But if it's aware, it can learn."

Hendry leant back in his chair.

"But now we've pulled back, Sir" said Chas. "We're not gonna be trying to defend scattered, isolated positions, just one. And we've got high ground, a lot of warm bodies on the deck, weapons and raw materials to build defences. And we've had a lot more combat experience than it has."

"Question is," said Ged, "how does that help us in long run?"

"Well," I said, "that's the big question, isn't it?"

"Fair enough." Ged toyed with an empty glass; probably wishing there was something strong in it, but resisting the call. Getting blootered now helped nobody. "What the hell can we do?"

"One, Parkes is on the radio, trying to hail Windhoven –"

"Done us bugger-all good so far."

"She's also hailing on all other frequencies. If there's *anyone* else out there, they might be able to help."

"Or they might be as stuffed as we are."

Christ, I didn't need Ged cracking on me. "We're not dead yet. Any progress with the Chinook, Sir?"

"Not as yet. Engineering's not my area. I think I might know what the problem is, but fixing it –"

"Understood, Sir. Just do whatever you can, requisition whatever you need. What I'm thinking is this. We set up defences fast. Pull everyone who's not actually going to be fighting those things to the most central location we can."

"The Hill, most likely," said Ged.

"Aye. So we block all approaches to that location with any-thing spare – any barbed wire left over?"

"Might be a roll or two."

"Break it out. We've got the Landrovers and their armaments. We've also got farming vehicles – tractors, mechanical diggers. We can use them to run over the bastards."

"What if Parkes can't raise anybody?" Chas spoke quietly. I looked at him. His eyes were wide. He was thinking of Jo.

"We're not dead till we're dead, Chas. The important thing is to get the Chinook airborne again. If we can do that, some of us can hold the ground here while we fly the rest out, then it can come back for us."

"Fly out? Where to?"

"Any stretch of land that's not occupied or surrounded. It's taken them time to get here. They've got to march like any oth-er army. So, we put distance between us. It buys us breathing space."

Chas nodded. After a moment, so did Ged. I was relieved to see he looked a little more energised.

"We build concentric lines of defence. They break through one, we fall back behind the next. The longer we can hold out, the better chance we've got."

Hopelessness folded round me, like pressure at depth. But I wouldn't, couldn't, *must not* give way. Don't think about the long game, Robbie, cos we all lose that in the end. Just think about the next problem. Except, like the nightmares, they just kept coming. No matter how many of them you dealt with there were always more, and bit by bit they wore you down. By sheer weight of numbers.

Because numbers always win in the end.

"If we can do them a lot of damage in that first engagement," I said, "From what we've seen, they'll pull back to regroup and reinforce. So the harder we hit them, the more time that buys us till the next attack. We need to show this Deep Brain it's got a fight on its hands, and we will not go down easily."

"Sounds great," said Chas. "How?"

"Simple. We invite them in."

We had SA80s, Minimis, sniper rifles, several Gimpys and the blooper. Plus some C-4 explosive and personal communicators from the army base. We still had a good supply of ammunition for each weapon, plus each man carried two frag grenades. The exceptions to that were Hassan, who had none, and Chas and myself, who carried three – frags, smoke, white phosphorous.

There were also shotguns, rifles and ratting carbines – .22 revolvers with ridiculously long barrels and wire-framed stocks. Not in the same league as what we had, but all it took to turn a nightmare's lights out was an accurate headshot.

Those who couldn't fight were put to work erecting defences. Barbed wire; furniture; farm machinery; unneeded cars. Anything that could block a path was dragged across it.

We had stocks of Molotov cocktails. Torn bits of fabric, old bottles – add something flammable and Bob's your uncle. Fuel siphoned from vehicles, bottles of spirits. Any spare reserves were now pressed into service to make more; I saved the last of the Inn's Isle of Jura for myself.

Katja was on lookout on top of the Hill. The Dinkies were back at the farmhouse, to be deployed where they were needed.

On the higher slopes, we'd set up fougasses for when – *if* – we were pushed back. A kind of improvised mine. Take one fifty-five gallon steel drum, readily available on any farm. Pack explosive at the bottom – C-4, fertiliser mixed with petrol – and pack the rest with pieces of metal, stone chips. Anything that would do damage. Bury in the earth with the open end sticking out, and then you just had to set it off and watch your enemies blown to shreds.

Chas was on Pendle Row, Jo round the opposite side of the Hill.

As well as guns, everyone carried a hand weapon of some kind. I had a hatchet tucked into my belt; others carried old police truncheons, baseball bats and pick-axe handles and spades and shovels, axes and hatchets, pitchforks. Even knives lashed to broom handles as crude spears. No-one was completely defence-less.

God help us if it got to that stage. We weren't special forces, knew nothing about hand-to-hand fighting. If a position was overran, you fell back and fired again. Hopefully driving them back.

But there were so many of them.

And we could only fall back so far.

Just north of the Hill the road leading towards Downham vanished into the sea; beside it lay a stretch of flat ground containing the two pools where the nightmares had attacked the night Tidyman died. The space was wide open, up to the encircling drystone walls, and below a wooded slope. From the water, all they'd see were two men with rifles – Mleczko and me. Not even a Minimi in sight. Short of putting up a sign saying *picnic area*, there wasn't a clearer invitation.

Behind the wall, however, Ged crouched with his shotgun beside me, and Billy with his beside Mleczko, gazing up adoringly. Mleczko did his best to pretend he wasn't there. Beyond them was a long line of villagers and soldiers with rifles and crate-loads of Molotov cocktails.

The rain intensified. A slow, low hissing from the blackening sky. A white fork of lightning left floaters in my vision – red, gold and green.

"Brace yourselves," I said. "Any minute now."

"How do you know, Sarge?"

"Storm's coming in, Mleczko. Heavy rain'll cut visibility and give them a better chance."

I could see the question in his eyes: *You really think they're smart enough to plan like that?*

Maybe not, but the Deep Brain is.

Stiles was in his caravan. Katja said he'd been brooding, silent. She didn't say she thought he might have an idea to save us, but I read the hope in her eyes. She was afraid to think about it, let alone give it voice.

The lightning flashed again, dazzling me. Mleczko sucked in a breath; in the murky distance dark, shadowy figures stood in ranks at the water's edge.

The thunder rolled in. The rain was driving down now with merciless force, pounding and hammering on my skull. Water danced on the ground, in puddles and on any hard surface. Splashing into my eyes. Hard to see through it. Visibility thinned down by the driving haze of it. The thunderheads were almost directly above.

Then a sound.

Like a huge breath, let out through a phlegmy throat.

Like a thousand hissing snarls, unleashed as one.

And the nightmares came for us.

Hundreds of the bastards. Closely packed. No room to manoeuvre.

"Hold on," I said to the men around me. "Hold on," I said into the communicator.

The nightmares staggered forward, forward, forward. Mleczko and I began firing. Some fell. But the army came on. Closer. Closer. So close I could see their faces.

"Sarge?" Joyce's voice crackled out of the communicator.

"Wait for it."

The front row of nightmares erupted into a run.

"Now!"

The men hidden behind the wall stood and fired, fast volleys. Two GPMGs laid down sweeping arcs of fire further down the wall, tearing into the nightmares still swarming out of the water. The nightmares were falling. But there were so many more.

Aim and fire.

Got one in my sights. God, that *face*.

The empty sockets of the eyes, round and pale and glowing.

I pulled the trigger. Its head snapped back, spraying dark matter. It fell.

Another in my sights.

Aim.

Fire.

Gunfire all around now, almost lost in the roar and the drum of the rain.

The panic burning, gnawing at your control. The urge to fire wildly, pray you hit something, anything to hold back the tide. So many of them, and for each one you dropped, ten more still surging forward.

Bodies jerking under the bullets that hadn't hit the mark, then carrying on. Bullets hit chests, stomachs, legs, arms – hit and changed nothing.

But other shots hit home. Retain control. Panic is a choice. I remembered Katja saying that. Her father had said it. He'd been a soldier too. "I think you would have liked him," she'd said.

I wondered if he'd have liked me.

Heads snapped back; brains flew; glowing eyes went out. Bodies toppled and crashed to the ground. The ones behind trampling over them.

Firing. Firing. A SA80 rifle holds a thirty round magazine. The bolt locked back. Empty.

Pulling out the magazine. Steam floating up from the barrel and breech as the rain hit it.

Ram the fresh clip in. Lightning flashed. Thunder rolling in and down.

And on they came, in rags of clothing, rotten and torn. Some naked. Maybe they'd died that way; maybe the clothes had rotted off. Irrelevant now. Some male, some female. Some showed signs of their former youth or age, under the green moss. But you hardly noticed now. Death the leveller.

A poem I'd read once – *Great Death hath made all his for evermore.*

If he hadn't yet, he was bloody well working on it.

Bodies piled on bodies like sandbags.

So many soldiers, expendable, uncomplaining, to be flung into the meatgrinder, again and again and again. I'd once seen a film about Stalingrad. The Germans kept on driving into the fray, the Russians too. Each more afraid of their own leaders than the enemy. Or drunk on their own propaganda.

But the living tire. Even the most professional soldier, or the most fanatical, runs out of steam. But not these. A General's wet dream. They'd never complain about inadequate equipment, never crack under the constant threat of destruction or seeing their comrades fall, never question the morality of their task.

Like I had.

After the desert road.

Baba. Baba.

Another face in the sights. Aim. Fire.

Now.

"Wall of fire!"

The Molotovs started flying. Two-person teams – one lit the cocktail, the other threw. The Molotovs hit the nightmares' front rank and erupted into sheets of flame.

Nightmares blundered through, aflame head to foot. No pain, but blinded. And the flame eating through soft tissues. A skull burst in the heat.

But there were always more.

They thought – the Deep Brain thought – there were still the numbers to push through our weak spot.

Which was the whole point.

I grabbed the communicator. "Joyce. *Now.*"

From the wooded slope above came the roar of engines.

Rotting heads turned.

They surged down the slope towards the nightmares. Tractors and mechanical diggers, scoops and ploughs extended. They drove into the nightmares' left flank.

The mechanical diggers' scoops scythed bodies in two, shattered skulls. Caterpillar treads rolled over what remained, leaving lifeless pulp.

The tractors smashing nightmares aside; the heavy wheels crushing, flattening.

They went down in droves. Severed limbs flew free. Survivors writhed and thrashed on the ground, still 'alive' but helpless.

Each driver had at least one armed man in the cab, who picked off any undamaged nightmares trying to attack. And from behind the drystone walls, still we fired.

Because there were plenty left.

The farm vehicles roaring in towards us. The men stumbling

back from the walls. Me yelling to Mleczko to move a dozen men further down, towards the water, and hammer any still emerging or trying to retreat. Hitting the ground as a tractor grates to a halt inches from my position. Joyce looking sheepish behind the wheel. "Sorry, Sarge."

The bodies, piled up across the once-green field. Well, it's still green, I suppose. Except where the nightmares had been burned black. Not the same kind of green, not the kind I wanted to see.

Scattered shots and bursts. Twenty nightmares left now. A dozen. Dropping like flies. Heads exploded as high velocity bullets smashed into them. Blood and brains, spilling over the grass and the dead in the rain.

A last one standing, weaving, twisting this way and that from threat to threat.

Half a dozen guns fired as one, and it toppled.

And then there was only the guns' fading echo, the thunder's distant rumble, the rain's relentless sound as it rinsed the clotted slurry of blood and brains into the clogged quagmire of the ground.

The ground was empty. Forty or fifty still stood in the water, silent, watching, but made no move towards the land.

I aimed. We waited. The gun's barrel hissed, steam rising; the rain beat down so hard I could only see the glow of their eyes.

Then, as one, they turned and walked back into the water.

"Yeee-hooo!" whooped Billy, in what he doubtless thought was a rebel yell. He leapt over the wall, danced a clumsy jig. Mleczko, jogging back from the water's edge, shook his head, grinning wearily. "All fucked off, Sarge."

"Good work."

A ragged cheer went up. Rifles and shotguns shaken in the air. From the distance came firing, scattered shots, but they died away.

"Chas? Jo? What's your status? Report. Over."

"Clear, Sarge. Over."

"Clear," said Jo. "Over."

"Good work."

The farm vehicles were parked up. Joyce climbed down, staring out over the torn, broken corpses.

Ged glanced over, smiled slightly, and began reloading the SPAS-12.

I could still hear cheering, through the whining in my ears, as Joyce's men waded in, finishing off the crippled nightmares with blows from rifle butts. A couple of shots rang out; Joyce's sandpaper voice, berating whoever wasted the ammo.

"Yee-haa!" Billy skipped and gambolled round the still-flaming patches of ground, in among the bodies, kicking at a torso here, a severed head there, waving his over-and-under shotgun in the air. "Got them! Got the smelly fuckers! Ha-haaa! All fucking dead! Got them!" He whirled back towards us, waving the gun in the air. "Got them, Danny! We got them all!"

"Billy!" I heard Mleczko scream.

On the ground lay a nightmare; everything gone from the waist down, guts trailing in the dirt, an arm and half its face torn away. But one eye still glowed, and one arm remained.

And jaws. It still had jaws.

The nightmares could move incredibly fast when they wanted, even in a state like that. Only in short bursts, but that was all it needed to grab Billy's ankle, yank itself forward, and bite into the meat of his calf.

Billy screamed, first in panic, then in pain. Mleczko yelled something and ran past me, dropping to one knee as the nightmare's head reared away from Billy's leg, torn meat hanging from its mouth. Blood spurted from the wound. Mleczko fired, and the nightmare collapsed.

Mleczko ran towards Billy. I followed; Ged too.

Billy was wailing, clutching his wounded leg with both hands. Blood streamed through his fingers.

"Ow, fuck! Fuck!" Fright stole over his face as it dawned. "*Fuck!*"

He looked up at Mleczko. "Help me. Please, Danny, help me!"

"Alright, mate," Mleczko said in an older, wearier voice than I'd ever thought to hear him use. "Alright."

Billy was crying. "You can make it better, can't you?"

No-one spoke. Like I said, he was simple. Not the full shilling.

What Mleczko later told me they called a 'not-right' where he'd grown up in Salford.

"You can, can't you?" His wide, wet eyes darted from face to face. "You can make it better." Poor bastard was blubbering openly, now. "Make it better, Danny, please. I don't want to die."

"You're not gonna, mate." Mleczko crouched beside him, squeezing his shoulder. "We'll get you right again, no worries. Not getting out of twatting those fuckers that easy."

I opened my mouth to speak, but Ged put his hand on my arm.

Billy was grinning, however tightly, through the tears. "You're gonna be fine," said Mleczko. "I hadn't shot the fucking thing, it'd've died from biting you. Fucking hell, I've been there when you've let one rip. Poison fucking cities, you could."

Billy was laughing, even as he cried. Mleczko patted his shoulder again. "You'll be right, pal. Just hang on. I'll go get Saddam to take a look at you."

"Saddam," giggled Billy, as Mleczko walked away from him. "Saddam. That's fu-"

The three-round burst blew most of his head apart on impact; the rest flew clear of the body.

I leapt back from the blood; with his head gone, it hosed and splattered the ground. The body dropped forward onto the churned, blackened turf.

Mleczko stood over him for a moment, as if computing whether he'd need to shoot again, then lowered his rifle.

Ged went to him, reaching out a hand; Mleczko twisted away with a warding-off gesture, and walked off, brushing by Joyce like he wasn't there.

Bodies choked Pendle Row.

The nightmares lay on tarmac and pavements, draped over the cars dragged across the road, crumpled against the walls where they'd fallen. Others lay scattered down Barley Road. Empty bullet cases crunched underfoot.

The bay's surface looked flat and innocent.

Chas came towards me, face furrowed and sombre.

"We lost four," he said. "All locals."

"Shit."

"Could've been a lot worse."

"Aye."

The rain hissed down between us. "Want me to clear this lot away?"

I shook my head. "They could be back any minute."

"Thought you said we'd keep them away longer like this."

"That's the plan, but they might have a different one."

Chas nodded. "Well, best get ready for them then, hadn't we?"

"Besides, we leave their bodies where they are, it'll slow them down. More to climb over."

"Every little helps. So what do we do about the next one, Sarge?"

"See if we can get 'em again."

"Same trick?"

"Aye."

"Think they'll fall for that twice?"

"We'll see."

"Same place?"

I shook my head. "Thought you could give it a try."

Chas looked dubiously up and down the Row. "Where'm I supposed to put a bunch of tractors?"

"The Newchurch Road. They can sweep down and hit them here at the junction."

"Try anything once. Stiles said anything?"

"He's out for the count. Checked before. Drank himself stupid."

"Maybe he's got the right idea."

"Fucksake, Chas."

"Sorry, Sarge."

"I need you of all people with your head screwed on right."

"Yeah, I know. Sorry." He grinned. "Fucking hell, Jock, I thought *I* was supposed to keep *you* on the straight and narrow."

"*Sergeant* Jock to you, grotbag."

The rain kept driving down, harder than ever before.

Still was two hours later, when they attacked again.

The second try...

God, just thinking about it...

The Deep fucking Brain.

It's learning fast.

They threw a big load at the Row, or so it looked.

Chas and his men did as we had, hid the main force and left a skeleton crew visible, then hit them hard with heavy fire and Molotovs before whistling the vehicles down. The nightmares falling back.

And then the second wave came out of the water.

They hit the farm vehicles. Overran them. Jamming the wheels and tracks with sheer weight of numbers – pushing, rocking – a tractor keeled over, a mechanical digger seemed to rear up and crash to the ground like some weird beast in its death throes. Most of the drivers got clear. Not all.

And then they overran the Row. Andrews, about twenty other defenders – all killed.

They fell back, laid down heavy fire. But they kept coming.

And next I knew, the call was coming out.

"Robbie! Robbie!"

Rapid, muffled explosions in the distance. "Chas?"

"They've taken Pendle Row. We couldn't hold them off. They've broken though onto the lower slopes behind it. Need help *now*."

"On its way."

Jo got the Landrover with the Mk19 onto the open ground behind Pendle Row. The nightmares staggered through in droves, but Chas scrambled aboard and opened up on them with the launcher, hitting them hard.

I brought Joyce, Mleczko, a good thirty defenders with me, all with SA80s, and it didn't look anywhere near enough.

The survivors of Chas's team were running back to us. Just him and Jo left on the Dinky covering their retreat, Chas firing the blooper into the nightmares' ranks, blasting fragments of them skywards, until –

It stopped firing. Chas grappling with the blooper. A jam.

And that was when the nightmares, milling closer, broke into a run.

Jo gunning the engine, trying to turn.

The nightmares smashing into the vehicle, tipping it over.

Jo on the ground rolling, scrambling to her feet with rifle raised as I screamed for covering fire.

Chas landing under its shadow as it toppled towards him.

Scrambling clear – almost made it – almost –

Almost.

The Landrover crashed down, belly-up to the sky, the full weight of it coming down on his right leg, just above the knee.

Chas bellowing, scrabbling at the earth, tearing his nails to bloody pulp. Jo beside him, firing this way, then that. A nightmare fell, then another – but never enough. There were always more.

Blood seeping out from under the Landrover. Chas yelling at Jo. Jo shouting back, shaking her head. He yelled again. She ignored him.

Leave me. Save yourself.

No.

Almost automatically, as if my hands were moving of their own volition, I found myself sighting on Jo. Her first, then Chas? Or the other way around? If she was going to stand her ground till they got her too, it'd be a mercy.

Chas tearing the WP grenade from its harness, pulling out the pin.

Jo staring back at him.

Click. I couldn't've heard it over the gunfire, the screams, the explosions, the dying, but I'd swear I did.

Click.

As he released the handle, it fell away and the fuse began to smoke.

Jo screaming.

Chas shouting at her to *go, go, go.*

Jo running – nightmares barring her path. Mleczko firing, me too, cutting them down.

But I didn't sight on Chas as he lay there, the grenade smoking as the nightmares rushed in on him and –

Mleczko pulling me down. A vivid sheet of flame, then the explosion followed by several others as the remaining grenades in the Landrover, the Dinky's fuel tanks, all went up.

I scrambled up. Flames. A gouged, blackened crater. The Landrover's wreckage crashed back down into it. Of Chas Nixon, nothing remained.

Jo lay on the ground, unmoving.

The nightmares pouring through. Mleczko yelling in my ear, wanting orders.

Joyce running forward, shooting. Nightmares leaping up at him, pulling him down.

Focus, Robbie.

The voice sounded almost like Chas. Except that he'd've said Jock, and – no. Don't think of that now. I aimed on one of Joyce's attackers and fired. Mleczko too. Joyce scrambling free, slinging Jo over his shoulder, staggering back, a wound gaping in the side of his face – half his cheek torn away. But he kept going, till other hands took the woman from him and carried her away, and then he turned and walked out to meet the nightmares, firing on them till the gun was empty and they pulled him down.

But before they could finish him, I did. I did what I'd been going to do for Chas, what I should've done for Billy. I sighted on his head and fired a burst that tore through his skull and that of one of his attackers. They both went down and the others swarmed all over Joyce, biting, tearing, chewing...

Aim and fire. Aim and fire.

I glanced left at Mleczko. His SA80's barrel moved this way, then that, shellcases jumping from the breech. Too fast, it seemed. He was firing wild. But when I looked, I saw a nightmare go down each time.

Fucking hell, he's good.

Aim and fire. Aim and fire.

The bolt locked back. The nightmares, yards away, wading in, jaws yawning open.

"Fall back. Fall back."

I heard myself screaming the words, but felt oddly calm. Everything moved slick and easy. The SA80's empty magazine sliding free as I ran. The replacement clip sliding neatly into place.

Turn to face them. Two nightmares closing in. I dropped the first, tracked right, fired again. The second one fell too.

But still they came.

"Grenades!"

I was already overarming the first one. Mleczko sent another sailing in. Then everyone dived to the ground and tried to burrow into it.

The two explosions sounded so close together it was like a single blast. I felt an intense wave of heat and could see the explosion even through squeezed-shut eyes.

"Fall back! Fall back!"

And so we did. We fell back up to the next line of defence and dug in.

And we waited.

But for now, they didn't come.

For now.

Jo sat in a corner of the farmhouse living room, blank-faced, rocking to and fro.

She'd dived for the ground before the blast went off. Knocked unconscious, but barely scratched. Hassan said she should be fine. But she hadn't spoken a word.

I crouched beside her. "Jo?"

No answer. Just rocking.

"Jo?"

Rocking.

"Joanne."

Endlessly rocking.

"Fuck you then."

A blink, a reaction; reddened eyes focussing on me.

"That all you're gonna do for Chas? Sit in a corner crying? That what he died for? Him *and* Joyce? What a fucking waste of two good men."

Her whole face flared, and her hand flew out. I caught it at the wrist – just. The fury, vibrating in her muscles, trying to tear free to try again.

"Better," I said.

Her voice was thick. "Bastard."

"Aye. I'm a bastard." I knew I was. But this had to be done. "I need you, Jo. I need your help. You'd've made one fucking hell of a good soldier. I can't afford to let that go to waste."

Eyes wet and bright; a shuddering breath. Then a sob and she pitched forward. I gripped her tight.

"I loved him," she whispered.

"Me too."

"I would've died with him. I wanted to."

"My best mate."

"I should've stayed. When he took the grenade out. I should've died with him."

"He gave his life."

"That's what you do if you love someone."

"That's what soldiers do."

"I should've stayed, but I ran."

"That's what he wanted. Jo, hen, I'm gonna need you to stay alive a wee bit longer."

I let her go. She sat back, looking at me. "What do you want?"

"I need someone to take care of the other survivors. The ones who can't fight."

"Katja –"

"I've other plans for her." She looked at me. I lit her a cigarette. "You're to keep them alive long as you can, if those things break through."

"When."

"If." I felt like the prize fool of all time for not just owning up and admitting the truth, but if I didn't act like we'd make it, who bloody would?

She opened her mouth to argue, then shrugged.

"If there's no hope left, it's your judgement what you do."

She nodded. A silence. "That everything?"

"Pretty much."

A knock at the door. "Who is it?"

"Mleczko, Sarge."

"One minute." I turned to Jo. "You up for it?"

"Alright."

"Get going." She nodded and stood. "Can you tell Katja I'd like to see her?" She nodded again. "Come in, Mleczko."

He stood to attention as the door closed behind her.

"You wanted to see me, Sarge?"

"Aye. At ease."

"She OK?"

"What do you think? Take a seat."

I uncapped the bottle, poured two Isle of Juras.

He grimaced, but choked it down. Strictly a lager man, Mleczko. Not like Chas. I almost smiled. Almost.

"Sarge?"

Focus, Robbie. Focus.

"I need a new Section Leader, Mleczko."

"Sarge?" Then it dawned. "Serious?"

"Seriously. Consider yourself promoted. Assuming you want it."

His face lit up. "Yeah, Sarge. Won't let you down."

"I know. You'll need a 2IC."

"Got anyone in mind, Sarge?"

"I was thinking of Katja." His eyebrows rose. "Any problem there for you?"

"No Sarge. She's good. I'd've gone for her myself."

"I'll bet." He was still young, after all. "Just keep your mind on the job, OK?"

"Course Sarge."

I nodded. "Get your head down, Corporal. Dismissed."

He got up, saluted, went out.

"What do you reckon, Chas?"

No answer; he was dead.

"You reckon he'll do?"

No answer; he was dead.

"I reckon he'll do."

No answer; he was dead.

"Fuck, Chas. What the fuck am I gonna do without you?"

No answer; he was dead.

"Fuck."

CHAPTER EIGHTEEN

The night has passed, thick with rain, lit only by lightning and dying fires.

They haven't come back yet. But they will. You can put money on it. It's the one inevitability left. Death isn't as final as it was, and taxes – well, there's always an upside.

I'm going to give this to Katja when I'm done. It's going in a safe place, along with her account and Stiles' notes.

Maybe they'll be of some use to someone. Maybe someone else will read them all one day. Someone from Windhoven, maybe.

Maybe this will just be a curiosity by then. Maybe the nightmares will be gone, or at least contained. I like the idea that this will run its course, and the dead'll be dead again. At last. Permanently...

Focus, Robbie.

I haven't much time. I want to explain something.

I want to talk about the desert road.

7th November. Winter back in Scotland, but in the desert, it was still hot.

I read somewhere that a breakdown isn't normally down to one single traumatic event. It's cumulative, like erosion – one thing after another. Maybe it'd been building for a while. I'd helped fight enough dirty little wars, after all. Sooner or later, questions get asked. If only in the silent places at the back of your mind.

The city had been under insurgent control from around the middle of the year, with the civilians caught in the crossfire. Rumours circulated; civilians with white flags fired on, ambulances fired on. We dismissed it as lefty propaganda. Civvies didn't understand war.

So the coalition forces were going in.

But I wasn't involved in any of the fighting. I heard the reports. But I can't say for sure what happened in there.

What I can say is this:

On the afternoon of November 7th, I was stationed on a small desert road leading out of the besieged city.

With me was a section of eight men. Among them Chas Nixon. My CO, Lieutenant Alderson, had given me my brief. No males 'of military age' were to be allowed to leave the city.

"Military age being, sir?"

"Under forty-five, Sergeant."

There was no lower age limit.

"These orders are specific, Sergeant. They're to be turned back. Not detained or held at the checkpoint. They could end up massing and pushing through the roadblocks."

Fuck. That'd been the plan forming in my head. Not letting them through, but not forcing them back into the killing ground either. Someone had thought of that. Someone wanted blood.

"We want to make a clean sweep of all insurgents, not let them scatter to regroup later."

The road was little more than a dirt track. Other units were tackling the main roads. We saw very little. The main attack force was staging to the north. From the city itself came sporadic gunfire – insurgents staging live-fire exercises.

Time ticked by, hot and slow beneath that burning sun.

Late afternoon.

"Heads up!" Chas Nixon shouted.

Men reached for their guns, stood ready. I held my SA80 at port-arms, ready to rock.

A group of people were coming down the desert road. Four women, two girls. Two men in their seventies. A man of about forty, holding the younger girl in his arms. A man in his twenties. Two boys in their teens.

I stepped forward, held up a hand. "Ads?"

Ads was our translator, a scared young local man. We called him Ads because it was all we could pronounce of his name.

The group stopped.

The man holding the child spoke. He looked tired. Blood on his hands and face.

"He says they want no trouble. They just want to leave the city before the attack starts."

"Ask him where the blood came from." It was a delaying tactic.

I had my orders.

Ads spoke with the man. "It's from his brother. He was hit by sniper fire."

"Insurgent?" asked Chas.

"Ours."

"No. I mean, was his brother one of them?"

"He says no. They were trying to get out, that's all."

It didn't matter. "The women and girls can go through."

Ads translated. The father looked from his family to us. He spoke again. His voice had risen. Chas stepped back, lifting his rifle. The older girl – about fifteen – screamed. The father shouted over her. Ads was still trying to talk to him. One of the women moaned. Another seemed to be praying.

Ads turned to me. "He says they're not insurgents."

"We've got our orders. Turn them back. The women can go through. Not the men. That's final. No negotiation, alright? You want to debate it, talk to whoever the fuck's in charge."

Chas glanced at me.

The strain was showing. Who the fuck *was* in charge? What

the fuck were we doing there? None of us seemed to know any-more. But here we were.

Ads stared back at me. What did he want me to do?

Of course, I knew. He wanted me to act like a man with a mind of my own. With some measure of fucking humanity in me. He wanted me to say *fuck my orders*. He wanted me to say *stand down, lads*. He wanted me to say *let them through*.

But I didn't.

Big soldier-boy, with his big gun, and a fucking coward under it all. Not even the guts to stand up to something a blind man could see was wrong.

I was a coward; Ads and the civilians had exposed it. And I hated the whole fucking crew of them for doing it.

I shoved him back towards the roadblock. "*Tell him.*"

Ads started talking. The father shouted over him. The little girl he was holding began to wail.

Finally, he thrust the child into one of the women's arms and turned back to us. Pointed at me. Shouted something.

The men had their rifles shouldered. I waved them back, but kept my own gun ready. "What's he saying?"

"He says..."

"What?"

Ads looked back at me. "He says you're sentencing them to death."

I moved closer to the barricade.

"He says if you're going to kill them, do it yourself. Get it over with. It'll be quicker."

The man was shouting the same phrase over and over. He had a beard, dark hair to his shoulders. Western dress – white shirt, jacket, trousers. No tie. The children were all fucking wailing now.

Later, Ads told me the man had been shouting *Do it. Do it. Just do it.*

The man reached out and shoved me.

"Tell him to fucking cut that out."

The man shoved me again.

"Ads!"

I jabbed the rifle towards the man.

He tried to knock the barrel aside.

I pulled the trigger.

A high velocity rifle bullet, fired at that range, let me tell you:

Going in, it makes a small, very neat hole.

The hole it makes going out is a different story.

Blood hit my face and hands, sprinkled my uniform. Blowback from the entry wound in the man's chest.

Blood sprayed out of his back, splashed the women, the children, as he fell and lay still.

One of the old men, behind him, screamed and fell too. The bullet had shattered his upper right arm. Must've hit the brachial artery; blood hosed out across the dusty road.

Screaming.

So much fucking screaming.

The teenage girl, the little boy – they fell on the body. The girl screaming, over and over: *Baba, baba.*

Daddy. Daddy.

Rifles were up and pointed, a hairsbreadth from cutting loose.

One of the older women – the man's wife, I was guessing, the man's widow – she was screaming at us. Ads didn't need to translate. I could guess.

Bastards. Cowards. Murderers.

Nothing I wasn't already calling myself.

The old man went into convulsions. I shouted to the section medic who ran to him, fending off blows from the women and the younger men.

Some tiny piece of mercy.

Too little, too late.

The old man died too. Shock and blood loss.

Desert spread out each side of the road. Scrub trying to hold the sand together. A crosswind blew plumes of sand across the road. It clung to the blood, soaked and blotted it. Crumbs of it clung to the dead faces of the men I'd killed. And to the blood on my face and hands.

The report said *suspected insurgents*. The report cleared me.

But I'd know. I'd always know.

How long listening to the women scream at me? How long wanting to shoot them, or myself?

But it ended.

They picked up their dead and walked back towards the city. All of them. A Muslim has to be buried within twenty-four hours.

They walked away down the road. None of them looked back. The sand plumes blew back and forth, obscuring them.

I was screaming after them, screaming at Ads that the women could go through.

Ads did as he was told. He shouted after them. But if they heard, they gave no sign.

One turned back and looked. Just once.

It was the older girl. Her face was blanched and streaked with tears. Hatred I could have borne. But all I saw was grief, and mute incomprehension.

She turned away and followed her family.

When she was older, she would have been beautiful.

If she'd lived.

The rumours of civilian massacres came out later, of course. And I saw with my own eyes the white phosphorous dropped on the town.

Estimated civilian casualties: 6,000.

Piss-pathetic by the standards of the flood and what's come after, I'm sure. But I'm guessing the population's much smaller by now. So it'll probably sound as bad as it deserves to.

I can't be sure they died. I only went into the city once, after the attack. I saw the shattered houses. The bodies piled up in the streets. The burned ones, bodies half-turned to ash, skin hanging off – the skin of the hands hanging down like gloves.

I couldn't speak of what I'd done. Not even to my wife. Especially not Jeannie. I couldn't bear to take comfort from her. I could *not*.

I had no right to it, not anymore.

She tried to stay the course. The drinking. The depression. The outbursts of violence and rage.

But one day I came home and found her gone.

No more than I deserved.

So now you know.

Pretty much done now

Dawn is breaking. I'm inside the farmhouse at the foot of Pendle Hill, finishing off. Just a matter of time now befo

"Sarge! Sarge!"

Fuck, I think, and put down the pen. Parkes, bursting into the room. "What is it?"

"We've raised Windhoven on the radio, Sarge."

"Fucking brilliant." I'm on my feet, energised. "Where?"

"Chinook, Sarge."

"Let's go."

On board – Hendry, hunched over the comms.

A woman's voice crackling out of the speaker. "Windhoven to Osprey. Osprey, this is Windhoven."

Hendry leans forward. "Osprey here."

"Who am I speaking to?"

"Flying Officer Hendry, ma'am. Also Sergeant McTarn – he's the ground commander here –"

"I know who McTarn is." Christ, my reputation travelled.

"– and Private Parkes." Which sounded too much like a bad joke.

"This is Captain Bowman. Where's Squadron Leader Tidyman?"

Hendry looks at me. "Killed in action, ma'am."

"Christ. What's your status?"

"Still on the ground at Pendle, with the surviving ground force and about a hundred civilians. Been trying to contact you for a while now."

"I was wondering where you'd got to."

"The Squadron Leader hadn't briefed us on your location. The paperwork was lost with him. Captain, can you give us your co-ordinates? We're under siege and need an evac."

"Not much point, I'm afraid."

A cold finger up my arse. "Ma'am?"

"Started showing up about a fortnight ago. Didn't do anything at first. Just wandering around. We shot a few. But then more turned up. We've got virtually the entire former population of the Thames Valley here right now."

"What's your status, ma'am?"

"Not good, Hendry, not good at all. Attack began in earnest day before yesterday. They've managed to breach the under-ground base, overrun the aircraft bays so we can't get out. We've been holding them off, but..."

She doesn't say more; just lets the hiss of static do that for her. Through it, I can hear distant gunfire.

"Can you get to the surface, Captain? We could fly in, hit them on the ground. At least give some of you the chance to –"

"Negative. We can't hold them. We're running low on ammu-nition, and they just keep coming. Soon, we'll be fighting them hand to hand. We'd be long gone by the time you got here. Be-sides, sounds like you have problems of your own."

"You know what they say, Captain; it's grim up north."

Bowman laughs. There's an ugly, jagged edge to it. "Any luck raising your regional control centre?"

"None, ma'am."

"Us neither. My guess is they've either gone under already or are in the same boat as us. I'm afraid you're on your own, Hen-dry. Take what action you see fit."

"Copy, ma'am."

A pause; muffled voices in the background. "I'm afraid that'll have to be it. They're breaking through. Must dash."

"God be with you, ma'am." I never pegged Hendry as religious. Then again, I never asked.

"You too, Hendry. Windhoven out."

The line goes dead.

"Sarge? They're moving."

This is it. This is it. The fuck do I do now? Chas?

I've got your back, Robbie. You need help, you got me. Alright?

I need help, Chas. Need it fucking now. Where are you? Where?

"Sarge?"

"Move..." *Focus, Robbie, focus.* "Move 'em out, Parkes."

"Yes, Sarge."

So, then. It's here. At last.

Outside, other survivors huddle under tarps. Those we've the space for – the women, the children – they're crammed into the farmhouse, or Stiles' caravan. The rest are out there, under whatever shelter we can improvise.

We won't need it much longer anyway.

The P226 at my hip. The SA80 at my side. Chambering a round as I go. The pages folded in a plastic bag, tucked under my arm.

Katja in the field, huddled under tarps with the rest. She gave up her billet for someone she thought needed it more.

You should have been in charge. Not me.

I walk to her. She stands. I give her the papers. We don't speak. There is nothing to say.

Stiles appears at the caravan door. He's pale. He half-raises a hand to me, in some kind of salute. But I'm already running.

On the side facing Barley, we found a couple of farmhouses – one a working farm, the other converted into a residence – made into an open space by a dirt road crossing them.

They stand just below a ridge of high ground with the footpath cutting down it. On the left side of it is a field ringed with a solid drystone wall, where we've taken up positions. We've got Gimpys, Minimis, rifles, Molotovs, a few grenades. On the right is a small, pointed plateau, where we've set up a Gimpy and a couple of riflemen.

The fields, meadows and other open ground below us are all as heavily mined as we were able to manage, enough that any of them advancing over the open terrain will be blown to fuck. Parkes is down there with Neil and Steve. The fougasses have to be detonated manually. That's their job. Their orders are to wait till the nightmares are in range, blow the charges and run.

If we can use the fougasses to force the nightmares onto the footpaths – like the one leading up to the farmhouses and the space between them – they'll pour out into what we'll be able to turn into a perfect killing zone.

In the farmhouses, there's Levene and a few of the better local rifle shots, to whittle the odds down as they come up the path.

It'll work as long as the fougasses keep them to the paths. Or until they realise there'll be no further explosions once the mines are blown; when that happens, they'll start using the open ground again, and our last advantage will be gone. All we can do then is hold position as long as we can.

I crouch behind the drystone wall. I can feel my hands shaking. *Fuck.*

Chas, pal, I need you here now.

Mleczko's good. But it just isn't the same.

He isn't Chas.

Even if we *can* get the Chinook up again, what then? A stay of execution? In the long run, the result's the same. We all die. Nothing lasts. No-one gets away. One by one, we all fall down.

The nightmares move so slowly – except when they come at you in those short, deadly, bursts – it's easy to believe you can outwit them, outrun them. But they're untiring, relentless. And sooner or later, you have to stop.

For nearly a minute, I just crouch there, terrified someone'll ask me for an order. Hopelessness is a huge fucking weight, crushing me so flat I can hardly breathe.

Come off it, Jock. You've got a job to do. Deal with each problem as it comes. Worry about this attack, then worry about the next one. Worry about getting the chopper off the ground again, then worry about where you're gonna go. And for fuck sake, Jock, stop fucking snivelling.

"*Sergeant* Jock to you, grotbag."

"Sarge?" Mleczko, blinking.

"Noth –"

And that's when the fougasses go off like a fucking cannon-ade.

Yelps, a couple of whoops. I peer over the wall. Plumes of smoke rising. Flames crackling further down the slope.

Levene's voice, crackling out of the communicator. "It's hitting the bastards, Sarge. Got to have taken out hundreds of them."

"Good. And the rest?"

"Hang on..." A tinge of excitement in the voice. For Levene, that's saying a lot. "Yes. They're taking the footpath. I can see them at it, Sarge. They're heading our way."

"OK." I raise my voice. "Everybody, weapons ready. Company's coming. Levene?"

"Sarge?"

"Hold fire. Let 'em get in close."

"How close do you want 'em?"

"Wait till they start entering the killing zone. Then hit the ones who're still coming in. Hit them too early, they might pull back. I want this to fucking *count*."

"Copy, Sarge. Just keep them out of here, OK?"

"We'll cover you, Levene. Just make sure you do the same for us."

"Copy that, Sarge."

We can hear them coming now. The tramping squish of feet in mud. The distant hissing sounds. I flex my hands on the SA80.

And the smell. The thick ripe stench of the dead. Like a finger touching the back of my throat. I gag, spit out bile. More coughing and retching further down the line.

"Our guests have arrived, Sarge."

No shit. "Everyone stand ready, but hold fire until my command. I'll fucking feed you to the bastards myself if you fire early. Clear?"

"Sarge," comes the echo down the line, even from the civvies. There isn't really that much of a line between us and them now. We're all in the same boat. And it's sinking.

"Wait for it... wait for it..."

Sighting over the wall. The green-stained bodies shuffling forward. Yawning faces, blackened teeth. Eyes glowing with green torment, as they close in with outstretched, grasping hands...

Closer... closer...

"Fire!"

I shout orders, point. But everything seems too slow, not quite in step. It's not them. It's me. I'm out of sync. Not fast enough.

Not now. Stay together. Focus. *Focus!*

They go down quickly. They don't fall back. They keep coming. Till they're all cut down.

There'll be more of them soon.

"Sarge! Sarge!" Parkes.

"Parkes, go ahead."

"They're back on the open ground. There's something different... oh shit."

"What?"

"Sarge, you're not gonna believe this."

"What is it, Parkes?"

"God almighty, there's gotta be thousands, but –"

"Spit it out!"

"They're spread out in groups of fifty or so. Big gaps between them. The fougasses'll hardly dent it."

"Looks like they mean business this time."

"What it looks like, Sarge."

"OK. Blow the remaining charges and get back here. Levene?"

"Sarge."

"Cover their retreat, then get back to the bastards on the footpaths. Fire at will. Let's see how far we can whittle them down." I raise my voice to the others. "All riflemen move forward. Get into a position where you can see the enemy. Take your time. Acquire your target. Be sure of your shot. And drop the fuckers. Make every bullet count. Every one we kill now is one less to deal with at close quarters."

"Like when they get here, you mean, Sarge?" Mleczko murmurs.

"Bang on, Mleczko."

The fougasses going off. Levene's rifles start firing seconds later. I move forward into the yard of the working farmhouse, sighting down on the nightmares entering the wide-open meadow below.

Parkes and the others are running. The nightmares are close behind though, closer than they should be. Some of them break into runs. One leaps on Neil's back and he goes down. Others falling on him. Neil screaming.

I aim, look through the sight. A face swims into focus. I centre the tip of the blade in the Trilux sight between its eyes. Squeeze the trigger. It drops.

Good shot. Now do it again. But even with that slow, shuffling pace, how long before they get here? And if they run...

Fire. Fire again.

Parkes and Neil scrambling up the meadow and into the farmyard.

And then –

"They're running!"

"Fuck!" Yelling into the communicator. "Levene, get out of there now! Fall back, we are falling back!"

I unpin first one, then the other of the grenades I still hold – one white phosphorous, one frag – and overarm them both into the advancing horde, then run as the explosions ring out behind.

Diving over the drystone wall. Aiming over as the nightmares come crawling up into the farmyard, onto the footpath – fucking everywhere –

Focus!

"Covering fire!"

The MGs chattering. Levene and the others pour out of the buildings. Two, from the farmhouse on the right, aren't fast enough. The nightmares pull them down. Mleczko running forward, firing from the hip, lobbing a grenade.

"Mleczko!"

An explosion. Mleczko ducking, the others running past him. Levene hanging back, firing at the nightmares, a rearguard –

Going after them. "Get back here, the fucking pair of you!"

Levene's trips, he falls. Half back on his feet when one hits him in a flying tackle. Two, three, four more hurl themselves onto him, grabbing, tearing. He screams.

"Levene!" Mleczko, turning back.

"You can't do anything! Get behind the wall! Hold the line!"

I cover him as he goes. Nightmares closing in. I shoot one in the forehead. Then another. And another.

I realise I'm laughing.

I realise I'm going to die. Here, today, now.

I realise it's what I've wanted for a long time.

The girl turning back, the last look on her face as she goes.

For a second I see her, and lower the gun.

For a second, it's her father, and I don't shoot. And it never happened. And I'm redeemed.

And then I realise it isn't her or him at all, it's a nightmare. It looks a little like the man I shot. Tubby, a beard, shoulder-length hair. What's left of it.

Its eyes, burning.

I point the gun.

I pull the trigger.

Click.

Fuck.

It jumps.

I'm drawing the P226, but it's on me, teeth going for my throat. I get my left hand under its chin as we hit the ground. Its jaws snap, its lips brush my cheek – but not its teeth. Pushing it away from me, pulling the Sig-Sauer free to kill it. Thinking: *Lucky bastard, McTarn –*

Still thinking how lucky when it twists its head and bites three fingers off my left hand.

Dark. Thick dull throb of pain in my hand.

My hand.

"Fuck!"

"Easy, Sarge." Hassan, pushing me back down on an improvised pallet bed. The ceiling above me. Spinning. I feel drunk.

"Alright. Alright. Get off." I put a hand to my forehead. It burns.

Gunfire. Close to.

"Where?" I bat Hassan's hand aside and sit up. My head and stomach roll.

"Sarge, take it easy."

"Bollocks." More gunshots. "Bastard things are right on top of us." I look at him. "Aren't they?"

He nods.

"What happened?"

He drops his gaze. "Mleczko killed your attacker, carried you back."

I remembered Levene. "I told the little bugger to leave the wounded. Still, if he knows when to disobey an order..."

Your attacker.

"Shit!"

"Take it easy, Sarge."

"Stop fucking saying that! Fucker bit half my hand off." I swallow hard. Nothing seems quite real. "I'm gonna become one of them. Aren't I?"

"You might have a chance."

"What do you mea..." I close my eyes and raise my hands to my face, but only one set of fingers touches it.

There is a swaddled stump where my left hand was. I hold it up, to be sure he's not just bound the undamaged fingers and thumb in tight. No. It's gone.

I let out a laugh that sounds odd and weak and strange to my own ears.

"Sarge..." Hassan, reaching for a needle.

"No!" I fend him off. "No time." I get off the table. My legs wobble. No. *Stand straight.* I'm in my underwear. "Get my fucking combats."

"Sergeant, you've just had surgery."

"I was bitten, Hassan. I'm fucked."

"We may have cut the infected tissue away in time. You might have a chance."

"Get me whatever pills and shots you need to keep me on my feet. I'm no fucking good to anyone in here. So do as you told. I'm giving you a fucking order."

Christ. I sound like Tidyman.

It hasn't worked. I can feel it. A terrible burning pain, in the stump of my wrist. Nausea, a pounding headache. I walk on.

Behind me there's the Hill, the farmhouse, Stiles' meadow. In front of me, another meadow, leading down to drystone walls and a gate. The defenders spread out along the wall. Mleczko at the gate, shouting orders.

Beyond the gate, down the path, they're coming in small, scattered groups.

Their eyes are glowing green.

Green like the sea. Like the deep sea.

I can hear, from far off, over the shouts and gunfire, the lapping of sea on the shore.

I reach the gate. Slump against it. Mleczko jumps, stares at me. "Sarge!"

"Mleczko. What's the situation?"

He looks older than before. Command'll do that. "They marched more of the fuckers up slower, while we were still fighting that first lot, so then they could go flat out. Full speed, you know? They were coming in on all fronts. Had to fall back, but soon as we got one defensive line, they were on top of us again. In the end, we didn't have anywhere else to go. So here we are." He rubs his face. "Lost a lot of people. Lot of kit, too."

"What we got left?"

"Still OK for rifles. Few Minimis, couple of Gimpys... pretty much it."

"Then we make them count." I look down the lane. There don't seem to be many of them. A few dozen, hanging back. They drop one by one as the bullets whine and crack out. "Doesn't look like much of an army."

"Not compared to what they were hitting us with before."

Green eyes glow down the path. I stare into them; they expand and swallow me up.

The sound of a huge ocean. Waves. But there's something else. Listen. *Listen.* I can hear voices. Human voices.

The refugees, back in the meadow...

No. Not them. This is different. I'm not even hearing the gun-shots anymore. I can only hear the sea. And the voices.

They're crying out. I hear men and women. Children too. Crying for mercy, for release. In rage, at lives cut short so soon.

The gnawing pain in the stump of my wrist, the thump of my heart squeezing new pain through my body. I can feel it spread-ing. They've slowed it down. But once it takes hold, there's no shifting it.

Mleczko's mouth moving. Saying something. But I can't hear. And now all I can really see, all that really matters, are those glowing green eyes.

And the light flickers and fades and contracts – shrinks from a glow filling the whole world to two dying bulbs, the eyes of a nightmare falling forward as it dies.

"Sarge? Sarge?"

I turn back to Mleczko. "Alright. Here's what you do. Hendry made any progress with the Chinook?"

"If he had we'd be airborne by now, Sarge. And I don't reckon he's got long to pull one out of the hat."

"What d'you mean?"

"I think I know why they're holding off."

I picked the right man for the job, because I think I know too. "They're going to wait till dark."

"Yeah. In my eyes, that's what they're gonna do. Keep throwing cannon fodder at us, tire us out, use our ammo up. But once it's dark and we can't see the fuckers, they'll rush us. The lot of them. And they won't stop."

My forehead's burning. Rain hitting it. "Right. Here's what you do. Start picking people for evac. Find out off what's the maxi-mum the Chinook'll carry. You're gonna have to pick who goes and who stays. Tell Hendry if the fucking thing's not ready to fly by dark I'll feed him to the nightmares myself."

Mleczko glances down the footpath. "What about..."

"I'll handle it here." He opens his mouth. "None of your lip. I'm not dead yet. Get your arse in gear."

I draw the Sig-Sauer and look down the lane, thumb on the hammer.

Dusk. The sky growing dim. A dulled sunset seeping through the clouds. Blood soaking through a bandage.

No word on the chopper. It was always a long shot.

They're gathering down the road. Clusters of tiny lights.

I've a splitting headache. The stump of my wrist throbs. Not just the stump, in fact. My whole forearm, now. The bandages are wet. Something seeping through.

Hassan gave me pills. Morphine and codeine. I dry-swallow two, think *fuck it* and down a third. Probably not a good idea for a man with a gun, but fuck it all over again. We left proper procedure behind a long time ago.

The lights moving. Shuffling forward. I can hear the sea again. Growing louder. The voices. Screaming. Moaning. Sobbing. Wailing.

Footsteps, coming up behind me.

"Mleczko? Hendry got that fucking chopper fixed yet?"

"No."

And it's not Mleczko, either. It's Katja.

She comes to stand beside me, watches the gathering mass below us. "Are you alright?" She shakes her head. "Stupid question."

There's someone else with her. His silhouette looks strange. Fucking drugs. I'm dizzy, weak. When the nightmares come I won't stand a chance. How much of them lingers on? Some fragment, some flicker of consciousness? I remember the empty farmhouse, the father staring up at his old home. The thought of being aware as my body kills and eats people I know...

Kills and eats Katja.

But it's not the drugs. It's...

"Stiles?"

"Yes." He looks very calm. Katja isn't looking at him.

He's wearing a wetsuit. An aqualung. A diving mask pushed up on his forehead. Boots, but a pair of flippers hang from his belt.

"What the hell?"

"He's going to get himself killed." Stiles reaches out and touches her arm; she pulls it away.

"Katja, we've talked about this. I have to try. It's the only chance."

"What is?" I demand.

"This."

He climbs over the gate before I can stop him, before I even realise what he's doing. "Stiles, for fuck sake –" I'm scrambling forward, to go after him. Down the road, the nightmares have started shambling forward.

But Katja stops me. She's crying. "No," she says. "Let him go."

I stop and stare. Confused? That's not the word for it. She turns and goes to the gate. He looks down the path at the nightmares.

"You're sure?" Her voice is tiny. Almost a child's.

"No," he says. "But I've got to try."

He turns back. They come together and kiss. I have to look away. Not out of jealousy. I'm past that now.

"I love you," I hear him whisper, and her whisper it back.

When I turn back, he's walking down the footpath. The nightmares have stopped their advance. They just stand and watch him, with their glowing eyes, in the deepening gloom.

Stiles reaches them and stops. For a frozen second, it's just them, contemplating each other.

The eyes of the nightmares in front of him begin to pulse, just like the ones back at the army base did. Stiles sways, nearly falls, but doesn't.

The pulsing stops, and –

The nightmares are parting. Stepping aside to leave a clear path. Stiles starts walking. They turn their heads and watch him go. Then they turn back to watch us.

It's like a ripple effect, extending as far down as I can see, as he goes. Until he's out of sight.

"What the fuck?" I say again. I tear my gaze from the nightmares and stare at Katja. "What the fuck is going on?"

"They want him," she says. "They always have."

"What?"

"His notes. Didn't you read them? It's all in there."

"What the fuck's he trying to do?"

"Save us all," she says.

"He's..." I remember the wetsuit, the equipment. "He's going diving?"

She nods.

"But I thought he couldn't. I thought he'd die if..."

She nods again. Then she turns and walks back the way she came.

I turn and stare out at the nightmares. They stand and watch us. Eyes glowing. As the darkness deepens.

A couple of minutes pass. I lean on the gate, shivering in the chill of the rain even as I welcome it falling on my burning forehead. A footfall behind me.

"Ged."

"Lad." He leans on the gate too, on folded arms. A farmer, surveying his land. The SPAS-12 slung across his back. "How you doing, lad?"

"How do you fucking think?" He doesn't answer. "Sorry."

Smiling slightly, he waves it away.

"I'm dying," I say at last.

"Aren't we all?"

And I have to laugh.

Ged chuckles as well. "So, what you planning to do, lad?"

"I'll stop here," I say. "This is it for me. Even if we get the Chinook airborne again, I'm fucked." I hold up the bandaged stump. Another sick, fevery shudder passes through me. "So I might as well go out on my own two legs, eh?"

Ged nods. "Good enough. If you've no objection, I'll join you."

I turn and stare at him. "Are you mad?"

He just looks at me.

"Ged, I'm not gonna be falling back, did you hear me?"

"I know the score, lad. They'll not get that chopper airborne again. We both know it. This is it for us all now. Barring miracles."

"Believe in them?"

"Oh, miracles happen." A smile softens his face. "My missus saying yes when I asked her to marry me, that were a miracle alright. And our Cl..." he trails off, the smile gone.

"I'm not holding my breath for any tonight."

"Nor I. If I've got to die, I'll do it here. This far and no farther, all of that. I've run enough from them bastards, killed my Clare."

There nothing to say to that. "Alright," I say. "I'd be honoured."

"I know, lad."

"Just one thing, Ged?"

"What's that?"

"Can you stop calling me 'lad'? My name's Robert."

"Alright then, lad. Robert it is."

The sun is nearly gone.

And so am I.

I can barely stand. The pain and the sickness are almost too much to bear. The stump of my hand is like a second heart, pumping poison. With Mleczko's help and a roll of gaffa tape, I've strapped the hatchet to the stump of my wrist. Makes it hurt all the worse, but at least I can do some damage.

My hand shakes. I'm sweating like a pig. When I wipe it away, my forehead's burning like hot coals.

They're just shadows now. Shadows with eyes. Their outlines blur and break up as the light fails.

A full clip in the P226. No spares. How the fuck am I supposed to reload? I have an SA80 too – propping it on the gate, I can fire one-handed.

Mleczko's on one side of me. Ged and Katja on the other. Others spread out behind the walls.

In the camp behind us, people are crying. Someone praying. A few ragged voices rise in a song. A hymn, a folk-song, or just something that was in the charts a few weeks ago. I can't make it out. But I can hear the sea. Louder and louder, trying to drown everything else out.

The sea, and the voices.

why me why me? i didn't want to die
no no no my baby my baby
bastards you bastards
for being alive
dear father in heaven

pater noster pater noster
hail mary full of grace,
the lord is with thee, blessed art thou amongst women, blessed is
the fruit of thy womb jesus christ, holy mary mother of god pray
for us poor sinners now and at the hour of hour of our death
want to live want to live want to live

no not like this not to die like this not
like this not like this

"Fuck," says Mleczko. "Here they come."

Down the road, the forest of glowing eyes is moving.

bastards bastards want to live why me and not you?
will live will live will live again kill you kill you KILL YOU
EAT EAT EAT EAT EAT

Like a tide.

A tide of souls.

Rising. Gathering. And then the wave breaks.

"Open fire!"

The GPMGs and Minimis sweep the advancing ranks. But the next wave just scramble over the fallen bodies. And that means you've got to aim up to hit them in the head. And the twilight makes accurate firing harder and harder with an automatic weapon.

Aim and fire. Aim and fire. They keep falling. But they keep coming too.

This is it. No matter how hard we hit them, they won't fall back this time.

Then they burst into a jerky, scrambling run. They're not coming direct for me. They're focusing in, closing on specific points, choosing their targets.

They're going for the machine guns.

Faces leap out, rotten. Aim and fire. Aim and fire.

Not one of you yet, you bastards, not one of you yet.

The answer is a furious wave that crashes on a sea wall. Their voices are screaming in rage. All the different voices, blending in and out. Now and again one voice leaps out. But it's a whole. An organ note. Sounding together. One voice. I stop shooting as I realise that. One voice blended out of many –

"Sarge!"

And if I listen to it closely I can hear what it's trying to say.

"Sarge!"

What?

"Robert!"

Katja's voice. Maybe the only one that could snap me out of this. As the wave of the dead crashes against the gate.

Firing. Bodies dropping. A nightmare trying to climb over, then jerking, falling past me, its skull shattered. They stumble back, bracing against the tidal force of the multitudes behind them. Hurling themselves forward again.

Screaming from further down, on either side. They've reached the machine guns, grabbing the barrels and dragging them down, leaping over the walls to fall upon the gunners. The other defenders firing into them, but it's not enough, never enough.

"Robert!"

Firing out the SA80, letting it fall –

"Back!"

They crash against the gate. I can hear it cracking, buckling.

"Back!" Mleczko, running. They're all running.

Except me. Me and Ged. Back a few paces to stand our ground.

Katja wrenching at my arm. "Robert! Robert!"

"No." My voice sounds thick and slurred. "Go. Go." I don't look at her. Can't. What must my face look like now? So sick, so sick. I'm full of it now, the sickness. The infection. All I can hear in my ears is the ocean's pounding roar. I can barely hear her voice.

Holy Mary mother of God, pray for us poor sinners now and at the hour of our death.

Ha. Funny, an old bluenose coming out with that at the last.

"Go on, lass," I heard Ged say.

"Go," I tell her. "We'll cover you."

I can't hear her reply, if she has one. But I feel the touch of her lips, a last kiss, on my cheek.

And then me and Ged are alone and the gate's giving way. They burst through and I raise the gun and aim on the first one and I pull the trigger and its head snaps back. And I aim again and...

We back away as they swarm through and over the gate, Ged still thumbing the last few shells into the SPAS-12, then firing, firing, firing.

Raising the Sig-Sauer, shoot - a nightmare close in - I swing at it, smash its skull with the hatchet taped to my wrist, shoot again.

Shoot and strike, shoot and strike.

The axe gone, buried in another nightmare's head, the bone locking round the blade, pulling me off-balance, the haft breaking. A nightmare diving on me; firing upwards, into its gaping mouth. Somehow I manage to stand.

The shotgun empty; Ged using it as a club, smashing skull after skull.

But there are so many of them. Too many. And then they're on him. He goes down, thrashing and fighting, and I hear a scream torn from his lips.

I aim and fire on him, hitting him in the head. He falls and I'm screaming now, firing into the face of another nightmare, and then another, and -

The P226's slide locks back. Empty.

Fuck.

They stop and stare, facing me.

I throw the gun aside. Can still fight. I grab at the ground. Fumble for a chunk of rock as they shamble towards me.

But my legs give way and I collapse as they gather round me with their burning eyes.

I grip the rock, somehow manage to lift it a few inches off the ground with an arm as weak as an old man's.

"Come on, then," I say, then shout up at them. "*Come on!*"

Ged rises, torn and ravaged, missing chunks of flesh and his eyes glowing, but still – just about – recognisable. And stumbles off after the rest.

A wave of sickness and shivering, a terrible weakness. I feel my bowels and bladder fail. A rush of shame, and then –

Screaming after them, but I can't even hear my own voice now it's so fucking loud, the sea, the voices

flesh and blood, flesh and bone –

> *make us whole*

> *again*

> *let us live don't want to die let us live*

rage rage rage against the dying of the light, against those still drawing

> *unearned breath on land*

> *leaving us down here in the darkness*

down here in the darkness cold and alone

> *alone*

> *ALONE*

– *drowning me out, eclipsing me, eclipsing –*

Who? What's my name?

WHAT'S MY FUCKING NAME?

I scream – soundlessly to my own ears ––and fall back to the earth. Too weak now. And they just keep coming on, stepping over or around me,

> *me,*

> *me,*

Me, Robbie McTarn

ROBBIE MCTARN MY NAME IS ROBBIE MCTARN

And I realise why as the sickness rises one last time like a wave and the pain washes through my body.

My heart is hammering hammering hammering, fastfastfaster, and I'm burning up, oh god I'm burning up.

And then the thundering jackhammer rhythm of my heart is all I can hear, even the ocean is gone and I hear the rhythm thunder thunder thunder

And skip,

falter,

> Stutter erratically
> and then,
> finally,

> it stops.

And I can't move my eyes, can't look beyond what's in front of me as I lie dying, dying, DEAD upon the dull earth, as dead men and women stagger past me, mind screaming, beating the bone walls of its cage as it dies from lack of oxygen, the lights going out for good.

Things slipping away from me. My dad, something about my dad... did I love or hate him? Can't remember now.

I want to scream out in rage at it. Scream out in the fear I feel. But can't.

All I can hear are the screams I can't utter.

The screams others are uttering for me.

rage rage rage

> *oh god no not me not like this*

And I'm falling, crashing down, plunging through a deep dark endless ocean, glowing green eyes and rotting hands and faces reaching out for me.

Screams and voices all around me. And they're all my own.

I can't remember my name anymore.

Vaguely I realise my limbs are moving but it's not me moving them, that this is the last awareness of my body I shall have. I can't remember can't remember anything I'm just the tiniest little spark of consciousness and all that is left is my rage and my terror to swell the waters of this ocean and I feel myself fading and when this is done I will not exist at all anym

PART THREE

Storm Surge – Fathom Five

...how is it
That this lives in thy mind? What seest thou else
In the dark and backward abysm of time?

Shakespeare, *The Tempest*, Act I, Scene ii

CHAPTER NINETEEN

Stiles

My air hose. That was where it started. I was exploring a wreck off the north-west Scottish coast, and I snagged it on a sharp edge of some kind. I didn't see what.

The hose snapped.

Bubbles everywhere. Silt billowing in the water as I scrabbled for a way out of the wreck. Banging into walls, practically blinded.

My life didn't flash before my eyes. Instead I thought about the life I *wasn't* going to live. I was thirty-one, with a PhD, and I spent my time, one way or the other, immersed in the sea. Pun intended. But I had a shopping list of other plans: marriage, kids, a house –

All going now in this storm of bubbles and silt. This stupid death. Stupid accident. *Stupid.* A pratfall, almost.

Not like this. Not like this.

Trying to grab the air-hose, feeling it flail away, pushed out by the jet of air. Bruising and slashing my arms and legs on the rusted, barnacled hull...

And then I was in open water.

It's blurred here, but I remember:

Holding breath. Lungs bursting. The air-hose, couldn't find the air-hose, hands scrabbling at the water for the FUCKING AIR-HOSE –

Blue water

    Rocks and sand, the sandy bottoms of the ocean

Up above

  above, light,

     coming down through the water

      Long away above.

        No time,

     no time

striking up for it.

    too deep, too deep – must decompress, acclimatise

But no time.

Swimming up towards the light.

And –

Look at a bottle of Pepsi, Coke, Irn Bru if you like. Whatever you prefer. An unopened bottle. It's not fizzy, is it? Not until you break the seal and release the pressure. At high pressures, gas dissolves in liquid. When you dive, when you go deep and stay there, the nitrogen in the air you breathe dissolves in your blood.

Clear so far?

When you surface, you release that pressure. Remember the bottle of Pepsi? Imagine that happening in your blood, lungs, brain, eyes.

Divers working at depth are supposed to resurface slowly. That way the nitrogen is released gradually and without causing any harm. If you surface too fast, the bubbles of nitrogen form inside your body. They can form in the brain, in the jelly of the eye.

Most commonly, they form in your bone joints.

Doctors call this condition decompression sickness or barotrauma, sometimes caisson sickness. Divers call it the bends.

But if you're forced to surface at speed, most ships equipped for diving carry a hyperbaric chamber. This is a sealed structure where gas can be pumped in or released to increase or reduce the pressure. Turn the pressure up, the nitrogen dissolves again. Then release it – *slowly* this time – and it's released gradually, like it should've been in the first place.

Do this, and all should be fine.

But this wasn't a diving ship, just a fishing boat I'd chartered for the day. I was on holiday. I hadn't dived in weeks, and I'd been impatient to get out there. I'd dived before, dozens of times.

Overconfidence. I forgot one tiny, massive detail. The sea is an alien world; we only exist in it on sufferance. One slip can be fatal. And almost was.

Sometimes, even now, I wish it had been.

The pain began as I ascended, and the gas bubbles expanded in my joints. Imagine your wrist trying to push your hand off; imagine your elbow trying to push your forearm down and away. The skin and muscle stops that happening. But the pain...

Lying on the deck of the ship. The agony was beyond anything I'd ever known. The boat turning coastwards – the reek of petrol fumes, the deck vibrating. My nose and mouth full of blood. Frothing. A taste of bitter iron.

"How are you feeling?"

The doctor went by the rather wonderful name of Naomi Scrimgeour. The first sounded very pretty and very gentle – which she was – while the second brought to mind a Viking raider come to remove vital organs with an axe. *Are you on the NHS, sir, or would you like an anaesthetic?* Old joke. Less funny than ever now.

"Fucking awful," I said. She looked down. I felt like a prize arsehole. "Sorry."

But, in truth, the pain was constant. Which she should have known. She was the doctor, after all.

There'd been damage to the nervous system. A common side-effect. Intermittent numbness, shooting pains, weakness down the left side of my body.

"What's the prognosis?" I finally asked.

They'd moved me into a private room, thankfully. The hospital was near the coast. I was never sure where. Outside, I could hear the cry of gulls.

She still wasn't meeting my eyes; her face was flushed. She shuffled the papers in front of her. "Um – well –"

Bad news she wasn't sure how to break. I'd pretty much guessed it already.

"Doctor. I'm sorry. But please tell me." My voice was a gravelly croak. I wondered if that was permanent too. "I respect honesty and directness. I try to deal with others on that basis, and I like the same in return."

If I'd felt like an arsehole before, I felt a prize ponce after delivering *that* one, but she looked up and smiled. Not an entirely comfortable smile, but a smile nonetheless. "Alright, Dr Stiles –"

"Ben."

"Ben." I'd tried to get her to call me by my first name on the half-dozen times we'd previously spoken. Success at last.

Dr Naomi Scrimgeour's glasses were small and neat. So was she, generally. Five or six years younger than me. Minus the glasses, her eyes were blue and tilted up at the corners. Short brown hair with subtle blonde highlights. A face made up of small, neat angles. Tiny bones. A rosebud mouth. Peaches and cream skin. A pimple just above her left eyebrow, a tiny mole above her right cheekbone; tiny flaws that made the rest more real.

Her voice was soft, gentle and low, but the content, as she'd promised, was blunt and to the point. "You've some nerve damage which will impair your dexterity, and will cause random shooting pains. The gas bubbles are trapped in your joints, and there's nothing we can do about them. The pain from them will be constant."

"Permanent?"

She looked back down at the papers in her lap and gave them a meaningless shuffle. "Permanent. There's medication to help you manage the pain. We'll probably prescribe DHC – dihydro-codeine – but there are other options available, up to and including morphine."

"Life expectancy?"

"Reduced."

"By how much?"

"Dr Stiles –"

"Ben."

"It's hard to be exact."

"You must have some idea."

She touched her hair. "A lot depends on how closely you follow the prescribed regime."

"If I do?"

"You'll live longer than you would otherwise."

"How much longer?"

She looked up at me, took a deep breath. Never easy, a job like this. "With luck and good pain management, you could reasonably expect to reach your fifties. Possibly even your sixties."

"My sixties."

"Or longer. It's hard to be exact."

"Appreciated."

"You asked me to be honest."

"I know. And I'm glad you were." I made myself smile, to sweeten the pill. "Just wish the news were better."

"If it's any consolation, so do I."

She was the kind of lady I would have asked out in a moment – attractive, intelligent, not too much confidence. Which hardly paints me in a good light, but I'm afraid it's true. Sara, my last girlfriend, told me that despite the whole 'New Man' act, what I still wanted was a traditional WIFE – Wash, Iron, Fuck, Etcetera. That was why I never lasted with women – I was after someone I could talk with as an intellectual equal, but who'd still be happy to spend her life either in the kitchen or popping out babies. I'd begun thinking I needed to change my ways, if I was to settle down and start a family as I wanted to. But there was still time, another six months, just to sow some wild oats –

But tomorrow, as my old mother used to say, is too late.

"Of course," she said, "they're making new advances in medical technology all the time."

"When they tell you that," I said, "you know you're fucked."

"All I'm saying is, you don't know what might be around the corner in terms of new treatments."

"I know. Just trying to cope with it. Humour, you know?"

She puckered her mouth and pretended to glower. "Is that what you call it?"

She sounded like my dad talking about my taste in 'music' – always in inverted commas as far as he was concerned – so I chuckled. Then silence. She looked down at her notes again.

I glanced at the bedside mirror, as I kept doing out of morbid fascination. I'd been considered good-looking, before. There'd been no serious relationship since Sara left, but no lack of one-night stands or month-long flings.

But the face looking back at me now was lined and creased like an old handkerchief. Gaunt, as well. I'd lost nearly two stone. Sunken, bloodshot eyes. And my hair, once a proud glossy black, was a greasy, tangled mess, at least half of it gone grey or white.

The girls would not come running anymore.

And never mind the pain.

There was something else. I knew the answer, but needed to hear it. "Dr Scrimgeour?"

She smiled at me. "I think you can call me Naomi now, if you want to."

"Thanks. Will I... I mean, is there any prospect... any chance... could, maybe, in the future..." She nodded, eyebrows raised, egging me on. That small, sweet, bright smile in place. Her lips, so red. I was staving off the inevitable here. Just do it, Stiles. "Will I ever be able to dive again?"

Her smile faded. Again, she struggled to meet my eyes. If I

hadn't known her answer already, that would've told me. "As a result of the accident, your blood's ability to dissolve nitrogen has been massively reduced. If you dive again, surfacing would kill you. So the answer is no, you won't. I'm sorry."

I felt my hands come up to cover my face. She spoke, but I didn't hear it. She must have realised that, because after a while, her hand touched my shoulder and squeezed lightly. Then she left.

A piece of rusty iron. A moment's panic. And everything changes. Go into the water with one life, come out with another.

"I've loved the sea since I was a kid. Whenever we went to the beach, my parents could never get me out of the water. I might still be able to swim, at least. If I'm careful. There's that at least."

"Well, that's good anyway."

Dr Whittaker shifted in his chair, an ageing teddy-bear in smart casuals. His office was like him – likeably cluttered, lived-in.

A clock ticked quietly on the wall. I lay back on the couch. Faint sounds of birdsong and distant traffic came from outside. It was early October, but the light filtering through the windows was still warm.

"Have you given any more thought to your future?"

What future? But that would be Negative. That would be A Bad Sign. He'd want more sessions. Fuck that. All I wanted now was just to get away. No more sympathy. No more understanding. Just leave me alone, *everybody*.

"Not as yet. It's hard to say."

"Well, no reason you can't continue your work as a lecturer, once you feel able. You said they were holding your post for you?"

My day job – lecturer in Marine Biology at Manchester University – was purely academic; I'd dived chiefly when I *wanted* to, in my own time. No. No reason I couldn't go back. Except the way the students would look at me, especially the pretty ones I would have flirted with before the summer break... a thousand years ago.

"Yes. Leave of absence. Get myself back in order."

"How long?"

"The next academic year, at least."

"Generous of them."

"Yes." I was reasonably popular, not bad going with half-a-dozen exes on the staff. But I was always good at staying friends. As a lover, I'd never been cruel. Just wanted more than they could give. Or they'd wanted more from me. Depends on who you asked.

"So, a year to recuperate and..." Whittaker spread his hands. "Chart some sort of course. Any ideas as yet?"

"Not for the long-term, not yet. But for now I've taken a lease on a place in Wales. Away from it all. The city's too..."

"Whereabouts in Wales?"

"Barmouth. Gwynedd coast. Nice place."

"The coast."

"Yes."

"Do you feel that's wise?"

"Yes. I do." I heard my voice rise. But I was tired of having my thoughts and motives picked over. Another reason I had to get away.

"Well, if you're sure..."

"I am."

"I'll give you my number, of course. Any time, night or day, if you have a problem."

"Thanks, doctor."

And I meant it, even though I had no intention of calling him.

"Ben?" I stopped at the door. "Is there anything else you want to discuss, before you go?"

I pretended to think it over, then shook my head. "No. Really. Thanks."

A lie, of course.

There were the dreams I kept having. I kept waking from them, sure I could still hear the sound of breaking waves. In the hospital I'd put them down to the sea's proximity, but they'd continued in Manchester.

So had the echo of voices, calling my name.

I told you my memories of the accident are blurred. In particular, what happened right after my hose broke. Bubbles and silt, blind panic, trying not to breathe in...

There were images in the dreams. Of the accident, except that I could see more clearly in the whirling dark. And there were faces in it, coming out of the darkness, out of the water itself.

Faces with eyes that glowed green.

I moved out of my flat in Didsbury village that weekend. Went round the place packing stuff. What to keep, what to throw away.

I took my old diving equipment. Wetsuit, aqualung, flippers and mask. I should have junked it. But somehow I couldn't. It was too final a goodbye.

One of my exes – a sweet, kind-hearted lady called Janet who I really should've appreciated more – drove me down one evening, saw me safely into my new home, pecked me on the cheek and drove home, gracefully turning down my offer of dinner.

Probably just as well.

I stood outside my front door gazing out towards the harbour. It was dark by now, but I could hear the break and hush of the waves. I stood there listening to them for a while, savouring the wind's salt tang, then went inside.

CHAPTER TWENTY

I woke on a cold November morning. When I squinted at the red numerals on the bedside clock, they told me it was actually a cold November afternoon.

I tried turning onto my back, and immediately wished I hadn't. Debilitating pain burst from every joint in my body and washed through me in a sickening wave. My stomach rolled slowly. I moaned and clenched my teeth. It was hard to separate the dull throb and nausea of my hangover from the constant joint pain.

I lay for a while in that particular circle of hell where the pain is prolonged because moving makes it worse. Finally, I grabbed the blister pack on the bedside table and fumbled for the water bottle beside the bed. Praise Jesus, it wasn't empty. I popped two of the waxy tablets into my mouth and washed them down.

I'd had trouble sleeping the night before, so I'd been up till the small hours watching DVDs, fortified with whisky. I hadn't made it to bed till 4.00 am. At least I'd managed that. Falling asleep in a chair left me in worse agony still.

I thought of showering, but it seemed too much like hard work – undressing, staying upright in the cubicle. Sod that. Instead I clung onto the banister rail and limped downstairs for coffee.

By the second cup, the pain was subsiding. The fridge yielded two rashers of questionable-looking bacon and three eggs. I put the bacon under the grill, broke the eggs into the frying pan and hunted down the heel of a loaf. Pepper and brown sauce made the whole lot vaguely edible.

Get out and about, lad. Come on.

It was almost 3.00 PM now. Maybe two hours of daylight left.

Just another day in my new life.

The pain was constant, as forecast, and as prescribed I'd 'managed' it with DHC. Although the lovely Dr Scrimgeour would've had a seizure if she'd known I was replacing it with gin and whisky of an evening. I had days where I'd skip the evening dose of DHC in favour of getting ratarsed instead. Unlike most opioids, alcohol didn't induce constipation.

A range of high, craggy hills called Dinas Oleu overlooked the town – in Welsh, 'the Fortress of Light' – but hill-walking was another pre-accident pleasure I could forget about now. The altitude change would expand the bubbles in my joints further, shifting the pain from 'medium, constant' to 'utter fucking agony.'

I walked every day, as much as possible. With the aid of a stick I got around reasonably well. There was still pain, but I blocked it out as best I could. I wasn't going to be robbed of any more pleasures than I had to be.

In short, I alternated healthy, outdoorsy stuff and exercise with getting thoroughly wrecked. I got by.

But I still had those dreams. Virtually every night unless I drunk myself unconscious.

I went to a couple of shops, replenishing vital supplies and dropping them back off at my digs, then wandered out again. I started at the harbour. Even at that time of year, it was picturesque. Fishing boats bobbing at anchor, Dinas Oleu and Cader

Idris looming above, the iron bridge across the mouth of the estuary. After that I walked down the promenade that cut the harbour off the from the beach. I had to use the top of the sea-wall, because the footpath was long gone, vanished under the piled-up sand.

The prom led to a long, stepped concrete jetty extending half-way across the harbour mouth. Broken mussel shells littered the jetty, dropped or beaten by gulls to smash them open. They crunched underfoot.

I reached the end and limped down the steps. A warning beacon stood at the bottom. I turned my back on the town and harbour till I could only see the steel-grey ocean. The sun was dying behind thick banks of cloud, but a dull red glow burned through and made the waters blaze further out.

The waves were breaking in a soft, lulling rhythm. I closed my eyes and tilted back my chin; the wind rose, blowing my matted, greasy hair back and chilling my face.

Above the sounds of wind and sea, I heard somebody crying out.

I opened my eyes. No-one in sight. A car moving along the coast road, under the hills, away from the town. The sea was empty too. But I could hear a voice. Two voices. Male and female. But not the words. I couldn't tell if the tone was anger or fear.

The wind was moaning. I had to shout over it.

"Hello?" I called out. "*Hello?*"

The wind died, and the voices with it. Waves burst on the sand.

I looked around, still saw nothing.

Carry on.

I didn't feel comfortable on the jetty anymore. Too open, too exposed. Too easy to go in. I knew how the sea could be. A huge predator, waiting for one mistake. I'd forgotten that once; look at me now.

"Well chuck yourself in then you bastard. Finish the job. Why should you be alive when we're not?"

I started, almost overbalanced. The voice was right in my ear.

But no-one was there when I spun around. And that last sentence – it *couldn't* be real. Maybe just my unconscious talking. Not necessarily a sign of madness.

Naomi had warned me that opioids like DHC occasionally caused hallucinations. But I'd been taking the stuff for months now; surely it would've happened sooner?

I walked back along the jetty and came down onto the beach. A ridge of dunes had built up between sea wall and shoreline in recent years, topped with coarse marram grass. I climbed them, as I did more or less daily, and walked towards the shore.

I felt the surf wash around my boots. Touched my fingers to the waters as they lapped round me, then to my lips to taste the salt. Felt the fresh briny smell blow in, the smell of rotten fish and seaweed too. But something rotten doesn't have to smell bad. The smell of autumn is of decay, of leaves rotting and mulching down, but you can't beat a walk in the woods. Not as far as I'm concerned, anyway.

I looked out towards the horizon. I don't know how to describe it. Perhaps... if I said it's like living across the street from someone you once passionately loved. Someone you shared everything with, every thought, every dream. You've slept together. You've seen them naked. You know their body, maybe better than they do. They know yours the same way. You know where and how to touch them, how they like to be kissed. And you'll never see them that way again, never sleep with them. You had that intimacy, but it's been withdrawn. Lost. Gone forever.

"Doesn't have to be," a voice said in my left ear.

No way could this be a hallucination. It was real. But something was wrong with it. Something missing. What?

"It doesn't have to be," the voice repeated. It was a man's. Scottish. "You can go back to her if you want."

I didn't turn around. Couldn't. I didn't understand why. It should've been simple. But I couldn't.

"It's *easy*," said a second voice. It was a woman's. An older woman, forties or fifties, husky and like velvet. "It's where you're happiest, isn't it? So why don't you?"

I didn't answer her either. There was something *wrong* about her voice too. I still didn't know what, but it was there.

"Benjamin?" Jesus Christ, even my mother didn't call me that any longer. "It's very rude to ignore people when they're talking to you. Wasn't this always where you were happiest?"

"Course it was," said the man. "We all know that."

"You loved her, didn't you?" The woman went on. Her voice was caressing and tender. "The ocean. She could take you deeper than any woman ever could. That's the real reason you've never married, isn't it? It's why Sara left."

I could feel them stood behind me. And I did *not* want to turn around, I did *not* want to see their faces. Mustn't. Because now I'd realised what was wrong with their voices. Their lips were so close they must be all but touching my ears, but when they spoke, I couldn't feel any breath.

"Course it was," the woman said. "She knew she'd always be second best. Didn't she?"

"What do you bloody want, boy?" the man asked. "Hobble around like this for however fucking long you've got left, pissed out of your skull so you'll not have to think about it anymore? Cos you're not just drinking to numb the pain, are you? Not the one in your body. No. It's because you can't be in there, isn't it? Can't be inside her like you used to. So are you gonna moon around like a lovesick teenager? Or are you going to be a man and go to her?"

"I can't," I hissed at last.

"But you *can*." The woman's voice was soft as feathers. It went with touching, somehow. I should have been feeling her fingers brushing down my arm, but thank God, I wasn't. "Just put one foot in front of the other. Just walk out into the water, and keep going."

"What?"

"You heard. She'll take you into her. You'll be inside with her always. That's what you want, isn't it?" The woman was murmuring into my ear now. That velvet voice. Despite everything, I felt my cock stir. "Go to her, Benjamin. Go to her."

"No," I said.

"You know you want to."

"*No.*"

"You're just making it harder for yourself in the long run, laddie," said the man, but there was an edge to his voice.

"Leave me alone."

"Go into the water, Benjamin." The woman sounded as though she was speaking through her teeth.

"Why the fuck should you get away?" demanded the man. "How fucking dare you be alive when we're not?"

"Go into the water." The woman, all tenderness gone. Her voice was a cold command. "Go into the water and *drown.*"

And at last whatever paralysis held me broke, and I could move. "Fuck off!" I shouted, and wheeled round, lashing out with my stick at –

Nothing.

Sweat clung to my forehead; my heart thudded against my ribs. The beach was empty.

I didn't look back at the sea, not then. I just stumbled up, back over the dunes in the gathering dusk, scrambling to the steps that led up to Marine Parade, firecrackers of pain going off in my shoulders, knees and arms. *That* was when I looked back.

A last gleam of dull red sunlight glanced off the water; then it dimmed and there was only the empty sea. But just for a moment, I'd seen something else. Only for a split-second, but just long enough to be sure it was there.

There'd been three, four, perhaps five of them, all standing in the shallows of the water. I couldn't see their faces, or even much detail about their bodies; that last dull blaze of sunlight had silhouetted them. But there had been something about them. Something... incomplete. But their hands had been outstretched. Beckoning me. And their eyes glowed green.

CHAPTER TWENTY-ONE

I didn't venture out the following day, or the one after. I could afford not to, as I now had all the relevant provisions – bacon, eggs, bread, milk – and most importantly a couple of bottles or two of cheap Scotch.

By the second night, though, I was climbing the walls and decided to risk one of the local pubs, the Royal. I walked down Marine Road before going over the railway bridge. As I did, there was a brief, soundless flash. I thought it was lightning, but the brief report that followed wasn't thunder. A firework? But it hadn't had the loudness of a rocket bursting, and all I could see was a single pale spark, sinking and dying against a deep blue sky. Besides, I realised, Guy Fawkes had been and gone

Signal rocket. I walked on because there was nothing I could do. The lifeboat would be going out if it was needed. Someone else would be fighting for his or her life. All I could do was silently (and drunkenly) wish them luck, whoever they were.

I only had a couple of pints in the Royal. It was more for the company, such as it was that time of year, than anything else.

The next day, for once, it wasn't an effort to get into the bathroom and shower. I even managed a shave beforehand. I'd been wearing the same clothes pretty much unchanged for the last two weeks; I threw them into the wash. I stripped the bed as well. This happened now and again; I'd experience a surge of revulsion at the state of myself, or the house, or both, and there'd be a burst of activity.

With that all done, I inspected myself in the mirror and pronounced myself almost presentable.

The mind, as somebody once said, is a monkey. I'd alleviated the boredom with imaginary conversations with people I knew – people like Dr Whittaker, Janet or even Naomi Scrimgeour, there was no-one I knew that well around here – about the incident on the beach:

"Ben, you know some opioids can cause hallucinations, DHC included. It's infrequent, but it can happen. If they come back, see a doctor."

"Naomi, I could *feel* them behind me."

"Did they actually *touch* you, Ben?"

"Well, no."

"There you go then."

"But I *saw* them, standing in the water."

"Only saw them for a moment, when the sunlight reflected off the surface. You said so yourself."

"... yes."

"Well, then. Look, Ben, you've been through a hell of a lot. And you've made a great deal of progress. But it won't all be plain sailing, and you won't get over it all overnight."

"Dr Whittaker is right, love. Give yourself some time. Get out a bit. Socialise. Last thing you want is to stay in and brood. Meet some people, make some friends."

"Janet, I'm fine."

"Then why are you sat around having imaginary conversations with us?"

I took my stick and went out.

On the beach, a bitter rain drove in from the sea like a cloud of nails. A tractor, a mechanical scoop at the front raised high, as if in triumph, trundled towards the water. It was towing a small, four-wheeled trailer. On it rested a bright orange inflatable dinghy with an outboard motor and RNLI on the bow, which pointed back towards the town. Four men, in the bright orange jackets and white headgear of lifeboatmen, sat aboard it.

At the water's edge, the tractor turned to face the sea. The lifeboatmen jumped out. A warning klaxon blared; the tractor reversed into the shallows. The lifeboatmen lifted the dinghy into the water, then clambered back aboard. Within a few seconds, they were speeding out into Barmouth Bay.

I was in no rush – it wasn't really an option, in my state – and dawdled to study any random object that caught my attention or just admire the view; I reached the concrete jetty about twenty minutes later. As I clambered over the jetty and walked down the half-buried promenade to the quay, I saw the dinghy coming back in. They seemed to be empty-handed. A practice run, maybe, training.

Or perhaps they'd gone out to try and rescue somebody and failed, without even a body to bring back.

Not a pleasant thought.

It was 2:30. Still time, just, for lunch at Davy Jones' Locker.

The Locker is a small building, built from grey Welsh slate and dating back to medieval times. A small open deck out front overlooks the harbour. Inside, the rough, irregular stonework is whitewashed, except for the huge fireplace at the very back, which retains its natural grey. Sadly it's not a real fire, just red electric light seeping through the chopped logs in the grate. A huge stuffed fish (*an allis shad*, the old marine biologist in me noted, *a member of the herring family*) hangs over the front door. Seafaring paraphernalia adorns the nooks inside, or hangs from the black-painted ceiling beams – green-glass buoys in nets of knotted brown string, old fishing nets, a spider crab, ship's wheels, lengths of chain, winches, lobster pots, model ships, propeller blades, a sawfish's snout (*rostrum, to give its right name*), a basket of dried starfish, sea-urchin and empty conch shells, and a brass diving helmet with its single, Cyclopean window at the front. Lighting came from old ship's lanterns hung from the rafters and lit by electric bulbs within them.

They don't serve booze, but I could get by without for now. I was more hungry than anything else, so I took a table near the fire and ordered ham and duck eggs. I got a coffee as well, and drank it slowly. Outside, gulls wheeled low, letting out their mournful, repetitious cries.

Sally, one of the staff, came up. "Want another?"

She was about eighteen, with dark roots showing in her dyed-blonde hair. In my bad old days, I'd been known to sail close to the wind when it came to some of my students. Not anymore.

"Please."

"Same again?"

"Thanks."

She went back to the counter. It wasn't common practice – customers normally went and got their own refills – but she knew me and liked to save me the trouble. That day, I could've quite cheerfully gone to the counter under my own steam, but it was still nice to be waited on by a pretty girl. Even if it was more out of pity than anything else.

The café was quiet, but far from empty. As well as locals, people still came to the coast this time of year. Not the family holiday crowd, but it was a nice time of year for hill-climbing and watching the late autumn leaves fall. When the weather permitted, anyway.

I ate slowly. No rush. Besides, despite the booze and smoking, I still had a sense of taste. Might as well enjoy myself. I finished my meal, and lingered over the second cup of coffee. Sally collected my plate and offered another refill. I dug out the crumpled paperback I'd stuffed in my coat pocket before venturing out. Time passed.

"Mind if I join you?"

I looked up, but even before I saw her face I knew I was caught. A long black dress clung to a sleek, curved figure. Small, pale hands; pink nail varnish.

Her face was a pale oval, black hair piled on top. Large, dark eyes, a red rosebud of a mouth, pencilled eyebrows. A sharp nose, high cheekbones. A strong, handsome face overall. Not my usual type, but still...

She didn't look like a Goth. Maybe she'd just come from a funeral? But I didn't get that impression, either.

I didn't answer at first. I was – struck. Actually, smitten might be the proper term. She cocked her head slightly; raised her eyebrows, parted her lips.

"Sorry. Yes. Please do."

"Thanks." She sat. "I won't disturb your reading –"

"No, it's OK." I closed the book. "Nice to have a little company."

She smiled embarrassedly and looked down. Christ's sake, Stiles; a *little* less forward would be nice.

"Sorry – I just meant –"

"No, it's OK. Really. It's nice of you. I'm here with friends, but... They have different interests to me."

"Oh?"

"Well, they're off quad-biking today. And tonight... tonight they'll be roaring drunk and stoned."

"Not your thing?"

She twitched her nose and shook her head. "I'm a quiet kind of girl. Very boring, I know. Much rather go up in the hills or the woods and stand there looking out to sea."

"Yeah. I'm the same."

A pencilled eyebrow arched up. "Really? Somehow I picture you as quite the party beast." She smiled. It was mischievous if not downright naughty, but most of all it was *real*. It also made the corners of her eyes crinkle in a very nice way.

I laughed. "Used to be."

"Not anymore?"

"I had an accident, few months ago. Have to take things easier than I did. But..." I smiled back at her. "... I'm starting to enjoy myself again."

"Glad to hear it."

"Need a refill, Ben?"

"Um no, thanks, Sally." I still had half a cup. Besides, any more and I'd be running back and forth to the toilet, which I didn't fancy. Unlike the lady in black. "Would you like –?"

"Oh, just a coffee, please. Black, no sugar."

Sally's mouth twitched at the corner, but she nodded, smiled and said: "Coming up."

"Something I said?" the woman asked, after Sally had gone.

I laughed. "No. She likes to save me the hassle because I'm not that mobile. But that's just for me, not every other punter in the place."

"Oh. I'm sorry."

"Don't be. My fault, not yours."

Sally brought the coffee over, gave me a mock glare and winked. *You're forgiven, but don't do it again.* I smiled and watched her go.

"I think she likes you."

"I'm old enough to be her dad."

"Funnily enough, I don't imagine that stopping you. For long."

"Ouch."

"Ben, did she say?"

"Yeah, that's right. You're –?"

"Ellen." She extended a hand.

"Pleasure to meet you."

"Likewise."

She sipped her coffee. I toyed with my cup. "Have you been up Panorama yet?"

"Where?"

"That's a no, then."

"I've only just got here." She took another sip, looked over the cup's rim. "But if you know of any good spots and don't mind showing me..."

Her eyes were very wide, very dark, and very inviting. A part of me wanted to make excuses. Run and hide. Too good to be true. Had to be some kind of a stitch-up. But I wanted to believe her.

"I'd love to," I said, and that sealed my fate. But of course it had been sealed long before then. "I can't take you there, though."

"Why not?"

And so I told her. Explained about the bends, how I couldn't travel to high altitudes.

She touched my hand. "Will you come some of the way with me? As far as you can? It would be nice to have the company."

What else could I say to that, but yes?

From the top of Panorama, which lies at the edge of Dinas Oleu, right above the Mawddach Estuary, we could see the hills rolling inland to our left, the grey ribbon of the estuary winding through the sandbanks, wormed with narrow creeks, on each side. Turning right, beyond the railway bridge the estuary opened out into Barmouth Bay and, beyond that, into the Cardigan Bay and Irish Sea. In the distance was the Lleyn Peninsula, the long arm of land reaching from the top of Wales, and the mist-shrouded contours of Anglesey.

We stood in silence. I'd seen the view before, but I was seeing it with Ellen now, through her first-timer's eyes. And of course, I'd never expected to see it again myself.

Teeth gritted, I'd started climbing the long, steep road up the side of Panorama with her, expecting the agony to explode in my arms and legs any second, doubling me up and humiliating me. And once it did stab me; I'd gasped, but she'd reached out a hand to steady me and... and the pain had ebbed away. She'd looked at me and smiled. "OK?"

"Yeah." And I was.

"Want to go back?"

"No. Not yet."

We'd gone higher than I'd ever expected to, past streamlets trickling down rockfaces into little drainage ditches, coming off the mountain road and walking past the farmhouse that lay before the woodlands around the summit. Fallen leaves, rust-red, rustled in the light breeze. Stones thick with moss. All of this, and the landscape glimpsed in snatches through the trees, soon to be seen in full. The anticipation of seeing it again. Then out into the open air; restraining myself from looking around because I wanted to wait now till I reached the summit, determined to get there even if the pain, long deferred, exploded full-force. The last dozen yards were very steep, but I'd managed it, hardly even limping.

"It's so beautiful," she said at last; her voice hitched as she said it.

"Ellen?" A tear trickled down her left cheek. As I watched, another ran down her right. "Jesus, Ellen, are you alright?"

"Yes. Yes. I'm fine. No, really Ben. It's OK. It's OK. Really." She smiled, wiping her eyes. "It's just so beautiful."

"You've never been to Wales before?"

She shook her head and looked inland across the mountains. "I've never seen this land before."

A funny way of putting it, but I liked it. For a second I'd thought she'd said *I've never seen land before.* My imagination. It wasn't always reliable. I'd have to tell her that, if I saw her again. I knew I wanted to.

But not right now. Not just yet.

Ellen put her hand to her mouth and sniffed hard. Then again. And a long, sobbing breath out.

I put a hand on her arm, without thinking. She took her hand from her mouth, dabbed her eyes with a tissue. "Silly," she said, looking down, not meeting my gaze.

I touched her chin, tilting her face up. "It's OK," I said. "It's OK." My voice shook a little; I could've cried myself. Maybe out of gratitude. Maybe it was just her company, or maybe she had some kind of healing touch – the kind of crap claimed by the kind of people I'd avoided as peddlers of false hope, exploiters of the gullible, determined to try and accept my fate with some kind of dignity rather than chase pointlessly after non-existent miracle cures. I didn't know or care; something had happened I'd thought never would again. I'd climbed a mountain. And for whatever reason, it was because of her. For that alone, I could have loved her forever, right then.

That moment. When the eyes lock. When you know, you just know, it's just a kiss away. And the kiss is coming, due within heartbeats.

I touched my mouth to hers. Soft, yielding. Then the touch of her tongue in my mouth, her tongue on mine. That first kiss. Like so much else, it'd become so common I'd stopped appreciating it. And like so much else, I was finding it fresh and new, with her, with Ellen...

... what *was* her second name?

No matter. There was time for all that. However long she was staying for.

Where was she going back to? She hadn't said. It didn't matter. It could be the grimmest place on earth, and I knew if she wanted, if she'd let me, I'd follow her there.

Christ, Stiles, is this love at long last?

A faint taste of salt in my mouth, in hers. The tears, perhaps. Finally she broke free, a gasp of breath, her hands on my chest, pushing me back. "Enough."

"Shit – Ellen, I'm sorry."

"No. It's OK. I just..." She touched my cheek, eyes crinkling with that smile of hers again. "You're very sweet."

"Sweet?" Christ. Kiss of death, a woman calling you that.

"Sweet," she said, and kissed my lips again, the merest brush. "We have time, don't we? Ben?"

"Yeah." I was smiling too, the biggest and stupidest of my adult life. "Much as you need."

"Good." She still smiled; the most amazing smile in the world. I wanted to see it every day for the rest of my life.

Shit, Stiles, this is *love and all.*

"So," she said. "Where now?"

We wandered some more over the hills, then down to the old slate quarry and the harbour, which nestles in the crook of the coast road. I kept expecting the pain to kick in, but it never did. Perhaps it was a once-only miracle, and if I tried this again I'd be in agony. Thinking that sharpened my senses; I don't think I'd ever been so aware of what's around me before. After a while I stopped worrying and lost myself in the moments.

We walked back to the Quay and up the High Street for a drink in the Tal-Y-Don. I don't remember what we talked about. Everything and nothing. All that young lover's stuff, except neither of us were that young anymore. Not old either, but I'd always thought myself long past being smitten like that, if I'd ever been capable of it to begin with.

We had dinner at the Last Inn, a restaurant just off the quay. I had baked seabass, Ellen steak and chips. Afterwards, as the night fell, I walked her home along the sea front, arm in arm.

"Won't your friends be worried about you?" I asked.

She shook her head. "They know I like to go off on my own."

The sky had cleared; there were few clouds and the full moon hung low over the sea, laying a silvery path from horizon to beach. A lover's moon, I thought, and said so.

"You old romantic."

We stood and looked out for a while. Then she turned to face me, taking a deep breath. Shit. Here it came. The bad news. She had a boyfriend, or a husband.

She looked up at me – those big dark eyes – and said: "Ben, I want to sleep with you."

The air left my lungs. Panic. What if she wanted to come back to mine? Despite my clear-out that morning, the place was still in no fit state to receive a guest.

"But not tonight."

I was half-relieved, half-disappointed. But, as she'd said, we had time.

"I don't want to move too fast," she said. "I want it to be right. Does that... make sense?"

"Yes." And it did.

"Good." She touched my face. "Ben..." She laughed. "I've just realised, I don't even know your surname."

"Stiles. What about you?"

The moon lit her face as she smiled. "Vannin."

"Unusual name. Beautiful, but unusual. Where's it from?"

Her eyes crinkled again. "That's for me to know..."

A last, deep kiss and she stepped away. "I'll say goodnight now. It's too perfect. Only be an anticlimax otherwise. Meet you tomorrow?"

"Sure. When? Where?" I was like a lovesick schoolboy all of a sudden. Addicted. I was addicted to her.

"The Locker? About eleven o'clock?"

"Sure."

"Goodnight, Ben Stiles."

"Goodnight, Ellen Vannin."

I watched her walking away. She looked back once, blew me a kiss, and then disappeared up one of the sidestreets. There were plenty of hotels along the seafront, but she wasn't at any of them. Another mystery to be solved. The click of her heels on the pavement faded.

Ellen Vannin. The name tripped off my tongue. It sounded familiar. From somewhere. God knew where. As long as she wasn't a convicted axe-murderer.

I laughed at myself and turned to go.

They stood in the surf.

There was a long line of them. A dozen, maybe twenty. As before they were silhouetted, but the light gleamed through them, in places. Through gaps that shouldn't have been in a living person's body.

Cold green light glittered where their eyes should have been.

The one in the centre extended a hand and beckoned. One by one, as I stumbled away, along the deserted seafront, the others beckoned too.

A cloud slid across the moon as I ran; the pavement darkened. When I looked back, it had passed, and the moon shone again on an empty sea.

CHAPTER TWENTY-TWO

The next fortnight was the happiest of my adult life. I dismissed the figures in the surf as another hallucination. I didn't dare tell Ellen. I trusted her – I thought I did. No, I *knew*. This was love. Total. All-consuming. I would die for her if I had to. I didn't think I could drive her away. But I didn't want to – *couldn't* – take that risk.

If you've ever been in love like that – and I pray you haven't because it can only lead to pain – then you'll understand.

There were no further hallucinations, anyway; no voices in my ear or figures in the waves. And so the only shadow that'd lain on me lifted, and the days and nights passed with Ellen Vannin. We walked the hills together, ate and drank together. And, yes, we slept together.

The first time, I was afraid my body would disgust her. I was scrawny and pale, arms and legs like pipe-cleaners. Even on my good days, I moved stiffly, and had the face of a man twenty years older.

Well, she'd seen my face and she knew my story. But even so, I worried.

The first night we slept together, she insisted on undressing me, peeling off my shirt, pulling off my boots, stripping me naked. As she did, she kissed my body – my nipples and stomach, my knees and thighs, even the insteps of my feet – before pressing me back on the bed, bending over and pressing her lips down on mine.

"Beautiful," she whispered.

I reached up to touch her breasts but she grinned and slapped my hands away, running her tongue over her top lip. "Naughty."

She kissed me deeply, and then worked her way down over my chest and stomach to my cock, kissing it gently, running her tongue up and around it. When she took me in her mouth, I cried out, grabbing fistfuls of bedclothes. "Stop. Stop." But it was too late. The orgasm was so intense it damn near hurt.

I sagged back with a moan. There was silence. Shit. I'd ruined it. Gone off like that. In her mouth as well; women didn't like that. I tried to mumble an apology, but she was laughing, wiping her lips.

"Well," she said. "I suppose I should take that as a compliment."

She stood up and released her long black hair; it fell around her shoulders. "Now," she said, "you've got no excuse. I expect you to last this time."

Her dress fell around her ankles, slithering down the pale slopes of her body smooth as water. She was naked, except for her black shoes. She kept them on throughout. "Touch me," she whispered, and guided my hand between her legs. She was already open and wet to the touch. With her free hand she drew my head to her breasts, and I took a nipple in my mouth as she stroked my hair.

My health, as if in response, was the best it had been since the accident. I reduced my DHC dosage, even skipped it once and suffered no ill-effects. That *was* only a one-off, though; on the whole, I still needed to take the medication, but less than before. I had no doubt it was down to Ellen in some way. How or why, I didn't know and I didn't care. I just wanted it to last.

We didn't talk about her friends. Throughout that fortnight, I never met them, not till the very end. They were just a vague reason that Ellen was here in Barmouth. A plot device. Nothing more.

We didn't talk about the future. I was afraid of finding out that it was all just a fling for her, a holiday romance, to be consigned to a shoebox full of memories, of things that once were but no more. I didn't want to know I'd be just another faded snapshot – *do you remember that time in Barmouth, in the autumn of...*

I wanted this to be forever. I wasn't going to make the same mistakes I'd made with Sara, with all the others. I was ready to commit. I was ready to change, whatever was necessary. Whatever it took. And I knew that was reckless, and I didn't care.

For a few waking hours a day I was on my own. She had to spend some time with her friends. It was a teenage thing, to want to spend every second together... but still I begrudged every minute of the day that wasn't mine.

Still, there were things to do. My house was almost unrecognisable now, it was actually *clean.* Clothes were washed and put away (occasionally even ironed), the washing-up was done daily, the carpets hoovered and cleaned. Parts of the place actually *gleamed.* It looked like a place fit to receive visitors. When I wasn't busy with the flat there was still time for a walk along the beach.

Or to surf the internet.

I didn't have a home computer. I'd rarely worked on the things even at University, unless I had to. I much preferred to write longhand. It was more portable, less likely to go wrong, it could be done anywhere. After all, given the choice, where would you rather work? A grubby, ratty bedroom, or a beach or mountainside? The defence rests.

But there was a coffee shop at the far end of Church Street that doubled as an internet café. I used it to make my occasional contacts with the outside world via the web. Generally I used it to follow current affairs, music, literature, general stuff really. Today, though, I had something different in mind.

Today, the last day of that happiest fortnight – although I didn't know that then – I was doing a little detective work.

It was the her name; the nagging familiarity of her name. I *knew* I'd heard it before. I'd asked her, but she shrugged it off; she was no-one special, she said (I disagreed) and she'd never done anything to lift her into the public eye.

But it wasn't a common name. You wouldn't forget it once you'd heard it. And I was sure I had... but I didn't know where.

And so I sat in the café, cup of coffee at my elbow, and typed 'Ellen Vannin' into a search engine. And watched the parade of hits come up.

For a start, the correct spelling was Ellan Vannin. In the old Manx tongue, it referred to the Isle of Man.

But also, there were two songs. *Ellan Vannin*, a traditional Manx song, the island's unofficial 'national anthem.' And another, more recent, by a Liverpool folk band called The Spinners: *The Ellan Vannin Tragedy 1909*.

The SS *Ellan Vannin*. One of the Isle of Man Steam Packet Company's fourteen mailboats, all named after some feature of the island. Snaefell, Tynwald, Ben Machree... the actual ships had changed over the years, but the names had been passed down. All except one.

On December 3rd, 1909, the SS *Ellan Vannin* had sailed from Ramsey Bay for Liverpool, with twenty-one crewmen, fifteen passengers, and a cargo of sheep and turnips.

The weather had been temperate enough when she set out, but rapidly worsened to a Force 11 gale driving twenty-foot drives. Having been on the sea myself, I knew that was like. The sad part was, she was close to port when it went wrong. She'd passed the Bar lightship and entered the Mersey Channel. Exactly what sent her down was never confirmed; most likely a massive wave had capsized her. There was no time to do anything. No-one made it out. All thirty-six people aboard her drowned.

It'd been the worst shipping disaster in Manx history. The name

Ellan Vannin was never re-used by the company.

It was coming back to me now. The Irish Sea around the Isle of Man is notorious for its shipwrecks, and I'd gone wreck-diving off there a few years before. There'd been a few of us. One evening, we'd been in the pub. One of the party was a bloke called Hughie, a Liverpool man. He'd had a guitar, and he'd taken it out and played the Spinners song. Told us the story.

There was no woman called Ellen Vannin. But of course, it might be a family name... somewhere. Could just be a coincidence.

Coincidence? When you see dead things calling you from the sea, when their eyes glow green like the ones you dream and nightmare of? Ever since you nearly died – in the sea, Ben. In the sea –

"Ben?"

I jerked round in the chair, fumbling for the mouse, as Ellen walked in.

"What you looking at then?"

"Oh, nothing."

Her eyebrows went up. "Nothing?"

"Honestly."

"Nothing, tra-la-la?" She was looking at me the way she did sometimes, head half-turned to look at me sideways, a teasing, I-don't-believe-you smile on her lips.

Shit.

Then she grinned. "Hope you weren't looking at porn there." She leant forward and whispered. "You'll get in trouble if you do that here."

I leant over and whispered back. "Why would I need to look at porn, when I've got you?"

"You old smoothie," she said, and brushed her lips across mine.

The tension had passed. "Just checking my emails," I told her.

"Anything interesting?"

"Bugger all."

"Oh well. I'm bloody starving. Lunch?"

"Why not?"

We ate at Davy Jones' Locker once more. It was a very mild day, so we chanced sitting out on the deck outside.

"Ben... I've got something to tell you."

My stomach lurched. Did she know I knew?

Know what? She's got a name that sounds like something else? Vannin's just her family name, Ben, that's all. It's coincidence.

But my eyes flickered out to look across the harbour where the tide had come in, sure I was going to see *them* rising up out of it.

Shit, she's pregnant, that's it, that's what she's going to tell you.

"I'm leaving tomorrow."

"Oh." A part of me was almost relieved for a second. Then it hit home.

"Shit."

Her smile was crooked and her eyes glistened. "Yeah."

"When... when are you..."

"Don't know exactly. Probably early on."

We looked at each other, neither speaking.

"Do you work?" I asked at last. Weird. I realised it'd been another question I'd never got round to asking.

"Why?"

"I just thought..." No, there was no other way, I had to ask her *now* "... If you don't have a job to go back to, you could stay here a little longer. I mean, with me."

She stared at me.

"I'm sorry. I didn't mean to..."

"No. No, it's OK. You mean that?"

I nodded. Her laugh was half a sob. "I thought – I was afraid you just – that you didn't want... I mean, long-term..."

Her hand reached out across the table; I took it. "I was afraid that *you* didn't."

She laughed again, dabbed her eyes. "We're both bloody stupid aren't we?"

"Yeah."

"But I can't stay here, Ben. I can't."

"Why not?"

"I just can't."

"A job?"

"Yes. No. Sort of. It's complicated. But... oh, God, I love it here. It's so beautiful. But I have to go back. At least for a while. But, would you consider..."

I wanted to hear her say it herself, but she left the sentence unfinished so long I had to do it for her. "Coming back with you?"

"Yes."

"Yes," I said. "I would."

"Yes? Really?"

"Yes."

"Ben, you don't know where I live. You don't know..."

"I don't care." I squeezed her hand. "Simple as. End of."

She wiped her eyes again with her free hand, and smiled. "You're sweet."

"Don't call a man sweet," I growled. "For God's sake."

"Oh for pity's sake," said Sally, collecting our glasses. "Get a room, you two."

The sun was going down; we walked along the sea-front, her hand in mine.

"Do you want to come back to mine tonight?" she said.

"Best had. My last chance, isn't it?"

"Mm?" She frowned for a second, then giggled. "Yes, of course. I was thinking you'll always be at mine after tonight." She looked ahead, and I glanced sideways at the sea; it was reassuringly empty. "Will you be OK?" she asked. "Just packing up and going like this?"

"Yeah. I'm used to travelling light." A thought occurred to me. "How are you getting back?"

"Mm?" For the second time she seemed distracted, thrown by what I'd said. Maybe the late nights were catching up with her. It wasn't as if we'd been drinking. We'd hardly touched a drop; my alcohol intake had fallen to almost nothing in the last two weeks. "Oh. Yeah. We'll be driving."

"I'll have to pack some stuff, that's all. Just wondering about room."

"There'll be plenty. Karl's got a van."

"Karl?"

"You'll meet him in a minute."

Dinas Oleu's outlines crumbling into the thickening dusk; a sharp tang of coal smoke in the air as we came down Marine Road.

The house stood near the railway bridge, one of a row of tall terraces, made up of bricks of grey Welsh slate. Ellen opened the front door.

"Hello?" she called. "We're back." She motioned me through, pushed it closed with her foot. Old newspapers were heaped up between the door and the wall.

The living room was on the left. The door was open. The light was off, and the only illumination was from the dim flicker of the TV. A woman with black, bedraggled hair slouched on the sofa.

"Carrie?" Ellen called. The woman didn't respond. "This is Ben."

The woman's head turned our way. The tangled mop of hair hid her face.

"He'll be coming back with us tomorrow."

Carrie nodded slowly. She half-raised a hand and made a faint noise that could have been, or meant, anything. Her skin looked very pale in the TV's flicker.

Down at the far end of the hallway, shoe leather scratched on linoleum. A tall, thin shape stood swaying in the kitchen doorway, backlit by the thin grey twilight. A second shape, smaller and plumper, shambled to stand alongside him with painful slowness. It wore an old print dress. The first figure put an arm around its shoulders.

"Ben, this is Donna and Charles."

Jesus, Ellen, who the hell are these friends of yours?

"And this is Karl."

She pointed up. The staircase to the right was very steep and vanished into darkness. Floorboards creaked. Another figure was coming down. He was very tall and very, very thin. He was bare-footed, wearing jeans and a white sweater. His hair was longer than Ellen's or Carrie's, and hung lank and heavy.

I couldn't see any of their faces.

Ellen's hand gripped mine tightly. "Are you still sure, Ben?"

"What?"

"Sure you want to come with us?"

"Yes..." Why was her hand so cold, suddenly? And clammily damp? I forced a smile and waved generally at the group. Charles raised a hand silently in greeting. Karl kept coming downstairs, slow and purposeful.

"Why are all the lights are off?" I asked. "Forget to pay the bill?"

Charles and Donna rocked back and forth in silence. As Karl reached the bottom of the stairs, he shook his head slowly from side to side.

"They don't talk much," Ellen said. "They can't. It was enough of an effort, just for me to..."

"What?"

I was turning to look at her, but then I stopped. Something I'd seen from the corner of my eye, in the hallway's grey crumbling twilight dusk –

Charles and Donna were trying to get to us. The space between the staircase and wall was too narrow for them to walk abreast, but they squeezed close together and shuffled forward. It was like watching a grub squirming. Karl had stopped at the foot of the stairs, and had turned his head towards them.

"I brought them with me," Ellen said. "In case I needed help."

"Help?"

"With you, Ben." Her voice hitched. "With you."

The hallway wasn't quite as dark suddenly. I could see Charles and Donna a bit more clearly. The more I saw, the more I wished it was still dark. The flesh of their faces were hanging off the bones, barely attached. They faded back into the dark as Karl turned towards me, but by then I was looking right into the light source, into the two discs of green light that should have been eyes, glaring through wet, tangled hair. His face looked grey. Something had eaten part of his nose. When his mouth opened, a hole gaped in his cheek.

Now Charles and Donna's eyes were glowing too, and their bustling down the hallway was like insects scuttling towards their prey. There was a thumping sound from the living room. I didn't look to see what Carrie was doing. Pain shot up my arm. Ellen's grip had tightened, and her hand was searing cold.

"I'm sorry, Ben."

"What?" I turned to look at her. Her profile was smooth, white, unmarked; eyes closed, a thin tear-track gleaming silver on her cheek. "What is this?"

"I'm sorry," she said again, as the green light began seeping through the join of her closed eyelids. Lighting up her face. The glow brightening as her eyes opened, as she turned to face me, the eyelids shrinking back and away like scorched polythene, the light blowing away softening shadows and comforting illusions and showing her face for what it really was, for what crabs and fishes and slow decay had left of it, the mouth snarling open into a scream full of blackened teeth as she lunged towards me.

CHAPTER TWENTY-THREE

I didn't scream as I staggered down Marine Road. I felt the pain exploding from my bone joints, but from a distance, like a report rather than the real thing. I vaguely realised I'd lost my stick and shouldn't really be able to move like this.

I didn't know, not then, that my jeans were sodden with my own piss.

I reached the intersection of Marine Road and Marine Parade, past the Sandancer nightclub and the amusement arcade. Beyond them were the seafront and the road to the quay. Waves were breaking; I heard them briefly over the roar of blood in my ears.

Not the sea. Not the fucking sea.

One lover betraying you is bad enough. But two is too much to bear. The sea always was my first love. Now that was gone too.

Barmouth was deserted. No sign of anybody. That wasn't right. It wasn't that late. There should be *somebody*. Somewhere.

Where now?

The police station. It wasn't far.

And tell them what?

The knowledge was in my head, never to be forgotten; it'd been branded into me in that endless moment before I'd – somehow – broken free of Ellen and her 'friends'. I knew the truth now, but even through the terror and the chaos, I also knew it was madness and that to tell a police officer was a short cut to a night in the cells at best, being sectioned at worst.

Home.

The railway crossing was clear. I stumbled across it, past shops and cafes all closed up for the night and right, down Church Street.

"Ben?" Ellen's voice, lilting coyly. A lover's coaxing, now obscene. "Be-en?"

They were coming round the corner, Ellen in the middle, hair wild in the wind and the long black dress flapping round her, eyes aglow. The others followed; Charles and Donna, still holding each other upright as they blundered like drunks over the pavement and the middle of the road; Karl's long gaunt frame, hair flapping loosely, arms stiff and swinging at his sides, hands hooked into claws, and Carrie, a thin, tiny shape, almost skeletal. Dear God, how old was she, how old had she *been*?

All their eyes glowing.

"Ben!"

I turned and ran. Pain stitched into my side, drove through my poor abused legs, but I had to keep going, had to keep going...

I didn't look back again. Didn't dare. God knew what I'd see. Karl, most likely. My one chance was the physical condition they were in, their shape. They weren't moving fast, not even Ellen. Maybe whatever had brought them back was weakening.

I reached my front door, shoved the key in the lock. My heart battered my chest; I thought for a second it'd burst. That would have been a bloody laugh, after everything else.

The shuffle and scrape of feet. *Don't look. Don't look.* The lock, not turning.

"Fucking twat!" I screamed at it, and the key revolved. The door gave and I shoved it wide. When I looked back, I saw they were closer than I thought, no more than ten feet off. Lamp-light hit Karl's face, or what there was of it. His arms were out-stretched, grasping.

I slammed the door shut, turned the key in the deadlock, put the security chain on.

The windows – I staggered to them one after the other. All locked. Hands thumped on the door.

Now I wasn't in flight, the pain hit me. The agony doubled me over. I climbed the stairs on hands and knees, every movement a wrench of pain, all the while promising myself just a little fur-ther, just a little further, just a little more.

"Ben?" Ellen was calling through the letterbox. "Ben?"

I collapsed at the top of the stairs, outside my bedroom door. I'd left the DHC in there, on the bedside table. I'd thought I didn't need it anymore. Maybe I hadn't, not then. I'd been drugged on something else. But that was gone now, along with all the other comforting illusions that had accompanied Ellen Vannin. Shoulders, elbows, wrists, hips, knees, ankles; they all grated and screeched like buggered hinges every time I moved. Even if I didn't. But I had to move to reach the painkillers.

I lay there, sobbing through my teeth. Mostly from pure physi-cal pain.

Mostly.

"Ben?"

I closed my eyes. For a few precious but horrible seconds, the pain in my body faded away, as the other kind kicked in.

Three-quarters of the planet are ocean. At least, they were back then. God knows what the proportions are now.

We've used it since we first came down from the trees. It's fed us for thousands of years. We've learned to travel across, over, even below it.

But it can't be trusted; it isn't our home. You can drown in a few inches of water; it's home to creatures that kill with a bite or sting, or just plain devour you. And the sea itself. We can't even drink salt water. It's as difficult and dangerous to explore as outer space. You need breathing gear and protective suits just as you would in space, and even then, you're only one mistake away from death. Or worse. I'd forgotten that and look what it'd cost me. It had mauled me like a cat toying with a mouse, then left me for dead. Bored with the new toy. Forgotten me.

So I'd thought.

How many didn't get away? Shipwrecks, drownings, suicides? Storm surges, tsunamis? How many dead?

When I was at school, somebody told me that ghosts were formed like this:

Emotion is a form of energy. Brain activity is electrical; thoughts are like tiny lightning bolts jumping around your brain. Something bad happens – something violent or terrifying, something traumatic (oh yes, I knew long words like that when I was eleven, I thought I was clever and knew everything, but of course I knew fuck all) and there's a huge *storm* of that energy. You used to hear words like 'thought patterns' in science-fiction books. I'd always visualised bright imprints on the retina, after-images left by intricate jumbles of electrical bolts, strange curlicues like Arabic writing or cuneiform.

Those patterns get thrown off, and they soak into the surroundings. An imprint. Like a snapshot of the soul. The same way sound, converted into electrical impulses, imprints a cassette tape. Waiting for something – the right kind of mind, a sensitive enough mind – to trigger it, connect. To complete the circuit. Heat energy is absorbed from the surroundings and converted, to make the recording run. This was why people who witnessed hauntings almost always reported a sudden drop in temperature.

A sort of tape recording basically. But, possibly, with some rudimentary life, or consciousness of its own.

Later on I was told that, scientifically speaking, this is total bollocks.

But what if it's not?

And if – just *if* – it's not:

How many deaths in the sea? Over millions of years, how many lives ended there, in terror and agony – and rage, at the ending of your life – while others live?

Why me and not you? Why you and not them?

Millions? Billions?

How can every molecule of that vast, rolling deep not be taint-ed?

Water evaporates and is carried away. Haunted lakes, rivers, streams... but it all returns to the sea in the end.

Last thoughts, fears, suffering, all flying back and forth. Isn't that all a mind is?

The sea is vast, but not infinite. Sooner or later there had to be a tipping point. Perhaps it was the sheer volume of deaths. No one event, no bolt of lightning in a castletop laboratory, just... that.

The sea is alive. It wasn't before, but it is now. It's awake, and all it knows is wrath and terror, agony and rage.

When I nearly drowned the sea reached out to claim me – the eyes, coming out of the darkness, the faces. Another mind, another soul. Because that was the worst of it. One mind – one single, planet-wide brain – and it was alone. Enough to drive anyone insane.

And Ellen... what was Ellen?

The Deep Brain – I had to call it something, and what better name than that? – was just becoming aware when it nearly took me. It had been... absorbing me. Taking me into itself. But awake now. Its mind had touched mine.

For the first time, it *knew* a living mind.

It knew something other than rage.

It was not alone.

But then I'd escaped, with my life if not much else. Back to dry land and stayed there for good. How could it reach me? The sea is governed by time and tide, the moon. It has no arms, no legs...

Only it does.

How many souls in the deep?

How many bodies drifting on the tides?

It had used them. Made them more fitting for its purposes – in Ellen's case at least, it made her pass for a living woman. And sent her out.

But it was young and new, its strength limited. It had sent out a few emissaries, to look for me. It could sustain the deception, for a little time.

So many millions, billions of others in the world. So many others drowning every day, but they died and were taken and were lost. They just added to its strength, became part of it.

It had no-one. Nothing to make it complete. So out of all the billions, on the earth, the sea had come for me and me alone.

It had wanted to seduce me. But it couldn't sustain the deception. Maybe didn't want to. Wanted me to know where I was really going. And like any clumsy, untried, inexperienced suitor, it had revealed itself badly.

I began to laugh, rocking to and fro on the stairs as Ellen called my name.

I'd once heard a song called *Marry The Sea*.

I laughed all the louder.

"Ben? Ben?" Ellen's voice calling through the letterbox. Outside, I heard hands thumping on the windows. "Ben, let me in. You promised. You said you'd go with me. You said you loved me."

The oldest and most painful one of all: *you would if you really loved me.* Never promise you'll do anything for a loved one, because sooner or later they'll demand the one thing you just can't do.

"Ben, it won't be like the others." Her voice was hitching. There was a clotted noise in her throat. "You'd become part of me in full. We'd be one. Isn't that what love is?"

What could she know about love? She must know something, I supposed. She'd have to, to do this.

"Please. Don't leave me on my own."

Something thumped at the window at the end of the landing. I turned and looked. Karl. He'd climbed up, clung on. He had spread flat against the window. His eyes glowed through at me.

"Ben? Ben?"

I didn't answer.

"Alright, then!" Her voice had a dull, cold finality, worse than any scream. "We're going. We can't stay longer, and we can't take you by force. It has to be of your own accord. But if that's the way you want it, fine. I can live without you, and I won't always be weak. I'm growing stronger all the time." She paused. I wouldn't look at the window, but a dull green glow spilt from it across the landing.

"The icecaps are going, Ben," she whispered. "They'll melt, all of them, and they'll cover all the earth. And when they do, I'll take *everyone*. It'll be soon. Sooner than you think."

The green glow vanished. Downstairs, the letterbox banged.

And the house was silent.

I stayed there all night and through into the morning. The agony got worse and worse. Finally, somehow, I made it to the bedside table and took the pills.

When I could walk again, I went downstairs. I opened the front door; the wood was scratched and scored.

It was early in the morning when I went back to Marine Road. The sun was rising over Dinas Oleu, which I knew now I would never be able to climb again. The sky was clear blue, soft pink near the horizon; the air was crisp and cold, the first snap of the incoming winter. The tang of coalsmoke hung in the air, and the long, mournful cries of gulls echoed in from the sea. They were the only sound.

There was a sign in the front window: AR WERTH. *For Sale.* The front door was slightly ajar. I nudged it open.

A thick, foetid smell washed out of the dim hallway to greet me; I pulled my sweater up to cover my mouth and nose. A thin buzzing sound. Flies.

I found a light switch and pressed it, but nothing happened. The buzzing came from the front room. A small, thin figure slouched on the sofa, head hanging forward and down.

Carrie.

She was alone in the room. Flies crawled on one dangling hand; it was bloated and badly discoloured. The hair that hung and hid her face was matted and dry. The stench hit me even through the sweater. Gagging, I backed out of the room.

The kitchen door was open. Some light came through the window in the back. Flies were buzzing in there too.

A small dining room adjoined the kitchen. A chair lay on the floor. Charles and Donna lay beside it. I recognised the stained, faded print dress Donna wore. There wasn't much else to recognise. Charles was little more than bones and ragged clothes; Donna was badly bloated and in the throes of black decomposition. The carpet around them was badly stained.

The house was bitterly cold. I moved back. I needed to get out. Away from the house, before I was discovered here. Away from Barmouth. Away from the sea.

But I needed to know.

I went up the stairs. There was dust everywhere. A few footprints and marks, but otherwise no sign anyone had been here in months, even years. In the empty bathroom, something dark and wet filled the toilet bowl, flies swirling above. I didn't inspect it any closer.

There were three upstairs bedrooms. I checked the one next to the bathroom first.

Karl lay sprawled on the bed. He looked quite recently dead. No bloating. His eye sockets were empty though. And there were the holes in his face. His nose half-gone. Eaten, I guessed, before he came back.

The other two bedrooms were empty.

I found no trace of the woman who had called herself Ellen Vannin.

I left Barmouth that night, and booked into a B&B in Manchester. While I was there, I wrote down what had happened. I had to try to make sure of it. I knew I wouldn't be believed, that it was the end of my career. But what was I supposed to do?

Wrote it, typed it, emailed it out. To the University and to a friend who worked in a government ministry.

And then I looked for a new place to live, cheaply, out of sight and mind. A place to hide, far from the sea I'd used to love.

I chose a village in north-east Lancashire, where there was no sea and hardly any people; I rented a static caravan and I drank and I drank. I wanted to kill myself, and put a knife to my wrist more than once, but I could never quite do it. So I drank instead, not caring about what it did with my medication. I was probably hoping the combination of the two would finish the job I couldn't. But my body seemed far more capable of absorbing the punishment I was doling out than I'd thought.

Through those years, whenever I was sober, I would hear the sound of the sea. And voices. Hundreds, thousands, millions of voices, calling my name. A murmur that rose and fell like the sound of the waves, till they couldn't be told apart, but growing steadily, relentlessly louder.

An incoming tide of souls.

There were rains, of course, and storms. Floods, too. At first, I'd been afraid, but after a while I dismissed them. False alarms.

But then the rains came and didn't stop. The floods got worse. The TV stations started going off the air, one by one, the remainder broadcasting old light comedy. When they're showing old episodes of *Morecambe and Wise* and it's not even Christmas, you know something's badly wrong.

And the sound of the sea grew louder.

When I heard shouts and screams in the distance, I ventured out into the rain and squinted down. Below, I could see where the waters had come in, and suddenly the sea, the voices, the souls, were louder than ever before.

I went back inside as the first shots rang out. The Deep Brain was testing its strength, and that of the defence. If the villagers put up a good enough fight, it would fall back, for a while. But sooner or later, it would come in force, and it wouldn't stop. And it would, most especially, want me.

Rain drummed on the caravan roof. In my head, the sea-sound was deafening. And the voices. All the screaming dead, all those last moments, caught like voices on tape.

It was when I heard a woman's voice say, loud and clear in my ear, as if it was next to me, "Ben?" and visualised Ellen, Ellen naked with her arms outstretched, and remembered her face, that last time I'd really seen it, that I decided I could do it now – and better had, while there was still time.

I lay down on one the divan with a bottle of whisky and drank most of it. It made the voices and the tide fade away, made sure I wouldn't hear Ellen's voice again. With the Dutch courage from that I could do it, and I wouldn't even feel what I was doing to myself, but I blacked out almost the second I cut into my left wrist. My next memory is of lying on the Chinook's deck, and Robbie McTarn standing over me.

CHAPTER TWENTY-FOUR

The footpath is steep, but that's not so bad, as I'm on the downslope. Trouble is, it's uneven, chunks of stone threatening to turn my feet as I go. Not easy with a limp.

Before the flood, the air was fresh up here. High above the world, far from the cities, *et cetera*. Oh, you'd catch a whiff of those nice agricultural smells, like silage and cowshit. But there'd be the smell of grass and fallen leaves too, wildflowers, new mown hay, all depending on the time of year.

Not anymore. After the flood there was a constant stench of sewage and decay, from everything in the water. That began going in the last week; the air was fresh again, the wind with a hint of saltwater. Yes: the sea I fled from has truly come to find me.

The smell's changed again now. I breathe through my mouth as I wind my way down, between the ranks of the walking dead. For most of them, that green mould, or whatever it is, has arrested the decay. But not reversed it. Even a fresh corpse needs some time in the deep, being charged up with whatever powers the Deep Brain possesses, to develop that protective coat. So I get the smell of the dead, along with the stink of that green stuff. I don't know what the hell it is – maybe I would have once, back in my old life with more brain cells left to play with – but it smells like the bottom of a drained pond.

They turn and look at me as I pass. There is nothing on their faces. Slack and empty. I'm used to seeing that now. On the faces of the living and the dead.

Smoke still rising in the distance. Beyond that, far down, lies the open water. I keep walking. And no-one moves. There is only the silence. The cold hard wind blows keen across the fell. And I walk on.

I spent the first night after the flood in an upstairs room at the farmhouse the soldiers commandeered. When I woke, I could still hear the sea-sounds. I went to the bar and got to work on the first available bottle. People glared at me at first; finally they just ignored me as best they could.

Later on, there was shouting in the distance. Gunfire. A few minutes later, McTarn came in, and he brought a woman. She was in her late twenties and tallish, with chestnut hair. She was half-soaked and shivering, too, but you could tell she might be pretty, or more than that, under it all. Everyone was staring at her. McTarn reached out to steady her, but she pulled away.

"I'm fine. I'm fine. I don't need any help. Which way is the toilet, please?"

McTarn pointed. When she'd gone there were sniggers, a few laughs. Taking the piss. Uncomfortable.

Over the past few years there'd been plenty of time for brooding. And I'd done a lot of that, about Ellen Vannin. She had, literally, been made for me. Soft. Alluring. And in the end, *submissive*. A little coy and teasing, but... she'd asked for nothing. Just come along and given things to me, done things for me. Wanted nothing for herself. So what did that say about me?

The bed-hopping, the never settling down... I understood now it was not because I had nothing to give, but because I *wouldn't* give. Oh, I told myself, and anyone who'd listen (less and less of them as time went by) I wanted to get married, settle down, but in the end all these women *wanted* things from me. Under the outdoorsy adventurer I played at, there was just a scared little boy who didn't want to get hurt again. That was who Ellen had been made for.

When I saw her – Katja – for the first time, I saw a woman who was the complete opposite of that.

When she came back from the toilet, a few minutes later, face scrubbed clean and hair scraped back, she didn't tell anyone anything. No effort to charm or flirt. I didn't understand why, not then.

I don't believe in love at first sight. It wasn't love. Not then. I just saw someone and realised I wanted something from her. Not sex. Just a pair of arms to hold me, to take the weight off my shoulders, soft hands to stroke and soothe the pain away.

I huddled down, away from the probing, demanding stares of all these people expecting me to pull some miraculous rabbit out of the hat. McTarn barking at me, spitting out his rage. I flinched from it; it added to the voices, calling.

And then I heard Katja saying "Please don't."

The sounds in my head subsided a little, as I heard her talking to McTarn that low voice, that accent. So gentle and so sooth-ing. The sea-sounds, the voices, were louder. I wanted to tell her. Warn her. I didn't know how. It hurt when I tried – the voices rose to a din.

Say something, Ben. You have to say something.

"They're calling me," I said to her.

She looked over at me, studying me. Those great dark eyes. "Who?"

"The voices. The souls. All the dead."

They roared. I gulped down whisky, refilled my glass. Pain stabbed behind my eyes. It faded when I drank.

"Go on," she said. It was a whisper. Soft as snow.

I shook my head.

"Please?"

"Can't."

"Why?"

"Hurts."

She sat there, waiting. I didn't want her to go. I started talking about the diving accident. And anything else I could think of. Maybe I could slip sideways onto the subject, tell her before the voices could realise and scream.

She listened; of course she did. In case I said something useful. Because she needed to be useful too. Be an asset, and not just a pretty face. There were too many men here, too much testosterone. Too much potential for things to turn ugly.

As it got dark, she walked me back to the caravan, up the dimming footpaths. I was very drunk. We didn't speak much.

I slumped on the divan. Katja sat on the one opposite. She smiled a little at me. Like at a pet, I thought.

"Will you..." I asked. "Will you do something for me?"

Her face lost expression. "What?"

"Just hold me." Her eyes narrowed. *Shit.* "I don't mean – not sex, I don't want sex." Although I wouldn't have said no. "I just want someone to..."

She pursed her lips. Thinking it over, calculating the odds. "All right."

She knelt beside the divan, held out her arms. I rolled into them.

Drifting off to sleep; cool fingers stroked my brow.

The two farmhouses. The scene of the last attempt to hold them off. Bullets have chipped the walls and the windows are shattered. Scorch marks. Scattered remains of people. Ours, theirs, it doesn't matter now. Gnawed bones, torn fragments of clothing. A group of *them* crouch over four or five dead sheep. One tears at a severed leg. Another lifts a tangle of intestines, looped around its fingers like a bloated, slippery cat's-cradle and tries to bite through it.

Some of the things are inside the nearest farmhouse. They're in the front room. I stop and look.

They're staring at the walls, looking around the way someone waking up after a long drunk might try to take stock, to understand where he is and what's happened. Take it from me on this one; I speak from long experience.

Another stands in front of the mantelpiece, staring at the pictures along it. It picks one up, holding it upside down, its head cocked to one side.

One of the sheep-eaters looks up from its feast. It's a fresh one, not covered in the mould yet. Blood smears its face. An eye has burst; the socket glows. The other eye burns dully, like a grimy light bulb. Its clothes are soiled with blood. So are its hands. Some of the blood might be its own; in places the clothing is ripped open. Its stomach is an empty cavity. The meat it's been chewing drops out of it onto the ground.

The other sheep-eaters are staring at me too. Another stands in the farmhouse door, watching. The ones in the living room are staring out through the glass, even the one with the photograph. It falls from its hands. Glass shatters.

Stop dawdling. Stop mooning. Go. Go now.

Is that my own thought, or the message in their eyes? Or someone else, calling me? I start walking again. They part to let me through, dead flesh brushing mine. I pass without incident, but feel their eyes on my back as I walk on.

When I woke next morning, I rolled over to see Katja with her foot braced on the opposite divan, lacing up a boot. It was one of mine.

"Where did you get those?"

She looked over at me. "We're the same size," she said. "I didn't think you'd mind. You've a few pairs. Is that OK?"

"Sure." Then I noticed something else. "Your hair..."

She half-smiled and ruffled it; she'd cropped it short. "I thought it was time for a change of image."

"OK," I said, feeling stupid and slow.

Katja sat on the divan and faced me. "I want to know what you know, if I can. Not for McTarn or the others. For me. I need to make myself useful around here. Otherwise, all I'll be, sooner or later, is another hole to fuck." Her face went hard, her voice too. "And I will not go through that again." She took a deep breath and relaxed. "I'm going to McTarn now – see what else I can do to help. I can use a gun. I can fight. I think he might find that useful, don't you?"

"Yes," I mumbled. I felt betrayed. Weak. I couldn't look at her.

Then I felt her hand squeeze mine. Surprised, I looked up. "Last night," she said. "You liked that, didn't you?"

I nodded. I couldn't meet her eyes.

"I have no problem giving you what comfort I can. If that's what you want. In exchange, you tell me what you can."

"Difficult," I said. "Hurts when I try."

"Try," she said. "It's all I ask. Alright?"

"Alright," I said.

She stood, hands on hips. "How do I look?"

I almost said *beautiful*, then realised it was the last thing she'd want to hear. "Like someone you shouldn't mess with."

She smiled. The first real smile I'd seen her give, and it was all mine. It lit her face up, and I could see what she'd been trying to hide ever since arriving. "Good answer," she said. "See you later."

The narrow footpath leads along a twisting, sunken stream. From the banks, trees lean over the waters, branches splayed out like twisted hands, roots writhing free of the earth as if poised to strike. One has fallen in the stream. The chill waters wash and lap over it.

It's quite painful now. Every step brings fresh agony from my knees and hips.

I dig a quarter-bottle of Bell's from a pouch in the wetsuit, and take a deep swallow. The liquor burns its way down to my gut. The joint pain loses some of its edge.

Not far now.

Drinking alcohol before diving is a very stupid and dangerous thing to do. But in my case, so is diving, full stop.

But then, I'm not coming back from this one. I've always known that.

I haven't seen any of them since the farmhouse, except for a couple in the meadows below them, chasing sheep. They'll go after animals if humans aren't available. Hot blood and living flesh. Something that can sustain the existence the Brain's given them. All that energy's got to come from somewhere.

The path is clear. They must have congregated higher up. Ready for that last big push. Why are they waiting? Maybe because they know I'm coming to them. And maybe not. It'll be dark soon. That'll make it easier for them.

Katja...

I put one foot in front of the other.

Then I hear footsteps. Slow and dragging. They're coming up the path one by one. Single file. Slow, plodding steps; there's no hurry now, no sense expending energy. They're coming straight towards me.

No weapons. Except my knife. No diver leaves home without one. To cut whatever you might get fouled in. I could, maybe, get one of them with a lucky stab, in through the eye sockets, into the brain...

And the others would pull me down and tear me into pieces. Maybe better to use it on myself.

There's nowhere to go. No point, no sense in retreating. If I don't get where I'm going, it's all over. It might be anyway. No guarantees this will work.

I grip the haft of the knife. I've run long enough. Not anymore. Not anymo –

The first has reached me. Literally inches away. It stops, staring into me with empty, glowing eye-sockets. And then it steps sideways off the path and crashes into the stream.

One by one, the others do the same. They clamber along the stream and then back up onto dry land as soon as they're past me.

My luck is holding. Or something is.

I press forward, starting to laugh as they drop out of my path.

A couple step aside, up against the chicken wire fence hiving the path off from the field alongside.

I keep going, because I have to.

Katja...

Quid pro quo. That was what she was offering.

Katja would give me what I needed, in exchange for the one thing I couldn't bear to do.

I sat on the divan after she'd gone, and I thought it over long and hard.

What decided it for me, in the end, was the thought of the look she might give me if I said no. Or if I said yes and broke my promise.

Despite her hard-facedness, I had an odd feeling she liked me. I didn't want to lose that.

So, about an hour after she'd gone, I began whispering to myself. I imagined Katja sat there listening, and I started telling her about the Deep Brain.

The voices began rising almost at once, and eventually I had to give up. I flopped back across the divan, moaning. My head rang and throbbed.

I lay there and breathed deep. Then, after a few minutes, I sat up and began again.

By the time Katja came back, I was exhausted and running with sweat, but I was, at least, able to utter those few words when I limped down to the Inn. I was able, at last, to tell someone else about the Deep Brain.

Death is coming. Not the most cheerful way of putting it.

I slumped into my chair afterwards, barely noticing it when Katja came to sit beside me. "Are you alright?" she asked.

I shook my head. "Managed to talk about it. A bit. Difficult. Hurts." I told her about my day. "It hurt like hell, but I managed more than I had before." The pain was bearable now. I wasn't taking directly about the subject, so it dwelt in the background with a vague suggestion of menace.

"I'm proud of you," she said. When I looked, there was something in her face, something I hadn't seen before. Respect? Something like that, maybe. She had some idea, anyway, what it cost me to speak.

She touched my hand. "Why don't you tell me something else now?"

"Like what?"

"Not about these things. Not about this Deep Brain. Tell me something about you, instead."

"Really?"

"Yes. I would like to hear."

So I started talking. I was more than a little hammered by then, so I'm not sure of all of it. I'm pretty sure it was a fairly, maudlin, rambling piece, most likely about my love life. I might have cried a little. I don't remember.

What I do remember is this: her taking my hand, stroking the back of it with her thumb. I didn't dare look up, to see her face, but I felt the warmth of her touch and thought that, perhaps, this was not an act.

I drank myself into a stupor that night, and so I didn't see much of her. Her and McTarn carried me back to the caravan. She came to see me the next morning, and held me a little while.

"Have you tried writing it down?" she asked.

"I did before," I told her. "When I sent in the report. But I destroyed my copies of it. There's nothing here." A pain unrelated to the hangover twinged at my temple.

"Perhaps you could try doing it again?"

"Perhaps."

Over the next fortnight, we spent more and more time together. After a few days, she began to volunteer information about herself. Where she'd come from, what had happened to her, the journey to Pendle. Her voice choked and halted at points; she didn't always meet my eyes, and I think once or twice she wept. Her hand was in mine throughout, and I no longer knew who was giving comfort and who was receiving it.

I make my way down the path where it rejoins the stream, and come out onto Pendle Row. The dead are shambling up; they bump and jostle me as I pass, but none of them offer any direct violence.

I step out into the road. There's more room now.

Smoke's still rising from the burned-out homes. I saw it from a long way off. The Inn is still standing, anyway.

Four of them are in the Pendle Tea Rooms as I pass, sitting at one of the tables. They look up and watch me as I pass, stepping over corpses and pieces of corpses.

The pain stabs at my joints. I sag against a wall, sinking down. The sun is sinking too. I must move on soon. And I will. But I have to rest. Just for a few minutes. I'm almost there.

Katja and I slept together for the first time about a week before she moved in with me.

I'd developed a schedule. After she'd gone for the day, I took pen and paper and wrote for as long as I could. Which usually wasn't very long. I'd have a drink, rest up, and then set to work where I left off. If I was lucky, I managed a third of a page a day.

Destroy it. Destroy it. Destroy it. I would hear a voice whispering that at least once a day, usually as the clamour of the voices rose to new, agonising heights, but always clear above them, and it was always the voice of Ellen Vannin.

But I didn't. I was, after all, used to living with pain.

I didn't talk to Katja about it. It took all my strength to focus on the subject long enough to write the day's quota down. The time I spent with her... that was for me.

"You're nearly done, aren't you?" she asked.

"About halfway," I told her. "But I'll get it finished."

She looked at me, stroked my face. I almost recoiled, it was totally unexpected. I was used to being held, to my brow being stroked as I drifted off. But this? "You are stronger than I thought," she said. "Ben..."

"Yes?"

"If you want to... you know... then we can."

I didn't know what to say. "But... but you said... I thought..."

"It would be..." she took a deep breath. "It would be because I wanted it too."

"Seriously?"

"Seriously."

"But... you were just... I mean, for the information, to be useful..."

"Things change."

It wasn't what you'd expect. You'd expect it to be pretty special, swinging from the chandeliers kind of stuff. I mean, despite my physical state, I knew what to do. Years of experience. And Katja – well, of course, she had a lot of experience too.

But it was different from that. More hesitant. This wasn't about her giving some punter his money's worth, or me showing what a stud I was. We undressed slowly and carefully. I folded back the sheets on the divan and climbed under them; Katja followed. We just lay there for a while, facing each other. I could feel the brush of her bare skin against mine.

"Kiss me."

I leant forward and put my lips to hers. I felt rusty, out of practice. Clumsy. Her too. Kissing was one thing she wasn't into. Each of us was afraid to make the first move, to start things, because we'd been something else before and that wasn't what we wanted to be now.

But once we started, we got there in the end. And, yes. It was good.

Jesus Christ.

It's almost dark. There should be lights coming on in the street. If this was the world we used to live in. But the only lights are from the figures walking up the road.

I stand. Joints scream in pain like rusty hinges. Start walking. Nearly there.

I reach the end of Pendle Row. Cross the bridge onto Barley Road. The road from the village descends and finally disappears, down into the water below. Dead men and women clamber out onto it and totter past me. Dead children. Further out, the converted mill sticks up; beyond it, the top of a drowned white house.

No dead animals, though. Odd. They'll kill and eat animals, and an infected bite'll kill a beast, but it won't come back. I don't know why.

This is it, then.

The night before they destroyed Roughlee, the sea-sounds woke me. Katja was a soft, warm weight beside me on the divan, but I knew we weren't alone.

Above the bed, a dark shadow moving.

Above the bed, two dim green points of light.

Above the bed, the figure leaning down, the glow brightening, and Ellen's grey and rotting face coming down out of the dark, blackened lips peeled back for a snarling kiss.

"*Ben.*"

I screamed. Katja woke. The room was empty. But all I could do was babble it, over and over and over again.

"Ellen. Ellen Vannin. She's found me."

I pull off the boots. Put on the flippers.

I walk down into the water. It laps coldly around my ankles. I can hear the sound of the sea breaking, hear voices moaning and crying. The water rises to my knees, to my thighs, my groin – *Fuck! My bollocks have just imploded* – then my waist, my chest.

I wet the diving mask and pull it over my eyes and nose, making sure the seal is watertight. Check my tanks.

"Ellen?" I shout it. "Ellen. I'm coming."

And I put the mouthpiece in and for the last time in my life, I dive.

CHAPTER TWENTY-FIVE

I unclip the diver's light from my belt and shine it ahead as I swim across the flooded road. The surface recedes, further and further above.

Eyes glow in the murk. Then the torch picks out their faces. They swim up, fast. One collides with me, sending me flying into the path of another, and for an instant I think they're turning on me. But they're not. They go past.

I'm feeling the pressure now. The pain begins. Up above me, dark bodies rise through the water, eyes green pinpricks, aiming for the dim, dying light above.

Ellen? Ellen? Where are you? I'm coming to you. This is what you wanted. Isn't it?

Ellen?

"Ben..."

Katja's eyes, bright with tears.

Outside, gunfire. McTarn and the others are further down, making a last attempt to hold the dead back. It's not going to work. We all know that. Why even try?

Because we have to. Because to give in goes against everything we are.

But giving in is what I'm talking about doing.

"You can't," she says.

"I have to," I tell her.

"You don't even know it'll work."

"If it doesn't, we'll be no worse off."

She wipes her eyes. "We'd be together. Don't you want that, at least?"

I take her hands. She pulls them out of my grip. "You know I do."

"Then –"

"I've got to try. It's what McTarn and the others came for."

"Fuck them."

"They came here because they thought I might have an answer. Well, I didn't. I don't now. Just an idea that might work."

"And it'll kill you."

"If it doesn't, those things will. If it does work, some of us might make it." I take her hands again. "You might."

Her eyes squeeze shut. Her lips peel back from her teeth and her head dips forward. "You bastard. God damn you, you bastard."

I grip her hands tightly. She grips back. There is nothing I can say that will stop it hurting. But that's the way of it.

"I'm tired of being a coward, Katja."

"You're not."

"Yes, I am. If I'd gone with Ellen, back at the start, none of this might have happened."

"That's stupid."

"If I'd gone with her, the floods might not have come. Or at least, not – what came with it. All I've done, all my fucking *life*, is run and hide. And I'm tired of it. Katja, I've got to try."

I hold my arms out to her.

And for the first time, it's me who comforts her.

Ellen?

Is it too late? There's no answer.

From down in the depths comes the breaking of waves. And the voices. Screaming and crying out.

don't want to die

> *bastards up there in the*
> *air and the light still*
> *breathing*

> *mother*

father

> *brother*

> *sister*

> *my daughter*

my son

I strike out. Pressure. Pain. Deeper. Go deeper.

I don't have long. And I don't know what to do. I'm accepting an offer that might not even still be valid.

Ellen?

The valley floor lies open below. Up ahead is the white house.

"Ben?"

I know that voice.

"Ben."

She steps into view, outside the white house. An arm extends, beckons. And then she disappears inside.

I strike down and as I do –

The voices explode into my skull like a grenade bursting, my barriers going down. I can't see straight – can't because I'm not seeing through my own eyes anymore.

It's dark. They move forward.

It's like a TV set picking up a thousand different channels. And someone's got the remote control, flicking from channel to channel to channel to channel to channel to –

The gate gives way. Ged goes down. McTarn – poor bastard, red and black rising across his face as the infection spreads– falls.

They don't touch him, because he's one of them now. And even as he realises it, his heart stops. I feel his death. Because I know him, perhaps, the cameras zoom in, to get it from every angle – his mind dying, swallowed up in rage and terror that's sucked into the Deep Brain to make it stronger – strength then funnelled into McTarn's corpse to make it rise and walk. He leaves his gun behind. He doesn't need it anymore.

Guns firing, little spots and flickers of distant light. Now and again, a camera goes blank as a bullet hits home. But still they advance.

Jo, Katja and Mleczko taking charge, getting the remaining defenders to round the survivors up. There's only one place to go now.

Can't see. Have to aim down, hoping I'm still on course. Swim and swim. Ignore the pain. Please let me be right. Please.

Hendry refusing to leave the Chinook, standing guard, firing his last bullets into the attackers before they pull him down. They swarm over the Chinook till it rocks and falls, rotors breaking on the ground.

The survivors back up the hillside, firing. The steps that lead up Pendle. So steep. The dead are climbing too. Slow. But relentless. The dead don't get tired or out of breath. And so they steadily gain.

Parkes holding position, firing down the steps, buying time for other survivors to get past. But the dead get closer, closer – and suddenly leap in one of their terrible flurries of motion. Parkes has no chance; she has time for a single scream before they pull her down. Nearly a dozen of them fall upon her. In their hunger, they tear her apart.

People fall behind, collapsing – but no-one can go back for them, can't slow down the group to save one. So the too-old, the too-young, the weak, the sick – they're left where they've fallen, begging for help – till dead hands seize them and dead jaws tear the flesh from their bones.

The lucky ones, if there's time, might get a bullet in the head, to spare them.

My hands plough into something soft. My body is alive with

pain, one long wire of it. I open my eyes and I can see properly. My fingers are buried in silt, lying thick over grass that comes loose in my hands, drowned and dead, the earth it's rooted in turning to slurry.

The house is in front of me. I swim for it.

I know I won't last much longer.

There's a door, and it's open. I swim down a flooded hallway, past a living room where a seat-cushion, bleached and bloated from its long immersion, drifts past.

"Down here, Ben. I'm here."

It's from the end of the hallway. Here's a door, ajar. I swim to it and push it wide.

The windows are shattered; drifts of silt and debris are piled everywhere. Cooker and microwave, washing machine and dish-washer, over there in the corner.

Ellen Vannin sits at a table in the centre of the room, in her long black dress. Her black hair drifts wild in the current. Her head rises. Her face is a grey, howling mask like perished rubber, fretted and holed, blackened teeth bared by fish-eaten lips.

I stopped finning and settle, let my feet touch the floor.

Her eye sockets blaze.

Her mouth tries to form a smile. "You came."

Yes. In the end.

"Thank you." She rises from the table. "You're sure about this?"

Yes.

She steps towards me. "The girl? Katja? You love her?"

I loved you too. And I can again.

She holds out her arms to me.

I unfasten the aqualung and let it fall, slipping the mouthpiece from my lips. A long stream of silver bubbles flies upward. I kick off the flippers and step into her embrace, lower my living mouth to her dead mouth, and breathe in.

And on top of Pendle Hill, Katja, Mleczko, Jo, Hassan and twenty or thirty other men and women can see out over half of what was Lancashire, for all the good it does as the dead swarm up it from all sides. Katja checks her pistol. Six rounds remain. She raises the gun and fires, hitting a dead thing between the eyes, thinking, four shots left. She hasn't miscounted. The four shots are for the dead, but this time, she knows who the last one's for.

It's over quite quickly, without pain. I/we watch my body and the body I/we knew as Ellen Vannin topples and drifts to the floor.

Then I/we turn my gaze outwards, out through the eyes of the myriad dead.

The survivors have huddled into a knot around the trig point on the summit. The dead are all around them.

In me/us there boils so much rage. The rage and the terror of all the dead. But now there is more. Now the Deep Brain is... a whole mind. At last. I am... not Ben Stiles anymore. But I am... was... him. Enough to know it is time to stop.

And so I reach out and I halt the dead in their tracks.

On the summit of Pendle Hill, a stillness falls.

Katja Wencewska, two bullets in her gun and only one for the dead things, freezes, looking sidelong at Jo, Mleczko, the others. Guns are held ready; axes, clubs, makeshift spears. All used and blooded. A steel baseball bat, buckled out of shape.

The dead surround them, unmoving.

All save one. One figure, shouldering through the ranks. At a first glance, you might almost think he was still alive. If his eyes didn't glow.

The body of Robert McTarn approaches; Katja aims at his face, finger tightening on the trigger.

The dead don't need to breathe anymore, but it's necessary for speech. I work McTarn's lungs to force out the words. Would he appreciate me using his corpse like this? Is anything of McTarn left, apart from the traces and echoes absorbed into the Deep

Brain? Even I can't answer that.

"Katja, it's me. It's Ben."

It's not really, not anymore, but I have to put it into terms that can be understood.

I tell her that it worked. That now I am the Deep Brain. And it is me.

That the dead are mine to command. That I will return them to the depths.

That the war is over.

But.

I warn her because I must. Because there are aeons worth of fury in the deep. I warn her because I cannot promise that I will remain in control forever. Because one day the rage might overwhelm me and the dead might walk again.

I will try to decommission my weapons. To let them die and decay. Most of them. But the Brain craves form, physicality, and I must give it that.

I tell her to be watchful, and to remember. I tell her to remember me.

And I cannot kiss her now, because the only lips I have the living would flinch from, but I kiss her in another way. Mind to mind.

Whispering, as I do: forgive me.

And then I turn the dead round and march them back, down the Hill. Back to the sea.

Until only the body of a man called Robert McTarn remains.

"I love you," *I say through him, and then he too begins the long walk home.*

And as he goes, I hear, above the keening of the wind and the wild laughter and rejoicing of those who have, at the last moment, been spared, the weeping of the woman I will always love.

EPILOGUE

Storm Warning - Ocean Rising

Ancient ocean, your waters are bitter.

Lautremont, *Les Chants De Maldoror.*

Katja

My name is Katja Mleczko. Today I am 43, making me the oldest person in the Pendle Islands.

When I was born, most people lived to at least 70. Even older. There were people more than 100 years old. Impossible to imagine that now, after the Flood and the Rising. Even to the ones alive before them, like me, it seems unreal, a dream. Our children, with little or no memory of the world as it was – for them, I think, it's easier.

This life ages us fast. My generation took it all for granted; spoilt. Now we're where our ancestors were two, maybe three hundred years before. If that. Our only medicines are the ones we make ourselves. There are folk remedies – a piece of mouldy bread on a wound makes a crude antibiotic, they used it for centuries before penicillin – but still, illnesses that would have been nothing when I was a child claim more lives each year.

I've had nine children. The first came eighteen months after the dead things went back into the sea. The last, eight years ago, almost killed me. After that, I took precautions, although I was widowed soon after. I have had no lovers since; I'm past that now.

I married Danny Mleczko. He took charge after the dead things went away, and I soon saw he was interested in me. He was still a boy, in most respects, but he was sweet, beneath his brashness. We became lovers; when I fell pregnant, we married. It wasn't much of a ceremony – there was no priest – but Hassan did his best. He was the next most senior soldier present, so he officiated.

The Chinook never flew again. Any other survivors we met we reached by boat, or they found us. The strangest were a small group from Manchester, who drifted to us on makeshift rafts. They were workers from the CIS tower, led by a bright young woman called Vicky. They'd survived on the roof of the building. Somehow she'd kept them going, fighting off the attacks, downing passing birds with lumps of stone. She set them 'targets' for the day (she was in sales.) When the dead things stopped attacking and the food got scarce, she made them build rafts from flotsam and jetsam. She was a natural planner and organiser; I remember her fiancé had survived, too, and no sooner had they got to Pendle than she started organising her wedding. I was one of the bridesmaids. Vicky's still alive. She's the second oldest person round here now. We've become good friends.

There's nothing much left to scavenge from the old world. We have what survival skills we've learned the hard way, or from books we salvaged. A few generations ago, my family would've known all this. Now we're learning it all again.

We rear sheep, raise crops, and farm fish. The waters are full of them now. We collect driftwood, cut peat, fell trees for fuel and to build small boats to commute between islands.

We survive.

We tried to raise Windhoven afterwards, in the hope the miracle might have come in time for them too, but we heard nothing. We never heard from anyone else. Perhaps we're the last humans of all... but I can't believe that. Or simply don't wish to.

Danny became a fisherman; one day he went out in one of the boats and didn't come back. It happened; still does. I married him out of necessity – we had to survive, raise children, make homes and communities – but I loved him in the end. But never as I loved Ben Stiles. I wish I could've; he deserved it. But such things are not a matter of choice.

Three of my children were stillborn. A fourth died in infancy – pneumonia – and another died in a stupid accident, running on a fell. He fell, broke his neck. He looked very like Danny. Bad luck in the Mleczko genes, perhaps. I don't know.

It hurts to remember these things, even now. But I must.

I have three sons still, and a daughter. Our population is growing slowly, but it grows, repopulating the islands.

We're nearly all gone now, the ones who were there at the start. Some have lasted longer than others. Jo died only a couple of years after that last battle; she never really recovered from losing Chas. Strange how, with so much changed, someone can still die of a broken heart.

Hassan died last winter. He was the last of the soldiers. He passed on all he could in the years before. The Islands have four healers now, carrying on what he taught them. My daughter is one of them.

She looks somewhat like my mother.

I called her Marta. The skies are always grey. I can't remember the last time we saw the sun, and it's almost always cold. The winters are bleak and killing, often claiming the old and very young. This winter may be my last.

But, little by little, the waters are relinquishing the ground they claimed, yielding new lands, thick with silt and richly fertile. Grass soon covers them.

I remember old nature documentaries from my childhood, of baby turtles hatching and scrambling down the beach to get to the sea. So few of them made it. Birds and crabs picked most of them off long before they reached the water. Darwinism in action. I am haunted, I suppose, by all the ones who never reached the sea. It's the price paid for having survived.

I suppose the regret will be bred out of us soon enough.

I wrote an account of the flood and my journey to Pendle shortly after arriving, in what little free time I had, so that at least other survivors would know what we'd gone through. It's the least you can do, for the dead.

Other than a bullet between the eyes, if that's what it takes to give them rest.

Not that we have any bullets left. Now it's back to bows and arrows, spears, crude swords and knives. With so much machinery obsolete from lack of fuel or ammunition, there's no shortage of metal...

Robert and Ben left their accounts too; I've put our stories together here. There are some parts of their stories I've written in myself.

When Ben died, he touched my mind, somehow. A last kiss, of sorts, I supposed at the time. But I saw – experienced – his death. And not just his: Robert's as well. Perhaps because Ben was speaking through the corpse, perhaps because Robert loved me. I'm not sure. I wrote down all that I could remember afterwards.

I thought long and hard about including them here, but in the end I decided to.

Writing materials are hard to come by, and we improvise. Parchment made from sheep's hide, ink from sloes gathered from blackthorn bushes. I've gathered the old, scribbled notes and transcribed them over the years. The ink is fading on them, the paper starting to crumble or become mildewed. It's important they be remembered, Robert and Ben. Between them, they helped save us all.

I played my part, of course; I saved lives and, without me, Ben wouldn't have found the strength to do what he did. But still, I've often felt like a witness rather than a participant.

Although that may be about to change.

There's a small island, one of the furthest out from us to be settled. One of our fishing boats made landfall there last week. There were half a dozen dwellings on the island, small stone and wood huts dotted round the slopes. All empty.

They found blood on the walls of one house. Most of the sheep were still there. A few had stampeded off one of the steep edges of the fell and had drowned, their bloated, bedraggled bodies floating in the shallows.

That last touch of Ben's mind when he died. *Forgive me.* At the time, I thought he meant for leaving me, for dying. But Ben knew that his remedy might not be permanent. Another reason for putting this record together.

If one day Ben started to lose control, if the Deep Brain's rage and fury began to surface again, the only chance to control it would be to take *another* mind into it as his had been taken. Strengthen the mix. The Deep Brain had forged a link with his mind. Ben would've had to do the same.

Forgive me.

I hope I am wrong.

Not just for my sake. If it's true, what happens when *my* control begins to slip? I'll have to forge the same link with someone else, to follow me when the time comes. Someone I loved. As Ben loved me. Someone with the strength to do what must be done.

And I think of my daughter, the healer, my best-loved child.

In ancient times, they made sacrifice to the sea gods. Is that our future? Have we come full circle?

I don't want to believe it. But sometimes, when I sleep, I think I can hear the sea. Even when I know it's calm and silent. I hear voices where there are none, *can* be none, because there's no-one there.

And... there is something else. That is why I am writing this last piece.

Last night, at dusk, I walked along the old Pendle Row, past the Inn's ruins to the bridge, overlooking the bay. It's receded in the last few years, but there's still deep waters out there. I saw movement down in the shallows, so I looked.

They were only there briefly, for a moment. Then the moon hid behind a cloud; when it came out again, they were gone.

There were three of them. One was small and lean, wiry and quick. Another was tall and gangly. And the third seemed to have long, wild hair, and when it – he – moved, it was with a limp.

The men in my life, taken by the sea.

They beckoned me.

And their eyes glowed green.

THE END

Acknowledgements

'Lady' Andrea Power provided, in addition to her kindness, friendship and support, her extensive knowledge of narrowboats. Her extensive knowledge of real ale also came in useful, if not for the present novel.

To Simon C, former Army medic, I owe a debt of thanks beyond mere words; without his advice on barotrauma, military procedure and mindset, *Tide Of Souls* would be a far poorer piece of work. That he found the time to help me during what was a period of great personal difficulty for him only makes the debt greater. Cheers, Four-Eyes, from The Bearded Lunatic.

Anything I've got right about the relevant subjects is due in no small part to these two; any errors are entirely my own. Likewise, I'm responsible for any liberties taken with the geography of Lancashire. The flooding that occurs in the novel is a scenario entirely of my own invention, and is not based on any theoretical models that I'm aware of. Unless there's a global warning 'nightmare scenario' that also features zombies...

Jon Oliver, naturally, for ringing me up and asking "So, would you like to write a zombie novel for me then?" Also to publicity maestro Keith Richardson and all others sailing in the good ship Abaddon.

Lorelei Loveridge and Jaclyn Smith, for bigging me up.

Joel Lane's friendship, advice and support have been invaluable over the last ten years. Bernard and Clare Nugent, Mark Phillips, Jenny Bent, Clare Moss and Darren Bland, Matt and Kathryn Colledge, David and Jane Southall, Rob Krijnen-Kemp and my parents and grandparents are just some of the many who've provided faith and support – emotional or practical – over the years. A big thank you also goes out to Gary McMahon, along with my heartfelt apologies to anyone I've missed.

Indirect thanks are also due to: New Model Army, Justin Sullivan, The Jan Garbarek Group, Dark Sanctuary, The Cure and The Sisters of Mercy for providing a writing soundtrack.

SIMON BESTWICK was born in 1974. He writes horror fiction and the odd bit of crime, and wonders, in spare moments, if there's any connection to the fact that he lives in Lancashire. His short fiction has popped up all over the place, in the UK and the States, and is collected in *A Hazy Shade Of Winter* (Ash Tree Press, 2004, www. ash-tree.bc.ca) and *Pictures Of The Dark* (Gray Friar Press, 2009, www.grayfriarpress.com.) He's also written some decidedly off-the-wall stuff for radio, mostly comedy, which you can check out at www.darksmile.co.uk. He's worked as a fast food operative, drama teacher, typist, insurance salesman (which taught him a lot about the dark side of human nature) and a call centre operator. Ideally he'd like to con somebody into paying him to write for a living, as it's so much better than a proper job. Find out more about Simon at http://simon-bestwick.blogspot.com

TOMES OF THE DEAD

Hungry Hearts

Gary McMahon

ISBN: 978-1-906735-26-5

UK RELEASE: November 2009
US RELEASE: January 2010

£6.99/$7.99

WWW.ABADDONBOOKS.COM

CHAPTER EIGHT

Daryl felt oddly safe out on the streets. Despite the lawlessness, the fighting and looting and displays of aggression, he now possessed a self-assurance that had eluded him for most of his life. Were these simply more personality changes due to Mother's grip slackening, or had something occurred at a more fundamental level?

On his back was a new rucksack, the straps tight across his shoulders and digging into his armpits. Inside the bag were his tools, along with the photograph of Sally Nutman. She was his guiding light, his sole aim in all this wonderful chaos. With the city erupting around him, no one would even hear her death rattle; the extinction of her life-force would be lost amid the flowering brutality of this strange new world, a world he felt curiously at home in.

Mother's house was located in a suburb not far from the centre of Leeds. Daryl did not own a car, and he doubted that any taxis would be operating with so much going on, but it was a short walk, really. He'd traced the route many times in the past, and knew every shortcut along the way.

The best way was to follow the canal into the centre. It was usually a dangerous place to be after nightfall, but tonight *everywhere* was dangerous – indeed, the canal was probably safer than the streets and estates right now.

The moon was a faded orb masked by heaving clouds. Starlight was negligible. The pathways were illuminated by the cold light of street lamps, and Daryl picked his way past wrecked cars, overturned bins and piles of shattered glass and rubble. The occasional scream leapt at him from the darkness, garbled words echoed along lightless ginnels and alleyways. Daryl kept moving, trying to blend into the night. He'd always been an unnoticeable figure, and tonight that anonymity was a weapon almost as potent as the ones in his rucksack.

He'd left Mother in her room, staring into the giddy blackness and fearing the sight of her own private Reaper. Perhaps it would have Richard Nixon's face, or maybe it would be dark and featureless, skulking in the shadows of her room. The latter thought pleased Daryl; because of Mother's fear of the dark, it suited that darkness would claim her.

The canal towpath crunched underfoot, pebbles and broken glass scattered across its narrow width. The black waters ran slow and sombre, with not even a duck or waterfowl about to mar its glassy surface. It *felt* like the end of the world.

Daryl hurried along the towpath, his thoughts filled with images of blood and the sound of muted screaming. He had another erection – this was a banner night for his libido. He wondered if Sally Nutman would recognise him, if she had noted his scrutiny at some point over the last few months. Part of him hoped that just before she died, her eyes would blaze with recognition. The other half of him prayed that she would die in utter confusion, not knowing who he was or why he'd decided to use her in such a way.

The waters shone blackly at his side, reflecting his desires. The canal was like a mirror; the images it contained matched those he'd carried around in his head since he was a child. It felt as if the landscape around him was shifting, altering to accommodate his new shape. The sky had lifted, allowing him to breathe, the trees and bushes bordering the path pulled back from his approach, the path itself twisted and undulated to meet his falling feet.

After years of feeling apart, isolated, he at last felt that he had a place in the world. A dark place, filled with demons.

It was only fitting that his first victim be as beautiful as Sally Nutman. He'd adored her features from afar, cementing that face in his mind. The slanted cat-like eyes, the firm jaw line, the long, graceful neck. It would not suffice to kill an ugly woman first; a beautiful act must be carried out on a special victim. He began to regret that this long-awaited act might soon be over. He'd spent so long fantasising about it, building the whole thing up inside his head, that he feared the actual kill might be an anticlimax.

But, no. It was stupid to think that way. Here he was, on the cusp of *becoming*, and all he could do was whine! He sensed the disapproval of his heroes, his masters; their long shadows followed him along the towpath, maintaining their distance but never slackening their pace.

He heard a splash as he walked beneath a low concrete footbridge. Graffiti adorned the abutments: crude drawings and obscene slogans meant to express a rage that could never otherwise be demonstrated. The splash came again, softer, as if moving away.

Daryl stopped and looked out at the water, trying to make out what was causing the sounds. His eyes fell upon a discarded shopping trolley tethered to the opposite bank by the knotted fronds of some riverside weed. Nearby, a child's doll floated in a slow circle, pink and naked and deformed. Then, turning his head to face eastward, he finally saw what was making the noise.

A fat white corpse was struggling to climb out of the canal. Water-bloated and covered in black silt, the thing kept gaining a few inches before slipping back down the bank and into the water. Daryl could see it from behind, so was unobserved. He watched it for a while, enjoying its struggling motion. The body was naked, its flesh puffy and discoloured. The fat arms and stubby hands looked as if they were made of dough as they grasped at the mud on the sloped side of the canal.

Daryl edged along the path, watching. It was an amazing sight, when you thought about it, like something from a nightmare. He supposed that the corpse must belong to a drowning victim who'd suddenly risen from the murky depths, heading for shore to return home.

He paused, and wondered why he'd accepted all this so readily.

Reanimated corpses. The living dead. Perhaps it took the truly insane to accept a truly insane situation?

The Michelin-man body rolled as it grabbed a handful off moss, its bulk turning in the water. The face was hideous: a mass of jellied flesh and fish-bite wounds. It had no eyes, which went some way to explaining why it found it so difficult to gain the canal bank. The nose was gone, too; all that remained was a clean but ragged hole through which Daryl glimpsed white bone.

The corpse opened its mouth as if trying to scream. Canal water slid from between its fattened lips, spilling down over its flabby breasts and corpulent belly. Its lower portion was obscured by the dark water, so Daryl could not make out if it was male or female. If he was honest, he'd rather not know anyway.

As he drew abreast of the corpse, a fortuitous accident occurred. Still caught in its slow roll, the body's momentum carrying it round in an agonising circle which pivoted at the thing's hand – which was still holding on to the side of the canal – the corpse began to slide towards a steel stanchion that stuck out from the bank.

Daryl watched in quiet awe as the stanchion pierced the side of the thing's head, just above the ear, driving slowly into the sodden skull as if it were paper. The head split, the length of steel tearing it so that the waterlogged contents of the brain pan spilled out into the canal.

The corpse hung there, twisting in the undertow. The split had stretched around the front of the head, connecting with the mouth, so that it resembled a smile. Or a salacious leer.

Daryl laughed, and then continued on his way. For some reason the whole episode felt like a prelude to something bigger. Knowing how silly it seemed, he felt that the drowned corpse had been sent to him as a sign to show him something he would only understand later, once he was indoctrinated into the league of killers he longed to join.

He passed a burned-out concrete structure, an old storage shed used now for drug taking. Dirty syringes littered the doorway, and something stirred within. Daryl glanced into the darkness and saw a thin figure sitting against the wall. Its white limbs were skinny as pipe-cleaners and pin-cushioned with needles as it searched for a vein.

He hurried on, processing the information in a rush.

Habit. It all boiled down to habit.

These dead things – these hideous revived remains – fell into the same habits they'd suffered in life. The drug addict returned to the needle; the mother came back for her babe; the victim of a drowning once more attempted to climb back on to dry land. Life, he mused, was full of such cycles. The living re-enacted their daily routines, their lives becoming like a film clip stuck on a loop. So when they came back from the dead, what else was there but to *resume* that loop, to climb back into the rut and carry on carrying on?

It made perfect sense to Daryl. The dead tried to copy the living. It was all they knew, all they had within them: primitive urges, tribal acts, a repetition of events tattooed onto their memories by social custom and workaday existence. Strip away the thought process and all we are is habit, routine, learned experience. Like a mouse stuck on an exercise wheel, the dead just kept on running, with no destination in sight.

He crossed the railway line and then doubled back in a loop, the city rising before him. He could see the lights – far fewer than usual at this time of night – and the rooftops of the higher buildings scraped the sky like glass and concrete fingers. He focused on his destination; one of the new Docks along this side of the canal, where developers had built apartment blocks and fitness complexes.

Allinson Dock was less than a mile away. He knew the spot by heart, had traced the route both in life and in his dreams too many times to even count. Further along the river, at Clarence Dock, he could make out the blocky structure of the Royal Armouries Museum, with its hexagonal glass and steel tower set amid a clutter of oblongs. The windows reflected the canal water, glittering like huge insectoid eyes. Daryl admired the illusion, enjoying the fantasy while it lasted.

He left the canal and cut across a short bushy verge, stepping over the town planners' idea of an urban green zone. Empty beer cans, spirit bottles and used condoms were scattered between the shrubs.

Heading uphill, he reached a smooth, flat road surface. The road led into the apartment complex where Sally and her husband lived; it terminated in a few parking spaces that flanked the entrance to the underground car park.

Daryl squatted in the bushes and waited, scoping out the site. He watched a dark figure as it scuttled on all-fours, heading for the canal. The figure – it looked like a woman crawling around in the mud – disappeared into the undergrowth, and there followed a single splash as she entered the water. Daryl held his breath; he heard nothing more of the curious figure.

Nearby, the burned remains of a car smouldered, the metal of the bodywork groaning and creaking as it cooled.

He stared at the apartment block, locating Sally's seventh-floor windows with ease. He knew exactly where they were. All the windows were dark, but that did not prevent him from identifying the ones Sally hid behind, thinking that she was safe and secure.

He smiled. The darkness nestled around him, wrapping him in a comforting cloak.

Minutes passed, but Daryl did not keep track of how many. Eventually his legs began to ache from sitting in the same position, his rear end held inches from the ground and all his weight taken on the annoyingly weak muscles of calves that simply would not develop no matter how hard he tried to train them. He stood, stretching, sucking in the night. Sally's windows remained black, silent, and blind to the terror he brought. The temperature dropped around him, the air becoming sharp.

After another few moments he moved on, cutting across the road and entering the landscaped area at the side of the building. A few night birds hopped between the branches of the low trees; something burrowed into the foliage at his feet. There might be rats this close to the canal, but it was probably something as harmless as a hedgehog.

"I'm coming," he whispered. "I'm coming, dollface." It was not the kind of casual language he ever used; the lines were taken from some film he'd seen. All of his best lines came from films, or books. Not that he ever spoke them to anyone other than his own flaccid face in the mirror, or perhaps Mother's closed bedroom door...

The main doors operated on an expensive security system, involving a pass code and a CCTV monitor, but there was a man who lived on the ground floor, in apartment Number 03, who habitually neglected certain essentials of home security.

He always left his bathroom window ajar, to help ventilate the tiny room. The man worked nights. Daryl knew this from his surveillance exercises; either unaware or uncaring of the dangers inherent in city living, the man never bothered to close the window when he left for his place of employment. Daryl stepped softly along the side of the building, ducking below the eye-line of the windows along this elevation.

Soon he reached the open bathroom window.

He reached up, slid his arm inside, and popped the catch. It was that easy: the fine line between entry and exclusion, life and death, was a scant few inches of air between sill and frame. It was almost absurd the risks some people took without ever acknowledging the possible consequences.

Daryl glanced along the length of the building, carefully inspecting the area for prying eyes. Then, satisfied that no one was around to witness him, he clambered up the wall, finding a foothold on the smart new cladding system, and forced his thin body through the window.

Once inside the bathroom he returned the window to its former position, being careful to ensure that it looked exactly as it had done before he'd utilised it to break into the property. Once he was happy with the window, he walked across to the door and stepped out into a long narrow hallway. The front door was located at one end of this hallway; the living room was at the other; two other doors led off the cramped space.

Daryl didn't bother to have a nose around the apartment. He simply walked to the front door, opened it, and let himself out. He moved swiftly to the fire stairs – the lift might not be working due to the power blackouts – and climbed to the seventh floor, where Sally was waiting for him.

He'd been inside before, sneaking in after another tenant as they typed in the code on the main door. He'd received a funny look, but was not challenged, even though he had stayed there for two hours, exploring the interior of the building and waiting for Sally's husband to return home from a day shift so he could study any idiosyncratic lifestyle patterns the man exhibited. Even then he was aware that the slightest piece of behavioural data might help him in the future, when finally the time came to put his plan into action.

He was breathing heavily when he reached the seventh floor,

and his lungs ached slightly. At home he lifted weights to add strength – but not bulk – to his wiry physique. He had the body of a distance runner: lean, powerful limbs, a hard, skinny torso, but his *lower* legs – specifically his ever-puny calf muscles – remained weak and his stamina was terrible. His upper body strength, however, belied the narrow build he hid beneath his baggy clothing.

He was certain that Sally would admire his physique. He would leave her no choice in the matter.

He approached the door to her apartment and stood outside, running his hands across the surprisingly lightweight wooden door. She sat behind an inch of hollow, low-grade timber, awaiting his ministrations.

"Oh, baby. Baby, baby, baby." He giggled, but made sure that he kept it low, under his breath.

Then, feeling an enormous surge of energy building from the soles of his feet and climbing the length of his body, flowering at the midriff, throat, and face, he knocked six times in rapid succession upon the door – exactly the way he knew that Sally's husband, that idiot copper, always knocked.

He repeated the jokey secret knock – again, just like the husband always did – and then stepped back to wait for Sally to open the door and let him in; a shy suitor nervously awaiting his reluctant paramour.

TOMES OF THE DEAD

For more information on this
and other titles visit...

WWW.ABADDONBOOKS.COM

Out Now!

Price: **£6.99 ★ $7.99**

ISBN 13: **978-1-905437-03-0**

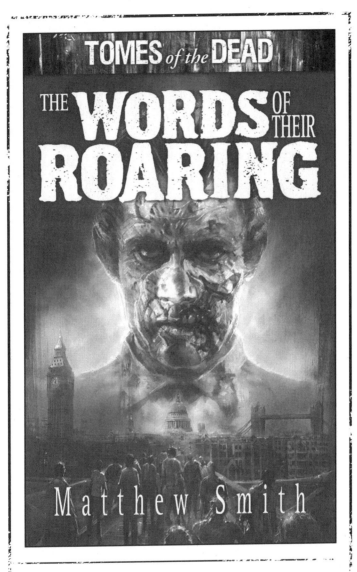

Price: **£6.99** ★ **$7.99**

ISBN 13: **978-1-905437-13-9**

Price: **£6.99** ★ **$7.99**

ISBN 13: **978-1-905437-72-6**

THE AFTERBLIGHT CHRONICLES

SCHOOL'S OUT

Scott Andrews

Price: **£6.99 ★ $7.99**

ISBN 13: **978-1-905437-62-7**

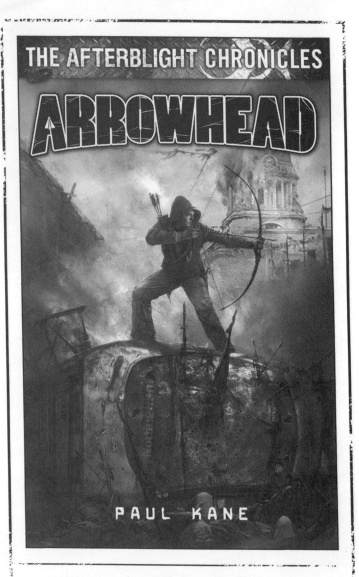

Price: **£6.99** ★ **$7.99**

ISBN 13: **978-1-905437-76-4**

Price: **£6.99 ★ $7.99**

ISBN 13: **978-1-906735-04-3**

THE AFTERBLIGHT CHRONICLES

AL EWING

DEATH GOT NO MERCY

Price: **£6.99 ★ $7.99**

ISBN 13: **978-1-906735-15-9**

PAX BRITANNIA

UNNATURAL
HISTORY

Jonathan Green

Price: **£6.99** ★ **$7.99**

ISBN 13: **978-1-905437-10-8**

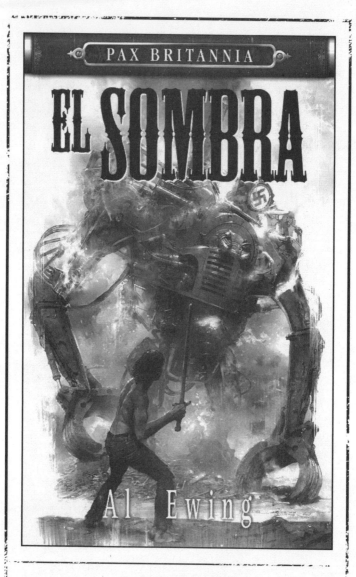

PAX BRITANNIA

EL SOMBRA

Al Ewing

Price: **£6.99 ★ $7.99**

ISBN 13: **978-1-905437-34-4**

PAX BRITANNIA

HUMAN NATURE

JONATHAN GREEN

Price: **£6.99 ★ $7.99**

ISBN 13: **978-1-905437-86-3**